Praise for John Gilstrap

END GAME
An Amazon Editor's Favorite Book of the Year

"Gilstrap's new Jonathan Grave thriller, is his best novel to date—even considering his enviable bibliography. *End Game* starts off explosively and keeps on rolling. Gilstrap puts you in the moment as very few authors can. And there are many vignettes that will stay with you long after you have finished the book."
—**Joe Hartlaub**, *BookReporter*

DAMAGE CONTROL

"Powerful and explosive, an unforgettable journey into the dark side of the human soul. Gilstrap is a master of action and drama. If you like Vince Flynn and Brad Thor, you'll love John Gilstrap."
—**Gayle Lynds**

"Rousing . . . Readers will anxiously await the next installment."
—*Publishers Weekly*

"It's easy to see why John Gilstrap is the go-to guy among thriller writers when it comes to weapons, ammunition, and explosives. His expertise is uncontested."
—**John Ramsey Miller**

"The best page-turning thriller I've grabbed in ages. Gilstrap is one of the very few writers who can position a set of characters in a situation, ramp up the tension, and yes, keep it there, all the way through. There is no place you can put this book down."
—**Beth Kanell, Kingdom Books, Vermont**

"A page-turning, near-perfect thriller, with engaging and believable characters . . . unputdownable! Warning—if you must be up early the next morning, don't start the book."
—*Top Mystery Novels*

NO MERCY

"*No Mercy* grabs hold of you on page one and doesn't let go. Gilstrap's new series is terrific. It will leave you breathless. I can't wait to see what Jonathan Grave is up to next."
—Harlan Coben

"The release of a new John Gilstrap novel is always worth celebrating, because he's one of the finest thriller writers on the planet. *No Mercy* showcases his work at its finest—taut, action-packed, and impossible to put down!"
—Tess Gerritsen

"A great hero, a pulse-pounding story—and the launch of a really exciting series."
—Joseph Finder

"An entertaining, fast-paced tale of violence and revenge."
—*Publishers Weekly*

"No other writer is better able to combine in a single novel both rocket-paced suspense and heartfelt looks at family and the human spirit. And what a pleasure to meet Jonathan Grave, a hero for our time . . . and for all time."
—Jeffery Deaver

AT ALL COSTS

"Riveting . . . combines a great plot and realistic, likeable characters with look-over-your-shoulder tension. A page-turner."
—*The Kansas City Star*

JOHN GILSTRAP

AGAINST ALL ENEMIES

PINNACLE BOOKS
Kensington Publishing Corp.
www.kensingtonbooks.com

PINNACLE BOOKS are published by

Kensington Publishing Corp.
119 West 40th Street
New York, NY 10018

All Kensington titles, imprints, and distributed lines are available at special quantity discounts for bulk purchases for sales promotions, premiums, fund-raising, educational, or institutional use. Special book excerpts or customized printings can also be created to fit specific needs. For details, write or phone the office of the Kensington sales manager: Kensington Publishing Corp., 119 West 40th Street, New York, NY 10018, attn: Sales Department; phone 1-800-221-2647.

PINNACLE BOOKS and the Pinnacle logo are Reg. U.S. Pat. & TM Off.

First printing: July 2015

10 9 8 7 6 5 4 3 2 1

ISBN-13: 978-0-7860-3505-2
ISBN-10: 0-7860-3505-6

Printed in the United States of America

First electronic edition: July 2015

ISBN-13: 978-0-7860-3506-9
ISBN-10: 0-7860-3506-4

To Hannah, Robbie, and Vivienne, the next generation

I do solemnly swear that I will support and defend the Constitution of the United States against all enemies, foreign and domestic; that I will bear true faith and allegiance to the same; and that I will obey the orders of the President of the United States and the orders of the officers appointed over me, according to regulations and the Uniform Code of Military Justice. So help me God.
—US Army Oath of Enlistment

Chapter One

Behrang Hotaki smiled at everyone who made eye contact with him. He knew some of them but many more were strangers, and if he was friendly, the merchants at the bazaar were more likely to take pity on him and share a plum or a tomato. Maybe some rice or some bread. For lamb or chicken, he would have to do something in return, and all too often that meant doing things he did not want to do. These people, villagers and merchants alike, would show him pity, but they dared not show him kindness, dared not show him friendship.

They knew him as an orphan, a waif, a boy whose family name may never be spoken. With the Americans gone, the old ways had reemerged, and the Taliban knew everything. Behrang understood that anyone who wished to see old age needed to assume that the monsters' knowledge was perfect.

He smiled, and they mostly smiled in return. To smile was to be polite, and to be polite was to be invisible. If a boy were shy enough—invisible enough—he could be forgiven the sins of his family. By demonstrating that he knew his place, the gifts bestowed on him might be more generous. Even Satan and the others understood that a boy his age needed some tiny bit of pity.

Behrang intended to hurt them all, to kill them if he could. Not with a gun or with a suicide vest, but with a betrayal of his own. He dreamed of the day when he might see all of these animals dead, their brains blasted from their heads. The slower they died, the happier he'd be. He wished he could watch as they had watched, but without that false expression of concern. He would not pretend to mourn for them as they had pretended to mourn for his family. If he were able, he would spit on their corpses, piss on their faces.

But that would not be possible. When justice finally came, he could not afford to be nearby. After Charlie—the last remaining American, who was even more invisible than Behrang—killed Satan and his leaders, the rest of the Taliban monsters would murder everyone in the village. Behrang would be far, far away when that happened.

And it would happen soon.

Among Behrang's greatest blessings was the gift of patience. Six years had passed since people in this crowd had betrayed his father—six years since his sisters and mother were raped while Behrang was forced to watch. Six years since the Taliban slipped the thin rope around his father's neck and hoisted him into the air, his feet mere inches above the ground. The jackals had laughed as Father had kicked and stretched to reach the gravel street that remained barely out of reach.

It had been six endless years since Behrang himself had become a toy of the Taliban monsters. They thought they owned him, that they could do whatever they wanted without consequence.

So many people here in the bazaar knew everything. They knew what his father had tried to accomplish—the education he'd tried to provide for everyone, girls as well as boys—and they all knew who, among them, had once been vocal supporters of his efforts. But to a person, they were cowards, unwilling to risk one one-hundredth of what Father had risked. Every one of them valued profit and their own safety above any point of principle. In the end, none of them rose to help, and now that it was all over and his family was dead, they dared to show pity to Behrang. In their minds, they were *better* than him because they had been too smart to be honest.

They all thought so little of Behrang that they would say things in his presence that should never be said in front of anyone. Because he was invisible, they assumed he was harmless. Perhaps they assumed he was deaf and blind. Either way, they talked in ways they shouldn't.

As a result, Behrang knew the secret of secrets. He knew where Satan would be tomorrow afternoon.

Behrang wondered sometimes if the man who called himself Satan—a blasphemy in itself—had a given name that was something different. He had to, didn't he? What parents could think so little of their son at birth that they would name him after the ultimate evil? Perhaps they could foresee the future. Or perhaps by giving him such a name they had shaped the man he would become.

Behrang had seen much cruelty in his thirteen years, but he had never seen anyone else who so enjoyed inflicting it. Satan showed no more emotion when he set a man ablaze than a merchant would show in selling a pomegranate.

Satan and the Taliban killed innocents for sport, for the sole purpose of turning children into orphans. The terror they inflicted was their greatest weapon, far larger and more effective than any cannon or bomb. Fearful people would stand and watch as girls—and boys—were raped, and they would do nothing as their fathers were lifted off the ground to be strangled to death.

Father would have told Behrang that he should not feel anger toward people who felt such fear, but rather that he should feel pity for them. *A man who lives in fear cannot live a full life,* his father had told him. *Fear is a slaveholder that turns good people into obedient pets. It is far better to live a shortened life in freedom than it is to die an old man as a slave to others.*

Behrang knew that the anger in his soul was wrong, that it would disappoint his father, but Father had found his relief from slavery so long ago. He had seen the world as a professor sees the world, through the smeared and foggy windows of a classroom, where lofty philosophy stirred the intellect of men and women living in comfort. As an orphan on the street, living off the pity of your family's murderers, the realities of life were gritty and painful and foul-smelling. Behrang had no room for theories and philosophy in his life. He had room only for living or dying, and the space between those two options was so small as to be unmeasurable.

He scanned the flood of people at the bazaar for the single face he needed to see. Somewhere among the dozens of farmers' and craftsmen's stalls, Charlie would appear, and when he did, the American would wink at him, and then they would wander off to somewhere safe. That's when Behrang would pass along his news.

Few people knew that Americans remained in this part of the province, and of those who did remain, Charlie said that all of them were looking for Satan. "If you see him," Charlie had told him, "if you even *hear* of him, I need you to tell me."

From the very first day they'd met, Behrang had suspected that Charlie was a soldier, but the man had never told him that. In fact, Charlie avoided saying anything about himself. He asked all kinds of questions, from who knew whom to how things used to be back when life was normal. Charlie was nice. Behrang liked the fact that he never pretended to be something he was not. While he spoke Pashto very well, he needed to be careful of his accent. On good days, Charlie's dialect was good enough to pass as a native, but there were certain phrases, particularly when Charlie was amused or angry, where his American roots would show.

Charlie's other problem was his blue eyes. They weren't unheard of in Afghanistan, but they raised questions. Behrang had pointed that out on their first meeting, and the next time they saw each other the American's eyes were brown and red and watery. Charlie explained to him that he wasn't crying, but rather that his . . . *contract windows* . . . hurt his eyes. Behrang could only imagine. If contract windows could change the color of your eyes, how could they not hurt?

Charlie knew things—the kinds of things that he couldn't possibly know. On the very first day they'd met—what was that, two years ago?—after Charlie had bought him a beautiful plum from the vendor's cart, he'd said to him, "I'm very sorry to hear about your parents and your sisters." Behrang had heard the foreign accent in his words.

Behrang's head swiveled to see who might have overheard. "Are you American?" he'd whispered.

"I'd like to speak with you," Charlie had said. He kept his voice low. "Away from these other people."

Behrang considered running away. The Americans had ruined his country, after all. They had killed so many people. But they had saved many, too.

"I want to hurt the people who killed your family," the stranger said. "My name is Charlie and I am your friend. You can trust me."

Behrang remembered smiling at those words.

And Charlie had smiled back at him. "I guess everyone you cannot trust tells you that you can trust them," he said, speaking Behrang's thoughts exactly.

Charlie's massive beard separated to show a happy display of white teeth. "The day comes when you have to trust someone," he said. "Why not start with the man who wants to make people pay for killing your family?"

From that very first meeting—the first of dozens—Behrang had trusted the big man with the thick neck and blue eyes. Charlie told him to meet in the fig grove north of the village. He said that Behrang should show up at eleven o'clock the next morning and wait. "If I do not arrive by eleven-thirty, that means it's not safe, and you should go on about your day."

Behrang remembered feeling his cheeks go hot with

embarrassment. "How will I know when it is eleven o'clock?" he'd asked.

Charlie's eyes softened at the question. "Do you know how to read a watch?" he asked.

"Of course." Behrang could read Shakespeare. Of course he could read a watch. There had been a time when he'd actually owned one. He'd had to trade it for a blanket last winter.

Glancing over his shoulder to make sure no one was watching, Charlie slid his own watch off his wrist and handed it to the boy. "Here," he said. "Take this one, courtesy of Uncle Sam."

Behrang also looked around for witnesses. "Your uncle will be upset that you gave away such a gift."

Something in those words made Charlie laugh. "Not this uncle," he said. "My Uncle Sam is a very generous man."

The way Charlie laughed made Behrang wonder if he was being mocked.

"It's fine," Charlie assured him. "I am not laughing at you. One day, you will realize why that is funny. Please take it."

"Then how will *you* know when it is eleven o'clock?"

"I will know. I have many watches."

Behrang nearly didn't go to that first meeting. All through the night before, he'd asked himself why he would want to expose himself to even the smallest risk in order to help one of the men who'd invaded his country. To be caught was to be killed in the most horrific way.

In the end, though, he remembered his father's impassioned speeches about principle. *Principle and con-*

venience are nearly always enemies, his father had told him. *As are principle and safety. One cannot be without principle and call oneself a man.*

Those words had so angered Behrang's mother. She'd called them arrogant. Could she possibly have known when she'd said, "Ideas like that will get us all killed one day," that she had foreseen the future? Father had insisted that Behrang's sisters, Afrooz and Taherah, go to the secret school in the basement of the old doctor's building so that they could learn and one day become doctors themselves. Such things were just not done. Not anymore, anyway.

Behrang had been only seven years old when Satan crashed through their door and tortured and killed his family, yet the sounds of the screams still echoed in his head every night. The image of the blood spray from their severed throats occupied the darkness when he closed his eyes.

If Charlie could avenge that—if there was even a tiny, remote chance that Charlie could kill the men who'd ravaged his family—then any risk was worth it.

Now, all these meetings later, as Behrang leaned against the Coca-Cola signpost among the sea of merchants and customers, he worried what might happen after this meeting with Charlie. Once they had their prize, what would become of his American friend? After Satan was dead, would they need Behrang anymore? Charlie had promised to make sure that Behrang would be sent to a safe place, but Americans were famous for making promises that they never kept. Father had been a lover of history, and he had told his family how the Americans had abandoned their friends in

Korea and Vietnam and he had heard stories of the people they'd abandoned in Iraq and more recently in Kabul. They promised to be trustworthy, and then they just walked away.

Surely, Charlie was the exception. They'd shared too many laughs—too many meetings that had less to do with the information Behrang brought than with just sharing time together—for Charlie to turn his back.

Surely.

Dylan Nasbe adjusted the *shemagh* at his neck and straightened his *kameez* so that he would look *just so* as he waded into the crowded bazaar. His heart raced as it always did when he mingled so close to the enemy. Because of the pressing crowd, he did his business without comm gear because even the smallest earbud could be seen in a crowd that was pressed this tightly.

He was also unarmed, at least by any reasonable measure of such things in a war zone. Again because of the tightness of the crowd and the resultant ease of casual notice, his only weapon was a hand-sized Smith & Wesson Bodyguard pistol, which he wore strapped tightly to his chest, virtually inaccessible through the shirt of his *kameez*. To draw it would require lifting his shirt and exposing his belly to expose the gun. Not a stealthy action in this part of the world.

Conscious that his accent was not always spot-on, and unable to tell the difference when he slipped out of dialect, he tried to say nothing, and as a rule, that was easy. In a crowd, a smile was usually enough. With his blue eyes camouflaged—he still blushed when he re-

membered the day Behrang had pointed out to him that
he had forgotten his contact lenses—he felt most self-
conscious about his size. This was a part of the world
where people barely subsisted, where heavily muscled
chests and necks were the kinds of anomalies that brought
suspicion. Suspicion, in turn, brought death—preferably to the suspector rather that the suspectee, thus the
S&W .380. As a hedge, he wore clothes that were too
big, hoping that the extra fabric would make him look
fat.

Afghanistan was a beautiful country when it wasn't
on fire or cluttered with corpses. While the roads
sucked beyond all comprehension, the landscape could
be beautiful. On days like this—market day—the village became a stunning display of colors and aromas as
vendors displayed their wares and hawked customers.
The air seemed fat with the perfumes of fresh car-
damom, cilantro, mint, and coriander, which combined
with fresh flowers and cooking lamb and chicken to
form a kind of atmospheric flavor that Dylan considered unique to this part of the world.

He prided himself in not understanding Afghan culture in too much depth—certainly not beyond the measure that was necessary for him to do his job. More
than a few of his Unit buddies obsessed over the cul-
tures into which they inserted themselves, but Dylan
considered it a liability to become too deeply involved
with anything that it was ultimately his job to destroy.

As far as Dylan was concerned, this entire mission
was a waste of blood and treasure. The instant politicians declared their intent to surrender and walk away,
every soldier left in harm's way became a pawn, and

every drop of blood spilled became a crime. But he was a soldier, and his was not to reason why. His was but to accomplish the mission and get the hell out.

Fifty meters ahead, he saw the Coca-Cola sign that was his destination. Yesterday, a surveillance drone had picked up the image of the broken bicycle in the ditch on the eastern side of the roadway leading into the village—the sign from Behrang that he had new information—and thus here he was, a week earlier than their routine meeting.

Just as it was a mistake to become too attached to the country it was your job to destroy, so was it a mistake to become attached to people who lived there. Success in war required a unique brand of mental disengagement. Success at Dylan's level of the game—the United States' most elite warriors—it was that and more. Sources of information were not friends, even though you made them think they were. They were assets to be exploited until they were dry, and then they were to be cast aside in favor of newer, fresher sources of even more valuable information. Dylan had done the drill a hundred times, maybe a thousand.

But he'd never before worked with an asset who was a kid—much less a kid with huge eyes and a bright smile and an infectious laugh. There was a toughness about Behrang that Dylan found inspirational. Life had dealt him the worst possible hand, yet the kid adapted. He survived. He'd learned to be angry without being bitter.

And in a few weeks, if a thousand things went right with nothing going wrong, Behrang would be safely in the United States. If another *million* things went right with nothing going wrong, he would be the newest member of the Nasbe family. After nearly twenty years in the army, Dylan had racked up a lot of favor chits, and he was cashing them all in on this one. He'd gotten the endorsements he'd needed from the Army, and another from the CIA, and now it all hung on a signature from some bureaucrat he'd never met from the Department of Homeland Security. Apparently, they knew more than the CI-freaking-A about terrorist threats.

It was a one-step-at-a-time process, and the idea had been in circulation for five months now. His wife, Christyne, was on board, and she assured him that Ryan was okay with it, too, though she discouraged Dylan from speaking to Ryan about it. That relationship was . . . complicated.

If Behrang bore the news that Boomer anticipated, the first step in the plan would launch immediately—getting the boy to safety. Once he'd been able to find out the location of the Taliban command structure, Behrang would disappear with the Unit's help to Pakistan, and from there, through a dizzying series of transfers, to foster care in North Carolina.

But first, Behrang needed to deliver. The Agency's endorsement made that as clear as crystal. As the chief of station had told Boomer to his face, "This isn't a charity case, my friend. This is a business relationship. The boy needs to earn his way to asylum."

Boomer believed that this would be the day when Behrang did just that.

Moving through this crowd was an exercise in capillary action—human peristalsis, maybe. He kept willing himself closer to the Coca-Cola sign, and he got steadily nearer. His approach was complicated by the fact that he didn't want to appear too focused. People noticed when others were trying to move to a particular location, and by noticing, that drew attention toward the target. Just try staring at the ceiling sometime and see how long it takes for others to wonder what's so interesting up there.

Afghanistan was a vigilant country. Constantly on the lookout for threats, residents had developed an instinct for sniffing out anything that was out of the ordinary, and once sniffed, that became the focus of attention and fear. Thus, Dylan pretended to shop. He kept his hands to himself and his mouth shut.

He'd closed to within fifty feet of the Coca-Cola sign when he caught his first glimpse of Behrang through spaces in the crowd. The boy leaned against the sign munching on a plum that dripped juice down his chin and onto the front of the rag that he called a shirt. He, too, kept a disinterested air about him, the posture of an orphan hoping not to be noticed.

Dylan was still thirty feet away when the commotion started behind him. The crowd surged toward him, nearly knocking him off his feet as people clogging the street hurried toward the sidewalk. To Dylan's left, a merchant's booth toppled over in the push of the crowd.

Not especially tall by American standards, Dylan was nonetheless taller than the average Afghan. As he stretched to his full height to see what the fuss was all about, his heart nearly stopped.

Satan was here. The highest of high-value targets was right friggin' *here*.

* * *

Behrang noticed the change in the rhythm of the day before he saw what caused it. The loud, vibrating sound of the assembled shoppers and merchants dipped suddenly, and then silence washed over everything. People parted from the street to move off to the sides. Someone might have screamed, but maybe it was just a loud gasp.

Instinctively, he wanted to run, but he stopped himself. To run was to get shot—if not by the Taliban or one of their sympathizers, then by a hidden American soldier or orbiting drone. As far as he could tell—and Charlie had confirmed it, though not in so many words—anyone who ran was automatically considered to be guilty, and therefore could be vaporized by a missile fired from so far away that no one knew it was coming until the shrapnel and body parts flew.

So he stayed where he was. What was the right move here? Should he gawk like all of the others, or should he pretend to be disinterested as he had been doing?

The best strategy was to blend in, so he pushed away from the Coca-Cola post and craned his neck to see—

Satan.

Fear twisted Behrang's insides as evil incarnate emerged from the crowd and walked right toward him, as if he knew exactly who he was looking for, and exactly where he could be found.

Blending no longer mattered. Running mattered. Survival mattered. He spun around to sprint into the countryside, but the path was blocked by another of the Taliban leaders. This was one whose name Behrang did not know, but he'd seen him in Satan's shadow many times. The man grabbed Behrang by his shirt and lifted him off his feet. The boy kicked to get away, but the man's grasp was too tight.

"Behrang Hotaki!" Satan yelled, silencing the crowd. "You stupid, stupid boy. Bring him here to me."

The arms that grasped Behrang around his middle clamped around him like an iron ring. The boy kicked and wriggled in an attempt to get away, but the grasp didn't weaken.

A wide circle formed around Satan as villagers and vendors alike watched with wide eyes. The man whose face Behrang could no longer see carried him into the center of the circle and dropped him onto the gravel road at Satan's feet. Pointy rocks ravaged his hands and his knees on impact.

"You are your father's son," Satan said in a voice so loud that it was clearly meant to be heard by everyone. "But you do not learn from your mistakes." From somewhere under his clothing, Satan produced a long, curved blade. Its razor-sharp edge gleamed in the bright sunshine. Behrang recognized it as the blade that had cut the throats of his mother and his sisters.

"This boy has betrayed me!" Satan said. "He has tried to kill me, and he has tried to kill you as well. I have shown mercy to him all these years, and this is what I receive in return."

The man who had carried him here now grabbed a fistful of his hair and pulled him erect, even as he stood on the backs of his knees to keep him from standing.

"No!" Behrang said. "No, it's not like that. I don't know what you're talking about."

Satan's eyes brightened as he stroked his thick black beard. He smiled. "Is this truly how you want to spend this moment?" he asked. He'd lowered his voice now. It was only the two of them talking. "Do you really want your last words to be a lie?"

Behrang's mind raced for something, *anything* that might save him. Ahead and to the left, he saw a man push himself through the crowd to the edge of the circle. The familiar face looked frightened. Angry.

Hope bloomed in Behrang's chest. "Charlie!" he yelled. "Help me!"

Three Years Later

Chapter Two

Jonathan Grave concentrated on his sight picture, forcing himself to ignore the heat of the afternoon sun that threatened to strip the skin off the back of his neck. In Virginia in July, the tropical sun was part of the deal. He lay on his belly on the mulchy forest floor, the forestock of his 7.62 millimeter Heckler & Koch 417 supported on a stack of three beanbags. He pressed the extended collapsible stock against his shoulder and split his attention between what his naked left eye could see and the ten-times magnified circle from the Nightforce Optics sight that dominated the vision in his right eye. Somewhere out there in the woods, roughly a hundred yards away, a target would present itself.

Soon.

Jonathan told himself to watch his breathing and to relax his hand on the rifle's pistol grip. When the target showed itself, it would take only a slight press from the pad of his right forefinger to send the round downrange. After that, it was all physics. He watched the movement of the grass for wind speed, and the—

His naked eye caught movement left to right, and he brought his scope to bear in time to see the black silhouette of a man streak from one tree to another. The target was back behind cover before he could commit to a shot, but at least now he knew where the son of a bitch was. If he moved again—

There! The target darted back to the left, taunting him, but Jonathan was ready for it. He led by a couple of feet and released a round. Then a second. The woods echoed with the rolling sound of the gunshot.

"Did I get him?" Jonathan asked.

"You were behind him by five inches on the first shot and probably twelve on the second." The critique came from his spotter, a giant of a man named Brian Van de Muelebrocke—aka Boxers—who had saved Jonathan's ass more times than anyone could count.

"Are you sure?"

"Would you like me to show you the scars in the trees?" Boxers monitored the action from Jonathan's right, his eye pressed to a Leica spotting scope. "Would you like a warning for the next one?"

Jonathan felt his ears go hot. "No, I don't need—"

The target darted out again from behind a tree, and Jonathan fired two more times. He knew even as the trigger broke that he'd yanked the shots wide.

"If I'm ever a bad guy," Boxers said, "will you promise to be the sharpshooter who takes me out?"

"Bite me."

"No, seriously. I'm tempted to go ride the target," Boxers went on. "I can't think of a safer place to be." As he spoke he pushed the joystick in his hand to the right, sending the target out of hiding again.

This time, Jonathan didn't bother to press the trigger. He knew better.

"Hey, Digger," Boxers said. "How 'bout I give you a baseball bat and you can beat it to death."

Jonathan released his grip on the weapon and squatted up to a standing position, leaving the 417 on the ground. "Okay, Mouth," he said, cranking his head to look up under Big Guy's chin. "Let's switch places. I'll take a turn at the stressful work of pushing buttons. Let's see you hit Zippy." The target—Zippy—was a converted tackling dummy that Jonathan had mounted on rails that could be laid just about anywhere. Powered by a remote-controlled electric motor, Zippy was a great training tool.

Boxers grinned. "Look at you bein' all threatening and shit. Do you want me to shoot with my eyes open or closed?"

Jonathan held his hand out for the controller, and Boxers gave it to him. Big Guy settled on his belly behind the rifle. The back of his T-shirt read, *Never run from a sniper. You'll only die tired.*

"Let me know when you're ready," Jonathan said.

"That's your call, not mine—"

Jonathan jammed the joystick to the left, and the target took off while Boxers was still speaking. The 417 barked twice. Half a second after each blast, Jonathan heard the faint *pang!* of a solid hit.

Boxers didn't bother to look up as he said, "Hey, Boss, did I hit it?" He rumbled out a laugh.

Jonathan pulled away from the tripod-mounted spotting scope. "I hate you," he said. Boxers was the most natural shooter Jonathan had ever known, and he'd been that way since the beginning. It was as if bullets responded to Big Guy's whims.

Boxers stood, brushed off the front of his T-shirt and jeans, and held out his hand for the controller. "I push the buttons because you need the practice."

As Jonathan handed over the box, his phone buzzed in his pocket. The caller ID said *unknown*.

He pressed the connect button and brought the phone to his ear. "Yeah."

"Yes sir, Mr. Horgan," a man's voice said. "This is Cale Cook at the western guard shack. There's a visitor here to see you. He identifies himself as a Colonel Rollins, and he says it's important that he speak to you now."

Jonathan didn't know the security team out here at the compound very well, so Cale Cook could have called himself by any name, but he knew all too well who Colonel Rollins was. "Take a picture of him and send it to my phone. I'll call you back when I get it."

Boxers' face showed that he'd been eavesdropping. "What's up?"

"Roleplay Rollins is here."

Boxers recoiled at the words as anger settled in his eyes. There was a time not too long ago when Big Guy would have hurried to beat the man to death, and Jonathan would have let him. The three of them had a history that involved Jonathan's and Boxers' last days with the Unit, and it had not ended well.

Jonathan extended his palm to settle his friend down. "Take it easy. Past is past. He saved our asses and we owe him a solid." His phone buzzed, and displayed a picture of the man the visitor claimed to be. Jonathan called the guard shack. "Send him up to the lodge and have him wait on the porch. We're on our way."

"Should we escort him?"

"Is he alone?"

"Alone and unarmed. I searched his vehicle."

"No," Jonathan said. "Let him go solo. It's hard to get lost when there's only one road." He clicked off and looked to Boxers. "This should be interesting," he said. "Let's pick up the weapons and ammo. We'll break Zippy down later."

Boxers pointed through the Hummer's windshield toward the front porch of the stylishly rustic structure that had started life a hundred fifty years ago as a log cabin, but whose original owners would recognize nothing but a portion of the western wall. "There he is."

Colonel Stanley Rollins, US Army, stood from one of the porch's cane rockers as they approached. He wore jeans and a white polo shirt, and an expression that was impossible to read.

"Looks like Roleplay is a civilian today," Boxers said.

"He hates that name."

Big Guy chuckled. "I know. That's why I like it."

"Don't start anything," Jonathan said. "Not until we hear what he has to say."

"I'll call him Stanley, then."

"He hates that even worse."

Boxers looked across the console. "Yeah."

Jonathan opened the door and slid to the ground. "Hello, Colonel," he called as he approached the lodge.

"This is a genuine surprise." He extended his hand as he closed the distance, and Rollins walked down the four steps to greet him.

"Hello, Digger," he said. His handshake wasn't the bone crusher that it used to be. "Nice to see you again."

"Stanley!" Boxers shouted, feigning delight. "Hasn't someone fragged your ass by now?"

Rollins didn't rise to the bait. "Big Guy," he said. "Pleasant as always." He pointed to the Hummer. "And still the environmental conscience that you've always been."

Dubbed the Batmobile by Boxers, the lavishly customized and heavily armored Hummer was one of Jonathan's favorite toys.

"Let's talk inside," Jonathan said. He led the way up the steps, turned the key and pulled the heavy wooden door out toward them. He stepped aside to allow the colonel to pass.

As he did, Rollins rapped on the door with a knuckle. "Impressive. What is that, oak?"

"Something like that," Jonathan said. "I believe in living securely."

Inside, the foyer led directly to a living room, fifteen by fifteen feet, beyond which a dining area led to a closed door that hid the kitchen from view. A stone fireplace dominated the eastern wall—the wall to the right walking in. Stairs in the far northwest corner led up to the sleeping levels. In decorating the place, Jonathan had leaned heavily on his experience at Colorado ski lodges. Woodsy artwork hung from exposed pine walls across the way on the north wall, while a rack of eight long guns took up much of the front, southern, wall.

"Wow," Rollins said. "I guess I keep underestimating just how friggin' rich you really are. What is this place?"

"Pretty much what it looks like," Jonathan said as he nudged a switch on the wall to wake up two dangling chandeliers made of antlers. "This is a place to escape to, to unwind. Two hundred twenty-five acres of seclusion."

"And a guard patrol?"

"When did you become a reporter?" Boxers asked as he pulled the door closed.

"Who would see this and not be curious?" Rollins said.

"Which is a good reason to have a guard patrol," Jonathan said. He motioned to the leather sofas and chairs near the fireplace. "Have a seat, Colonel. Suffice to say that things happen out here that are best not witnessed by curiosity seekers. Think of it as my company's testing grounds." He let the words settle in. "Can I get you something to drink?"

Rollins waved the question away. "No, I'm fine, thanks."

Big Guy was already halfway to the wet bar in the back corner of the dining area. "I'm not," he said. "You want your usual, Boss?"

"Please." On his own, this would be the time of day for a martini, but since Boxers was tending the bar, that meant a couple fingers of Lagavulin scotch. Boxers didn't have the patience for the delicate chemistry that was a good martini.

Jonathan settled himself into a chair, crossed his legs, and locked in on Rollins's eyes. "You know, Colonel, I don't think either one of us wants the charade of small talk. What say you get right to what you have on your mind?"

Rollins leaned forward in his chair and rested his elbows on his knees. "I presume you remember Dylan Nasbe."

"Boomer? Of course I do." Dylan had joined the Unit shortly before Jonathan was on his way out, but it was a small, tight community. Plus, Jonathan had had some recent dealings with Dylan's wife and son. "Is he okay?" The scotch floated over Jonathan's right shoulder, clamped in Boxers' fingers.

"No," Rollins said. "He's gone rogue."

"What does that mean?" Boxers asked as he took the sofa for himself.

"It means he's killing off Agency assets."

"Bullshit," Boxers said. "He was a good kid. No way would he do that."

"And yet he is."

"Why?" Jonathan asked.

Rollins shrugged. "Why does anyone do anything like that? Something went crosswise in his head, and he started wasting people."

Jonathan and Boxers exchanged looks. "I'm not buying it," Jonathan said. "I mean, I can imagine him whacking Agency guys—who among us hasn't considered that a time or two?—but I don't buy that he's crazy. He's got a reason."

"Lee Harvey Oswald had reasons, Dig," Rollins said.

"So did John Wilkes Booth and Charles Manson. But so what? Murder is murder."

"The Army is up to its nipples in shrinks these days," Boxers said. "*Somebody* has to have wondered the obvious."

"You already know some of it," Rollins said. "Those assholes who came at his family undoubtedly screwed him up at least a little."

"No," Jonathan said. "Well, of course it was traumatic, but I spoke with Boomer not long after that. He was okay."

"His deployments, then," Rollins said. With an acknowledging hand to Big Guy, he added, "Nipples-deep in shrinks as we are, there are no doubt hundreds of possible diagnoses, but none of them can be tested because we haven't been able to talk to Boomer because we don't know where he is."

"Why does it have to be Boomer?" Jonathan pressed. "You've got a couple of dead Agency guys—"

"Three," Rollins interrupted. "*Three* dead Agency guys, and they were all in the same AO as Boomer during his last deployment."

Jonathan recognized the acronym for area of operation. "So? After we punted on Iraq, Afghanistan was the only AO we had left. There have to be thousands of cross-links between the Agency dead and soldiers in country."

"And what makes you think they weren't killed by the Taliban?" Boxers asked.

"You're both getting defensive," Rollins said.

"Of course we're defensive!" Boxers yelled. Jonathan could tell he was spinning up to a bad place. "And why aren't you? Haven't you turned you back on enough of your brothers over the years?"

Jonathan extended a hand to calm his friend down. "Not now, Box."

"Screw you," he snapped, and his face instantly showed horror. "Not you. Him. Not only do you lay this on your own Army, you have to lay it on our Unit brother."

"If you'll calm down, I'll explain it to you!" Rollins shouted. He could get spun up, too.

Jonathan knew it was time to play peacekeeper. "Quit shouting, both of you. Colonel, I encourage you to make your case quickly, and with minimal bullshit, and as you do, keep in mind that you're talking about a friend who's given a hell of a lot for his country."

Some of the red left Rollins's face. None of it left Boxers'.

"Some bad things happened on Boomer's last tour," Rollins said. "I can't go into details, but he'd been working a source for quite some time, and then the source was killed. We think he blamed his CIA counter-parts."

"Why would he do that?" Jonathan asked.

"Because we blame the Agency for everything," Rollins replied. "Some things never change."

"There's a giant step between blaming and killing," Boxers said. "What proof do you have?"

Rollins looked to the ceiling and scowled, as if to divine his next words. "There's proof, and then there's *proof.* We don't have any of the latter. What we do know is he came home, walked away from his marriage, and disappeared." His eyes bored into Jonathan. "And I mean *disappeared.* Off the grid."

"You know, we're trained to do that, right?" Jonathan said. "In fact, we're *paid* to do that when we're in hostile territory."

"But domestically? Who would do that?"

Jonathan waited for him to get the absurdity of his own question.

Rollins acknowledged with a nod. "Okay, other than you, who would do that? Within a few days of his disappearance, the first of the Agency guys was killed, shot with a five-five-six round from a long ways away. Over two hundred yards, as I recall. He was on his way to his car in the driveway, and it was a perfect head shot."

Jonathan felt tension in his chest. That wasn't the kind of a shot most amateurs could make.

"Three days later, the second agent was taken out as he exited a coffee shop outside of Fredericksburg, Virginia, not far from your stomping grounds. Five-five-six again, center of mass, hollow-point round. Perfect shot and no one heard it."

Boxers' ire had transformed to concern. "Was this a coffee shop he went to regularly?"

Rollins nodded. "Every day. How did you know?"

"Was the first guy—the head shot—a hollow point?"

"No." Rollins smiled. He saw that Boxers got it.

"He was worried about collateral damage," Big Guy said. He looked to Jonathan. "He'd studied the guy's routine and used HPs as a safety."

"What about the third?" Jonathan asked.

"Another head shot," Rollins said, "again from long distance. The interesting thing there was that the shooter showed great patience. The agent had been standing for ten minutes with his kid at the end of the driveway, waiting for the school bus." He looked to Boxers. "Like before, this was a daily routine. He waited till the little girl was on the bus, and the bus was on its way before he shot. No one heard or saw anything. By the time his wife woke up and noticed he was missing—and then found the body—he was already stiff."

Jonathan took a pull on his scotch as he pushed the pieces into place. "That still doesn't mean Boomer did it," he said. Even he heard the weakness of his words.

"Doesn't matter," Rollins said. "The Agency thinks he did, and they'll move heaven and earth to find him and take him out."

"What about due process?" Boxers asked.

"Where have you been the past few years?" Rollins countered. "The alphabet agencies stopped caring about due process when the regime changed. That was about the same time when beat cops started riding around in tanks. This isn't your childhood America anymore."

"So, we've got a lot of conjecture and assumptions," Jonathan summarized. "Cut to the chase, Colonel. Why are you here?"

Rollins cast a nervous glance to Boxers as he said, "We want you to find Boomer and bring him home."

"Well, that's not gonna happen," Boxers said. "I don't hunt down my friends."

Jonathan said, "By 'bring him home,' do you mean alive or dead?"

"Preferably alive."

"But dead would be okay, too." Boxers growled.

Rollins worked his jaw muscles. "No, dead would not be *okay,* Box. But don't forget that every Agency wet work contractor is out looking for this guy. If they get him, he's toast."

"Then why not just leave it to them?" Jonathan asked.

Rollins recoiled. "You said it yourself, Dig. He's family. Boomer deserves better than a bullet. I don't care what he did, he deserves better than that. If you can get to him first, maybe you can talk him down. If he hears that you're the one hunting for him, maybe he'll take the time to at least tell his side of the story. This is serious stuff."

Jonathan leaned back into his seat and crossed his legs. The math here wasn't working for him. "You said bad things happened to him over there on his last tour. I won't even ask you for those details—at least not yet—but if the bad stuff is traceable to specific interactions with specific Agency assets, then I presume the remaining assets have become much harder targets."

"All the targets have been eliminated," Rollins said.

Jonathan exchanged a confused look with Boxers. "Then what's done is done," he said. "Good reasons, bad reasons, that's for others to decide. I'm not a cop. I'm not going to traipse all over hell's half acre to bring a colleague into custody."

"It's more than that," Rollins said. "The killings are real—they really happened—but that's not the punch line."

"Good Christ, Stanley," Boxers said with a derisive laugh. "Can't you just for once in your life deal from the top of the deck? Why does everything—"

"He's a traitor, guys," Rollins said. "He's selling secrets to the world."

Jonathan's heart skipped. "What kind of secrets?"

"The most damaging kind you can think of," Rollins said.

Chapter Three

"**I** can think of some pretty damaging secrets," Jonathan said.

"And with all due respect," Rollins said, "the ones you know are pretty old and yet they're still damaging if released. Boomer had access to the same smorgasbord of highly classified, compartmentalized information, and his are brand spanking new."

"*Traitor* is a big word," Boxers said. "Why haven't I read about any of this in the news?"

"Because he's not leaking to the news," Rollins said. "He's leaking directly to foreign intelligence services, and they know better than to cut off the gravy train."

"Meaning that they haven't told the press?" Boxers asked.

"Exactly."

"Well, that won't last for long," Jonathan said. "Not all intelligence apparati leak as badly as ours, but they all leak, sooner or later. Are we talking deployment strengths and launch codes, or are we talking the president's high school yearbook photos?" Among the worst-kept secrets in the world, as far as Jonathan was concerned, was the fact that the United States considered far too many trivial details to be highly classified. It was no soldier's prerogative to make such a judgment on his own, but by casting such a wide net, the government had deflated the value of classified labels.

"Somewhere in the middle, as far as we can tell," Rollins said. "The worst we've seen so far is a list of Agency assets in various countries around the world."

"Wow," Boxers said. "You're telling me that he's doing the same thing that you say prompted him to kill when it was done by others?"

"More or less, yes."

Jonathan's hand shot up. "Ding-ding. Bullshit bell. You said, 'more or less,'" Jonathan pressed. "That's a hedge. Give me both the more and the less."

Rollins sighed, clearly caught in an obfuscation. "There are differences," he said. "We think Boomer killed because the Agency gave up civilian assets. Boomer, on the other hand, is only giving up career assets."

"In what part of the world?" Boxers asked. From the look on Big Guy's face, Jonathan believed that Boxers was beginning to see the same crack in the story.

Rollins looked up at the ceiling. This guy had tells on top of his tells, always had. "No especially hot spots," he said.

"Be more specific," Jonathan pressed.

"Okay, he's given up France, Switzerland, and Italy, so far. But that's not the point—"

A laugh escaped from Jonathan's throat before he could stop it. "That's a lot less than more, Colonel. Jesus, how can you equate Paris to Kabul?"

"I don't," Rollins said. He appeared to be embarrassed. "But my bosses do. They think that he's only toying with us, that sooner or later, he'll start releasing the truly damaging material."

"How do you know he's even got it to release?" Boxers asked.

"Because we know which databases and files he stole," Rollins said. "And it goes way past Agency assets. We're talking war plans here, guys. We're talking every bad thing you can imagine."

Jonathan laughed again.

"This is funny to you?" Rollins said.

"Hell yes, it's funny," Jonathan said. His volume rose with his blood pressure. "How many times do you guys need to learn the same lesson? How did you let one guy—I don't care who the hell he is—access that kind of data and not know he was doing it?"

"Because he was with the Unit!" Rollins boomed. "We're the best of the best, remember? The most trusted of the trusted! Can you think of a single time that you were denied access to something you told your boss you needed to see when you were in country? It's not like you have to open every file. You just copy everything and look at it later. This is *huge,* Dig. It's beyond huge."

"If he turns himself in, he'll go to prison forever," Jonathan said. "How can we talk him into that?"

"It's better than getting murdered."

"Is it?" Boxers asked. "Given the choice, I'd take the bullet over a concrete hole."

Rollins stood, prompting Jonathan and Boxers to share a glance. If Jonathan hadn't received assurances that the colonel was unarmed, he'd have interpreted the movement as an aggressive act, an effort to gain physical advantage.

"That brings me to the next point," Rollins said.

"You ever notice there's always a next point when you're talking with Roleplay?" Boxers quipped. Rollins's shoulders stiffened at the use of the name he hated.

"I have," Jonathan said. He was *this close* to kicking the colonel out of the compound. "Just tell the whole damn story."

"It's the question you just asked," Rollins said. "How was he able to do steal what he stole? We don't have the answer to that question. Our tech guys can't figure it out. We need to know how he got the information."

"So you want to squeeze him before you put him in a hole forever," Boxers said.

Rollins squared off opposite Big Guy, staring him directly in the eye. "Yes, Box, that's exactly what I want to do. I want to squeeze him for information. I have every right to want it, and I have every intention of getting it."

"Why not just do it yourself, then?" Jonathan asked. "Get somebody with stars on his shoulder to cut the orders and you go in with the Unit and grab him."

Rollins took a few seconds to settle down, then returned to his chair. "That's not possible. The president will never approve a move like that."

"But he'll approve it for the CIA?" Jonathan asked. "What's the difference?"

"There are places where the Agency can go that the US military cannot."

"Do you even know where he is?" Boxers asked. "I kind of got the impression that you were clueless."

"We have reason to believe that he is somewhere in Central or South America."

"That's good, limiting the search parameters to six, seven million square miles," Boxers said. "With eighty million dollars' worth of Unit training in his head, that's a big playground to disappear into."

"I think the colonel is telling us they think he's in a part of the six or seven million square miles where the military cannot go without igniting a war," Jonathan said.

Rollins confirmed the guess with his eyebrows.

"And that means Cuba?" Boxers said.

"Or Venezuela," Jonathan said. "I think Colombia is our friend now. Or maybe that was yesterday. It gets so confusing after a while."

"So now you know why I'm coming to you," Rollins said. "Plus, that part of the world is your old stomping grounds."

Early in their time with the Unit, the squadron Jonathan and Boxers had been attached to had in fact stirred a lot of trouble south of the border.

"Are you saying that Boomer sought and received asylum from Cuba?" Jonathan asked. This was getting weirder by the second.

"We have no evidence of that," Rollins said, "but that is definitely a concern. Armed with the information he has, he'd be a big score for any of our enemies."

"I'm still confused on this," Boxers said. "Who's he leaking French and Austrian secrets to?"

Rollins pointed at Big Guy, acknowledging a good point. "Excellent question. I should have mentioned it earlier. Every release that we know of has been very specifically targeted. He sent the French information to the Russians, and only the Russians. The Austrian secrets went exclusively to the embassy of the Czech Republic. That's why I think he's playing with us, testing his strategies before sharing the really damaging information."

It was Jonathan's turn to stand, and he took his scotch with him. "This is different from the other blanket leaks of secrets, then," he said. "Edward Snowden sent his to the press for the specific reason of exposing secrets for the sake of exposing them. By targeting them like this—"

"—only a small population of people know that the secrets exist," Boxers finished.

"That's what I mean when I say that I think he's testing his systems. He doesn't want to tip his big hand until he knows he can pull off everything he wants to pull off."

"Which would be what?" Jonathan asked.

"I don't know." Rollins glared at Boxers. "Thus the desire to squeeze him for information. We don't even know for a fact that he's working alone."

Jonathan thought it through. "You know, it's not easy to pull off the kind of snatch and grab mission you're suggesting in another country. The logistics are difficult and the costs are high."

"We're not expecting you to do this on your own dime, Dig," Rollins said.

"Oh, I already knew that. The question is, who *will* be paying for it?"

"Your dear Uncle Sam," Rollins said. "Over the years, we've accumulated stashes of cash that Congress doesn't know about. There's enough to do pretty much whatever you want. We'll place what you need in an account of your choosing and under a name of your choosing. You draw from the account as you see fit. When the mission is over, it's over, and the remainder is yours to do with as you please."

The number Jonathan asked for needed to be a big one. Not only would he have to arrange for noncommercial transport in and out of the country, he'd have to arrange for weapons and identification, and all the other moving parts that went into operating that far away from home.

"Just to be clear," Jonathan said. "Will we have any government cover at all?"

"Absolutely not. If asked, this conversation never happened, and your kind Uncle had no idea where you were or why you were there."

"And when we locate Boomer, what then?" Boxers asked. "Who do we contact and where do we take him?"

"You'll have a contact protocol," Rollins assured. "If it comes to that, it'll be handled efficiently."

"Who else knows about this?" Jonathan asked. "Not officially, but in reality?"

"My boss knows," Rollins said. That would be the commanding general of the Unit.

"And what about his boss?" That would be the secretary of defense and on into the leaking civilian structure.

"I can't imagine a reason why he would be clued in," Rollins said. "Especially since this conversation never happened, and the cash we'll be transferring never existed."

Jonathan looked to Big Guy, whose expression looked oddly like JoeDog's when she thought it was time to go on a ride in the car. *Let's do it, let's do it, let's do it . . .*

"You'll stay out of my way in the planning?" Jonathan asked.

"Even if you call, I will not answer," Rollins said. He made a cross with his finger over his heart. "Scout's honor."

Jonathan weighed the options one last time. "What the hell?" he said. "You gotta die of something. Deal."

They shook on it.

Chapter Four

Haynes Moncrief acknowledged the maître d' with an arched eyebrow and headed for his regular table in the back left corner of the dark and opulent dining room, past the private wooden wine lockers of the establishment's most pretentious patrons on the left, and past the expansive display of wines for sale on the right. Morton's Steakhouse at Connecticut Avenue and Seventeenth Street, Northwest, had been his favorite spot for far longer than his celebrity had made him recognizable. His table made him invisible from the door, though not necessarily from the rest of the diners, but he'd found that by the time most people were seated and engaged in their own conversations, they had little inclination to break away to talk politics.

If he truly wanted to be invisible, he could sit with his back to the room, but he'd spent too many years under fire in too many corners of the world to not keep tabs on the people around him. Besides, since the murder of Congressman Blaine from Illinois remained unsolved, the Hill security apparatus had redoubled their efforts to get people like Haynes to pay more attention to their surroundings. He so loved getting lectures from tough-looking kids who were younger than Haynes's oldest pair of underpants.

He'd just pulled his phone from the inside pocket of his suit jacket when he saw his Manhattan on its way. More specifically, his *perfect* Manhattan—Maker's Mark plus equal shares of sweet and dry vermouth—with a twist instead of the cloying cherries that were the normal garnish. Too few bartenders knew how to pour a decent drink anymore, and Pierre was one of them.

Luis Martinez carried the silver tray with the drink perched in the middle, like the hub of a wheel. "Good evening, Senator," he said as he approached. "I took the liberty." Luis placed a napkin on the charger plate in front of his customer, and the drink on top of the napkin.

"Thank you," Haynes said. He took care lifting the conical martini glass, concentrating on not spilling a drop of the nearly overflowing drink.

"Are you ready to order, sir?"

"Tell Pierre he did it again," Haynes said as the drink warmed his core. "I don't think I'm ready just yet. I'll take some bread, though, and a glass of water."

"And are you expecting guests this evening, or should I take these other settings away?"

"I hope I'm dining alone. But leave one extra place." He winked. "You never know when some beautiful young lady might want to discuss politics over dinner."

Luis smiled. "Of course, sir. I'll check back with you in a few minutes."

"Luis, I'll tell you what. When this glass is empty, bring it a little brother, and then we'll talk food."

"Absolutely, sir."

He took another sip, placed the drink on its napkin, and turned his attention back to his phone. He'd been working hard to fully embrace the twenty-first century, and part of his commitment was to depend more and more on electronic readers as his source of news. While he missed the rustle of the newsprint, he didn't miss the inconvenience or the ink-stained fingers, so he figured he had a decent shot at successfully making the transition. The question now was which site to read first, the news outlet that portrayed him as a hero, or the one that portrayed him as an asshole. He decided on the latter to see what the president's media buddies were up to.

The update on the *Washington Enquirer* site read, "Moncrief Vows to Undermine President."

He'd done nothing of the sort, of course. Rather, he said in session that the president's plan to reduce military spending would undermine the security of the Free World, and that as long as he, Haynes, held the position of minority leader, his caucus would do everything in its power to block him. Partisanship aside, Haynes could not wrap his head around why the president and his party felt so uncomfortable showing international leadership. Whereas the Monroe Doctrine professed to protect the United States from all incursions into our hemisphere, President Darmond's doctrine seemed to be all about apologizing for past successes and surrendering against future victories. How that ass hat was able to get reelected after all the scandals of his administration remained one of life's great mysteries.

He'd just clicked on an article about the non-progress on the Blaine investigation when a shadow loomed over his table. He looked up to see the face and then he groaned.

"Excuse me, Leader Moncrief, but I need a moment of your time."

It was Mark Reeder, a longtime political gadfly, who now served as deputy assistant under chief special counselor to the president. Or something like that. Skinny and bald, he sported a ring of white Larry Fine hair above his ears and a Fagin beard.

"Mr. Reeder," Haynes said. "Having dedicated a great deal of time in recent months acquainting myself with new technology, I understand that a Mr. Alexander Bell from up your way in Yankee country has invented a device called a telephone. Have you heard of it?"

Reeder pulled out the chair to Haynes's left and sat. "May I join you?"

"Apparently so." Haynes checked his watch. "You do know it's seven-thirty, right? In a mere four and a half hours, you'll have a whole new day for working."

"This is important, Haynes."

The senator pressed the button to darken his phone and slid it back into his jacket pocket. "I prefer *Leader Moncrief.* Make it short."

"The president would like to speak to you about—"

"I believe he has a telephone, too. Even has my cell phone number. If it was as important as you purport, His Highness could be talking directly to me, and you could be at home with your dogs." Reeder famously preferred the company of dogs to human relationships. It made him the perfect White House staffer.

Luis reappeared. "Excuse me, Senator. May I get your guest something to drink?"

"He's not staying," Haynes said.

Luis blushed and looked to the floor. And vaporized.

"What are you so pissed off about?" Reeder said. "You're jumpy."

"I'm not *jumpy,* Mark. I'm tired and much more sober than I care to be. You want to talk about work, when in fact, I just left fifteen hours of work."

"That's the job when you're at the top of the heap."

Haynes took another sip of his Manhattan. A much bigger one. "Right now, Mark, I feel like hitting you in the face. I'm tired of the games your team has been playing."

"You'd feel differently if yours was the side that was winning."

"That's the thing, Mark. Until your regime moved into 1600 Pennsylvania Avenue, both sides understood that the game really was anything *but* a game. We have serious jobs to do, with serious consequences if we do things wrong. You guys just want to throw socialist, populist bullshit to the masses, and then call us names in the press when we save you from yourselves."

"If it's so bad for the country, why not just let us win?"

"Because you guys don't blink. You're already in your second term, and you know damn well that the damage you're doing will be delayed in its effect, and then, when we take back the White House in four years, you'll point to the new guy and the public will blame all the problems on him."

Reeder grinned. "You're right," he said. "You really

aren't drunk enough yet. Still, my boss wants you to re-consider your resistance to the Defense bill."

"That's fascinating. Have your boss talk to my chief of staff, and we'll arrange a special appointment for him to kiss my ass."

"Jessica Reinhardt," Reeder said.

The name hit like a gut punch. Haynes tried not to show it, but he knew he flinched. He said nothing, but as he lifted his drink, he saw the slight tremor in his hand.

"She was only sixteen," Reeder went on. "Her son, Lance, found out who his father is, and he contacted us with the news." He leaned in closer. "Turns out he's a populist-socialist, and the stuff he's reading about his daddy does not make him proud."

Haynes felt his ears going hot. "This Lance fellow," he said. "How old is he?"

Reeder shrugged. "Thirty-ish. Thirty-one, I think."

"And I'm forty-nine."

Reeder chuckled. "Ah, you want me to do the math. Yes, I understand that you were only eighteen yourself, but statutory rape is statutory rape. I don't believe there's a statute of limitations for sex crimes in Virginia."

Haynes felt the room narrowing, the light dimming. You didn't get to his heights in the political stratos-phere without expecting cheap shots, but this one had come out of nowhere. Jessica had been his high school squeeze, and when they'd first done the Big Nasty, they'd both been minors. Then his birthday came first, and the rest was named Lance. Last time he'd heard, Jessica had married a lawyer in North Carolina and

was living a happy life. She'd never sought anything
from him. And now this.

"There's a demand at the end of this," Haynes said.
"Understanding that I'm neither confirming nor denying, why don't you cut to the chase?"

Reeder's face peeled back into its lobbyist sneer as he
leaned back in his chair and crossed his legs. "You are a
cynical, cynical man, Senator Moncrief. I'm merely here
to give you a heads-up on a threat that seems to be looming over your sterling reputation."

The steak knife at Haynes's left hand called to him.
In a single stroke, he could drive it through the soft
spot under this chickenshit's jaw and into his brain
stem, disconnecting his melon from the rest of his
body before he'd even know to flinch.

"You're attempting to blackmail me on behalf of
your boss. Be careful, Mark. He has a security team.
You don't."

"Did you just threaten me?"

Haynes leaned forward until his arms were on the
table and glared at the little man with the big beard. "I
would never do such a thing," he said.

Reeder leaned back farther. "You don't scare me,"
he said.

"Yes, I do. And if I don't, you're more of an idiot
than I think you are."

"I don't think you entirely grasp where you are, Senator."

"Leader Moncrief."

"Haynes. This story hasn't hit the media yet because
we talked your baby boy Lance into keeping it quiet
until we could talk to you."

"Which brings me back to your last lie," Haynes said. "What do you want?"

Reeder took his time gathering his thoughts. "Pretty much anything we want," he said. "We don't want you to do anything overt, nothing affirmative. Just stay out of our way."

A punch to the throat would kill him, too. Haynes felt his fist tightening as that thought passed through his brain.

Yet he relaxed his posture. He'd fought too many battles over the decades without a major loss to concede defeat to this chicken-neck asshole. "Give me a second," he said. He reached into his pocket and withdrew his cell phone again.

"Take your time," Reeder said. His face showed equal parts confusion and discomfort.

Haynes pushed a speed dial and waited, confident that the party on the other end would pick up before the third ring. "Stella Pence," a voice answered. She had been Haynes's chief of staff for as long as he'd had a staff that needed a chief.

"Hi, Stella," he said. "Mark Reeder invaded my space at Morton's. Tony Darmond knows about Lance Reinhardt."

"Oh, no. Really? I'm so sorry."

"Don't be," he said. "It had to happen sooner or later. Sorry to put you on this particular spot at so late an hour, but make the calls you need to make. We're going nuclear."

Stella fell silent on the other end of the phone. "Are you sure?" she said. "There's no going back."

Haynes let her words swirl in his head for a while, mixing with his fantasies of reducing Reeder to a lifeless lump of tissue. "You've got a point," he said at length. "Can I ask you to hang around your phone for a few minutes? I'll get back to you one way or the other."

"Of course. Do you—"

He clicked off, slipped the phone back into his pocket, and smirked at Reeder, who he knew had heard his conversation.

"What?" Reeder said. "Clearly, I'm supposed to be even more afraid than I wasn't before. You've got a *nuclear* plan." He feigned a body-wide shiver. "Ooh, how scary."

"Did you know that the First Lady used to be a terrorist?" Haynes asked. "She killed people on behalf of her old friends from Russia. She also had an affair with Douglas Winters. You remember him, right? He *committed suicide* a while back?" He used finger quotes as he leaned on those words.

Reeder's steely façade twitched. "I have no idea what you're talking about."

Haynes allowed himself a laugh. "Wow, that surprises me. Well, be sure to watch the morning news shows tomorrow. It's a very cool story." He looked up for Luis's attention and beckoned him over. "I might even mention something about a story you're going to leak in a foolish effort to discredit me. I'm sure that the thirty-year-old innocent sex story will resonate far louder than the president's wife trying to topple the government."

Luis arrived at the table.

Haynes pointed to Reeder with an open palm. "My pale, trembling friend here was hoping someone could escort him to the door."

Luis looked terrified. He clearly had no idea what to say.

"Are you okay, Mark?" Haynes asked. "You don't look well." He made eye contact with Luis, and indicated with a twitch of his head that he should make himself scarce.

When they were alone, Reeder said, "If you had evidence, you would have revealed it by now."

Haynes sat taller. "I've known about your boss's transgressions since he first decided to transgress. I haven't revealed what I know because I thought it would harm the country that I actually love. That's hard for you guys to swallow, I know, but there it is."

"Yet despite this patriotic fervor, if we threaten to come at *you*—"

"I will tear off your head and shit down your neck," Haynes said. "Count on that."

"We'll take you down with us."

"No, you won't," Haynes said. "Despite all the tummy rubs you give to your lapdogs in the press, they'll tear you apart to get to the kind of raw meat I'm prepared to dangle. It's not as if the stage hasn't already been set. Remember those 'disproven' blog posts from a while ago? That fire went dark, but I bet it would be easy to rekindle."

Reeder looked deflated—literally, like he needed air. "Is this really the way you want to play the game?"

Haynes laughed long and hard. "Really, Mark?

That's your question to *me?* Do you remember who invaded whose private space here?"

Haynes could almost hear the gears in Reeder's head grinding for an exit strategy.

"Tell you what, Mark," he said. "Why don't you leave me alone?" He checked his watch. "I don't want an answer from you now. I'll give you till eight-thirty to say that you're sorry and that I never have to worry about some bogus statutory rape charge. At eight thirty-one, I'm going to tell Stella to start calling news-rooms."

Reeder sat there, looking dejected, as if the evening had gone any way but how he had anticipated, which was no doubt the case.

"This is your time to walk away," Haynes said. He motioned for Luis to show Reeder the door.

The meal tasted even better than usual. In addition to being one of the final bastions that recognized a perfect Manhattan, Morton's likewise understood the meaning of medium rare—it meant just north of rare, not just south of medium. When applied to a good cut of beef, the difference meant everything. Haynes received the phone call he'd been waiting for at eight-fifteen. The timing itself confirmed the value of the information he guarded. Nowhere else on the planet did the old saw, *information is power,* resonate louder.

With his belly full and his head appropriately buzzy, he stepped off the escalator into the lobby of the building that housed the restaurant, and from there, out into the stifling humidity of the evening. He turned right onto Connecticut Avenue and headed toward Farragut Square, beyond which another escalator would take him down to the subterranean bunker that was the Farragut West Metro station. His status as Senate minority leader qualified him for a car and a driver and a security detail, but he'd never wanted any of that. The voters he served were commuters themselves, and he'd hung at least two reelection bids on the fact that he endured what they endured every day. Oh, that the clueless, tone-deaf management structure of the Washington Metropolitan Area Transit Authority could find a way to make the nation's second-busiest commuter rail run on time with equipment that worked. Haynes had actually asked the question, in session, why it was that Metro officials granted themselves raises when fifteen percent of their elevators and twenty percent of their escalators were out of service on any given day.

He'd been shamed into abandoning that theme when someone on Twitter made the news by asking why he should be paid at all, given the dysfunction of Congress. It was the kind of taunt that felt like it could have legs, so he abandoned the Metro theme before the media forced him into an unfortunate sound bite.

Now that the public was politically illiterate—where sound bites on the bedtime comedy shows were the largest source of news for the under-thirty crowd—there was no longer such a thing as an innocent slip of the tongue.

He was making this walk through Farragut Square later in the evening than he'd planned. The indigents and homeless were reappearing from their daytime

hideouts and beginning to set up camp. At an intellec-
tual, intuitive level, Haynes understood that these poor
souls were largely harmless, but he also understood
that a good many of them would be better off in a mental hospital than on a filthy tarp on the grass. They
made him uncomfortable.

As he traveled the brick walkway, he kept his hands
in his pockets, his right fist wrapped around the grip of
his Ruger LCP .380 pistol. He carried it in a pocket
holster that always rested on his right thigh—literally
inside the pocket of his suit pants. He never told anyone about it because it was none of their business, and
he could get away with carrying it to work because
members of Congress bypassed the magnetometers
and security checkpoints. He harbored no fantasies
about shooting it out with bad guys, but if an active
shooter got loose inside the Capitol, or some nut job
started shooting up a rally, he at least wanted a fighting
chance if the murderer made eye contact.

Haynes knew the raggedy man up ahead was trouble
the instant he rose from his bench. It was something in
the way the man carried himself. His posture was too
good for a homeless guy, his neck too athletic. His eyes
too intense. And he was looking directly at Haynes.
And he wasn't dressed properly. No one needed a coat
when it was this hot outside.

Haynes knew that he was about to get mugged. He
stopped and set his feet for a fight.

The raggedy man clearly saw that Haynes had made
him, and he sped up his pace to close the distance. He
reminded Haynes of a torpedo in the water, its course
set and its mission irreversible.

Haynes reacted without thinking. The LCP was out of his pocket and in his hand. His left hand joined his right for support, and he bent slightly into an isosceles stance, just as he'd been trained, and just as he'd practiced.

"Stop!" Haynes shouted. He was way too loud because he wanted witnesses to know that this was not a fight he'd picked. "I don't want to hurt you!"

The man stopped forward progress, but his arms moved in a blur. A stubby sawed-off pistol-grip shotgun appeared from under his coat and he swung it up toward Haynes. The attacker said nothing.

Haynes pulled the trigger—there was no squeezing the little pistol's heavy trigger—and the pistol bucked. Blinded by the muzzle flash, he fired again, two shots in two seconds. Homeless people and pedestrians screamed and scattered, but the raggedy man in his sights just stood there.

If the shotgun had gone off, Haynes hadn't heard it—and he didn't feel any holes in his gut. But he also saw no holes in his attacker. The man wobbled a bit, seeming to have difficulty raising his shotgun again.

Haynes considered taking another shot, but then the attacker listed to his left and fell like a tree onto the grass.

Consumed by decades-old training, Haynes dropped his aim to the low-ready position and scanned left and right, searching for additional threats. Seeing none, he pivoted a one-eighty and scanned for threats that might be behind him. In his immediate vicinity, he saw only people on the ground or running away. In the farther vicinity, a few clueless Metro riders continued their casual stroll in his direction.

No one else seemed to be posing a threat. Instinctively aware that he had only five shots left if bad things happened, he shifted the pistol to his left hand, and with his right, he pulled his cell phone from its pocket inside his jacket.

This was going to be a long night.

Chapter Five

Security Solutions, Inc., was more than an official cover for Jonathan's covert activities—although it was certainly that. Renowned as a high-end private investigation firm, Security Solutions operated out of the top floor of a converted firehouse in Fisherman's Cove, Virginia—along the Northern Neck of the Potomac River—that also served as Jonathan's home, which took up the first two floors.

Security Solutions worked miracles for some of the biggest corporate names in the world, but for the most part, those investigations bored Jonathan to tears. As owner and CEO, he had to sign the checks and sit through the update meetings, but he lived for the juice of the 0300 missions—those jobs that separated good guys from the bad guys who had taken them hostage. These missions tested skills that he had learned at great taxpayer expense during his years in the United States Army and its most secret covert Special Operations unit. Once it was in your blood, it was there to stay.

The covert side of the business had no name, and

did not officially exist, though given the talent he hired for the overt side, some of those brilliant minds had to wonder what went on beyond the perpetually guarded door to The Cave, the section of the office's footprint where Jonathan's and Boxers' offices were located, along with that of Venice Alexander. (It's pronounced Ven-EE-chay, by the way, and if you don't have time in your schedule for a long lecture, you'd best not get it wrong a second time.) Nearly nailed as a felon in her younger years for causing mischief with her computer skills, Venice was now Jonathan's hacker-in-chief, and she'd never let him down.

At Jonathan's request, they'd gathered this morning in the War Room, the teak conference room within The Cave that Jonathan had stuffed with every techno-toy that Venice ever requested. Jonathan didn't even try to understand what most of it did. Venice sat at what Jonathan called the captain's station. Located at the far end of the rectangular conference table from the massive 106-inch projection screen, her spot was adorned with multiple keyboards, computers, and monitors— and maybe even a coffeemaker, as far as Jonathan knew. He might be the boss, but only a lunatic with a death wish would touch Venice's toys.

The other seven seats around the table had their own computers and monitors, too, but only Venice could patch them to the main screen, which currently displayed two pictures of Dylan Nasbe. The one on the left showed him kitted up for duty in Afghanistan, his face all but obscured by an uncontrolled growth of beard, while the one on the right was his formal Army portrait—the one that would have been shown on the news if he'd been off'd in combat. Universal camouflage ACUs (Army Combat Uniforms), thick neck, square jaw, tan Rangers beret set just so.

"How come you guys never smile in these photos?" Venice asked.

"Because we're killing machines," Jonathan said without dropping a beat. "Machines don't smile."

"So, that explains Boxers," she said.

"Hey," Big Guy said. He'd been concentrating on stirring his coffee. "Is that really how you want this meeting to start?" He flashed a ridiculous, slightly frightening pantomime of a happy face. "Is that better?"

"You said something about invading South America again," Venice said. "Is this gentleman the reason why?"

"He is."

"Well, at a glance, I've got to tell you that he looks like he can fend pretty well for himself."

"It's not an oh-three hundred mission," Jonathan said. He took ten minutes to fill her in on the details she'd missed yesterday afternoon.

While she listened, Venice pulled up a map of the world and made it spin to the Western Hemisphere, and from there zoomed in until Venezuela, Jamaica, Haiti, the Dominican Republic, and Cuba filled the screen. When Jonathan finished, she said, "So, let me get this straight. One guy is hiding out somewhere in this general area. What is that, only five percent of the world's land mass?"

"I think that's high," Boxers said. "I say three percent." This time, his smile was genuine.

"It makes the most sense that he would be in Venezuela," Jonathan said. "I don't see Boomer defecting to the Cubans, Jamaica is too full of tourists, and no one in their right mind would hole up in Haiti."

"Plus, the Cubans are about to be our friends again," Venice said.

"And there's that," Jonathan agreed.

"It's easy to live like a king in Haiti," Boxers said.

Jonathan coughed out a chuckle. They'd spent some time in Haiti a few years ago while in service to Uncle, and even the presidential palace was a dump in comparison to other such accommodations in the world—and that was before it was devastated by an earthquake. "I'm gonna trust my gut on this one," he said. "He's not in Cuba."

"How are you going to narrow it down?" Venice asked. "I mean seriously, you can't just go on a random search of the Caribbean."

Jonathan had already thought this through overnight. "I need you to pull up what you can on Boomer's family," he said.

Venice's jaw dropped. "Oh, my God, Dig. They're going to freak out if they see you again." Jonathan had rescued Christyne Nasbe and her son, Ryan, a while ago, in a particularly violent shootout. "Didn't Dylan tell you himself that they were having a hard time adjusting?"

"Yes, he did," Jonathan said. "But that was before he went rogue and started killing CIA assets. That's kind of a rule changer."

Venice's shoulders sagged as the reality washed over her. "That poor boy," she said. "How much can one family take?"

Jonathan bristled. "There's a place up the hill that's

filled with kids who show an amazing ability to adapt to adversity," he said. Resurrection House—the place up the hill—was a school Jonathan had founded anonymously as a residential facility for the children of incarcerated parents.

"Point taken." A few more keystrokes. "She's still in Fayetteville. She rents an apartment." Fayetteville was the home of Fort Bragg, which was the home of the Unit headquarters.

"Is she working?"

Venice shot him a look. "Give me a minute."

"Take your time," Jonathan said. "I don't mean to rush."

She rattled off a few more keystrokes, and then punctuated her work with a triumphant finger-poke to the keyboard. "Time!" she said. She pointed to the big screen with her forehead. "There it is. She's got a job at a lawyer's office."

"Really?" Boxers said. "She's not with the Unit?" The elite Special Forces organizations had a long-standing tradition of protecting their own. Many an administrative job was held by a son or daughter or wife of a fallen or retired operator.

"Sad, isn't it?" Venice said. "She moved off-post about three months ago. Ryan is in a public high school down there."

Of all the news Jonathan had heard that contradicted his memories of Dylan Nasbe, this was the most damaging. It took a lot to reach the status of *persona non grata* within the Unit. The only cases he knew of personally were assholes who took secrets public—and with one notable exception, all of those assholes had been Navy SEALs.

"Is it a good job?" Jonathan asked.

Venice laughed. "Good Lord, I wish I had the skills you think I do," she said. "I will send her apartment information to your GPS."

"Thank you."

Venice stopped typing and stared at her screen for a few seconds before giving Jonathan a scowl and leaning back in her Aeron chair.

"What?" he said.

"What makes you think she's going to tell you anything?" Venice asked. "What motivation could she possibly have to help you close the loop on her husband?"

"We're kind of her best bet," Boxers said.

"Silence seems like a very viable option," she countered.

"Only at first glance," Jonathan said. "I believe Roleplay when he talks about the Agency wet-work yay-hoos breaking their necks to kill him. If Christyne stays silent, she only helps the killers."

Venice wasn't buying. "That's what *you* say. I don't doubt that you're right, but how will she know that? The last time she saw you—"

"We damn near died saving her," Boxers said.

Venice went back to her keyboard. "I'm just saying that if I were her, based on what you shared about that night in the mountains, any vision of you is going to be pretty hardwired into bad times. I don't see that as a basis for great trust and sharing."

"Then I just need to be convincing," Jonathan said.

Venice looked back to him again. "I can see it now," she said. "Hi, Christyne. Last time I saw you, I was pulling you out of a river of blood, but now I want you to help me save your husband from a different river of blood."

"I think I'll use different words," Jonathan said.

"Of course you will," Venice said. "But will she hear them? And what about that boy? How are you planning to deal with his trauma?"

Jonathan saw the precipice of his patience approaching. "You're treating this as if it's a social visit, Ven. It's going to be an *awkward* visit. Our past history notwithstanding, there's the inherent awkwardness of Boomer betraying the nation he was sworn to protect."

"If that is, in fact, what he did," Venice said.

Jonathan conceded that part of her point. He still could not wrap his head around the notion that Dylan would do such a thing, but neither could he ignore the evidence that had been presented to him.

"Let me throw something into the debate," Boxers said. "Suppose Roleplay is just friggin' lying to us? Suppose Dylan never did anything remotely like the things he says he did, and this is just some kind a witch hunt they're wanting us to take point on?"

In all candor, Jonathan had not considered that possibility, at least not at that scale. He expected some of the details to be incomplete or misrepresented, but not the entire incident. "Why would he do that?" he asked.

"I don't know. It wouldn't be the first time Stanley's lied to us."

Without question Stanley Rollins's association with the truth was tenuous—perhaps even adversarial. But a lie of this magnitude—involving a fellow operator— would be of a scale that Jonathan could barely comprehend. "No," Jonathan said. "Rollins is an ass, but he's an ass who saved our lives. He came to us on this. I don't buy that he would be that dismissive of our safety."

Boxers raised his eyebrows and leaned back further into his seat. "I'm just sayin' . . ."

"And I'm just saying we made a commitment."

"Trust, but verify," Big Guy said.

"Always," Jonathan conceded. "And Ven, if it helps, I'll plan my visit to Christyne to make sure that Ryan is nowhere to be found. I'll do it during school hours."

Venice said nothing, but he saw the smile. It disappeared as her computer dinged, and her attention was diverted to another screen. "Huh," she said. "Don't you know Senator Haynes Moncrief?"

Jonathan nodded. They went way back. They were in Ranger school together, but Haynes hadn't made the cut for the Unit. Now he was a bigwig in the United States Senate. "Yeah, why?"

"I got an alert from ICIS," she said. Pronounced EYE-sis, the Interstate Crime Information System was a largely unknown post-9/11 system that was put in place through funds distributed by the Department of Homeland Security to keep various jurisdictions informed of criminal investigations real-time. "He was arrested last night for discharging an illegal firearm in DC."

Jonathan recoiled. "Discharging . . . What, was he shooting at streetlights or something?"

Venice read a little more. "No, he was defending himself against an alleged attack."

"What's an *alleged attack?*" Boxers asked, leaning on the words. "Seems to me somebody is attacked or they're not."

"I'm just reading you what I see," Venice said. "It says here that the man he killed had a sawed-off shotgun on him, but that it hadn't been discharged. The senator shot him twice in the chest and killed him."

"Haynes always was a good shot," Boxers said.

"Who attacked him?" Jonathan asked. "Was it an assassination attempt like that other congressman, or a random street crime?"

Venice read some more. "The record is still new, so it may be too early to know much for sure, but it seems to be leaning toward the senator as the aggressor."

"That's ridiculous," Jonathan said. "He's the Senate minority leader. Not exactly the profile of an active street shooter."

"Do you want to know what ICIS says or not?" Venice snapped.

Jonathan and Boxers exchanged looks. *Whoa.*

"So far, the investigation is focused on the fact that Senator Moncrief had a heated exchange over dinner with some White House official—"

"How could he even digest anything after breaking bread with one of those assholes?" Boxers said.

Venice continued as if uninterrupted. "—and he had had a few drinks." She looked up. "That's not the best set of circumstances after you shoot someone."

"Didn't you say that someone tried to shoot him first?" Jonathan asked.

"Some witnesses say that the senator drew his gun first—a gun that he was breaking the law just to have on his person."

"So, he should have shown the courtesy of letting himself be killed," Boxers said.

"Witnesses say that he made no effort to run away."

"From a *gun?*" Jonathan said. His voice had spiked an octave. "How fast a sprinter do they think he is?"

"Remember that I'm just the messenger, okay?" Venice said. "The police narrative emphasizes that the senator challenged his victim, drew his gun first. If he hadn't done that, then the victim would never have felt compelled to draw his gun to defend himself."

"The dead guy," Boxers said. "Was *his* gun legal?"

"Of course not," Jonathan said. "This is all politics. I say Haynes is screwed."

"I hate DC," Boxers growled. "It's a den of rats, every one of them waiting to feed on the mistakes or misfortunes of others."

Jonathan and Venice gaped in unison.

"What?" Boxers said.

"Mistakes and misfortunes of others?" Jonathan parroted.

"Positively eloquent," Venice said.

Boxers blushed. "Y'all suck."

Chapter Six

Lieutenant Colonel Ian Martin's heart sank when he saw the man enter the Washington Metro car at Foggy Bottom. Reflexively—instinctively—he saved the document on his laptop to its heavily encrypted home on his hard drive. When the computer sensed a connection, the drive would upload to the World Wide Web and then cleanse itself.

This was the third time in two days that Ian's path had crossed with this guy. He was on the tall side of average height and the thick side of average build, with a shaved head whose ring of shadow above his ears spoke more of male pattern vanity than tough guy fashion statement. A voice inside his brain told him that he was just being paranoid, but far fewer graves were filled with the bodies of paranoid people than people who chose not to trust their instincts.

Paranoia had been a driving force in Ian's life in the months since he'd launched his Uprising website. He'd covered his bases as best he could, thanks to the unwitting assistance of Uncle Sam's bazillion-dollar encryption software, but everyone knew that there was no such thing as true anonymity on the Internet. Ian wasn't even sure that he'd broken any laws—at least not yet—but just the notion that he might have meant that it was a good time to listen to the paranoid voices when they sang a unison chorus in your head. He just wished that the paranoia would be less of a shadow over his life.

Ian had started the Uprising website as a lark, maybe even as a joke—a place to anonymously post his frustrations as an army officer under the clueless leadership of the Darmond administration. It was hard enough to cast one's lots as a pawn to political gamesmanship, but Ian wondered if there'd ever been a time in modern history where incompetence had touched the clueless-ness of this team. The asshole in the presidential palace—and let's be honest, that's what the White House had become—was ready to surrender to any-body at the slightest provocation, and as a result, the world hailed him as the new prince of peace. Just be sure not to ask the residents of fallen democracies in the Middle East or the former Soviet states. They might confuse the American sense of peace with thou-sands of deaths and hundreds of thousands of refugees. But apparently, they weren't the United States' prob-lem, either.

The fact that the media so loved Tony Darmond, de-spite all of the scandals that had plagued his adminis-tration, frightened Ian more than the incompetence itself. The media lauded peace at all costs. The media outlets that had noticed the Uprising had already la-beled the site as a terrorist link, and painted those who'd joined Ian's side to be anti-American racist ho-mophobic killers of senior citizens. Or something like that.

As a military officer, Ian had dedicated his life to turning a blind eye to politics. He'd been sent to good wars and he'd been sent to stupid wars, and the secret to escaping the meat grinder with a sane mind was to embrace the truth that his was not to reason why. His job was to salute and make sometimes stupid stuff happen. To be a warrior for one's country was among the noblest callings a man could answer.

Until the orders he received tilted away from the lawful and reasonable. Once that line was crossed, Ian's duty to protect and defend the Constitution of the United States against all enemies, foreign and domestic, trumped the orders of the day.

As the rules changed around him over the five decades he'd walked the planet, Ian was reminded of the old story of the boiled frog. Put a frog in boiling water, and he'll jump out to save his life. Put him in cool water, however, and heat it around him, and he will allow himself to be boiled to death. So it was with the American people, who continued to sit passively as their God-given rights were stripped away by ambitious politicians.

Ian hated the thoughts and the feelings that had come to dominate his days. He hated the perpetual anger and the pervasive sense of helplessness as he watched with the rest of the silent masses as day after day evil triumphed over good. He knew there was a better way, and he knew that he was the one to spearhead it.

His plan was a simple one, requiring only a small band of loyal followers with very specific skills. He needed muscle, and he needed brains, but most of all he needed anonymity for everyone. His plan involved no invasions and no shoot-outs in city streets. Shots would need to be fired for sure, but if things went as he envisioned them, those shots would be fired one at a time, and a single box of ammo could accomplish everything that needed to be done.

The Uprising message boards had been his recruitment tool. By laying out red meat for people who were as frustrated as he, he'd baited a trap that would snare the kind of talent he was looking for. But he had to sift through the trolls and the nutjobs to single out those who truly were what they claimed to be.

The Uprising didn't need an army. It needed a *team,* a handful of maybe one hundred operators who could, in coordinated surgical attacks, eliminate the structural barriers that kept voters from having the voice they earned. It wouldn't be that hard, not with the right cadre of professionals. On Ian's side was the fact that the Department of Homeland Security was a muddled, bureaucratic mess, and the US military—one of the last bastions of sensible organization, albeit impossibly fat and inefficient in its own right—was forbidden by *posse comitatus* to do battle on American soil.

Among the delicate balancing challenges Ian had had to manage was how to share enough of the plan to attract good recruits, yet keep it secret enough that no one operator would ever have adequate information to betray him, the Uprising, or its other members. It had been a stressful few months feeling his way through new territory where the tolerance for a mistake was exactly zero. His efforts toward strict operational security had left no traceable bread crumbs—he was sure of that—but with each new human being in the mix, with their own personalities and weaknesses, bread crumbs began to form and multiply. Thus far, while he knew the true identities of the recruits he'd signed, none of them yet knew the identities of each other, but as their numbers swelled, that anonymity would become unsustainable.

And that was why the third sighting of the man on the Metro was so disturbing. In their first encounter—in a Starbucks—the man had attracted Ian's attention with a loud sneeze, and then had made a point of steadfastly avoiding eye contact as he read his newspaper upside down. Their second meeting played itself out in a CVS Pharmacy where Ian was picking up some nasal spray as a hedge against his summer allergies. There, the stranger hovered over the candy selection while Ian checked out, and then he followed him out of the store, only to peel off and go the other way once they were on the sidewalk.

And now this. The man stared with a malevolence that was intended to intimidate, and it was having its desired effect. Ian tried to appear disengaged, unconcerned, but as the man continued to stare, Ian could no longer fight the urge to stare back.

Finally, as they approached the Rosslyn Metro Station on the Blue Line, the man stood from his seat and approached.

Ian searched his memory for his quick-response training from long ago—a place to seek refuge from the fight he knew was coming, or, alternatively, some form of advantage over the attack. But there was nowhere for him to go, and it had been far too long since he'd thrown a punch to entertain a fantasy about throwing one now.

Whatever was coming was going to take its course without Ian having a vote.

At five foot nothing, Stella Pence was hands down the most intimidating person per cubic inch in the entire United States of America. She was already perched in her seat in the Leader's conference room when he entered at the appointed time. "Really, Haynes?" she said as his six-five frame cleared the door. "You had to shoot the guy? There wasn't an alternative?"

"Good afternoon, Stella," Haynes said. He helped himself to his seat at the end of the long table. As many staffers had suspected, his chair was in fact about an inch taller than the others.

She pantomimed for him to zip his lip and then she threw away the key. "You be quiet. Do you realize how much trouble you have caused? For us?"

Haynes let the words hang for a few seconds. "You can't want answers if you tell me to be quiet," he said.

Stella turned purple. Well, *more* purple. She'd been the heart and head of every one of his campaigns since the beginning, which felt like sometime around 1904. He understood that he owed her better than this.

"Look," he said. "The guy came off the park bench with the intent of killing me. I was faster than him. That's all there is to it."

"Not according to the Metropolitan Police," Stella said. "They remember something about laws that make it a felony to carry a weapon in the District of Columbia. What were you thinking?"

"Mostly about survival," Haynes said. "He was going

to kill me. I realize that this situation is an annoyance, but remember that my demise would leave you totally out of a job."

"Don't kid yourself," Stella snapped. "There are roughly ninety-nine senators and four hundred thirty-five members of the House who would fire everyone to hire me." It was more true than false.

Haynes laughed. "Truer words," he said. "So, how are we going to control this?"

"I told you that that gun would get you in trouble one day."

"Which part of 'it saved my life' are you having trouble with, Stella?" Haynes didn't mind tolerating a bit of grandstanding, but there were limits to everything.

"Are you armed again today?"

"That's an inappropriate question, and I will not answer it." Translation: Of course he was. The MPD had confiscated the LCP from last night, but there were more in his safe where that one came from. "Where we stand right now is that the Senate minority leader is alive despite DC's gun laws, and, parenthetically, no doubt contrary to the desire of the fellow in the Oval Office. I have been released on a one-hundred-thousand-dollar bond, and I will stand trial in three or four months. We have exactly that long to change the focus of the debate. That, in fact, is my plan."

"Have you spoken to John Bevis about this yet?" Stella asked. A steadfast contributor to Haynes's campaigns over the years, John Bevis was also the best defense attorney in Northern Virginia.

"He'll be fine with it," Haynes said.

"Are we taking bets on that? If so, I'm in for a grand."

Haynes was done with the banter. "Objections noted for the record," he said. "Now, let's shift from what I did to what you should be doing. Tell me about the man I shot last night."

Wherever Stella went, she carried an enormous leather portfolio that was half as thick as she was tall, and had to weigh more than she did. Haynes had never dared to look inside, and feared to ask what it held, but he imagined that it was the Holy Grail of the political opposition. Though Haynes was far from the most progressive member of the Senate when it came to technology, his limited knowledge made Stella's system look like stone tablets and an abacus. She opened the black leather monster and read from the page on the top. She always read from the page on the top.

"According to the coroner, your attacker's name was John Doe. Cause of death was a bullet through his heart, though she speculates in the report that the bullet through his liver would also have been fatal, though arguably at a slower rate. I don't believe that you're smiling."

"I'm sorry," Haynes said, though he was anything but. "It's gratifying to know that I hit what I was shooting at. Did I mention that I wasn't killed? Tell me about John Doe."

Stella went back to her papers. "He's an unknown quantity," she said. "No ID in his pockets, no hit off of the fingerprints. He's completely off the grid, and according to the Metropolitan Police, the Capitol Police, and the FBI, no one knows who he is. He never existed."

Haynes knew what that meant, and he suspected that Stella knew as well. "No one's invisible these days unless they are intended to be invisible," he said.

"What are you suggesting?"

"I don't have a specific suggestion," Haynes said, "but I know that Congressman Blaine's body is still warm, and no one has yet to identify his shooter, right?"

Stella's face darkened. "Are you suggesting that they're one and the same?"

Haynes shrugged. "I'm suggesting that they could be. How would we know when one shooter is a ghost and the other—the one who actually takes up physical space in the physical world—is dead? As a result of some admittedly expert shooting."

"Does the thought of jail appeal to you, Haynes?"

"Actually, it repels me," he said. "But for the now, I live in the glow of having beaten the mysterious bad guy to the draw. What's our next step?"

Stella looked horrified. "You're asking me that question? I was going to ask you that question."

Haynes took his time considering the problem. Anywhere else on the planet, the fact of his survival while under attack would grant him a free pass, but this was the District of Columbia, where juries tilted in bizarre directions that allowed drug dealing tax evaders to serve on the City Council without consequence while slamming hundreds of dollars in fines against people who parked in spaces where the meters had been broken for weeks. A prominent politician who dared to live might well be at a disadvantage. The fact of his

gun would likely be the deciding factor, and the city fathers were likely to take a hard line.

"I think our best bet is to nationalize the issue," he
said. "But for my illegal gun, I would be dead now. It's
an argument that will get us a lot of national attention."

"I think you're right," Stella said. "The problem is
that your jury is going to be composed of DC residents
who will indict whomever the prosecutor tells them to
indict, and then the trial jury will be composed exclusively of people without enough clout to get out of their
jury duty, and every one of them will be positively giddy
at the prospect of sending a senator of your political per-
suasion to jail."

Haynes let the words hang, then said, "Have you
considered a career in motivational speaking? Your op-
imism in the face of difficult news is stunning."

"You make light," Stella said, "but just wait until—"

"We've got time," Haynes interrupted. "We need to
find out who the assassin was."

"The FBI doesn't know who he was," Stella said. "If
they don't know, how on earth are you going to find
out?"

When she framed the question that way, the answer
was as obvious as the sun in the sky. "I know a guy
who knows a girl," he said.

Chapter Seven

To call Christyne Nasbe's place of residence a house would be an overstatement, but neither was it a trailer by any reasonable definition. A single story tall, it was squat and long, perhaps three-quarters as deep as it was wide. Their place sat in the middle of a long line of similar abodes, on a residential street that reflected the tastes of the working class. The tiny lawns were uniformly trimmed to be neat, but nothing was expensive. Jonathan imagined it to be a neighborhood filled with enlisted folks who did not make the cut to live on post.

Christyne lived in number 104, which was set off the road by maybe twenty feet of grass, surrounded on the sides and back by a chain-link fence. Yellow flowers that Jonathan recognized but couldn't name grew along the base of the structure in the front, and the windows all but vibrated with colors from bouquets of flowers that cascaded from window boxes that could barely contain them. The place wasn't much, but it was well cared for.

Boxers drove the Batmobile past the house on the left to the end of the street, where he turned around and parked on the Nasbes' side of the street, but five doors down. "Want to watch for a while, or do you want to get right to it?" he asked.

Jonathan reached into a pocket and pulled out a two-by-two-inch leather pouch from which he withdrew a tiny wireless transceiver. He inserted it into his right ear, while Boxers did the same. He turned the knob of the radio on his right hip and then pressed the transmit button on the earpiece. "Mother Hen, Scorpion. Do you copy?"

A few seconds passed before Venice's voice said, "Loud and clear."

"We're on scene at the Nasbes'," Jonathan said. "I don't anticipate this being a hot op, but I wanted you to be in the loop."

"Understood," Venice said. "Is Big Guy on the net, too?"

"Right here," Boxers said.

"Here's to success," Venice said.

With that, the stage was set. Jonathan checked his watch. Two-fifteen. "How old do you suppose Ryan is now?" he asked.

Big Guy shrugged. "At least seventeen," he said. "Maybe eighteen. Why?"

The last time he'd seen Ryan Nasbe, the kid was spattered with strangers' blood and damn near crippled for life as he was being hustled to safety by even more strangers. Jonathan had never had the chance to explain the details of why he was there to rescue him, which was exactly the way it was supposed to be. The last thing he wanted to do was go eye-to-eye with this kid again and ignite old memories. Especially under the circumstances.

"No reason," Jonathan said. "I was just curious."

"I imagine he's still in school at this hour," Boxers said. "I know that would make Mother Hen happy."

Jonathan looked to his friend and smiled. Big Guy got it. "All right, then," he said. "Let's go."

They locked the Batmobile behind them and as they walked casually up the sidewalk, Jonathan knew without doubt that the phone trees had begun to buzz. In a military neighborhood like this, where roughly fifty percent of the population was on deployment somewhere, anything that was out of the ordinary attracted its share of attention and then some. While Jonathan and Boxers had both dressed to blend in, the temperature was too hot to justify the denim vest Jonathan wore to conceal the .45 on his hip, and Boxers was so large that everybody noticed whatever he did, wherever he did it.

"Do you miss it?" Boxers asked as they strolled the sidewalk.

"Parts of it," Jonathan said. "But not this part at all. I never felt comfortable with the secrecy of deployments." It had cost him his marriage, in fact. "Do you?"

"Every friggin' day."

"Even the bullshit?"

"I don't even remember the bullshit. I just remember the job."

Jonathan craned his neck to look up at Big Guy. "It's not a lot different than the job you have now."

"It's a *hell* of a lot different," Boxers said. "Back then it was for God and country."

"Until," Jonathan said.

"Exactly," Big Guy said with a chuckle. "Until God watched the country diddle us in the ass. I didn't enjoy that part so much."

"You can't have one without the other," Jonathan said. "It's all one big diddle."

He shifted to more serious issues. "I want you at the back door until we know what we've got. No weapons showing, and I don't for a minute think this is going to go violent—"

"But nobody ever died from abundance of caution," Boxers said. "You know I was here last time we did something like this, right? What do you want me to do if somebody bolts?"

"Try to stop them. But don't hurt anybody. I don't want to be a source of escalation. Yet."

Big Guy tossed off a half-salute and peeled off to take a position in the back.

Jonathan pressed his transmit button. "Be advised we're at the house," he said. "I'm going to the front door."

"I copy you're going to the front door," Venice said. The radio protocols could be a burden on simple operations like this, but the attention to detail kept everybody from becoming complacent.

"Big Guy?" Jonathan asked over the air.

"I'm in place on the back side. Be ready for a big dog. Big piles out here."

That was an interesting data point, Jonathan thought. While there was a better than average chance that one day he would be ejected from this mortal coil by a bullet, he had no intention of letting his insides spill outside at the whim of a canine attacker. It wasn't a threat worthy of drawing down on approach, but it was something to be on the lookout for.

Jonathan pressed his transmit button. "I'm going to the door now."

It was a delicate moment. On the one hand, he needed to be aware, but on the other, he wanted to draw as little attention as possible. All he wanted to do was talk. When the talking was over, he wanted to leave the Nasbes in peace, absent the need to explain weird stuff to neighbors. He felt dangerously exposed as he stood directly in front of the door to knock. It was the way regular people knocked, but it was also the best way to guarantee a gut full of buckshot if the party on the other side was having a difficult day.

He rapped five times with the knuckle of his middle finger. Nothing urgent, certainly nothing police-like. Just an old friend dropping by to say hello. When no one answered after thirty seconds or so, he knocked again.

"I see movement inside," Boxers said in his ear.

Jonathan saw it, too, a shadow moving behind the sheer curtains. "I'm coming!" a voice called from the other side. It was male and it sounded young.

Oh, shit, Jonathan thought.

The door opened to reveal a tall, skinny kid of maybe seventeen. His eyes were a lot brighter than the last time Jonathan had seen him, and his face bore a lot more color. Ryan Nasbe looked remarkably like his father, but about fifty pounds lighter. A trail of dark fuzz down his jawline and under his chin marked the place of a future beard. Recognition came after maybe three seconds of confusion, and then all the brightness went away.

"Hi, Ryan," Jonathan said. He mustered a kind smile.

"Scorpion."

"You remember. Nice to see you again. You look well."

"He's not here," Ryan said.

Jonathan cocked his head. He knew what the kid was talking about, but he didn't want to let on.

"My dad," Ryan clarified. "He's not here."

"I know," Jonathan said. "We're not here to talk to him. We're here to talk with your mom."

"We?" Ryan craned his neck to see around the visitor at his door to look out toward the street.

Jonathan pressed his transmit button. "Come around to the front, Big Guy," he said.

And now the pallor returned to Ryan's face. "That guy's here, too?"

"I never leave home without him," Jonathan said. It was supposed to be a joke, but it fell about a mile short. He cleared his throat. "We're a team. Is your mom here?"

Ryan didn't move out of the door opening, and he didn't say anything. He looked confused and frightened.

"We're not here to cause any trouble, Ryan," Jonathan said. "I promise you."

"Ryan, honey, who's at the door?" a woman's voice called from down the hall. Because he knew who it had to be, Jonathan recognized the voice, but he probably wouldn't have without that prompt. After a few seconds, she tried again. "Ryan? Who is—"

Christyne Nasbe turned from the cross hall into the living room and stopped dead. Her jaw dropped. "Dylan's not here," she said.

Movement from behind told Jonathan that Boxers had arrived. "Hi, Christyne," Jonathan said. "You're both looking well."

"I said he's not here."

"I know that, ma'am. We're not here to see him. We're here to speak with you." By now, Boxers' shadow had joined his across the floor of the foyer.

"About Dylan?" Christyne pressed.

"Can we come in, ma'am?" Jonathan asked. "I swear to you we mean no harm."

Ryan looked back to his mom for direction, and she remained frozen in place. Neither pretty nor not, Christyne bore the weathered look of an exhausted homemaker with a teenaged son. "Let them in, Ryan."

"They want to hurt Dad," he said.

"It's actually the opposite of that," Boxers said, his first words since appearing in the doorway. "We're here to help him."

The Nasbes stared in unison.

"We've driven a long way," Jonathan said, "and Big Guy needs to pee. If he does it out here, he'll kill the plants."

Boxers growled.

Ryan smiled in spite of himself.

"Let them in, Ry," Christyne said.

"Fine," Ryan said, though clearly it was not. He stepped aside.

"Thank you," Jonathan said, and he stepped past the teenager into the foyer, which was really just an extension of the living room, which in turn was an extension of the dining room. Everything appeared to be as neat and organized as the exterior, but the furniture all seemed too big for the space, leading Jonathan to wonder if the move here had been sudden, and by extension, if they considered it to be just a temporary relocation.

"Nice place," Jonathan said.

Ryan didn't drop a beat. "No, it's not. It sucks. The bathroom's down there." He pointed to a hallway on the left.

A lot transpired in the two-second silent exchange that followed between Jonathan and Boxers.

I don't have to go.

Yes, you do.

Asshole.

Punctuated with a grin from Jonathan. Hey, the kid had called his bluff. What else could he do?

As Boxers disappeared down the hall, Jonathan turned back to Christyne. "May we sit?"

She didn't move. "I don't know. Tell me why you're really here."

Jonathan took a step backward so he could see both Nasbes in the same glance. He couldn't tell if the kid was doing it consciously, but by hanging behind Jonathan, out of sight, Ryan was making him very uncomfortable. "I'd prefer you'd stay where I can see you," he said.

"Why?"

Jonathan's shoulders sagged. "Please let's not make this a confrontation. We really are here to help Dylan. But to help him, I need information from you."

"You want me to tell you where he is," Christyne said.

"Mom!"

A toilet flushed.

"Do you know where he is?"

Boxers reappeared. "Well, this hasn't progressed very far," he said. "How's the arm, Ryan? Last time I saw you—"

"It's fine."

"It's still not a hundred percent," Christyne clarified. "But it's going to be."

"A lot better than being dead, huh?" Boxers said. Their previous encounter had indeed been traumatic.

Jonathan watched the realization wash over Christyne. No matter what followed, she owed them more than nasty aggression. "Come in and sit," she said. "Please."

"Try not to break the furniture, Big Guy."

"Ryan!"

The kid's smile made Jonathan laugh.

Truth be told, the furniture was anything but fragile. Stoutly constructed and heavily cushioned, Jonathan figured that Dylan must have picked it up in Germany. TDY, maybe—temporary duty.

Christyne sat with her son on the sofa while Jonathan and Boxers each took a chair. "I am grateful to you for your help before, but you are wasting—"

Jonathan held up a hand for silence, and reached for the television remote control. Someone had muted the third reel of *Saving Private Ryan,* and Jonathan cranked up the volume to a level north of loud, but barely south of painful.

"Jesus!" Ryan shouted. "What the—"

Jonathan held up a hand for silence again. He motioned for everyone to lean in closer. "You need to assume that your house is bugged," he said.

Christyne's hand shot to her mouth. "Oh, my God."

"Are you shitting me?" Ryan said.

"I can't say for sure," Jonathan said, "but for this conversation, it's not worth the risk." He shifted his eyes to Christyne. "So, let's get to it. Do you know—"

"Uh-uh," she said, and she held up her own hand. "No answers for you until we get some. Why is the world looking for Dylan?"

The question seemed to come from an honest place, and it took Jonathan off guard. "You really don't know?"

"You're asking questions out of turn," she said. "This is answering time."

Jonathan shot a look to Ryan. He might be older than last time, but he was still a kid, and there were some things that a boy should never hear about his father.

"All Ry and I have left is each other," Christyne said. "What you can say to me, you can say to him."

Jonathan didn't approve, but it wasn't his call. "Big Guy and I were approached by his former commanding officer," he said.

"Colonel Rollins," Ryan said, as if to emphasize that he already knew some of what was going on.

"Exactly," Jonathan said. "He, uh, well . . . Oh, crap. There's no soft way to say it. He accused Dylan of murder and treason."

"Bullshit." Mother and son said it together.

"I'm reporting, not accusing," Jonathan said. "And it doesn't matter what you think. What matters is that that's what the government thinks, and they've dispatched shooter teams to kill him."

Ryan's eyes glistened red as he retreated into the sofa's back cushion. "They're trying to kill my dad?" He pivoted his head to engage his mom, who to Jonathan's eye looked sad yet not shocked. "Mom?"

"Either you want to hear this or you don't," she said. Jonathan doubted that she wanted her words to sound as cold as they did.

Ryan redirected to Jonathan. "Who do they think he killed?"

Jonathan watched for a reaction from Christyne as he said, "Some CIA agents."

"You can't believe that," Ryan said. "You know my dad. He would never murder anyone."

Jonathan said nothing. It was *because* he knew Boomer that he knew that he likely did do the killing—for precisely the reason why Jonathan had himself killed so many people over the years. There were bad guys in the world whose positions shielded them from the rules of justice that governed everyone else.

Addressing Christyne, Jonathan said, "Colonel Rollins mentioned some *unpleasantness*—his word—that transpired during Dylan's last tour of Afghanistan. Do you know anything about that?"

Christyne's face remained blank as something passed behind her eyes. Jonathan interpreted it as a flash of panic. She recovered by looking heavenward, as if to receive a divine answer. "No," she said.

She was lying. Jonathan drilled her with a glare, yet said nothing.

"No," she repeated, as if to fill the silence. "I don't know anything about that."

Ryan clearly read the body language the same way Jonathan did. "Mom?" he said. "What happened?"

Christyne showed fear. She'd been caught unprepared. She'd allowed a peek at her cards, and she clearly did not know how to recover.

Jonathan let the silence rule. Ryan's question had accomplished more than anything he could say.

Christyne's shoulders sagged. She was done. "Ryan, I want you to go to your room."

"The hell I will."

Jonathan's peripheral vision caught Boxers' flinch. He didn't like it when kids cursed at adults. But Big Guy didn't say anything.

"You don't need to hear this," Christyne said. Something inside of her seemed to have broken. She seemed close to tears.

"You said we were a team. You said I could hear anything." He was close to tears, too. "I'm staying."

Christyne looked to Jonathan for help.

"Nope," he said. There was exactly zero upside to getting sucked into a family dispute. His vote had been overridden once. It made no sense to walk into the same propeller a second time. Besides, it appeared that one way or the other, he was going to hear the story he'd come to learn.

"Please, Ry. I don't want—"

"No!" He nearly shouted it. "We're talking about *Dad*! I'm not going anywhere. It's not fair for you to ask me." Tears overran his eyelids and tracked down his cheeks. "This can't possibly get worse than it already is."

Christyne considered her son for a solid thirty seconds. Finally, she inhaled deeply. "Okay," she said. "His name was Behrang, an Afghan boy, an orphan. The Taliban had slaughtered his family. His code name was Bulldog."

"An informant," Jonathan said.

"That's how it started, for sure. Dylan developed him. I think that's the right term."

"Close enough," Boxers said. His tone told Jonathan that Big Guy had arrived at the same unhappy conclusion to which Jonathan had already jumped.

"He developed him over multiple deployments. We'd actually—" A painfully uncomfortable look to Ryan. "We'd actually put the wheels in motion to adopt him."

"Oh, God," Boxers said. Jonathan's insides churned. It was the ultimate of terrible mistakes. Informants were resources, objects with heartbeats. Their purpose was to propel the larger mission, and then to be discarded if necessary. The relationship required abject coldness—the very opposite of what Christyne was revealing.

Ryan gaped. Clearly, no one had told him that he'd been scheduled to be a big brother.

Christyne continued. "We were almost to the finish line during Dylan's last deployment. The paperwork was processed, and we were *this close* to everything coming together. Behrang had one last task to do. He knew a Taliban commander who was at the top of the Most Wanted list. The worst of the worst."

"Satan?" Jonathan guessed.

"How did you know?"

"I try to stay plugged in," he said. He knew that this story wasn't going to end well.

Christyne said to her son, "Are you okay?"

"I don't know. I haven't heard any of this before." He cocked his head. "I was going to have a *brother?*"

Christyne offered up a kind, motherly smile and touched Ryan's face with the tips of her fingers. *You're sweet.* She returned to her story. "Dylan was scheduled to meet Bulldog in a town square or something—a bazaar, I guess—and they were within sight of each other when Satan arrived."

"Did Dad shoot him?" Clearly, in Ryan's mind, there was only one right answer.

"He had orders," Christyne said. And then her voice stopped working.

"It works that way a lot," Jonathan explained. "On an intel operation like that, the rules of engagement almost always preclude enemy contact unless fired upon first."

Christyne pointed her agreement at Jonathan. Her voice was still not accessible to her.

"Did Bulldog get killed?" Ryan asked. His nightmares continued to bloom.

Christyne nodded some more and pleaded to Jonathan with her eyes. *Please don't make me do this.*

"You're making this harder on your mom than it needs to be, Ryan," Jonathan said.

"I don't care. This isn't about Mom or her feelings. This is about my *father.* You had a father once, right, Scorpion? I have a *right* to know this."

The kid had no way of knowing that Jonathan's father was serving a no-hope life sentence at a supermax prison—or that he should have been sent there a hell of a lot earlier than he was.

Christyne's eyes continued to plead for Jonathan's intervention. Finally, he said, "I don't know what you want me to say, ma'am. If you send him to his room, do you really think that you're not going to have to fill him in eventually? It's inevitable, and when you do, the pain of the message is going to be compounded by the pain of the insult." She shouldn't have played the *we're a team* card if she wasn't willing to see it through to the end.

"Yes," she said. "They killed Behrang. They . . . killed him." In the hesitation, Jonathan saw the flash of an additional detail nearly shared but then abandoned.

"How?" Ryan asked.

"Oh, for Christ's sake," Boxers said. "Give her a break. This is hard enough."

Hearing it come from Big Guy must have made a difference. Ryan's shoulders relaxed and he leaned back into the seat cushion. He looked spent.

Jonathan let silence reset the emotion in the room. As much as he did not want to be a bully, the conversation had to go on. For the next part, he'd have paid Ryan ten thousand dollars to leave the room. He cleared his throat, then went for it. "Did he blame the CIA for the boy's death?" He avoided using the name in hopes of gaining some distance from the horror of the event.

Christyne seemed spent as well. "He never *said* that."

"But he implied it?"

She looked to the ceiling. "Well, no. Not really. Not in so many words."

"Come on, Christyne," Boxers said.

"I'm really not trying to be difficult. Given the stakes, I want to take care to stick with what I *know* before I get to what I *feel*."

Jonathan got it. He resented the waste of time, but he got it. When it came to husbands and wives, intuition almost always trumped the bare facts.

"Over the years, I lost track of the number of times Dylan was deployed," Christyne explained. "You know how it is. One time he'd be gone for a week, and then he'd be gone for three, four, six months. It's the job. And I presume he was good at it. There was always a hard separation between his work and his life. He never brought the work home."

But this time was different, Jonathan thought.

"But this time was different. He was so *angry*. So disappointed. I knew it was about Behrang, but I sensed there was more. For weeks, I begged him to tell me, but all he would say was things like, 'I hate those assholes' and 'the spooks are running the military.' But there were never any overt threats. Yes, he was angry, and yes, he's clearly capable of violence, but he's been angry before and he's been trained in violence for a long time."

"We were told he abandoned the family," Boxers prompted.

Christyne cut her eyes toward Ryan again, but he seemed lost in a place inside his head. "I wouldn't call it *abandoned*," she said. "He told me that he was going to be going away for a while."

"Why?" Jonathan asked.

"He said there was something that he had to do."

"Did you know that he had left the army?" Jonathan asked.

"Yes."

"Was that a sudden decision for him? Did it surprise you?"

"He'd been in for a long time," Christyne said. "He'd done his duty."

"But he was less than a year shy of his twenty," Boxers said. "That's a lot of retirement to leave on the table."

"I'd rather have him alive than retired," Ryan said.

Jonathan was grateful that Boxers let it go. Much of this conversation was beyond the understanding of a teenager.

"Clearly he was agitated," Christyne said. "I think he'd just had his fill and was ready to move on."

"To where?" Jonathan asked.

Christyne's jaw locked and she looked to the floor. This was the step too far, apparently.

"You're in this far, ma'am," Jonathan prompted. "You wouldn't have told us what you have if you didn't trust us to help him. Trust us for the next part, too. Where is he?"

Silence. She seemed to be on the fence, struggling deeply with the whole trust thing.

"Is he in the country or out of the country?" Jonathan pressed.

"Out, I think," she said. "I'm really not sure, but that's what I think."

Jonathan saw that as a point of confirmation for what they already thought they knew. "Is it Venezuela?" he asked. As an added precaution against suspected listening devices, he more mouthed the word than spoke it.

The flash behind her eyes told him what he wanted to know, even before she could mount an effort to deny it. Which she didn't. "How did you know?"

"Because I think that's where the feds are looking for him. I assume you have the means to contact him?"

Stone face.

"Of course you do," Jonathan said. "Tell him to remember Acid Gambit. There's a huge graveyard across from where the Commandancia used to be."

"Acid what?" Christyne asked.

"Gambit," Ryan said, his first words in a while. "Like the X-Men character?"

"Sure," Jonathan said. He had no idea. "G-A-M-B-I-T. Acid Gambit."

"What does it mean?"

"Dylan will know. And there's no way to miss the cemetery. It's huge."

"The Commandancia? What's that?"

"He'll know. Trust me, he'll know. How much time will he need?"

"For what?"

"To get mobilized to meet us in Panama."

Christyne stewed. "A week," she said.

Jonathan said, "Fine. Have him meet us there one week from today. At noon."

"What happens after he meets you?" Christyne asked. "If I can contact him, that is. And if he agrees."

"We talk," Jonathan said. "After that, the rest is up to him."

"How will he know it's not a trap?"

"Because we all have to trust each other right now."

"No police, right? No FBI or CIA?"

"Cross my heart." Jonathan made a giant X over his left chest. "Our mission is far enough off the grid that we wouldn't want their involvement any more than Dylan would. And by the way, make sure he knows that one mistake will ruin everything for him. He needs to be careful."

"Which brings up another point," Big Guy said. "I get it that you love Dylan. I get that he's your husband and your father, and that you'd do anything to protect him, but I want to make one thing as clear as it can possibly be. If you intentionally mislead us, jam us up and get us into trouble—if you set us up for some kind of a double-cross—I'll forget all about you being part of the Special Forces family. All I'll remember is that you tried to hurt us, and trust me when I say that that would be a terrible, terrible mistake." He bored his eyes through Ryan. "The kind of mistake that keeps a teenager from seeing drinking age. Am I making myself clear?"

Air leaked from the room as the reality of Big Guy's threat made its mark.

"I think that sounded more threatening than Big Guy meant it to be," Jonathan said, aware that his statement was more lie than truth. "But this is the worst possible time for you to lie. If you have no intent of contacting Dylan—or, worse yet, if you intend to betray us—this is the time for you to tell us to walk away."

Jonathan pointed to Christyne with his whole hand, as if it were a knife blade, or maybe a karate chop. "You know that we work hard in what we do, and you know that we will fight to make things right. You don't want to be the thing that is wrong. Tell me you understand that."

A new level of fear invaded Christyne's face as she nodded emphatically. "I do understand. Just as you understand that if you ever harmed us, Dylan would not rest until you were dead."

Jonathan smiled. "I wouldn't have it any other way."

Chapter Eight

"**V**ictor Carrington," the man said as he took the seat next to Ian. "You look frightened. Don't be."

Victor Carrington was Ian's avatar on the Uprising boards. Alternatively, he called himself the Commander. "What would I have to be frightened of?" Ian said. He thought he'd pulled off the causal disinterest thing pretty well.

The man visually scanned the inner circle around them, as if looking for eavesdroppers. "I think that high treason would be a good start," he said. "Most people I know in your line of work get jumpy at that one."

Ian felt an icicle form in his chest. He chose to say nothing.

"David Little," the man said, offering his hand. "Sorry to be so confrontational, but I wanted to make sure I had your attention."

Reflexively, Ian accepted the man's handshake. "I don't . . ." His voice trailed away.

"I know," Little said. "It's a tough thought. Life imprisonment. Death penalty. It's a lot to absorb."

"Why are you here?" Ian managed to ask.

"I'm going to convince you to take a walk with me. If only as an alternative to the above."

"Where are we walking to?"

Little allowed himself a smarmy smirk. "Wherever I take you. I don't mean to be an alarmist, but sometimes there are no delicate ways to say something. If it helps, I think you will find the trip to be a worthwhile investment of your time."

"Who are you really?"

"I don't have the authority to tell you that," Little said. "And whatever conclusion you can draw from that statement will no doubt take you very close to the answer."

Ian's brain worked the problem in a second. The guy had a name—or at least a pseudonym—but he had no authority to offer more. Put that in context with the thick neck and the fact that he didn't bring a contingent of cops with him, and Ian's instincts brought him to some form of covert operator. What he didn't know—and apparently wouldn't know until the appointed time—was for which agency. "You have my undivided attention," he said.

"Right answer," Little said. "Really, this is good."

No one could possibly understand the garbled nonsense that poured from the loudspeaker, but Ian knew from experience that they were at the Rosslyn station, and when Little rose from his seat, so did he. Like every other corner of Washington, DC, and its surrounding suburbs, Rosslyn, Virginia, was the repository for a lot of spooky activity. Crystal City in Arlington housed much of the Navy, the farther-flung suburbs of Fairfax and Chantilly and Centreville housed the really scary parts of the CIA and the National Reconnaissance Office, and the really, *really* scary stuff was in far-flung areas of western Virginia and eastern Maryland. That left Rosslyn with the lesser-terrifying elements of a dozen different alphabet agencies. In his mind, Ian imagined that each of the long-term leases for those agencies was officially registered to Acme Greeting Card Company.

Little said nothing as he led the two-person parade out of the Metro car and up the escalator to the concrete canyon that defined this northernmost part of Northern Virginia. Ian squinted against the sunshine and pulled to a halt as they stepped out onto the sidewalk on Wilson Boulevard.

"Your head's in the wrong place," Little said, apparently reading Ian's thoughts. "You're thinking that you're somehow being kidnapped, or led away against your will. What you should be thinking is that you're very, very close to achieving your dream."

If that was supposed to make things clearer, it missed the mark.

"Is the Uprising real or isn't it?"

Ian's insides seized. *He knows.* He said nothing.

"Of course we know," Little said.

Christ, he can read my mind!

"Relax. We're on your side."

"My side of what?" Ian said, floating a bluff. "And who's *we?*"

Little chuckled. "The first question insults my intelligence, but I get that you're vamping for time. And when you follow me, you'll see the answer to your second question." He thumped Ian playfully on the arm with his elbow. "Come on, Colonel. You're a soldier. You're supposed to embrace new adventures."

"Suppose I refuse?" Ian said. "What happens if I say no?"

Little scowled with mock earnestness. "Hmm. Well, I'm not going to hurt you, if that's what you're worried about. But between you and me, how long do you really think you would last in the general population in Leavenworth?"

Ian's heart and head raced in near-panic mode. This was the nightmare, the unthinkable. Getting caught had always been a risk, but it had been such a different one, such a manageable one. And he'd been so careful. Now his world had been reduced to only two terrifying choices: he could try to run, or he could follow. But they already knew so much.

"It's just up here, Colonel," Little said. "And I swear to God that no one's going to hurt you."

"And that's precisely what you would say if you were going to hurt me."

Little laughed. "Yes," he said. "Yes, I suppose it is. But here's a little detail for you: My boss needs you too much to let you get hurt."

"Yet he'll let me rot in prison."

A shrug. "In ten minutes, this will all make sense." Little waited for Ian's answer. He seemed to have all the patience in the world.

"I have no choice," Ian said aloud.

"I don't see much," Little agreed. With that, he started walking up Wilson Boulevard.

Ian followed. Just past the Hyatt, Little turned right into a towering office building that had seen better days, and led the way inside without bothering to see if Ian was following. Truly, he had no choice. The lobby security guy looked up as they approached, but after a brief dip of his head, he turned back to whatever interested him on his desk.

"If I'm not out in a half hour, call the police, will you?" Ian said. He tried to keep his tone light enough not to be alarming, but serious enough for the guy to give some thought if he in fact did not reemerge from wherever they were going.

The guard made no indication that he'd heard Ian, but the words caused Little to stop, turn, and smile as he waited for Ian to catch up. He said nothing as he pressed the Down button on the elevator.

Of course it would be the basement.

The car dinged, the doors opened, and Little motioned for Ian to enter first. The interior walls of the elevator car were draped with dark green quilted moving blankets, typical of any elevator used for freight. Ian wondered if the blankets would also muffle the sound of a gunshot. Little pressed the button for B3 and the doors closed.

Fully aware that any escape option—as fragile and unlikely as they had ever been—had now evaporated, Ian concentrated on slowing his racing heart. He took a deep breath through his mouth, held it, then released it as a silent whistle. Whatever was coming, he needed to think clearly, and that wouldn't be possible if he didn't do something to contain the surging adrenaline.

The elevator jerked to a halt and the doors opened onto a concrete tomb of rooms that clearly were never designed for paying tenants. With dingy tile floors and battleship-gray concrete block walls, the low-ceilinged corridor reminded him of a hospital morgue, or maybe a bunker.

"Out and to the left," Little said.

Ian complied, and was oddly relieved when Little accompanied him.

"Third door on the right." Painted the same color as the walls, the doors down here were all made of smooth steel.

Ian stopped at the appointed place. "Do I need to knock?"

Little reached around him and rapped lightly with the knuckle of his middle finger. "No, I got that."

Five seconds passed, and then the knob turned. The door opened to reveal a man who could have been Little's clone—thick neck, wide shoulders, shaved head, and very serious eyes. A black T-shirt clung to a heavily muscled torso. Unlike the man who'd escorted him to this spot, however, the greeter at the door openly carried a pistol on his hip. It looked like a government-issue Beretta M9. Ian wasn't sure where the mounting evidence was pointing him, but he was growing more and more uncomfortable.

"Really?" the new guy said. "This is him?"

"Victor Carrington in the flesh," Little said.

Unsure whether that was his cue to introduce himself and shake hands, or merely to stand quietly, Ian chose the latter.

The guard stepped aside and let them enter. "The old man is waiting," he said.

The phrase resonated with Ian. In military parlance, "old man" was synonymous with commanding officer. Everything about this so far had screamed military, and that was just one more confirming element.

The inside of the room looked like the office of a busy blue-collar worker. Work orders dangled from pins on a full bulletin board, and where the floor was not taken up by mismatched gray and beige file cabinets, they were cluttered with cleaning supplies, air filters, fluorescent light tubes, and various other items critical to the maintenance of an office building. Ian's escorts (captors?) indicated an inner door.

"In there," Little said.

Ian hesitated. "Who is it?"

"Open the door and you'll know."

Steeling himself with another deep breath, Ian squared his shoulders and pulled the door open to reveal another office, this one only slightly nicer and neater than the anteroom. The man who'd summoned Ian stood from a wooden chair in front of the cluttered desk that dominated the room. "Thank you for coming," he said. "I apologize for the theater, but surely you understand."

Ian thought he recognized the face, but when he heard the voice, he knew for sure. His heart rate doubled. Again. "Holy shit," he said. Then, very quickly, he added, "Sir."

General Manfred Brock, United States Army chief of staff, seemed amused by Ian's rush of recognition. "You look frightened," he said. "There's no need. We are all here to commit the same crime."

Ian feigned ignorance. "Excuse me?"

General Brock bore none of the physical stature of his lofty rank. At five-six and maybe one hundred thirty-five pounds, he'd famously commissioned customized stars for the epaulettes of his uniforms because there simply was not enough room from his shoulder to his neck to accommodate the standard four-star array. There was nothing youthful about the man, from his sun-leathered flesh to his close-cropped white hair, but nor was there anything elderly about him. This afternoon, he wore civvies, blue jeans with a denim shirt, both components sharply pressed.

"You know the old expression," Brock said. "Never bullshit a bullshitter. We can dance all day around the fact that you are the father of the Uprising, but you need to know that I know the truth. In fact, I believe that that is the true source of your unease right now. Are you going to tell me I'm incorrect?"

Ian didn't bother to try. "How did you find out?"

Brock sat back in his seat, gesturing for Ian to do the same in the adjacent chair. "I presume you're aware that I have a lot of very smart people working for me," he said. "At last count, about three hundred fifty thousand of them. Though if Tony Darmond and his puppets have their way, it will be a lot closer to two hundred twenty thousand. Among those smart people are folks who are quite adept at computer wizardry. You in fact are one of them, are you not?"

Ian settled into his seat and crossed his legs, trying his best to appear casual and calm. "I believe you know exactly what I'll do for you, General."

Brock waved at the air. "No *general* in this room," he said. "In fact, no rank at all. If this goes bad, we'll all hang from the same size rope."

Ian felt his cheeks flush. He looked to Little and his

clone, but got only stone faces in return. "What exactly are we talking about, Gen . . . Sir?" There were limits to the suspension of honorifics.

"Treason, of course," Brock said. The words spilled from him lightly, as if he'd just named his favorite color. "Isn't that what the Uprising is all about?"

Ian hesitated before answering. Truthfully, he'd never allowed himself to think in such blunt terms. "I suppose it could be considered that," he said.

"Do you prefer terrorist activity?" Brock asked with a broader smile. "That is, after all what the Brits would have called the Minutemen had the term existed in the eighteenth century. We get to call them patriots because our side won. It's all semantics. It's all just words. They don't matter."

But they do matter, Ian thought. He understood the general's point, but why did he find it so offensive? "I'm not a terrorist," he said.

"Murderer, then. And conspirator. Once you start down the road of capital offenses, the titles get progressively more offensive."

Ian gaped. He found himself breathing through his mouth.

"You are responsible for the murder of Congressman Blaine, are you not?"

Jesus Christ, how can he know?

Brock crossed his legs as well, and laced his fingers across his lap. "I sense that I'm making you more nervous. That's not my intent. In fact, my intent is quite the opposite. I want you to know that I am impressed with your activities so far."

Ian's head swam in confusion. "Impressed? I don't understand."

"It's not a ten-dollar word, Ian. Excuse me, in this context I suppose you prefer Victor. Impressed. I am impressed."

"At what?"

"Your ability to pull off what so many of us have been considering, but have not had the guts to try."

Ian continued to stare. This was the kind of topic where an incorrect guess could have devastating consequences.

Brock sighed. He seemed genuinely frustrated that the conversation was not going the way he had planned. "Let's take a step back," he said. "We can agree that the Darmond administration is the worst in history, can we not?"

Ian considered that. He felt comfortable saying, "Certainly since the Second World War."

"Okay, fine. I'd actually go back to the beginning, but we can start with World War Two if that makes you more comfortable. Can we also agree that if he is not stopped—if he is allowed to continue down the current road for another three and a half years—the damage to the republic will likely become permanent?"

These were exactly the points he'd made through the postings of the Uprising. "I can agree with all of that," Ian said.

Brock clapped his hands lightly. "Very good, then. If we project the logic out to the end of its tether, it becomes clear that as patriots—*not* as the terrorists that the media will portray us to be—our duty is to ensure that Darmond and his agenda are stopped."

Ian cut his eyes to Little and Clone.

"They're both on our side," Brock assured. "It's safe to speak plainly."

It was insane to speak openly of such things. And to hear the words coming from the senior-most flag officer in the United States Army made Ian wonder what kind of trap this was. "Sir, I am really not comfortable answering these questions."

Brock sighed noisily. Famously impatient, he seemed ready to blow. "Fear of being charged with mutiny, no doubt," he said.

"Fear of being charged with *treason,* sir."

"For Christ's sake do you believe what you publish or do you not?" As soon as the question was in the air, he held up a hand to cut off any response. "Of course you do. You've already admitted to being the leader of the Uprising, and that alone is enough to get you court-martialed and locked away for the rest of your life. Do you believe for a second that I would be here, this exposed, having this conversation if I did not have the appropriate leverage over you? I was hoping for a cooperative spirit, but if it needs to be strong-arm tactics, I can do that, too. As you might guess, I am a busy man, and this kind of bullshit not only wastes my time, it frankly pisses me off. Are we clear so far?"

The change in demeanor and approach startled Ian. His silence now was less recalcitrance than vocal paralysis. This man was chief of staff for the entire friggin' United States Army. *Holy shit.*

"I'll take your silence as agreement," Brock said. He'd settled back into Nice Guy mode with an ease and speed that was every bit as startling as the previous transition. "I apologize for being so blunt, but as you can imagine, these are anxious times, and the clock is ticking. In fact, it's ticking faster than I had intended, thanks to your efforts."

"I-I'm sorry?" Ian stammered. The quick transitions were making him dizzy.

"Apology accepted, but I stipulate that you had no way of knowing what you were doing. The good news is that there's still time to fix it." He stood from his chair and Ian followed to his feet reflexively. "Spend some time with Little and Biggs here. They'll spell out what we need from you." He extended his hand. "Pleasure to meet you, *Mister Carrington.*"

Ian accepted the hand, even though he was certain that his own was cold and wet.

As Brock headed for the door, he said, "As Benjamin Franklin once said, we must all hang together or most assuredly, we will all hang separately." Everyone in the room but Ian found that funny.

When the door closed behind the general, and it was just him and the thick-necks, Ian realized that it was time for him to piss on a fire hydrant to establish some measure of control over his future. Figuring both of his new companions to be noncoms, he played their deferential instinct to his own benefit. "Have a seat, both of you," he said, gesturing to the two chairs while he helped himself to the leading edge of the metal desk. If nothing else, his perch gave him the benefit of height when the two men finally settled themselves into place.

"First things, first," Ian said, following whatever random thought his brain injected into his consciousness. "Before we get into whatever the plan is, you really couldn't do better than Little and Biggs for avatars? You should be ashamed."

Little gave a smile that was ten degrees more menace than mirth. "Tell you what, Victor," he said. "We can talk all about that as we take our little drive out into the country."

Chapter Nine

"**H**aynes Moncrief wants me to do *what?*" Jonathan asked. He'd returned from Fayetteville to Fisherman's Cove to prepare for the trip to Panama. The seven-hour drive had left him a bit brain-numbed.

"You heard correctly," Venice said. They spoke in the armory-slash-vault that resided under the parking lot that separated Jonathan's home and office from the property belonging to Saint Katherine's Catholic Church. "He wants you to intercede on his behalf with Wolverine." Venice had never liked it down here. The fact of her presence told Jonathan that this was important.

"He's the Senate minority leader, for crying out loud," Boxers said, never looking up from his task of selecting weapons from his locker and arranging them in their appropriate duffle bags. "I give good odds that she'd take his call." Wolverine was Jonathan's code name for Irene Rivers, the director of the FBI, for whom he'd done quite a lot of off-the-record work over the years.

"I dunno," Jonathan said. "He's something of a political turd ball now that he shot the guy in the park.

Nobody wants him to rub off on them." He pulled a Heckler & Koch M27 from the rack, cycled the bolt a couple of times and dry fired it. "In fact, I'm kind of in the same boat. Why did he call us?"

"Apparently because he knew you and the director were friends," Venice said. She spoke from the doorway, half in and half out of the vault.

"You know we've got seats, right?" Jonathan said. He indicated the stools that lined the Velostat-covered aluminum workbench.

She crinkled her nose. "I don't like the smell," she said.

"Blasphemy," Boxers said.

"The senator is in a difficult place," Venice said. "Apparently the guy he shot does not officially exist. Completely off the grid. He wants to know why."

"Why does he think?"

"He says he doesn't know," Venice said. "And on the heels of Congressman Blaine's assassination a few weeks ago, the lack of a known identity is particularly troubling."

"The Fibbies aren't idiots," Boxers said. He cycled an HK417, and apparently liked what he saw and felt. "I'm sure they're troubled by that, too."

"He thinks that the administration will either drag their feet or withhold information that would exonerate him," Jonathan guessed.

"Wouldn't be the first time," Boxers said.

"You make Darmond sound like the most corrupt president ever," Venice said. She'd campaigned hard for him in his first term, and twisted herself six ways from Sunday to ignore the obvious during Darmond's campaign for a second term. She needed evidence north of fingerprints and photographs to believe the man could do any wrong. Venice held steadfast to her belief that the president was an innocent victim of the bad people around him.

Jonathan let it go.

"But you're right," Venice confirmed. "That is what he thinks."

"If he doesn't trust the FBI, what does he want Wolfie to do?" Jonathan asked.

"I think he figures that she can counter any neglect he might suffer at the hands of the attorney general."

At face value, Jonathan thought Moncrief had a point. They had served together a thousand years ago, back when the now-senator had been a then-Ranger, and they'd kept in touch. Haynes was a hothead and he loved to hear himself talk, but he was a good man at his center, and Jonathan thought he had every reason to dread some form of lynching from the Darmond regime.

"Tell you what," Jonathan said. "I'll see if Father Dom can set up a meeting before it's time for us to take off for Panama. If we can, we'll meet, if we can't, then Haynes Moncrief will have to fend for himself for a while."

"How, exactly, did you land on Panama as a meeting place?" Venice asked.

"I've been a little curious about that myself," Boxers said.

Jonathan reached into the locker for his MP7, the wicked little machine pistol from Heckler & Koch that had become his favorite left-thigh sidearm for hot operations. "I was shooting from the hip, pardon the pun." He worked the action to verify that it was unloaded, and then he laid it into the duffle next to the M27. "Operation Acid Gambit is the stuff of history in the Unit. It was one of our first and most successful ops—one that people who'd never participated would know the details of. I figured the meet needed to be in neutral territory—I sure as hell have no desire to go to Venezuela—and Panama is more or less in Boomer's backyard."

"Assuming he's in Venezuela," Boxers said. "Mrs Boomer never confirmed that."

"She never denied it, either. I think it's worth the risk."

"And how are you going to get there?" Venice asked.

"We've got time left on our access to Mannix's Lear."

"Too much time," Boxers said. "It's like flying a tuna fish can." Free access to the Lear had been part of Jonathan's fee when repatriating Mannix's daughter from a religious cult a few years ago. It replaced a much more spacious Gulf Stream from a previous mission, and Boxers had a hard time getting comfortable in the tight environs of the flight deck.

"A first world problem," Jonathan said.

"But you're going to a third world country," Venice added. "How are you going to pull that off?"

Jonathan said, "We've contacted friends on both sides of the border." It was tough going for a while after the United States surrendered the Canal Zone to Panama in 2000 in accordance with the deal engineered by Jimmy Carter twenty-odd years before, but now the country was finally rebounding, and Jonathan maintained personal relationships with a number of

Panamanians who retained good feelings about their distant northern neighbor. Truth be told, as Darmond's America drifted away from its traditional philosophical underpinnings, it was more difficult for Jonathan to find allies in Washington than it was to find them abroad.

"Did you obtain clearance for your weapons, too?" Venice asked.

"The weapons, too," Jonathan confirmed.

"We are what TSA agents have heart attacks over," Boxers said with a laugh.

"Do you have a plan?" Venice asked. "I mean a meeting place is different than a plan. How are you going to make contact?"

"I'm going to stand there and wait for him to come to me," Jonathan said.

"You're kidding."

"It's the only way I can think of," Jonathan explained. "He knows that the Community is looking to hurt him. If I arranged a dead drop or something else that's spooky, he'd never sniff the bait. He'd assume that we'd be watching the site because that's exactly what we would be doing. Nothing shows vulnerability quite like standing out in the open."

"Even you admit that he probably killed those CIA agents, Dig," Venice said. "Are you really comfortable making yourself another target?"

"He won't be alone," Boxers said. "I'll be watching."

"You can't shoot a bullet out of the air," Venice said.

"Boomer won't snipe at me," Jonathan said.

"You're assuming," Venice said. "And betting your life in the process."

"There's no reason for him to," Jonathan said. "He's got no beef with me. I'm hoping Christyne will make it clear that we come in peace. If he doesn't trust us, then he just won't show up. He's got no reason to kill me."

Venice looked to Boxers. "Then why will you be ready to snipe Dylan Nasbe?"

"I'm just there to finish any fight that Boomer starts," Boxers said. "I agree with the boss, though. There's no reason for him to come at Digger. There's certainly no reason to piss me off. He knows that I would make a very bad enemy."

"So he's afraid of you," Venice said.

"He *respects* me," Big Guy corrected. "I'm confident that he's scared shitless of what I can become with the proper motivation."

Jonathan smiled at his partner's words. Boxers was one of a small handful of people on Earth who could say stuff like that and make it sound like a casual part of doing business.

"So, your plan is just to fly into Panama City International Airport—or whatever it's called—and drive off?" Sometimes, Venice underestimated Jonathan's abilities to plan things without her assistance.

"That's where those friends come in again," Boxers said. "There are some old Spec Ops sites that still have life in them."

"But you're still going to get picked up on radar, right?" Venice pressed. "I mean, you can't just invade a sovereign nation and not be detected."

Jonathan and Big Guy shared a smile.

* * *

Ian had lost track of where he was. Riding in the backseat of the Kia Sorento, he knew that they'd headed west on Interstate 66, spent a little time going south on I-81, and then it was westward again into the mountains. After that, turns onto small two-lane roads led to more turns onto two-lane roads, and occasionally, the two lanes looked more like one lane. Little drove while Biggs rode shotgun. While they didn't treat him as their prisoner—they were polite if guarded, and no guns were pointed in his face—he felt like a prisoner nonetheless. Perhaps that was what happened when you were being driven to an unknown place by unknown people, all of whom shared a secret that was worth killing for.

West Virginia was a beautiful state. Green and lush—wild and wonderful, just as the license plates advertised—these hills and the people who lived in them were the very soul of the United States. Continuing west and south for hour after hour, Ian knew that they were entering Coal Country. The woods were so thick and tall that the Kia drove two or three miles at a stretch without ever catching a glimpse of unfiltered sunlight.

Ian enjoyed the company of people like those who lived in these parts—God-fearing patriots whom the Northeastern elites—President Darmond and his crowd—dismissed as ignorant rednecks. The residents of these woods might never in a lifetime see the money that an ex-secretary of state could earn in a single speech to a trade association, but they found a way to manage and thrive. They laughed with their children and partied with their neighbors, and did their best to cope with the crap that the elites flung their way from Washington. These mountain people, along with their kindred spirits in the Southeast and the Midwest and the Southwest and the Northwest—the hundreds of millions of people who never dined in a five-star restaurant and never cared to—were the backbone of this nation, and they were being railroaded by bureaucrats who derided them.

The anger among residents of Coal Country and the Rust Belt was palpable. Ian had heard from hundreds of them through the Uprising boards. How, they wondered, could the government care so little about them? Was it really as simple as punishment for the fact that residents here rarely voted for people of President Darmond's party? Work here was already scarce. For the people of Coal Country, where savings accounts were stripped bare, unemployment meant foreclosure. And foreclosure meant humiliation because people who actually worked for a living still prided themselves in their responsibilities to provide for their families.

After all, what did a senator from New York care about starving children in West Virginia or in Louisiana or in Indiana? The fact that the starving children in West Virginia were mostly white—and therefore outside any usefulness in reelection campaign advertising—made them doubly forgettable.

As Ian and his keepers drove deeper into Coal Country, Ian was pleased that General Brock and his team had either been reading his Uprising posts very closely, or, more likely, that the general had drawn similar conclusions to his own. It was significant, he believed, that whatever planning the general had put into place would be focused in the heart of areas most oppressed by the Darmond regime.

During the drive, he'd made some assumptions that he hadn't bothered to confirm because he'd know soon enough whether he was right. The first assumption, building on the presence of Little and Biggs, was that the general was building an army. If the general had been reading Ian's posts, he would know that the army needn't be a big one. One hundred, two hundred fifty soldiers at most. And they would need training. Training, in turn, would require a training location, and what better location than the Coal Country of West Virginia? Country folks knew to keep to themselves. Other people's business was not their own.

Yet somehow, because the communities were small, word always leaked. People in small towns learned things that star reporters from the *New York Times* would never be able to pry out of the locals. And therein lay the real genius of placing the training operation in the middle of the communities that were most oppressed by Washington. If word leaked—no, *when* word leaked—it would be the rare bird in this part of the world who would pick up a phone and call the authorities.

"How close are we?" Ian asked.

"Have you got someplace else to be?" Biggs asked back.

"Well, technically yes, but I can only assume that General Brock will make sure that I'm not brought up on charges of desertion." Actually, the charge would be absence without leave, but he preferred the comic value of desertion.

"I'm pretty sure that the general can make happen just about anything he wants to make happen," Little said.

"There's also the matter of needing to use the bathroom."

"When we get to a turnout I'll pull over."

"Thank you. And you never answered my question. How close are we to our destination?"

Neither of the men in the front seat said anything.

Chapter Ten

Our Lady's Chapel in Saint Matthew's Cathedral in downtown Washington, DC, was the most acoustically pristine spot in North America, thanks to renovations a few years ago that were sponsored by the United States Federal Bureau of Investigation, under the leadership of Irene Rivers, who had served as director for ten and a half years, and had just scored a second ten-year appointment from President Darmond. Thanks to a unique combination of insulation, scanning, and jamming, sound generated inside this space could not escape to the rest of the world.

Jonathan Grave was one of precious few people who knew that the space existed, and while he was annoyed by the long drive from Fisherman's Cove to the District, he felt the same tug of excitement that he always felt when he visited here. In a town like Washington, which valued secrets more than gold, some things could not be discussed in official spaces, and some people could not be logged in to official buildings.

Jonathan and Irene went way back, to the days when

he was still in the Army, and she was still a field agent for the Bureau. They'd broken a lot of laws together over the years, but always for the right reasons. Irene was among the last of a dying breed of bureaucrats who understood that true justice often lay in the white spaces between the lines of codified laws, and she was willing on occasion to work with contractors to secretly accomplish tasks that the government could not officially sanction. Ever since Darmond and his gang had taken office, every operation was a cause for a press conference. The man had an insatiable appetite for cameras and microphones.

Irene rarely called press conferences, and Jonathan never did.

The sharp contrast between bright sunlight and sudden darkness blinded him as he entered the cathedral, enough that he had to stand still for five or ten seconds to let his senses adjust. When they finally settled, he allowed himself to be taken in by the beauty and grandeur of the place. A nominal Catholic since birth, Jonathan had sine-curved in and out of the faith and currently found himself more in than out, hoping that at the end of his days, God would understand the righteousness of what he did for a living. As a lover of beautiful things, he could not help but be overwhelmed by the opulence of the cathedral.

Once he could see, he pivoted his head to the right, toward where he knew the chapel to be. If he counted right, this was his fourth, maybe fifth visit to this spot for a similar purpose. Two rod-straight toy soldiers in business suits stood astride of the chapel, so directly out of the Central Casting catalog for *security detail* that they might have been wearing T-shirts from The Bodyguard Store. Jonathan recognized one of them from a previous meeting, but if the guy remembered—the one on the left—he made no indication.

"I'm sorry, the chapel is closed," said the one on the right as Jonathan approached.

"I'm here to see an old friend," Jonathan said. "I believe she's waiting in the chapel for me."

The bodyguards exchanged a glance. "And what's your name?"

His neck bristled. "Is the director expecting a lot of visitors?"

Color invaded the bodyguard's face. Before he could say anything, a familiar voice from beyond them said, "Let him in, fellas."

The fellas were not pleased, but they knew an order when they heard one. They parted in unison, like automatic doors, to let him pass and then they closed ranks again.

Irene Rivers rose from her chair in front of the Virgin Mary as Jonathan entered the chapel. Attractive for a woman of her age, Irene wore an elegantly tailored dark blue suit, her strawberry blond hair pulled back in a ponytail that had never seen a television camera. Her smile was as bright as polished marble. There was a beauty about her that somehow escaped the lens when she was photographed.

"Hello, Scorpion," Irene said. "You look well."

"As do you, Wolfie." Her Wolverine handle went all the way back to the first time they'd worked with each other. Jonathan always sensed that she sort of liked it.

"Please have a seat." Irene gestured to the assembled hard-backed chairs as if they belonged to her.

Jonathan waited until Irene selected a seat, and then chose one in the same row, two to the left.

"It was so nice to hear from Dom," Irene said. "A phone call from him often means that my day is going to become interesting." Jonathan's long-time friend and confessor Dominic D'Angelo had first introduced him to Irene, and as the nature of his professional relationship with the FBI director matured, all face-to-face appointments between the two were arranged by Dom. While all calls to Irene's office were logged, and her cell phone data was subject to subpoena, the discussions between even the FBI director and her priest were beyond legal discovery.

"How is Venice?" Irene went on. "It's been so long. And how are Mama and Roman?"

Small talk was part of every meeting everywhere. Something to be endured before getting down to business. "They're all fine," he said. "I think Roman is closing in on fourteen now, and Mama still thinks she runs the world."

Irene laughed. "Mama *does* run the world." In Fisherman's Cove, there was only one Mama. Like Oprah, she was a one-named force of nature to whom everyone showed respect. Not because she was frightening, but because she was so damned nice. And frightening.

"You know that one day I'm going to lure Venice away from you and into my shop, right?"

"Trust me. Uncle Sam can't afford her salary," Jonathan said. There was also the fact that Venice had never liked Irene. She'd tried to explain it to him a couple of times, but he didn't get it. Actually, he couldn't swear that the explanation had ever held his interest all the way to the end.

"I imagine you must be pretty busy," Jonathan said.

Irene laughed. "Enough with the small talk, eh? All right, then, down to business. You want to know about one Mister John Doe."

"I do."

"Why?"

"Because Haynes Moncrief is an old friend of mine, and he's heard a rumor that I have connections."

Irene's features darkened. "Rumors? From where?"

Jonathan waved her off with a flick of his hand that might have been shooing a fly. "Relax, Madam Director. Not that kind of rumor. The three of us occupied the same space a couple of years ago at the Fairmont Hotel. A cocktail reception before the Resurrection House Foundation dinner."

Recognition dawned. "Of course," she said. "Sorry for the flash of paranoia."

"These are paranoid times." He held out his arms as if to display the room. "Note the venue."

She offered a teasing smirk. "It's nice to know you approve. Now, about your John Doe. As you had been led to believe, he doesn't exist." Irene said that with a full stop. As in, end of story.

"He's a real corpse," Jonathan said. "He's got real bullets in him that made him truly dead."

"At least as dead as Julius Caesar," Irene agreed. "But according to official records, the fellow who once occupied the bag of skin that is now his corpse in fact never walked the Earth."

"How about according to unofficial records?"

"Ditto." Irene crossed her legs. It was a sexy leg-cross that never failed to get Jonathan's attention. "The man that Haynes Moncrief shot might just as well have been you or Big Guy. He was never born." As she said that last part, Irene's face turned stony.

"Are you telling me that the assassin was a military operative?"

"No," Irene said. "I'm telling you that he is invisible to a level that is nearly impossible to achieve without the involvement of key elements of the federal government." She shot her eyes toward her bodyguard, and lowered her voice. "And I'll tell you that there are disturbing similarities between the attempted murder of Senator Moncrief and the successful murder of Congressman Blaine. The press hasn't picked up on it yet, but they will before long."

Jonathan wasn't buying. "You're telling me that the entire intelligence apparatus of the United States can't determine the real identity of a man they made disappear in the first place?"

"I don't think you realize how good we are at these things. You in particular should be encouraged by that. I can tell you for certain that he was not a Justice Department asset—or, at least we were not the ones who effected his identity change."

"Who does that leave, about a thousand alphabet agencies?"

Irene glanced at her guard again. "You need to understand that over the past four years, the intelligence-gathering community has evolved into something very strange. As the administration gets a free pass on spying on our own citizens, the bad guys seem able to peek under our national skirts at will and examine lots of dirty bits. What they can't find on their own, somebody on the inside leaks out from our end. People are dying from this, Dig, and I don't see the political will to do what's necessary to stop it. The will doesn't exist because the people aren't forcing anybody's hand. Honest to God, it's getting to the point where I don't recognize the country anymore. That leaves it to the dedicated professionals to limit the scope of the damage. For some of our most important HUMINT assets, that means total, irreversible destruction of their true identities. If the records don't exist, they can't be hacked or stolen."

Jonathan scowled. "You've always had a cynical bent, Wolfie, but I think this is new territory for you."

"This is a terrible way to speak of the man who just reappointed me, but Darmond is an empty suit with a pretty smile. That's why I accepted his nomination. At least I can run some interference from my little corner of the federal apparatus."

A scary thought dawned in Jonathan's mind. "Are you suggesting that the president is somehow behind Blaine's assassination and the attempt on Moncrief?"

Irene took her time. "Let me tell you what I *don't* think. I don't think that the attack on Senator Moncrief was a random act, and neither does Ramsey Miller, my Secret Service counterpart, yet I'm disturbed by the vigor with which the administration is painting it that way."

"We've been around this block in my shop as well, Irene, and I'm not comfortable with the notion of the president as assassin."

Irene raised a hand for silence. "Please don't put words in my mouth," she said. "I do not think that the president is trying to kill people. Congressman Blaine was of his party, remember? And quite the supporter."

"Then what *are* you suggesting?"

"I'm suggesting that assassination is a very dangerous business. We don't yet have proof enough to even suggest that Blaine's murder and Moncrief's attempted murder are related, but I'll bet you a hundred bucks right now that they are. Call it a gut feeling, but my gut has done well for me over the years."

Jonathan thought it through for a few seconds. "If you're right, they'll be coming for Senator Moncrief again."

"Probably."

"Have you spoken with him about that?"

Irene scowled deeply. "Let's think that headline through, shall we? *Senate minority leader seeks help from FBI director in murder case.* Um, no. Given the nature of the charges against him, we can't go near him."

Jonathan got it. "That's for me to do."

A pressed-lip smile. "I'm sorry that I don't have anything more concrete for you."

"Hey, it is what it is." Jonathan started to stand.

Irene put her hand on his shoulder. "One more minute, please," she said.

Jonathan waited.

"I confess that I was expecting a call from your side of the world, but this was not what I expected the content to be."

Jonathan cocked his head. "What did I forget?"

"I thought this was going to be about an old friend of yours," she said. "Remember a fellow named Dylan Nasbe?"

Jonathan prevented his face from showing the message that his gut was sending. "Sure, I remember him.

We were in the Army together. But just for a while. He came in shortly before I left."

Irene gave him her cat-eyed look. "Don't be coy with me, Scorpion. You served in the Unit together."

Jonathan shrugged. "If you say so. You know I can neither confirm nor deny. In fact, I am officially unaware that there is even such an organization as the Unit."

"Okay, fine," Irene said. "We'll pretend that we're on the other side of the broad denials. Did you know that he's gone rogue?"

Jonathan held fast to his poker face. "What does that mean?"

"It means that he's working against us. He's leaking classified materials to the enemy."

He noted that she made no mention of killing Agency assets. Was she unaware, or merely playing a careful hand? Maybe he'd never know. "I find that hard to believe," he said. "Why haven't I heard about it on the news?"

"Because we've successfully kept a lid on it thus far."

"And why are you telling me?"

She gave him a long, hard look, clearly trying to see through his mask. "It's been my experience that when Unit members get into a jam, they somehow find their way to you."

"Well, I haven't seen him. I haven't heard anything about this."

Irene shifted in her seat and recrossed her legs. "Digger, we've plowed far too many rows together for you to start lying to me now."

She had something on him. He knew it just from the smug set of her mouth. He had to be very careful not to burn a very important bridge. "The only way I could imagine lying to you is if you tried to put me into a corner where I felt trapped."

Irene uncrossed her legs and leaned in closer to him. "Why did you visit Christyne Nasbe the other day?"

Jonathan kept his face impassive. He said nothing.

"Shall I show you the surveillance photos?"

Jonathan remained silent. He had no doubt that she possessed the photos, just as he had no doubt that he had broken no laws.

"Curiously, it seems that after some initial banter, the family decided to watch a war movie with you. At very high volume. Digger, I'm telling you, this is not some charity case that you want to get involved in."

Jonathan reached out and placed one hand on Irene's knee. It was a gesture of friendship, not romance, and she would understand the difference. "As you say, we've plowed a lot of rows together. All told, I think I've earned the right not to have surveillance on me. And I've earned significant benefit of doubt."

"So you *are* involved with Nasbe."

"I didn't say that. But let's stipulate to two things. One, that there is no greater patriot than I."

"Are you going to tell me again that you're on the side of the angels?" Irene said with a roll of her eyes. "That one is getting old."

"And it is no less true than when you first heard me say it. I encourage the Bureau and the Agency to do whatever you feel is necessary as far as Nasbe is concerned, but leave me out of it."

"That's easiest to do if you're not in it in the first place."

The discussion was about to become circular, and Jonathan had neither the time nor the patience. He stood and offered his hand. "You owe me this much, Irene."

She hesitated, then took his hand. "Just promise me you'll stay out of the way."

"No watching?" Jonathan said. "No following?"

She nodded. "No watching, no following."

Chapter Eleven

Another hour passed and as the shadows lengthened and the roads continued to narrow, Ian picked up the sounds of distant gunfire. It was too far away to pose a threat—and in this part of the world, gunfire wasn't exactly out of the ordinary—but the cadence of the shooting, the sheer volume of it, told him that it wasn't just a bunch of country boys having a good time. It didn't sound like warfare, either. The sounds were too ordinary for that, too regular.

"We're approaching a shooting range, aren't we?"

Nothing.

He took that as a yes, if only for the lack of emotion shown by either Little or Biggs. Ian assumed from that that the gunfire was a typical part of a typical day, and that meant they were approaching the end of their trip into the mountains.

The final turn—a left—required Little to bring the Sorento to a complete stop before negotiating the otherwise invisible space through the trees that put them on a road so narrow that it might have been a deer trail. To make the turn even more treacherous, its angle from the main road—if that's what you could call it—was considerably sharper than ninety degrees. Nearly a U-turn. Given the size of the vehicle, Ian was impressed that Little could negotiate it without tearing the mirrors off.

The deer trail lasted for what had to be more than a mile, through impenetrable walls of trees and bushes along either side.

"You ever get errant hunters up this way?" Ian asked. He was tired of riding in silence.

He was equally shocked when Biggs actually spoke. "Not for long," he said. "Visitors are made to feel very unwelcome."

Roughly a hundred yards later, Little pulled to a stop and Biggs opened his door. "Stay put," he said to Ian. He left his door open as he disappeared behind a tree ahead and on the right. While Ian couldn't see the soldier's hands, body language told him that he was speaking on some sort of telephone. The entire transaction lasted less than ten seconds, and then Biggs returned to the front seat and pulled the door closed. "All set," he said.

"What just happened?" Ian asked.

"You ask a lot of questions, don't you?" Biggs said.

"And I'm used to getting a lot more answers," Ian replied. "No offense, but you guys suck as hosts."

Little pulled the transmission back into gear and they started moving again. Around the next turn, a pair of heavily armed men in camouflaged battle gear stood abreast of a gate that blocked the road. The gate itself appeared to be part of a fence that extended into the thick foliage. Again, the vehicle stopped. Little and Biggs both rolled down their windows and instructed Ian to do the same.

As he complied, Ian took note of the guards' kit. The pattern of their cammies was at least one iteration older that the current military standard, maybe two. Each wore body armor that had to be punishing this time of year and each carried an M4 rifle. The pouches on their vests bulged with additional ammo. Whoever they were, they were prepared for some serious fighting.

"Good evening," said the guard who approached the driver's window.

"I'm back," Little said.

"I still need to see your card, sir."

Ian noted that the guard on the right side of the truck—Ian's side—hung back a few feet, and stood with his feet planted in a deliberately wide stance. If things went ugly, he would be in a better position to bring his rifle to bear and eliminate the threat.

Little undid his seat belt and leaned over onto one butt cheek to gain access to his wallet. From it, he removed a red, black, and white laminated card that was roughly the size of a credit card. The guard took it and examined it closely, and then studied Little's face.

"How long have you been off the compound?" the guard asked.

"Fifty-seven days."

The guard on the driver's side stood tall again, and the one on the passenger side relaxed. Ian surmised that the answer to the question was in fact a password.

The driver-guard leaned closer to the window and squinted to see into the backseat. "This him?"

"This is our guy," Little said.

"You've checked him?"

"He's good. No weapons."

Ian waved at the sentry and got a disdainful grimace in response. "Okay, open the back gate. Let me take a look and we'll get you on your way."

As driver-guard moved to the back, passenger-guard repositioned himself for an angle on whatever the lifting gate might reveal. Given the air of tension, Ian opted to sit still and keep his mouth shut. He listened as they rummaged through stuff—he'd been in this car for how many hours, and he'd never even thought to see what was behind him. Clearly, it had been too long since he'd been in the field.

The tail gate closed, and then the sentries returned to their original spots. "Okay, folks," driver-guard said. "Have a good evening."

Little tossed off a casual, very unmilitary salute, and they were moving again.

Through more woods. Lots and lots of woods. Easily another mile. Finally, they reached another gate, and the drama repeated itself. Only this time, the casual answer to the casual question was that they'd been out to see a movie. After the vehicle search, a second gate opened, and within a hundred yards, the woods thinned to reveal acres of open spaces populated with dozens of temporary structures that resembled single- and double-wide house trailers arranged in what could have been a neighborhood pattern of streets.

While his head buzzed with questions, he'd reached the point of not wanting to give Little and Biggs the pleasure of ignoring him.

As they cleared the patch of trailers, the terrain opened up to reveal a parade ground—that's all Ian could think of. A wide open space that would be ideal for marching at parade, but where there should have been grass, there were instead long stretches of exposed rock. Beyond the flat space, a terraced hill rose forty or fifty feet, where there appeared to be more buildings atop another cleared area.

"This is a strip mine," Ian said.

"Used to be," Biggs replied. "Part of it, anyway. Now it's our training facility."

Ian caught the casual use of the plural possessive but opted not to press. Gates, guards, volleys of gunfire, and barracks were pretty much all he needed to know. This was getting very real very quickly. And he suspected that the guards at the gate were as intent on keeping people in as they were keeping people out. Any chance of backing out had probably evaporated by now. The thought actually soothed him. Once choice was taken away, doubt evaporated with it. It made no sense to fret those things over which he had no control.

They drove for a good long way across the compound and up the hill to the elevated clearing he'd seen.

Here again, the buildings gave the feel of something temporary. Eight office trailers—the kind you'd see at a construction site—were arranged in a single precise row. Each flew the American flag from identical holders attached to the structure of the trailers. Painted a gleaming white, everything about these structures sparkled, from the ultra-clean windows—not an easy task in so dusty an environment—to the stone pathways that led from the parking area to the front doors. Only one appeared to be different than the others, and the difference had everything to do with the uniformed men standing on either side of the short flight of stairs that led to the front door. Each carried an M4 rifle battle-slung across his chest, muzzle pointed at the ground. Their faces gleamed with sweat, but neither made any attempt to wipe it away.

Little swung the Kia into a spot between an old Ford Explorer and a Toyota pickup truck. "This is it," Biggs said. "You can get out now."

The automatic door locks popped and Ian let himself out.

"Follow me," Biggs said, and he started walking toward the toy soldiers. After a few steps, Little joined him, and they more marched than walked toward the men with the guns.

Ian found every bit of this to be surreal. Soldierly, yet not in a meaningful way. Everyone wore cammies, but the patterns were all over the place. The sentry to the right of the door might have been wearing a hunting shirt.

The sentries closed ranks as Ian approached with his attendants. "Halt," said the soldier on the left. "State your business."

Ian chewed a lip to stifle a laugh. *Who talks like that?* He suspected that perhaps they'd been watching too many movies.

"We're here at the old man's request," Biggs said.

The guards exchanged glances and separated. "You can go," the left one said. Up this close, he looked to be maybe twenty years old.

Ian followed the others through the front door into exactly what he expected he would see. Cheap paneling covered the walls and cheap carpeting covered the floor, all of it lit with stark fluorescent light. A very young man in digital camouflage sat at a desk just inside the door. The surface was a mass of papers, and as he stood, an eight-by-ten sheet floated to the floor.

"Can I help you?"

"Tell the old man we've got Victor Carrington with us."

The kid picked up the phone and dialed. Ian could hear the phone ring on the other side of the flimsy interior wall behind him that stretched the width of the building. He could also hear the "old man" as he told the kid to send them in.

"You know, it would be a lot easier if you just opened the door," Ian said. He didn't know what was going down, but he did know that it was time for him to start taking some measure of control.

"You should shut your mouth," Biggs said.

Ian pointed to the door. "I'm assuming you want to lead," he said.

Biggs took a step forward, and Little stayed put, placing Ian in the middle as the door opened to reveal more of the same, just with slightly better furniture. The man at the desk sat between two American flags, behind a desk that was too cheaply made to pull off the "carved" scrolls and filigree. Ian sensed that the desk's occupant was going for a tribute to the Oval Office's Resolute desk, but the tribute fell in a heap in an Ikea parking lot.

The man behind the desk might have been forty-five years old or he might have been thirty-five. He had that deliberately youthful look that made Ian think plastic surgery. Thick dark hair almost merged with his thick dark eyebrows, all of which framed a face that saw a lot of sun and a neck that saw a lot of exercise. The digital-pattern uniform he wore was closer to current Army standards, and the rank patch at his breastbone showed four stars.

Biggs and Little snapped to attention and saluted. "Sir, reporting as ordered with Victor Carrington, sir."

Ian intentionally kept his posture neutral, though instinct was hard to fight.

The man at the desk returned the salutes with a two-fingered flick from his eyebrow. It was the indelible mark of an asshole. "Mr. Carrington, I understand that you're used to calling yourself the Commander," he said. His Uprising avatar.

Ian stood still and stayed quiet. It was a question to which no answer could do anything but hurt him.

"Answer the general," Biggs said.

Ian remained silent. He had but one chance to make a first impression, and he was not going to cower.

Color rose in the general's face as he awaited an answer. He shot his eyes toward Biggs and gave subtle nod.

Biggs drew his M9 pistol from his holster and pressed it to Ian's right temple. "I told you—"

It was a step too far. Ian struck like a snake, pivoting his body to the right and swinging his left hand in a wide arc to grasp Biggs's gun hand. He twisted it viciously backward against itself, entwining the two bones in the man's forearm nearly to the point of breakage. With his right hand, Ian easily plucked the pistol away. He kicked Biggs to the floor and leveled the firearm at Little.

"I gotta tell you," Ian said. "I am officially tired of this. The next person who points a firearm at me is either going to kill or die. Are we clear on this?"

The kid from the front desk materialized in the

doorway, and Ian pivoted to cover him as well. "You're not immune from dying either, son," Ian said.

The kid's eyes swelled to saucers and he froze in place.

Having made his point, Ian broke his aim, dropped the magazine out of the pistol's grip, and racked the slide to eject the bullet from the chamber. He tossed the magazine into the corner behind Little and placed the Beretta onto the general's desk.

"Sorry about that, General, but I'm used to being treated a certain way, and I haven't seen any respect from your minions." As Biggs picked himself up from the floor, and Little continued to stare, clearly unsure what to do, Ian said, "I hope we understand each other."

The general seemed amused by the entire scene. He pointed to Little and Biggs. "Consider yourselves dismissed," he said. "You, too, Tommy." That sentence went to the adjutant, if that was what he was called.

Thirty seconds later, Ian and the general were alone in the cramped office. Ian helped himself to a folding metal chair in front of the general's desk.

"You're not the commander anymore," said the man behind the desk. "I am the general. You are the *colonel*." A little twitch of something behind the Desi Arnaz eyes spoke of suppressed craziness.

Ian felt a rush of unease. "Meaning no disrespect," he said, "what are you the general of?"

The general made an expansive, sweeping motion with both arms. "This," he said. "All of it."

Ian cocked his head. "All of *what,* sir?" He tossed out the *sir* as a peace offering in case the guy went all Kim Jong-un on him.

"The Patriots' Army," he said. "The force that will

return the United States to its people. It's the force that will deliver your ideas to the citizenry."

In the distance, the shooting range started to pop again.

"Forgive me," Ian said. "I'm not sure what we're talking about. No one has told me anything substantive about anything that is going on."

The general waved at the air as if shooing a fly, a gesture of dismissal. "Don't worry about Little and Biggs. They are loyal soldiers. They do what they are told, but they are not responsible for making decisions on their own."

"Let's be clear," Ian said. "I wasn't worried about them. I was annoyed by them. And not just because they're knuckle-dragging mouth-breathers. They essentially kidnapped me and took me to a place I don't know to do something that I don't understand. What—or maybe the better question is *who*—is the Patriots' Army? I get the take-back-America part—well, not really, but that's for later. Literally, who are they?"

"They have no names," the general said. "They are loyal patriots drawn to the common cause of revolution."

"Against the United States?"

"Yes."

"The most powerful military force on the planet."

"Precisely."

Ian scowled against the absurdity. "How?"

"You're not listening," the general said, with a slap on the desk. "Through revolution. Exactly the kind of revolution that you have been preaching through your Internet postings."

Ian folded his arms across his chest and crossed his

legs. "My Internet postings are all about the Casual Putsch—an elegant takeover via surgical assassination. With all respect, I've seen some of your soldiers, and they don't impress me. They are enthusiasts who play soldier, but they are far from being a competent fighting force."

"Which is exactly why you are here," the general said. "Your mission is to train them."

Ian felt as if he were falling deeper and deeper into a rabbit hole. "To do what? To revolutionize?"

"Yes."

"I meant that as a joke, General . . . what is your last name, anyway? Sir. If I may inquire."

"I am General Karras."

Ian narrowed his eyes. "Your real name?"

"At least as real as yours, Mr. Carrington."

Ian acknowledged the point with a twitch of his head. "Fair enough. And do you, in fact, have any military training yourself, sir?"

"You're becoming insubordinate, Colonel."

"All respect, sir, I haven't yet signed on to be a subordinate."

Karras's expression changed. It was nearly imperceptible, but Ian got the sense that he'd said something that the general had been waiting to hear. Karras rolled his chair back far enough from his desk to accommodate crossed legs. "Actually, Colonel, you have indeed signed up. General Brock assures me that he knows precisely who you are and what you have done. All the evidence he needs to see you prosecuted for murder. I am confident that General Brock will see to it that there's a military prosecution as well. Are things becoming clearer for you now, Colonel?"

Karras tented his fingers across his chest and waited for an answer.

Ian's head raced. So did his heart. Just like that, he recognized the box he'd been put into. He chose to say nothing as he searched his options—or, more appropriately, as tried to think of an option to search.

"So, just to be clear," Karras went on, "here is where you stand. General Brock has decided that your plan is better than his, and the Patriots' Army is the organization you will train to execute your plan."

"Articulate for me, please, exactly what you think my plan is."

Karras uncrossed his legs and leaned forward until his forearms were resting on the edge of his desk. His features darkened as he grew serious, and for the first time, Ian saw that there might be some military presence within those boyish looks after all.

"President Darmond was not reelected by the nation," he said. "He was reelected by New York City, Chicago, Boston, and California. He does not serve the interests of the average American. He serves his own interests and those of his elitist friends. Fifty-one percent of this country did not vote for him."

Such was the quirk of the American electoral system, Ian knew. Electoral votes meant more than the popular vote, and Darmond's team worked the highly populated border states like a political master. On television networks around the world, the election night rally boards made it look like a landslide, despite the fact that he lost the popular vote.

"Meanwhile, he and his Socialist agenda are focused on dismantling two hundred sixty years of American excellence. Internationally, we turn our backs on our friends and we embrace our enemies. We apologize to terrorists, we surrender hard-earned territory, and we give the finger to revolutionaries in other countries who are trying to convert their governments to the kind of democracy that the United States used to be."

Ian grew impatient. He'd heard and thought this all before, but he still was not a syllable closer to knowing what was expected of him.

The general had built up a head of steam. "That son of a bitch has three and a half more years to go. His puppets in the House and Senate won't see another election for eighteen months. The United States cannot endure for that long. They're already listening to our phone conversations. They know who has how many guns, and where they live. The Department of Homeland Security is buying literally billions of rounds of ammunition just to keep it out of the hands of the citizens who might fight back. I believe that we are merely months away from the ultimate power grab that will end this nation as we've known it and loved it."

Ian held up his hand to slow the general down. "You're telling me things that I might have written myself. What do you expect of the Patriots' Army?"

Karras breathed deeply. "Washington is a Hydra. It is a snake with many heads. They must all be removed."

Ian nearly reminded him that that was precisely what he was trying to do when he was so rudely interrupted and dragged out to West Virginia.

"General Brock feels that you cannot succeed one shot at a time, one shooter at a time. Attacks need to be coordinated and they need to be simultaneous. And in the end, while killing the president would be a great triumph, he is not the primary target. His security is too tight, and his assassination would consume too many resources, even as the chances for success would remain very low. Without a cabinet, however, he would be largely powerless. Take away congressional leadership and the Supreme Court justices, all of whom have ridiculously little security, and Darmond would be powerless to get anything done.

"And this is where the Internet comes in," Karras went on. "As the assassinations are being carried out, we will let that fifty-one percent of the nation who were betrayed on Election Day know that a new world has arrived. We will demonstrate that Americans are governed by consent, not by decree, and that the time has come for them rise up and be heard." The general's eyes grew glassy with emotion as he clearly saw the Great Day on the movie screen in his mind. "Once again, Americans will triumph over tyrants."

In his heart, Ian knew that Karras was speaking the words of a madman—that there was zero chance of success in a plan that pitted so few against so many. Ever since that terrible day in 2001 when all of America grieved, and in their grieving decided to surrender liberty in return for faux-security, the government of the United States had dedicated trillions of dollars and gallons of blood and hundreds of millions of man-hours to protect the government from its people. Much of that money—from additional security personnel to concrete security barricades to elaborate spying on "suspected terrorists"—was directed specifically against the very kind of insurgency that Karras spoke about.

Against the very Uprising that Ian wrote about.

Beneath the madness of the general's proposal, though, was a kernel of truth. With a larger assault force, the Uprising would have a greater chance for success, if only because more targets are harder to hit.

On the other hand, more conspirators are easier to detect. And once detected, the entire movement would be a single strike away from annihilation. "Tell me about your physical security here," he said.

Karras hesitated.

"I'm on board, okay?" Ian said. He crossed his heart and raised three fingers in a Boy Scout salute. "Cross my heart and hope to die."

"I'm not sure I understand the question," Karras said. He seemed off-balance, unsure whether or not to trust his newest recruit.

"What's to understand?" Ian said. "Physical security is physical security. I passed by the armed guys at the two perimeters—I like the two perimeters, by the way—and clearly there was a fence, but what else is there?"

"That's all that we can afford at the moment."

"Then afford more. Who's financing this thing, anyway?"

"That's none of your concern."

Ian stood, bracing his hands on the front of Karras's desk, and leaning over until they were nearly face-to-face. "We need to come to an understanding, General," he said. "Let's start with the fact that *you* reached out to *me,* not the other way around. I don't know if that was the doing of General Brock, or how it came about, but that fact alone puts me in the driver's seat. At least for a while. You want me to train your troops to do the impossible, following a strategy that exists only in your and my imaginations. I will do it, but you and I will have no secrets. That's not negotiable."

"You haven't earned that level of trust, Colonel."

"I have been *granted* that level of trust, General. We established that the moment you brought me here. Now, what is the source of the money that runs this outfit?"

Karras appeared to be caught in a crack, unsure what to do. If Ian had had any doubt before regarding this man's dearth of military training, that moment—that look in his eyes—eliminated it. "Give me a few minutes," Karras said. "Step outside and wait. I need to make a telephone call."

It turned out that "outside" meant all the way outside, into the heat and the humidity, and the watchful eyes of the hunters-who-would-be-sentries. He figured it had something to do with the thinness of the interior walls. He walked to the base of the stairs, took a single step farther, then pivoted to face the two uniformed boys. They both stood at a stiff and unsustainable port arms.

"My name is Colonel Carrington," he said. He glared into the eyes of the sentries one at a time, giving them a good ten seconds of heat apiece.

Each tried to keep his eyes straight ahead, but the temptation was too much.

Ian side-stepped to his left to confront the left-guard, nose-to-nose. "Are you eyeballing me, soldier?"

The kid looked confused. And that was, after all, the point.

"I cannot read your mind, soldier. Are you eye-balling me or are you not?"

The kid cut his gaze to the left, but they were so close that it was impossible not to look at each other. "I'm trying not to, sir."

"You are a sentry," Ian said. "You are responsible for protecting the life of your commanding officer from anyone who might do him harm. Why are you not eyeballing me?"

The kid clearly wanted to formulate an answer to the unanswerable, but the effort left him speechless, with his jaw moving up and down.

Ian shot his head around to face the other sentry, who stared ahead intently. Ian went for it. He turned and took two large steps to confront the kid's right ear. "And what about you, soldier?" he said. He didn't shout. He kept his words clipped and his tone quiet. Partly because he thought much of the Marine Corps' drill sergeant cliché was bullshit, but also because he didn't want to draw undue attention from the people inside the trailer. "I just told your buddy that he has a responsibility to protect your boss, yet you're not looking at me, either."

The soldier cut his eyes toward Ian. "I-I'm not sure what you want me to do, sir."

"What's your name, son?" Ian asked.

"Parnell, sir. Parnell Hall, sir."

"Nice to meet you, Parnell Hall, sir." Ian launched the statement as if it were an accusation. "What were you doing for a living this time last year?"

"I worked in the mines, sir."

Ian whipped around to confront the left guard. "And what's your name?"

"Christian Hall, sir. And I worked in the mines, too."

"Which mines?"

"The Abenkee Mine, sir."

"Is that close to here?"

"Yes, sir. Within a mile or two."

Ian turned back to Parnell. "Is it a coincidence that you two share a last name?"

"No, sir," Parnell said. "We're brothers."

"Twins, sir," Christian added.

That certainly explained their similarity in appearance. "Fraternal, then," Ian said.

"Excuse me?" Parnell said.

"You're not identical."

"No, sir."

Ian took four steps back to allow the sentries to see him in focus. "Y'all can stand at ease," he said.

The boys looked confused again.

"Relax a little," Ian said. "Let your weapons fall against their slings. All tensed up like that, you're going to pass out in the heat."

They hesitated in unison. These were two boys who had spent a *lot* of time with each other growing up. That wasn't a criticism; in fact, it was a detail that could make them ferocious fighters.

"Really," Ian said. "This isn't a trap."

Parnell said, "All respect, sir, how do we know that you're who you say you are?"

Ian clapped his hands together once, and pointed at Parnell's nose. "Exactly the right question," he said. "I'm glad you brought that up. Let's reason it through together. When I first arrived, I wasn't by myself, was I?"

They shook their heads. In unison.

"No, I was under guard. And what happened to the guard?"

"They left, sir," Christian said. He seemed excited to have an answer.

"Exactly. They left. In fact, they left me alone with whom?"

"General Karras," Parnell said. Maybe a competition was brewing among the brothers for correct answers.

"Bingo," Ian said. "And who is General Karras?"

"The commanding general of the Patriots' Army."

"Bingo again." Ian clapped Christian on the arm as a reward for the correct answer. "Under what circumstances would those bodyguards *not* have left me alone with the commanding general?" He understood the risks inherent to asking a question in the double negative, but this was, after all, an exploratory mission.

The brothers seemed appropriately confused. Ian gave them time to sort it out. Parnell held up his finger, as if pointing to the proverbial lightbulb over his head. "They would not have left you there if you were a danger," he said.

"Exactly. And because they did leave . . ."

It was important that they figure it out for themselves.

"Then you are not a danger to the general," Christian said. He showed genuine pride, and a part of Ian felt proud for him.

"Exactly. Therefore, you should not feel nervous around me."

Tension relaxed from the sentries' shoulders. In unison.

"So, Christian," Ian said. "Why are you here?"

"Excuse me, sir?"

"Why are you here? You had a job with the mine, I'm assuming you had a future with the mine. So, why are you here instead of there?"

Parnell's features folded into confusion, as if the question did not make sense to him. "How could we not be here, sir?"

Christian said, "With all the bullshit that's going on in Washington—pardon my French—somebody's got to stand up. Somebody's got to do something."

"This is the beginning of the revolution, Colonel," Parnell said. The brothers had fallen into a pattern of finishing each other's sentences. "You must know that, or you wouldn't be here, either."

Ian smiled. He found their enthusiasm inspiring. "How did you hear about the Patriots' Army?"

The brothers exchanged a glance. Christian answered for the two of them. "Well, sir, this isn't a very big area. We cover a lot of ground, but there's not a lot of secrets. Once Mr. Wainwright put out the word, it spread pretty quick."

"And what word was that?"

Another glance, this one more uncomfortable. "Who did you say you were, Colonel?"

"I said I was Colonel Victor Carrington. General Karras has appointed me as the man to train you soldiers into a real army."

"And why are *you* here, sir?" Christian asked. He shifted his hand ever so slightly on the grip of his M4. The move was so slight that Ian imagined that he didn't know he'd done it.

"In time, soldier," Ian said. "And I'd appreciate it if you would move your hand away from that trigger.

We're on the same side." He waited for both of them to comply. "You were going to tell me about Mr. Wainwright passing the word."

"Yes, sir," Parnell said. "He passed the word that he was raising an army to rise up against the assholes in Washington. Pardon—"

"Your French is forgiven," Ian said. "Now and every other time you might be inclined to tell me that. I'm not from these parts, so forgive me for asking obvious questions. Who, exactly, is Mr. Wainwright?"

The Hall boys were clearly dumfounded by the dumbness of their new visitor—or maybe their commanding officer. "He's Mr. *Wainwright,* Colonel. He owns this part of the mountain. Hell, he own the whole mountain as far as I know."

"So, he's wealthy," Ian guessed.

The Hall boys laughed. In unison. "Yeah, he's rich," Parnell said.

"Rich don't touch it," Christian added. "Him and his kin have been the most important family in this county for hundreds of years. He's a good man. A great man. We got nothin' around here if it wasn't for him."

"That's the truth," Parnell said. "Schools, churches, hospitals, everything is here because of him."

"So, he's a philanthropist," Ian said.

"Um . . ."

"He's charitable," Ian clarified. "He gives money away to good causes."

"Hell yes, he does." They said that in unison.

Ian's head swam with questions, but he sensed that his time was growing short, so he kept the focus narrow. "Is that why everyone who's here is here?" he asked. "Because Mr. Wainwright spread the word?"

They nodded. "Well, I suppose some people might be here for other reasons, but that's the reason most are here."

"Are you paid to be here?"

"No, sir," Parnell said.

"Well, we get food and a place to sleep," Christian said. "All the ammo we want to shoot, and lots and lots of training."

"What does the training consist of?"

"Right now it's mostly shooting," Parnell said. "I mean most of us are redneck country boys to begin with, so we can shoot, but we ain't used to shooting together. And we sure ain't used to the explosives and stuff."

That phrase definitely caught Ian's attention. "What kind of explosives?"

Christian said, "We've got grenades, RPGs—"

"Plastic explosives—"

"Yeah, that C4 stuff."

Ian asked, "Have you learned how to use those things?"

"Well, we're learning now."

"What are you going to do with them?"

"Shoot 'em at people, I guess," Parnell said.

Christian added, "What else would you do with them?"

Ian smiled. "I guess you have a point," he said. "There are relatively few uses for a rocket-propelled grenade."

The trailer door opened, and Karras's aide—Tommy, if memory served—motioned for Ian to come back inside. "The general wants to see you again," he said.

* * *

"I've given this matter some thought," Karras said.

"You mean you spoke with your father," Ian countered. They'd reassumed the same positions as before, the general behind his desk, Ian in front of it.

Karras's face twitched just enough to convince Ian that he'd struck the right nerve. "What are you talking about?"

"I'm guessing that the name Wainwright somehow figures into your family tree. I don't know the whole background, but for some reason, you were given a very grave responsibility absent many of the skills that are necessary to make it all work. That sounds like the gift—or the curse—of a father to his son."

"Where is this information coming from?"

"The basics—the fact that a Mr. Wainwright is the benefactor here—came from the Hall boys out front. The rest was sort of a guess on my part. Seems I did pretty well." Ian gave him a few seconds to absorb and react. "Now, what did you decide about sharing information with me? Am I staying and helping or am I walking away?"

The general seemed to have not yet recovered his footing from being blindsided. He just glared. Ian let him take his own time.

Finally, Karras said, "I am to share with you whatever you want, but only after you take the Oath of Allegiance."

Ian reared back in his seat. "Seriously? An oath? Is there a secret handshake, too?"

Karras's eyes cleared as if he had finally found his way back to territory where he felt comfortable. "No handshake," he said. "Just an oath."

"And to whom will I be pledging allegiance?"

"To the Patriots' Army. To your brothers in arms."

Something flipped in Ian's stomach. "I've already pledged an oath," he said. "To the United States of America. To protect it against all enemies, foreign and domestic. That's why I started the Uprising, and that's why I have chosen to stay."

Karras shook his head. "That's not good enough. Sooner than later, if you do your job correctly, this revolution will become real. Bullets will fly and people will die, and the people on the other side will have sworn the same oath you did, and will use those words to justify being our enemies."

Ian considered the subtext, and then he understood. "The oath to the Patriots' Army gives justification to punish those who might betray you. Us."

"That's it exactly," Karras said. "And as you might guess, given the fragility of our operation here, there really is only one punishment option for those who betray us."

"Execution," Ian said.

A smile confirmed his guess as accurate. "Shall we get started, then?"

Chapter Twelve

When flying below two hundred feet at three hundred fifty miles an hour in blacked-out conditions, Jonathan preferred blindness to the enhanced imagery of NVGs—night vision goggles. At that altitude, every ground condition affected the performance of the Learjet, and Boxers was having the time of his life. They'd been doing it for the last two hundred miles to stay under the coastal radar as they raced toward a jungle airstrip that was really just a set of coordinates as far as Jonathan was concerned.

"Haven't had this much fun in years, Boss," Boxers said through a smile. The aircraft took a big bounce, and he blasted a boisterous laugh. "This was a great idea. All we need are incoming tracers, and it would feel like the old days."

Boxers was the best pilot Jonathan had ever flown with, outside of the wizards of the 160th Special Operations Air Regiment. If it had wings or rotors, Big Guy could get it airborne when others couldn't, and land it where it wasn't designed to go. Sometimes the landing left a divot, and sometimes it didn't. Jonathan vastly preferred the non-divot landings.

"How far out are we?" Jonathan asked. Among what he considered to be his greatest weaknesses was his penchant for air sickness. Right now, he was willing his dinner to stay put, but the dinner was fighting back.

"We've been feet dry for ten minutes," Big Guy said. "That's why it's so bumpy. We've passed Ancón, but we buzzed it low enough that I fear we might have alerted the authorities."

Jonathan chuckled. "That means we might trigger the Panamanian Air Defense Force?"

Boxers returned the laugh. "I'm thinking barrage kites and severe bad wishes." Like much of Central and South America, Panama loved to beat the drum of sovereignty, but without an adequate defense to repel invaders, the word was more a debating point than a threat. Translation: no one was going to shoot them down.

But that didn't mean that they wouldn't be arrested when they touched down. "How far are we from the field?"

"I figure two, maybe three minutes."

"We're landing in a goddamn jungle," Jonathan said, "based on a series of numbers that someone said pointed to a particular spot on terra firma. The correct answer is something like two minutes and thirty-seven seconds."

"Okay," Boxers said. "Two minutes and thirty-seven seconds. Feel better now?"

"Have I mentioned that I hate you?"

"Just don't puke on the inside of the airplane. We

don't have time to clean it up, and it stinks like shit after it's baked in the sun for a day."

Look up Brian Van de Muelebroecke in the dictionary. You'll see Boxers' picture there as the definition of compassion.

"Seriously," Big Guy said, "If you don't mind putting on your big-boy underpants for a minute, I really could use a second set of eyes. We are in fact very close to the field."

Jonathan didn't bother to respond as he lifted his NVGs off of the top of the control panel and slipped the band over his head. He flipped the switch, and instantly, the absolute blackness became a tableau of finely detailed green landscape. Boxers had pulled back on the throttles, but the ground speed seemed ridiculously fast.

"You don't like giving me time," Jonathan said, "so how about you give me distance. How far are we?" He feigned annoyance in part to regain the upper hand in the dick-knocking.

"About five miles, give or take," Big Guy said. "I'm too busy flying to watch the GPS. You can do that, though."

Jonathan lifted the GPS finder from its position forward of the throttles and looked at it. The ridiculously expensive computer collected positioning data and combined it with speed and altitude to deliver a real-time image on a virtual map to tell them where they needed to be. "This shows two miles," Jonathan said, "and three degrees off the right-hand side."

The plane banked ever so slightly to the right.

Their contact on the ground was supposed to place

an infrared strobe on both ends of the runway to establish the straight line that would define the landing strip. This was madness. Every now and then, Jonathan wondered if it was time to take down his shingle and stop doing this craziness that he called a job.

Below, the lights of Panama City had disappeared, resolving to an unbroken tableau of very dark jungle. All the better to spot a flashing strobe. This trust thing was among the most difficult elements of his job. Because of the tight time frame, Jonathan had had to work through proxies for this op—friends of associates— and that didn't allow for the kind of vetting that typically was his preference. He'd been burned on such things in the past, but it didn't happen very often. The last time involved an arms supplier he'd dealt with for years in this part of the world who'd betrayed him in favor of a better offer from a man who frightened him more. That had proven fatal to everyone on the wrong side of the deal.

"This jungle's damned thick," Jonathan said. "Unless the runway is wider than I'm expecting, it's going to be a real trick seeing the strobe through the undergrowth."

"Have a little faith, Boss. Have I ever hurt you before?"

Jonathan didn't honor the question with an answer. The reality was so far into the yes column that he knew the question to be a joke. The good news was that the number of times Boxers had saved Jonathan's ass far outstripped the occasions when he'd bruised him.

Big Guy leaned forward in his seat and reached for the control panel, where he spun one of the radio receivers to a new frequency. "The strobe has a homing signal, too, though we don't often use it."

"Because everyone else can hear it, too?"

"Exactly. But you never know. What's the GPS telling you now?"

"One point one miles."

Boxers pulled back on the throttles and dropped the flaps to slow them down, then executed a wide turn to the right. "Keep an eye out to the starboard side, Dig. I don't have a lot of margin for error here. At this altitude, I can fly in the night or I can scan in the night. I can't do both."

Jonathan shifted his whole body in his seat and settled his NVGs more securely on his head. They'd been using the new four-tube arrays for a while now, but he still marveled at the panoramic view they provided, much more detailed and natural than the two-tube arrays that had been his mainstay for so many years.

The jungle was unrelenting, an unbroken sea of treetops that undulated in what appeared from here to be a soft breeze. Jonathan kept his gaze at a spot that was equidistant between the side of the aircraft and the horizon. If he looked straight down, he'd lose too much detail in the speeding scenery, and he'd become airsick. Boxers understood this, and if he'd chosen the correct path, and if the GPS was correct, and nothing went wrong, Jonathan would be able to pick up the flash, either by looking straight at it, or—

His peripheral vision in his right eye caught the flash. There was nothing subtle about it. The white-green strobe blinked frenetically, probably ten or twelve cycles per second. There was no mistaking it for any kind of natural occurrence.

He pointed. "There it is. Call it two o'clock, about midway to the horizon."

"Got it," Boxers said. He increased the bank of the aircraft and pulled a tighter turn. "Good eyes, Boss."

Once you knew it was there, you had to wonder how anyone could miss it. As Big Guy buzzed the airfield to survey it before landing, Jonathan reeled at the size of the slash through the underbrush. It was certainly wide enough—thirty or forty yards, to Jonathan's eye— and it appeared from a couple hundred feet to be fully paved.

"You think it's long enough to land?" Jonathan asked.

"Landings are easy," Big Guy said. Jonathan could hear the smile in his voice. "It's the takeoff that needs the room. I guess we'll find out the answers to both."

Sometimes, a simple yes was too big a challenge for Boxers.

Three minutes later, they'd circled the field, and Boxers lined up for his approach. The fuselage rumbled as the landing gear deployed, and the plane slowed noticeably.

"Have you got enough airspeed to stay in the air?" Jonathan wondered aloud.

"You said you wanted to land." Boxers laughed. Next to blowing stuff up, making Jonathan squirm was Big Guy's favorite thing. "The runway is adequate, but I don't want to push it. I'm gonna land just above stall speed."

"And to think that airline pilots get to use runway lights," Jonathan said.

"Airline pilots are pussies."

Jonathan fought the urge to remove his NVGs again to deny the reality of the lumbering approach, but at this stage, the landing needed to be a team effort, one flying, the other scanning. As they descended to treetop level, the nearest strobe dropped out of view, obscured by the tree line, and then the wheels found pavement. The Lear hit with barely a bump, and it felt to Jonathan that Big Guy hit the reversers even before the nose wheel was on the ground. The deceleration pressed him against his seat restraints and caused his NVGs to shift on his head. He touched them with his forefinger and thumb to keep them from flying off entirely.

Then they were stopped.

"Pretty damn good if you ask me," Big Guy said. He pointed out the windscreen. "And look how much runway I have left."

Jonathan had been too busy keeping himself tethered to his seat to notice that half the runway stretched out in front of them. "What the hell was that about?"

Boxers just rumbled out a laugh.

Their ground asset—he had no name as far as Jonathan knew, and in fact had no face and he could have been a she—had come through perfectly. After the Learjet was secured in the leafy bunker that was designed for exactly that purpose, he and Boxers hiked with full rucks for a little over a mile to find the rattletrap Jeep Cherokee that had been stashed for them off the side of a little-used road. Dressed all in black, with balaclavas covering their faces, they were invisible in the night.

They pitched tents and camped army-style till morning. When dawn arrived, they plowed through an MRE breakfast and set out on their day.

"It's been a couple of years since I ate this shit," Boxers said.

Jonathan didn't reply. He actually sort of liked the MREs. Some were better than others, but although he lacked the specific frame of reference, he didn't think that any of them tasted like shit.

When the meals were finished and hygiene issues taken care of, they cleaned up any sign of their presence, and killed the remaining couple of hours before heading out reviewing and re-reviewing their plan. Then it was time to go.

The keys to the Cherokee were stashed right where they were supposed to be, behind the spare tire that uglied up the tailgate. They drove it into Panama City, through the Ritzy part of the city—if any part of the city actually qualified for such a lofty description—into El Chorrillo, a slum that made South Central Los Angeles look like Hyde Park. Back in 1989, this neighborhood had been Ground Zero for the invasion of Panama, code named Operation Just Cause. The main targets of thousands of round of expended ammunition were gone now—Manuel Antonio Noriega's Comandancia (command post) and the shithole prison known as Carcel Modelo—replaced with shitty abodes that were only slightly more hospitable than São Paulo's tarpaper favelas. Jonathan had spent more time in Central America than he cared to think about—and he and Boxers were therefore as fluent in Spanish as any native. He wished he could take all of it back. Every nation and every culture had its good guys and its bad guys, but here in Panama, the default mind-set was to rip off the unsuspecting. Perhaps that was a natural offshoot of three hundred years of perpetual invasion.

They parked the Jeep at Calle 23 Oeste—West 23rd Street—and Calle B—B Street—in front of a bar that was still churning at 11:30.

"This is a lot of people, Boss," Boxers said.

"Nothing we can't handle," Jonathan replied. "You stay put. I'll buy us some security."

Without waiting for a response, Jonathan opened his door and stepped out into the thick, fetid air. Sometimes he wondered why the work he did was always and forever rooted in stinking hot environments. Sure, the Middle East provided that "dry heat" that desert dwellers loved to brag about, but a hundred degrees Fahrenheit was a hundred degrees Fahrenheit, and that was, by any reasonable standard, really freaking hot. The only difference was soaked clothing versus dry clothing and crusty sinuses. At the end of the day, the difference didn't matter.

Four dark-skinned men in their twenties took immediate notice as Jonathan stepped out of the Jeep. It was an expensive car for this neighborhood, and he was five shades lighter than the dominant skin color. Unlike Los Estados Unidos, where such aberrations were deliberately ignored in deference to political correctness, here in Panama, differences were recognized as the warning signs they were. Jonathan understood the men's concern every bit as much as he understood the danger he faced as he approached them.

"Good morning," he said in Spanish. They would recognize his dialect as more Colombian than Panamanian, but there was no downside in that. He still wore all black, but he'd shed the face covering and donned a New York Yankees baseball cap. The Yankees were America's team, even in Central America. His shirt covered the Colt 1911 .45 that was nestled cocked and locked in a holster inside the waistband of his trousers.

"Hello," one of them said. The speaker was tall for a Panamanian, and his skin shimmered with sweat. He wore a threadbare once-white guayabera and khaki pants. "I don't know you."

"Should I expect any trouble from you?" Jonathan asked. In this part of the world, a direct question was a statement of strength.

"Why would we give you any trouble?" the young guy asked.

"My name is Richard," Jonathan said, extending his hand.

The other guy looked at his hand for a solid ten seconds, but never returned the gesture. "My pleasure," he said.

"I didn't catch your name," Jonathan said.

"I didn't give it to you."

So this was how it was going to go. "That's a question and a statement that have gone unanswered," Jonathan said. *What the hell? If there's gonna be a fight, let's get on with it.* "What are your intentions?"

"You're not from here." The other three men fanned out in to surround their American visitor.

"No, I'm not. And I don't want any trouble. I'm begging you not to start any." He glanced over his right shoulder, and then his left, calculating the distance and postures of the men in his blind sides. He sensed defensive postures, not offensive ones.

"I will start nothing," the spokesman said. "You approached us, remember? This is your encounter to make violent or keep peaceful."

Jonathan narrowed his gaze as he evaluated the man on the other side of the conversation. He was not a thug, at least not in the typical sense of the word. Clearly, he was a resident of El Chorrillo, which meant he had to be tough, but there was a crispness to his diction and a brightness to his eyes that spoke of education.

"You're right," Jonathan said. "I apologize for coming on so strong. Meaning no offense, this neighborhood has a reputation for violence, and I wanted to head it off."

"So, I'll ask again. Why are you here?"

"Can you give me a name first?" Jonathan asked. "Please?" He'd learned decades ago that anonymity made violence easier. Once people knew each other's names, things got more personal. It's harder to hurt a person with a name than one without one.

"Call me Miguel," the man said, but he did not extend his hand. That, apparently, was a step too far.

"Miguel, then." Jonathan turned to the others. "Would you mind staying where I can see you? It's troubling to have you behind me."

"I think you should get on with an explanation," Miguel said. His teammates didn't move.

"I would like you to protect my vehicle for an hour or two," Jonathan said.

Miguel scowled and cocked his head. "Protect it? What do you mean?"

"You are from El Chorrillo, are you not?"

"I am. I was a little boy when people who looked much like you killed many of my neighbors and set many fires."

Jonathan shook his head. "You know that wasn't done by people who looked like me," he said. "That was done by people who looked like you. They set the fires and blamed the Americans. That's one of the reasons why Noriega is still in prison. Either way, that was a long time ago."

Miguel didn't argue.

Jonathan scanned the other faces. "You are from El Chorrillo, too?"

"Why does this matter?" Miguel asked.

"It matters because you know people. You are connected. I want you to use your connections to make sure that my Jeep is not vandalized or stolen."

"Why don't you watch it yourself?"

"I won't be able to," Jonathan said. "I'll be busy. But when I need the car, I will need it to be here."

"You're making me think that you are going to bring trouble to my neighborhood," Miguel said. "The kind of trouble that no one wants."

"If there's trouble, I won't be the one who starts it," Jonathan said.

"Then maybe I should just call the police."

That made Jonathan chuckle. Apparently, Miguel also saw the absurdity, because he chuckled as well.

"So you know about our police," Miguel said. "You look like you might be police yourself. American FBI, or perhaps CIA."

"I promise you that I am neither."

"Are you intending to break the law?" Miguel asked.

Jonathan bobbled his head and continued to smile. "Probably," he said. "But only in the strictest sense of the term."

"We shouldn't be listening to him," one of the others said. "He's trouble. He'll bring the police here."

"I'll pay you for your efforts," Jonathan said.

Miguel's eyes lit up. "How much?"

"Five hundred dollars," Jonathan said. An enormous sum in this part of the world—at least a week's pay. "Half now, and half when I'm ready to drive away." He heard involuntary gasps from the men in his blind spot.

"That is a lot of money," Miguel said. "This must be very important business. If it's worth five hundred dollars, then it must be worth one thousand dollars."

"I can always park somewhere else," Jonathan said. "Five hundred dollars is a lot of money for watching a car."

"If you have that kind of cash, we could just take it from you."

Jonathan winced. "No, that's a bad idea. You'd die trying."

Miguel laughed. "It's four against one."

"Four against two," Boxers called from the car. He'd unfolded himself from the driver's seat and puffed himself to his full girth.

"He counts as three," Jonathan said. He kept his tone light, his smile bright.

"Suppose we are unable to protect the car?" Miguel asked. "This is a dangerous neighborhood. There is only so much we can do."

"That would make me think that you had stolen it," Jonathan said. "You would never be safe again." Still light, still bright.

"One thousand dollars," Miguel said. "All of it up front."

"That's ridiculous," Jonathan said. "Why would I consider paying it all up front? Then you just run off."

"We must trust each other," Miguel said. "I sense that when the time comes for you to leave, you may be leaving in too much of a hurry to remember to pay."

Jonathan stewed on the words, and then he laughed. "I can't argue that point," he said. He dug into his pocket and withdrew a wad of greenbacks. He peeled off ten one-hundred-dollar bills and held them out in his left hand. As Miguel reached for them, Jonathan pulled them back out of range, and then extended his right hand. "We have to shake on it," he said.

"Excuse me?"

"A deal made on a handshake has the force of law," Jonathan said. "I've done my part, and now you are bound to do yours."

Miguel hesitated, but in the end, he shook. When Jonathan had him in his grasp, he closed his hand tightly and pulled the other man closer. "Do not make this deal lightly, Miguel," he said. "No windows broken, no tires flattened, nothing stolen from the inside. That's the deal. You do not want to cross me."

Anger flashed in Miguel's eyes, but then it faded. "If you do not believe I am a man of my word, then you may shove your money up your ass."

Jonathan laughed. "Exactly what I wanted to hear," he said. He released the man's hand and handed him the cash. "Have a good day."

He turned to walk back to the Jeep. Boxers had already begun to unload the rucks.

Chapter Thirteen

The cemetery in El Chorrillo sprawled for acres in all directions. One small step north of a potter's field, tilted and crumbling gravestones mingled with newer models to create less a sense of peaceful repose than one of desolation. Devoid of shade—how was that possible in a country so perennially hot and wet?—most of the grass had died, leaving a crumbling tableau of yellow and beige gravel.

Venice had found the perfect spot for the rendezvous, a mini-mausoleum more or less in the center of the cemetery that was marked with the name Velazquez. Made of black marble, the tomb rose six feet off the ground and glimmered in the sunshine. From the markings on the front wall, Jonathan determined that the monument held the remains of seven Velazquezes, their ages at death ranging from eighty-three years to four days. That last number made Jonathan feel momentarily sad. He felt some relief, however, when he noted that the date of the child's death preceded any recent military action that had involved the United States.

"Try to stay away from the north side of the tomb," Boxers' voice said in his ear. "You're hard to see when you're back there."

"Copy that," Jonathan said softly. He had his radio set to VOX, meaning that everything he said would be transmitted without him having to touch a transmit button. "Are you there, too, Mother Hen?" he asked.

"I'm here and I'm watching you." The SkysEye satellite network happened to be doing its official job of searching for petroleum fields, and as luck would have it, the eyes in the sky happened to be focused on Venezuela. It hadn't taken all that much coercion to convince Jonathan's old buddy Lee Burns to reprogram the satellite for a peek at Panama for a few hours.

Even though their radio channels were heavily encrypted, they avoided real names, lest the NSA got distracted from listening to Americans' phone calls and actually got to the business of spying on others.

The plan was straightforward. Jonathan would wait in plain sight, and Dylan Nasbe would or wouldn't show. Boxers had taken up a position atop the tallest building in the area. At twelve stories, it provided him with a panoramic view of the cemetery and its surroundings. Jonathan knew he'd be scanning through the scope of his HK417, which was more than capable of snuffing any threat that may arise on feet or wheels.

"Tell me what you see, Big Guy," Jonathan mumbled. With the humidity so thick and the ground so flat, he worried that his voice would carry farther than he wanted.

"A lot of nothing," Boxers said. "To your eleven o'clock, call it seventy-five yards, there's an old lady and a priest laying flowers at a gravesite. To your seven, seven-fifteen, a groundskeeper is working on what looks like a sprinkler system."

"Well, they certainly could use it," Jonathan said. "Are they paying attention to me?"

"Don't seem to be. Outside the cemetery, you've got people going about their business on the sidewalk. The dead seem to still be dead. But I'll let you know if a zombie thing happens."

"Remember the head shot," Jonathan said, smiling. "You need a head shot to kill a zombie."

"On the larger picture, I don't see anything out of the ordinary," Venice said. She hated witty banter during a hot operation, and was known to interrupt it. Unless she was the one being snarky, in which case all sins were forgiven.

"Copy that, Mother Hen." The SkysEye satellite network was a true blessing to Jonathan and his team. Providing imagery that was sharper than state-of-the-art when Jonathan separated from the Army, it was limited only to stills, and had a refresh rate of four minutes. When searching for oil deposits, that was a fine renewal rate, but when monitoring a dynamic environment, it was frustratingly slow. But it was a lot better than nothing. Plus, Jonathan imagined that it helped Venice immensely to have some idea of what they were doing when they were out causing trouble.

"Okay, Scorpion," Boxers said. "I think I might have something. Someone has definitely noticed you. She's coming at you."

"She?"

"Affirmative. She. I'm guessing ten years old. Maybe

twelve. Watch your two o'clock. If you can't see her yet, you will in a few seconds."

Jonathan shifted his gaze a few degrees to the right. He saw her right away. The girl's jet-black hair hung to her shoulders and looked as if it had not been washed in a while. Nor had it been combed. She wore a brightly patterned dress in red and white and green, and she wore sandals on her feet. Jonathan knew right away that she was Dylan's messenger, just as he knew that she was inexperienced in the intelligence game. She made no pretense of looking elsewhere as she approached, instead staring directly at him.

When she was still twenty feet away, Jonathan made a point of smiling as he said, "Hello, young lady. That's a very pretty dress."

The girl suppressed a smile and folded her hands in front of her. "Many thanks," she said. "Are you Mr. Scorpion?"

"I am."

"Are you here to meet a man with a big beard?"

Jonathan couldn't help but laugh. "I guess that depends on what the bearded man's name is."

The girl looked confused, as if she'd forgotten her lines. "Mr. Boom-boom?"

She had eyes the size of saucers, and prominent dimples in her cheeks that begged for a hug. "I guess that's close enough," Jonathan said. "Did Mr. Boom-boom send you to meet me?"

She nodded.

"Okay, then, here I am," Jonathan said. "Are you supposed to take me somewhere?"

The girl pointed to a spot behind her. "There's a car," she said. "A red one. You're supposed to go there."

Jonathan stood tall and strained to see into the distance. "I don't see a red car," he said.

"It's there," the girl said, but she looked at the ground.

"Little girl?" Jonathan said.

She looked up.

"Is there really a red car?"

She looked down again and didn't answer.

Jonathan softened his tone. "Hey," he said.

She looked up again.

"Did Mr. Boom-boom really send you?"

"Yes, sir." That came with eye contact. This kid should never play poker.

"And is there really a car?"

She looked away. Not to the ground this time, but definitely not in his eyes. "He said there was."

Jonathan thought about that. "But you didn't see it, did you?"

"No, sir." Eye contact.

"But did you see him? I mean really see him, eye -to eye?"

"Yes, sir."

"Was he nice to you?"

She nodded emphatically. "He gave me money." She pulled a twenty and some singles out of her pocket.

"Just for you to come and speak to me?"

She nodded. The smile was sparkling.

"And what are you going to do with all of that money?"

"Mama and my brothers need it."

Jonathan felt something sag in his heart. He reached into his pocket, pulled out his wad of bills and peeled off a twenty. "Tell you what," he said. "You do exactly what you said you were going to do with the money from Mr. Boom-boom. Make sure your family gets it. But I want you to promise me that this twenty dollars goes just to you, okay? You can save it, or you can spend it, I don't care. That's none of my business. But it's just for you." He held it closer to her. "Will you promise me that?"

The saucer eyes got even larger, as if that was even possible. "Yes, sir," she said.

"Okay, then," Jonathan said. "Run along. Take the money to your family. You've done your job. I can take it from here."

She hesitated.

Jonathan made sure to smile. "What's your name?"

"Margarita."

God, could you get any cuter? "Margarita, you are beautiful young lady, and you've been very, very helpful. Now, I need you to go home, okay?"

The dimples became canyons. "Yes, sir." And she was gone.

"You are such a sap for dimples," Boxers teased.

"Who are you and what have you done with Scorpion?" Venice said.

In a distant corner of his mind, Jonathan wished he had had kids. His deceased wife had had a son who was killed in an accident, but Jonathan had never had a chance to bond with him before he died. At one level, Resurrection House scratched that itch for him, but it wasn't the same. Not by a long shot.

"I'm walking toward the alleged car," Jonathan said. "Do either of you see anything that looks like a red vehicle?"

"Negative for me," Boxers said.

"I can't say," Venice said. "Red is not an uncommon color for a car, but I don't see anything poised particularly near you. The image I'm looking at is only two minutes old."

"Here we go then," Jonathan said.

"Hey boss, there's a tree line to your right, about twenty yards. Try to stay to the left of that. I'll have a full view."

"Roger."

There's something inherently creepy about a graveyard, even in the daytime. It's filled with people who don't want to be there, many of whom arrived by violent means. Jonathan didn't believe in the woo-woo shit of the afterlife, but there was no denying the raised hairs on the back of his neck as he walked north at a measured pace, neither slow nor fast. The intent was to appear perfectly normal. It was the most awkward feeling in the world.

"Break, break," Venice's voice said. "Scorpion, Mother Hen. Emergency traffic."

Jonathan stopped in his tracks. "Go."

"I just did a thermal scan," she said. "There appears to be a man hiding behind a tree downrange to your right."

"How far?"

"I don't know. The image refreshed forty-five seconds ago."

So, how far had he walked in forty-five seconds? Answer: a long friggin' way.

Boxers said, "Give me something, Mother Hen. A

map grid, maybe? Third tree to the left of the fourth gravestone?"

The airwaves went silent as Venice tried to work the problem. Meanwhile, Jonathan didn't move. Instead, he pretended to be interested in the gravestone to his left, Pedro Carraba, aged eighty-four years when he died in 1928, felled by tuberculosis. Those hairs on his neck that were thinking about standing up were on their feet now, cheering for attention. He felt ridiculously exposed, and he fought the urge to draw his weapon.

Ten feet ahead and to his right, a familiar figure stepped out from the cover of the trees into the open. Jonathan jumped a foot, and while his hand went to his weapon, he didn't draw. That was good, because Dylan Nasbe had him dead to rights with his Beretta M9.

"Hi, Dig," Dylan said. "Your team's pretty good. How did they find me?"

"Do me a favor and holster up," Jonathan said.

"So Big Guy doesn't separate my head from my shoulders?"

"Something like that."

Dylan laughed and waved at the horizon. "Am I in the general direction?" he asked.

"He'll see you. The holstering part is really important, though."

Dylan performed a dramatic bit of theater where he held both hands far out to the side, the M9 in his right and his left hand empty. He held that pose for a couple of seconds, and then he reached with his left hand to lift the tail of his shirt on the right-hand side so he could insert the weapon into a holster inside his belt. When it was all tucked away, he said, "A little bird told me that you wanted to have a discussion." On his left side, opposite his gun hand, a worn leather messenger's bag hung from a cross-shoulder strap.

Jonathan regarded his old friend. There were several ways to go with this conversation. He could be oblique and poke around the obvious, or he could go right for the jugular. "What kind of game are you playing, Boomer?"

"A damned dangerous one, if I read the tea leaves correctly," Dylan said. He'd gotten soft of middle since Jonathan had last seen him. He wasn't fat—not by a long shot—but he'd lost a lot the muscle tone that came with being part of the Unit. He'd trimmed his beard, too, to look less like the untamed growth that Afghanis expected and more like a civilized Central American. There was no denying the red, though. Or maybe it was orange. Certainly, it was the opposite of Latin. "And I don't go by Boomer anymore. Dylan will do. My Unit days are behind me."

"Talk to me," Jonathan said. "What's in the bag?"

"Are you here to arrest me?" Dylan asked. "Because if you are—"

"No," Jonathan said. "I'm not sure why I'm here. I don't have a good idea of what success looks like for this mission. But I know for sure that I'm not here to—"

"You've got trouble, Boss," Boxers said in his ear.

"Get down!" Jonathan snapped at Dylan, making a wide waving motion with his left hand as he drew his 45. "Arm yourself."

Dylan dropped to a knee, his M9 ready. "What?"

"I don't know yet."

The sharp crack of a rifle pulsed through the cemetery.

"The groundskeeper was armed," Boxers said. "He's not a threat anymore. This would be a great time for you guys to scoot."

Jonathan locked his gaze on Dylan. "Either you were followed or we were," he said. "We're made. Time to dee-dee mow." As he said the words, he wondered if the younger man would have close enough ties to Vietnam to recognize the vernacular for "get the hell out of here."

"What's happening?" Dylan asked, not moving. "Who just got shot?"

Jonathan scanned one hundred eighty degrees to his six o'clock, looking for threats. "Apparently a groundskeeper was more than he pretended to be," he said. "Where there's one shooter, there's always more."

"You're shitting me."

"I don't shit people." Jonathan ignored the absurdity of the phrase.

"You've never been a dull guy, Dig," Dylan said. "I'll give you that. What's the plan?"

"Big Guy, what's the plan? Do we have a clear lane out of here?"

"Tell me there's someone in your ear," Dylan said.

Jonathan gave him a thumbs-up, and then pressed a finger to his lips. He recognized that Dylan was trying to keep things light, but he had a job to do right now and there was a time and a place for everything, including shutting the hell up.

"Sorry, Boss, I've got nothing for you," Boxers said. "The priest and the mourner are just gone. I didn't see where they went." His voice was leaden with sadness and anger. "I think your best bet is to head south—directly toward the exfil vehicle. I'll keep an eye out for threats."

"You need to start heading down to the street, too," Jonathan said. "If this goes hot, it's going to be tough waiting for you."

"Don't wait then," Boxers said. "I can find my way back to the wings. I'm not leaving you without an observer."

Jonathan considered arguing, but knew it would be wasted breath. "Copy that," he said. Then, to Dylan, "Do you mind walking backward? We're going to head due south, but we don't know where the threats went. I've got a car waiting, but there's a fair amount of real estate between us and it."

Dylan moved at a high squat to join up with Jonathan. "Like the old days," he said. "What are we shooting at?"

"Anybody or anything that looks like it's thinking of shooting at us."

"Who are they? Whose side?"

"All I know is that a priest and a mourner used to be visible but aren't anymore," Jonathan said. "Besides, I thought you were the one to ask about who the enemies are."

"Frankly, I've lost track," Dylan said. "I've got way more enemies than friends these days."

Jonathan pivoted to look his old acquaintance in the eye. "One favor," he said. "Promise me that I'm not on the wrong side of the good-and-evil continuum."

Dylan crossed his heart. "We've got a long conversation ahead if we don't get killed by a priest and a mourner."

"Just so I can sleep tonight, let's stipulate that if the priest has a gun, he's not really a priest."

"All the cool kids are in Hell," Dylan said.

Jesus, this guy is another Boxers, Jonathan thought. *The world doesn't need another Boxers.*

"If you're set, we're moving," Jonathan said. As he stepped forward, his pistol at low-ready, he sensed Dylan walking with him in unison. The vista to his right was all tombstones and the occasional tree, while the area to his left was crowded with trees, presumably providing shade to the deceased. As he advanced, Jonathan tucked his weapon steadily closer to his body in order to look less concerning to any casual observers.

"Scorpion, Mother Hen," Venice's voice said. "My view just refreshed and I count five—no, seven heat signatures of people among the trees. I show the closest maybe fifty feet ahead of you, and twenty feet to your left.

"Stop," Jonathan said, and they both halted.

"Got something?"

Jonathan repeated the update to Dylan.

Dylan pivoted to be aiming parallel to Jonathan. "How do you want to play it?"

"I think they're waiting for us to wander into view and ambush us," Jonathan said. "I think there's a good chance that they're hiding from the sniper who sheared their buddy's head from his shoulders." That very mangled corpse lay between two tombstones just twenty feet ahead of them. Blood had pooled into a small stream that flowed ever so slowly in the direction they were traveling.

Jonathan grabbed a fistful of Dylan's shirt and

pulled him closer. At a whisper that he knew the rest of his team could hear—but the bad guys couldn't—he said, "We'll move into the tree line and then hook to the right. If we engage, we'll engage with the benefit of cover."

"Who are we engaging?"

"Anyone who tries to shoot us."

"You mean me," Dylan said.

Jonathan scowled.

"I just wanted to be clear. They won't be shooting at *us,* they'll be shooting at *me.* Not you."

"Then they miscalculated," Jonathan said with a wink. "I signed on to the mission, I signed on to the getting-shot-at part. Ready?"

Dylan confirmed with a single dip of his chin. It was time.

"We're moving, Big Guy," Jonathan said to the ether. "Did you hear the plan?"

"All I heard was that you're wandering exactly into the spot where I can't help you," Boxers grumbled.

"Take that as a sign," Jonathan said. "Abandon your spot and move to the exfil vehicle. I'm thinking if we get that far, we're going to want to move in a hurry."

"I'll think about it," Big Guy said.

It was more commitment than Jonathan could hope for, under the circumstances. If this turned into a real shooting war, having a marksman high and away could be a lifesaver, but if it turned into a ground slog, those four wheels parked in El Chorrillo would turn out to be more valuable than gold. Jonathan saw both sides, so he deliberately chose not to issue an order. In the end, this would evolve into the incident it was meant to be.

Jonathan led as they sidestepped their way into the trees, which were spaced far more widely than they appeared from outside the grove, which meant that there was significantly less cover than he'd been hoping for.

Jonathan pressed a finger to his lips, and then motioned for Dylan to move forward with him. They advanced in a shooter's stance, strong side elbows locked—right elbows in both their cases—and weak hand providing support to the grip. Jonathan scanned one hundred eighty degrees of horizon as he advanced, his focus wavering between the front sight of his 1911 and what lay beyond it. He fought the urge to look down at his feet, trusting them to find a path through the undergrowth that would not cause him to fall, or, perhaps more important, not make too much noise. Dylan stayed with him, step for step.

Ahead and to the right, maybe twenty feet away, movement caught Jonathan's eye. He froze, and on his command Dylan did the same. He couldn't put his finger on what it was, exactly, but it registered as something out of the ordinary, and in these conditions, that meant everything. Jonathan pointed to the tree where he'd seen the anomaly. Maybe a branch had moved.

Or maybe someone had exposed the barrel of a rifle. Between the two, only one of those assumptions would keep you from being dead.

Without moving his eyes from the presumed target, Jonathan waved his left hand to get Dylan's attention, then tapped his own chest to indicate that he would be the one to move, and then pointed to the tree with a wide arc that indicated his intention to flank his target to the left.

Dylan confirmed the plan with two taps on his shoulder.

His 1911 still up and at the ready, his finger hovering over the trigger, Jonathan began his advance. In the distance, he heard the sound of sirens, and assumed that it was a response to Boxers' shooting of the guy among the tombstones. He hoped it wasn't the case. Jonathan had a long-standing rule that he would not engage in lethal combat with public servants like local cops, but in a cesspool of a country like this, he'd suspend the rule if it made a difference. He just hoped he wouldn't have to.

Jonathan fanned out to his left, crouched and ready as he continually scanned. His progress made noise, but he didn't think it was audible above the blowing breeze. And, of course, he could be totally, tragically, wrong.

More movement.

In his imagination, a man was hiding behind that tree, a rifle poised vertically in front of his body. It was the posture of an assassin waiting to roll out and snap-shoot the idiot who was approaching so stealthily through the woods. Jonathan pointed again. Certainly, if the hiding target—

The attack came from the left.

Jonathan recorded it again as motion, but this time deliberate and big as the form of a man revealed himself from behind his cover and leveled a rifle.

Jonathan's pistol bucked twice in his hand, and the shooter dropped dead into his own shadow. Even as his brass was twirling to the ground, the target he'd originally been hunting revealed itself. Herself. Tall for a woman, she had an M16 variant pressed to her shoulder, and Dylan took her out before she could touch her trigger.

"We're under fire," Jonathan said. "Two down, good guys okay."

"I don't see any targets," Boxers said.

"Get to the goddamn car!" Jonathan shouted. Once triggers had been pulled, stealth didn't matter anymore. To Dylan, he said, "We're out of here."

"I'd lead if I knew where we were going," Dylan said.

"Then follow."

Venice had said that seven people lurked here in the trees. Assuming they were all bad guys, that left five, and if they were hired assassins, they were five talented shooters who no doubt had figured out that three of their buddies had already been off'd. That would give them pause, but it would also make them think. Surely, they had comms, and that meant they could coordinate.

"I need more gun than I have," Jonathan said to Dylan. "Cover me, will you?" He didn't wait for an answer. He advanced on the body of the man he'd shot. It hadn't been practical to wander through the streets of Panama City with a rifle in his hands, and if he had, chances were that Dylan would never have had the little girl approach him. Now he was stuck with his pistol and a total of fifteen rounds—thirteen, now—split between two magazines, and that wasn't nearly enough firepower.

The dead assassin carried a battle-slung FN P90, which he'd dropped to his side as he fell. Jonathan was both impressed and bothered. A favorite of elite US government agencies—most notably the Secret Service and the CIA—the P90 was an ugly third cousin to his beloved MP7, firing a wicked 5.7 millimeter round at twenty-three hundred feet per second, and the weapon's popularity had a lot to do with its ultra-diminutive size. Only twenty inches long and weighing just a little over five and a half pounds, in automatic mode the weapon fired at a rate of 900 rounds per minute. This was not a thug's gun.

Jonathan examined the clear plastic 50-round box magazine and was pleased to see that it was fully loaded. He holstered his .45, threaded his arm through the P90's sling, and thumbed the selector just be sure that it was set to full-auto. "How are we doing, Boomer?"

"It's spooky," he said. "I don't see anybody. I mean, nobody. I want to move."

"A few more seconds," Jonathan said. He searched the dead man's pockets for some form of identification, but found none. He did find an extra fifty-round mag, though, which he stuffed into a pouch pocket on his thigh. That done, he pulled out his smart phone, brought up his fingerprint app, and photographed the thumb and forefinger on the dead man's right hand. It was far from perfect, but it was a pretty effective way to identify people.

He returned the phone to his pocket, brought the P90 to his shoulder, and then looked back to Dylan. "Your turn," he said. "Get the lady's gun and check for ID. I'll cover you."

With the tiny rifle pressed to his shoulder, his finger poised over the trigger, Jonathan crouched to one knee and pressed his back to a tree to cover his six o'clock. He scanned the woods in front of him for anything that looked like a target. Nothing.

Dylan was right. The degree of calm was downright creepy. He'd seen this happen in war zones as a prelude to some of his most intense firefights. Locals disappeared to stay away from the shooting they knew was on the way.

"I'm done," Dylan said. "Let's go."

Jonathan handed him his phone, the fingerprint app already up. "Do me a favor and press the thumb and forefinger of her right hand onto the little square. Hit save after each one."

"Jesus Christ, Scorpion, we're wasting time."

"I want to know who's trying to kill me," Jonathan said, never looking away from his scan of the trees. "I'm funny that way. That being the given, you're the one who's wasting time."

Fifteen seconds later, Dylan proclaimed, "Okay, I'm done."

Jonathan held out his hand for the phone, and then slid it back into his pocket. "Be careful when you move," he said. "I haven't looked behind us in a while."

Again, he didn't bother to watch the other man. He was either good at his job or he wasn't. They would come out of this healthy, or they wouldn't. Dylan had always been good at his job.

"Still clear," Dylan said. "And silent."

"This feel like a trap to you?" Jonathan asked.

"Yup."

"Scorpion, Mother Hen," said the familiar voice in his ear.

"Go ahead, Mother Hen," Jonathan whispered. The acknowledgment wasn't necessary, but he wanted Dylan to know that he was talking to someone back home. He motioned for them to drop back down to a deep crouch.

"The satellite view just refreshed," Venice said. "From the radio traffic I've been eavesdropping on, I assume that you and Dylan are both at the base of a tree near a body?"

"That's affirm."

"Okay. You can't progress to the south. I show a cluster of heat signatures less than twenty yards from where you are right now. They're gathered in a group of two and a group of three. It's just like you said. They've laid a trap for you."

"Do you have a suggested option?"

"Head west," Venice said. "You need to put distance between you and them."

"That will take us into the open."

"Okay, then, you pick," Venice said. She didn't like it when her advice was sought and then argued with.

"Stand by one." He caught Dylan up on the new intel.

"We can always move north," he said. "At least we'll keep the cover from the trees."

Jonathan sighed. "That'll move us farther from the exfil site," he said. "And increase our wandering time. Assuming these guys are professionals, they're going to regroup. Our best route to survival is to get out of here."

"But among all those squatty gravestones, we'll be completely exposed."

"Yeah, but they'll still be in the trees where they won't be able to get a good shot."

"Until they move."

"Then we just have to move faster." Jonathan used his sales smile.

Dylan didn't seem moved. "This is crazy."

Jonathan smacked his arm. "C'mon, it'll be fun. Just remember to zig a little and zag a lot."

Dylan looked at him as though he'd grown a second nose. "This is suicide."

"Tell the kid to grow a pair," Boxers' voice said in his ear, "You draw 'em out, and I'll knock 'em down."

Jonathan grinned. "I thought I told you to bug out."

"Yeah, we can talk later about the wisdom of that order," Boxers said. "And since when did I ever listen to you?"

Jonathan addressed Dylan. "I've got Big Guy in my ear. He's monitoring us and will provide cover fire if we need it."

Dylan still didn't appear to be sold.

"It's not like we have a lot of options," Jonathan said as his final pitch. "I don't mean to throw a guilt thing on you, but I feel compelled to remind you that these guys are really here to kill you, not me. And not insignificantly, we came here to save your ass."

Dylan smirked. "Are you sure you're still young enough to run fast?"

"I heard that," Big Guy said. "Shoot him."

"On my count," Jonathan said. "Three . . . two . . . one . . ." There was no need to articulate the word *zero*. On that metronome beat, they both darted forward like track stars leaving their marks. Jonathan cut left first and then jinked right, varying the number of strides in each angle as well as the angle itself off of due west. The idea was to be fast and unpredictable, so that even if a shooter were taking the proper lead with his sights, the target would no longer be where the bullet was when it arrived.

He estimated he was fifty yards downrange before he heard the first report of a gunshot from behind. It must have been significantly wide because he heard nothing of the characteristic whip crack of a bullet passing nearby. He threw a glance to his right to make sure Dylan was still okay, and was pleased to see the wanted man vaulting a tombstone without breaking stride.

The next shots came in rapid succession, and from a variety of weapons. This time, a chunk of marble erupted from a memorial obelisk ahead and to his left, and a second bullet pounded past his left ear. Next came a very brief burst of automatic weapons fire that sent him diving for cover. Throwing himself to the ground was as instinctive as it was stupid. Because bullets travel two or three times the speed of sound, the act of hearing the shot without first feeling the impact meant that you were okay.

"Keep running," Big Guy said in his ear. "That shooter's down. I believe I can smell the other one's shitty underwear from here."

Jonathan had never heard Boxers' kill shot.

By the time Jonathan found his feet again, Dylan was easily a hundred yards ahead and still going. Before taking off after him, Jonathan pivoted back toward the trees and fired a long burst, sweeping once to the right and then to the left. He hated being shot at, and he needed to make the point. Then he was off again.

"That make you feel better, Boss?" Boxers asked.

Jonathan didn't bother to answer. Within twenty seconds, Jonathan was on the far side of the graveyard and in the middle of El Chorrillo slums. He allowed himself to slow to a businessman's walk, not just to call less attention to himself, but because he felt they were beyond the effective range of the enemy's small arms, particularly with Big Guy keeping their heads down.

Dylan was waiting for him in the doorway of a peeling low-rise tenement. His chest heaved from the run, making Jonathan feel better about his own breathlessness. "What kept you?"

"Let's get to the far side of these buildings," Jonathan said. He wasn't going to spar with this guy. He hadn't earned it yet. "I don't think they can get a reliable shot from this range, but I'd be happier with hard cover."

Jonathan led the way half a block south until they got a break in the façades, and then he hung a sharp right. "You might want to camouflage that rifle," he said.

Dylan kept his hand wrapped around the grip, but held it at his side, in line with the rest of his body. It was still visible, but you had to be looking for it to see it. There was a time when the residents of this neighborhood were used to seeing such things, and the sight wouldn't have raised too much suspicion—certainly not the kind of suspicion that would drive them to call the authorities, because the authorities were the people they were most afraid of. In more recent years, as a more peaceful corruption had embraced the people of Panama, Jonathan wasn't sure what the reaction would be.

Two gringos with firearms. What could possibly go wrong? He felt like he was in enemy territory.

The neighborhood was a dump. The vivid pastel paint jobs that were such the rage in Central American cities had faded and turned chalky. Where fences had been installed—always chain-link—the gates all hung by a single hinge if they hung at all, and it appeared that three of every four windows were broken. Pot-holed streets gave in to buckled sidewalks. As they moved farther away from the cemetery, people became more common. Four boys paused their soccer game to eyeball the gringo strangers as they passed, their faces showing the kind of studied disinterest that dominated civilians in every war zone in the world.

"What do you bet phone calls are being made?" Jonathan mumbled to Dylan.

"You're assuming they have phones," Dylan countered. "I worry more about the rumor mill. It's more efficient and way faster."

When they made it as far as the next street, they hooked a left and started moving south again. The scenery changed even though it didn't. The architecture remained downtrodden, though shanty houses were morphing into shanty businesses—bodegas and bars mostly, with customers gathered outside in the sweltering heat that was at least less sweltering than the stagnant air inside. The front of one property led to the rear of another, lending a haphazard, airdropped appearance to the community.

Their destination was Avenue A, one hundred yards distant, and from there they would turn left and head back to the vehicle that they'd stashed under Miguel's protection. Total distance, all turns included, couldn't have been more than a half mile, but as they closed the distance to the Avenue, a crowd began to form ahead of them. Locals spilled into the street from both sides, mostly men and mostly in their twenties—the sweet spot age for young and stupid.

"This doesn't look good," Dylan observed.

"Just keep walking," Jonathan said. "Keep the pace purposeful, and keep eye contact. Don't speak unless they speak first." He'd learned a long time ago that a purposeful stride scared the shit out of people who were trying to intimidate. If you behaved as if you belonged, and made no attempt to explain, even as your eyes dared others to ask, seven times out of ten you could preserve your Alpha Dog status. The other three times out of ten things turned ugly.

"If it comes to it," Jonathan continued, "you're responsible for the bad guys on the right, and I'll take the left." Dylan was among the most professional of professional soldiers. Jonathan did not insult him by explaining that any form of violence was strictly a last resort.

Jonathan's P90 dangled by its strap under his armpit, muzzle pointed toward the street. To be totally neutral—to convey a totally peaceful intent—he would have just let it flop there as he approached, but that wasn't the right move for this group. As the locals closed ranks and pressed together to form a human roadblock, Jonathan rested his right hand on the weapon's grip, effectively mimicking Dylan's posture with the M16.

"They're tightening ranks," Dylan said under his breath, barely audible.

Jonathan looked to his right toward Boxers' position in the sniper's nest and confirmed that they were out of his sight line. That meant they were alone. "Keep walking," Jonathan said. "Slow and steady. Do not stop and do not step out of the way."

"You're picking a fight."

"Nope," Jonathan said. "I'm stopping one before it starts. Just keep your face stern and maintain eye contact. Don't make any threatening moves, but don't tolerate any, either." While their paths had crossed briefly during Jonathan's days with the Unit, he and Dylan had never fought together. He understood that the man was well trained, and the fact that he was still alive spoke to a certain talent at surviving, but among the new generation of warriors, he'd found that subtlety had taken a backseat to outright aggression. That was one of the prices to be paid for fifteen years of constant warfare.

Twenty yards separated them from the locals. Ten. These were tough, territorial young men who may or may not have heard the shooting earlier, but who understood above all that the gringos with the guns didn't belong, and that they wanted them to leave. They needed to put on a good show of defiance. Jonathan hoped that they didn't cross a line that couldn't be uncrossed. He'd be happy to brush shoulders and exchange stink eyes, but if someone produced a gun, or slashed at him with a knife, that someone would die. And if past was precedent, that single event would create a convulsive reaction from the crowd that could only end in a bloodbath.

The crowd had formed a ragged rectangle that was roughly the width of the street, and maybe fifteen feet deep. As the distance closed to zero, Jonathan pointed himself toward the sliver of space that separated the two men in the front of the crowd. That's where he would part them. He drilled the two young men with his eyes. "We're leaving now," Jonathan said in Spanish. "Don't try to hurt me, and I won't try to hurt you."

He didn't slow, and because of that, shoulder-to-shoulder impact was inevitable. But the youngsters rotated out of the way, lessening the impact. Jonathan took that as a peace offering. They needed to bluster, but they were willing to avoid a fight. This might turn out well for everyone after all.

To check on Dylan's progress would mean looking behind, which would be a show of weakness, so Jonathan kept his eyes forward, scanning the eyes of everyone he confronted. Most looked away in less than a second. The tougher ones took two or three seconds. By the time they'd made it to the back of the crowd, even the shoulder-knocking had stopped.

And then they were in the open, and Calle B lay ahead. One of the most frustrating features of Panama City—actually, Panama in general, in Jonathan's experience—was the nonsensical logic of street numbering and naming. How was it that Avenue A ran parallel to B Street? In North American cities, streets and avenues were different, if only to conform to an organized layout of roadways. In this stinking corner of the world, there was no such thing as consistency.

"I'm really not sure what just happened," Dylan said as they were clear of the crowd.

"Boxers calls it gun-barrel diplomacy," Jonathan said. "But we're not in the clear yet." He sensed a change of posture in Dylan. "Do not look back. We are one hundred percent sure that we don't have a care in the world."

"And if they shoot at us?"

"Then we'll shoot back," Jonathan said. "We do not hold a position of strength, but they haven't realized it yet. You don't want to do anything to clarify the reality."

"How far to the exfil site?" Dylan asked.

"We turn left here," Jonathan said, executing the turn, "then we take the next right and the vehicle is parked on that block." He held up a finger as a *wait a minute*. "Hey, Big Guy. Where are you?"

"So, you *do* remember me," Boxers said. "I'm down on the street, four blocks from the exfil site. I think I might have picked up a tail, though."

"What does that mean?"

"It means other gringos that look like agency pukes walking in the same direction as me."

"Are they preparing to engage?"

"I don't think so. I'm pretending not to see them so I can't really turn around and glare, but they haven't made any threatening moves."

"Well, don't divert from the exfil," Jonathan said. "If we need to deal with them, we'll deal with them, but it's time to fly away."

"Roger that."

"Hey, Scorpion, we've got company," Dylan said. "That whole crowd is following us."

He spoke the words just as they were approaching the right turn onto West 24th Street, so Jonathan could catch the reflection in the window. It seemed that *literally* the whole crowd was following them.

Nothing good could come from that.

Chapter Fourteen

Jonathan picked up his pace as he turned the final corner, and he sensed that Dylan was relieved to do the same. They still didn't run, but it was definitely no time to dawdle. Half a block away, Miguel and his buddies had formed a roadblock of their own, more or less surrounding the exfil Jeep.

"Where are we going?" Dylan asked. His voice carried a nervous edge. "This is a trap."

"I don't think so," Jonathan said. He picked up his pace even more. As he closed to within a few hundred feet, he called, "Miguel! Do you know these people?" He tossed a thumb back at his pursuers.

Miguel stepped forward from his buddies and squinted to see the approaching group, a gesture that registered as nearsighted, though Jonathan couldn't imagine how that tidbit of intel could possibly help. "Some of them," Miguel said.

"Then tell them that we are good guys. That we're on their side."

"You know him?" Dylan asked.

"We're old friends," Jonathan said. The separation

distance closed even more. He kept his eyes on Miguel. He trusted this kid to do the right thing. He hoped he wasn't being foolish.

"Hey!" Miguel called, raising his hand as if to be called on. "Give these guys a chance. We should listen to what they have to say." Then he pointed at Dylan. "I don't know this one."

"He's with me. Big Guy is on his way." He used the phrase *el gordo* to refer to Boxers, which translated to "the fat one." He knew Miguel would get what he was talking about, and Boxers wasn't here to take exception.

Jonathan pulled to a stop when he was separated by, say, fifteen feet from Miguel, and then he turned to face his pursuers. "We are not here to hurt anyone," he said.

Someone yelled, "Then why do you have guns?"

"The American CIA is trying to kill us," Jonathan said. He didn't know for a fact that that was the case, but he felt it was close. And there was no better way to fire up a civilian population in any third world country than to invoke the name of the Central Intelligence Agency.

"We heard shooting," Miguel said.

"Some of that was us," Jonathan said, "and some of that was them. We were better at it."

That brought a smile from Miguel, and he heard a ripple of laughter from the newcomers.

Jonathan sensed opportunity. "I don't have a lot of time," he said. "We are Americans, but we do not work for the American government. We are not police. We are being pursued by government agents who want to kill us."

That brought a rumble of discontent. And excitement.

"We need your help to get away," Jonathan continued. "In a few minutes, a very, very large man will come this way. He is our friend, and I need you to let him through. But there are others—men and maybe women with guns—who will also be coming this way. I need you to surround them. Don't harm them. Don't push them. But surround them and slow them down. They will try to intimidate you, but they have orders not to hurt any local residents. They may make threats, but they will not follow through with them."

Heads nodded. Elbows prodded the ribs of people standing nearby. "How do we know that we can trust you?" someone asked.

"He has money," Miguel said. "Lots of money."

Well played, Jonathan thought. He reached into his pocket for the wad, and offered it to the presumed leader of the pursuing group. "I think this is three thousand dollars," he said. "It's all one hundred dollar bills, but I gave some to Miguel and I didn't count it all that closely." That was both a peace offering to Miguel and a threat. Peace offering to let it be known that Miguel's group had already been paid, and threat to let the new guys know that the folks on the other side had money to spread around. And of course, there were the guns.

The leader of the pursuers stepped forward and reached for the cash, but Jonathan pulled it back. "I need to know your name," he said. Some drills never changed.

"Roderick," the man said.

Jonathan felt himself twitch. It wasn't the kind of

name he'd been expecting. "Nice to meet you, Roderick." He held out a hand in friendship.

Roderick took it, and Jonathan squeezed just tightly enough to make sure the other man couldn't pull away. "Understand," he said in a voice that couldn't possibly be heard by anyone standing more than three feet away, "that by taking this money, you're making a business arrangement. You will allow my big friend to pass, and you will stop the CIA killers from approaching. If it all works, you will never see me again. If you betray me, will kill you first, and then I will make it my life's work to kill everyone else who is with you." When Jonathan said stuff like that, he had no idea how much was hyperbole and how much was real, and at one level, that didn't matter. What mattered was that the other party believed it to be true. "Do we understand each other?"

Roderick's expression never faltered. He didn't even flinch. "I take your money for myself and my friends. will do my part. And if you ever threaten me again, will cut your throat." He closed the deal with the kind of smile that signaled a fight to the death.

"Here's hoping that it never comes to that," Jonathan said. His smile was genuine. This was the last man he ever wanted to fight, but he admired his attitude. If you're going to trust your life to a stranger, it always paid off to trust it to a tough guy.

The deal was done. Jonathan turned to Dylan. "We just bought some time," he said in English. He knew the locals likely spoke the language, but by switching he felt his words would be less threatening. Anything for an edge. He pointed to the Jeep. "Those are our wheels."

He pulled on the door handle and stopped. *Shit.*

"Really?" Dylan said. "You don't have the keys, do you?"

Jonathan felt himself blushing. "Yeah, well. He was supposed to get back here first."

"Yeah, I heard that." Dylan laughed. "Well, Scorpion, I'll hand it to you. My life has never been more exciting than the twenty minutes we've been working together."

Jonathan laughed, too. "Evidence to the contrary notwithstanding, we really are very good at what we do."

"I've heard," Dylan said. Then he put a hand on Jonathan's shoulder—a gesture of friendship. "Actually, I know. What you did for Christyne and Ryan . . ." He trailed off.

"That was a hell of a fight," Jonathan said. "A lot went right that night, but only after everything went wrong."

"If you boys are gonna kiss, will you promise to get it done before I arrive?" Boxers said over the radio.

"How close are you, Big Guy? You heard the protection deal I made, right?"

"Affirm. My Company shadow is still with me. I'm about a quarter-klick out. If your friends are gonna warm, this would be the time to start."

Jonathan turned to the Panamanian crowd and pointed to the distance over their heads. "They're coming."

They turned. After a few seconds of confusion, with a little light shoving and pointing to coordinate the movement, Roderick and Miguel got their teams organized, and they moved out—slowly at first and then they gained momentum as they surged like a single organism up the street.

"Well, this looks like it could get ugly," Boxers said

"Remember, they're on your side," Jonathan reminded.

"I haven't drawn down on them yet." A few seconds later, Big Guy turned the final corner and became visible, head and shoulders taller than anyone else around him. The crowd flowed past him as if he were a boulder in a stream. As he approached even closer, Jonathan made a wide sweeping motion with his whole arm to get Boxers to pick up the pace. "I said we bought *some* time," he shouted in English. "Not all day."

"You know you're still on VOX, right?" Big Guy asked. He picked up his pace a little, but not enough to make it look like he was caving.

"Switching off VOX," Jonathan said, and he reached for the switch. And he waited, contemplating the vast number of ways that interaction with an automobile was dependent upon access to the key.

Chapter Fifteen

an drove the bare-bones Chevrolet SUV to the first gate and pulled to a stop. A camouflaged sentry stepped forward as Ian rolled the window down. "Good afternoon, Colonel," he said.

"Hello," Ian replied. He reached to his back pocket for his wallet, and presented his identification card. "I'm sorry, I don't remember your name."

"I don't think I ever told you my name," the sentry said. He examined the card closely. "Where are you going, sir?" This one was older than the average soldier in this army, and he exhibited much more attitude. And not in a good way.

"How is that your business?" Ian said. Attitude begot attitude.

"Well, sir, it's my business, sir, because I man this gate, sir. And I have standing orders from the general not to let anyone out who does not have a good reason to leave. Sir."

"I'm guessing you don't come from a military background," Ian said.

"You might be right. So, sir, are we going to do this all day, or are you going to answer my question?"

At one level, Ian admired this guy. In a world steeped in bullshit, the soldier tolerated none of it. The real Army could use more of that, Ian thought, especially in the senior ranks. "I'm going into Whitesville for a money order," he said. It was the God's honest truth.

The answer seemed to confuse the nameless sentry.

"It's like a check," Ian explained. "I have bills to pay. One of the best ways for me to stay under the radar to do my job here is to make sure that my bills don't go into default. Don't you think?"

The guard thought a little longer. "How long will you be gone?"

"As long as it takes. Two hours? I don't even know how long the drive is."

"About a half hour."

"Okay, then, a half hour there, a half hour back and an hour to do what I've got to do. If I did the math right, that's two hours."

After another few seconds' consideration, it appeared that the explanation was adequate. "All right," the sentry said. He nodded to the other man on duty, who leaned on the counterweight that lifted the gate out of the way. "I'll call down to the other gate and tell them that you're coming through."

Ian started to roll the window back up.

"Oh, and Colonel?"

Ian stopped cranking.

"Remember your oath, sir. You don't want me coming to look for you." He smiled. "Have a nice day, sir." There was no salute.

Ian was not a fan of the compound's apparent dual

role as a prison for those who'd volunteered to the cause, but he understood the need for limiting access to the rest of the world. People liked to talk, after all, and given the youth, inexperience, and exuberance of the rank-and-file, he cringed at the boasting and pillow talk that would run amok if the soldiers were allowed to run free.

The pillow talk, though—particularly the lack of it—would become a problem before long. Libido was a constant among young men, and without relief, morale could become a problem. But as problems went, that was the least among them. Discipline was the issue at the top of that particular list. The troops assembled at Camp Wainwright had not signed on for a career of disciplined war-fighting, but rather for a quickly executed revolution. He sensed that they would not have the patience—and that the Patriots' Army did not possess the finances—to train to the level of professionalism that he wanted to see.

But those were concerns for later. Right now, he had some life chores to take care of.

Whitesville, West Virginia, lay along the Coal River, nestled in a valley among valleys. Difficult to get to in the summer, Ian couldn't imagine what a challenge it would be with snow-covered roads. He had no idea what the population of the place might be, but he couldn't imagine that it was more than a couple hundred souls. Low-rise, well-worn, old-construction commercial buildings lined both sides of the road, which itself tracked the western edge of the river. This was a place for locals, he could tell—what tourists would ever find the place? The pharmacy sat next to the Shell gas station, beyond which was the Whitesville Grocery and Mary's Diner.

On the opposite side of the street—Coal River Road—closest to the water, he noted a hardware store an attorney's office, and the Whitesville Medical Building. The sign in front of the hardware store screamed GUNS AND AMMO!! Ian imagined that for many of the locals, the availability of guns and ammo made the difference between eating and starving. Ditto the availability of fishing tackle.

More people milled about on the streets than he would have anticipated for two o'clock on a Tuesday afternoon, but since this was his first trip into town, he conceded that he had no good point of reference. He pulled the Chevy into an empty spot in front of a stately yet weather-worn structure sporting the sign WEST VIRGINIA COMMERCE BANK. He noted the irony of his parking space's proximity to the last place he would go to get money these days.

Money orders were one on the last reasonably anonymous financial instruments left in America. Wander into any store that sold them—and there were many from big-box retailers to local mom-and-pops—and you could lay down as much as $1,000 in cash and walk away with a check that was nearly as secure as bank-issued certified funds. Purchasers of money orders didn't have to designate the payee in front of anyone, and because the transaction could be completed with cash, there was no record of who ordered the funds Even banks didn't require identification, but they were so heavily monitored by video cameras that anonymity was impossible. The National Security Agency had re cently initiated programs of active facial recognition at banks, airports, and other public venues that would have been illegal under previous administrations.

The hot sun and thick air embraced Ian like an unwelcome hug as he climbed out of the air-conditioned cab and surveyed his options. The pharmacy was more likely to have video surveillance, he imagined, because of the availability of narcotics, so that was out. He decided to give Bud's Hardware a try. He adjusted the 9 millimeter Walther PPK/S that was hidden by his shirttail, made sure that it was still concealed, and then strolled across the street.

A dangling string of sleigh bells slapped against the glass as he entered into what looked like a photograph from his childhood. This was a working man's hardware store, free from the bright lights, wide aisles, and tall ceilings that had run stores like this one out of business. In Bud's Hardware, where the air barely moved and smelled of fertilizer, paint thinner, and insecticide, the aisles were too narrow for two men to pass without each turning sideways, and the shelves were stacked and packed with all manner of tradesman's tools and household gadgets. In a single gaze, he saw a dozen different kinds of rodent traps and poisons, insecticides in a variety of different forms—from buckets to aerosol cans—a bicycle, and four different types of lawn mowers. For him, it was love at first sight.

"Howdy," said a ruddy-faced old guy with a grayringed bald head and substantial gut. He wore a blue denim shirt with the sleeves rolled up to his elbows and a pair of jeans that hadn't been laundered in a while, which he held up with a set of navy blue elastic clip-on suspenders.

"Hi," Ian said. "Love the store."

"Good to hear. After thirty-seven years, I've kinda come to hate it." He spoke the words with a smile and punctuated them with a throaty, juicy laugh. Smoker.

"It's like walking back into my childhood," Ian said. "Are you Bud?" He walked toward the glass-topped counter, under which an assortment of pistols lay on display. As he neared, he noted the massive Taurus Judge revolver holstered on the man's left side. Perhaps that explained the belt and suspenders.

"I am he. What can I do for you?"

"You sell money orders here?"

"I think I sell a little bit of everything here," Bud said. "Folks in these parts don't have a lot of shopping options, so I'm kinda it."

"That means yes?"

Another juicy laugh. "Yes, that means yes. I guess I got off point a little there. How many do you want and for how much?"

"I need five of them." Ian pulled a list out of his pocket, unfolded it, and placed it on the glass counter. On it, he'd placed only the amounts. They totaled just over eight hundred dollars.

"I can do that," Bud said. "Just give me a minute to pull the forms out of the safe." He disappeared into a tiny room all the way in the back of the store, and returned less than two minutes later with the money order forms in hand.

"I assume you'll be paying in cash?" he asked as he began the tedium of filling out the forms and writing in the amounts.

"I will indeed," Ian replied. He didn't venture to display his cash yet, though. In a strange town, it was wise to take a few extra precautions. "Just out of curiosity, why would you assume that?"

Bud chuckled but didn't look up. "I've lived in these mountains a long time, son. You learn to read the signs."

Bud seemed willing to leave it at that, but Ian couldn't let it rest. "Signs?"

Still no eye contact. "Yup. You ask for my name yet don't offer yours. I'm across the street from the bank, yet you come here to get money." Finally, he looked up from his work. "And I ain't never seen you before. Which brings up the issue of strangers in a town like this."

"There's an issue with strangers?"

Bud's lips pulled back to reveal an uneven row of mostly yellow teeth. One on the bottom left was missing. "Let's just say we got folks who live here, and folks we only see once or twice. I have you pegged for one in the second group."

"And why is that?"

Bud put his pen down and rested his palms on the gun case, his elbows locked. "I'll give you this," he said. "You talk a lot more than the others. I put you in the one-to-two visit group because you don't look like you come from here. You sure as hell don't talk like you come from here. Your hands are clean and your clothes are ironed, and you walk like you got a rod up your ass. No offense intended."

Ian realized that his jaw had dropped before he could stop it. He shut it again.

"You look like military to me," Bud went on. "And I been seein' lots of folks once or twice recently who look just like you. Any stranger's unusual in these parts, but strangers who look like each other is particularly unusual." His eyes narrowed as his gaze heated up. "Remember, you asked."

It was hard not to look away, but Ian forced himself.

Bud went back to the paperwork. "I hear the shooting up there. Sounds like a durn war sometimes."

"What do you suppose is going on?" Ian asked.

"I suppose that it's none of my business," Bud said. "I also suppose that you're asking me a lot of questions and I'm giving you a lot of opportunities to clarify things and you ain't havin' none of it." He looked up again. "I suppose that I don't trust you very much, but that I'm doin' business with you because you're gonna pay me cash money, and after that I don't care that I don't trust you. For credit, I need trust. For cash, I don't even need a smile."

Ian smiled anyway.

"And one more thing before I get on with this paperwork and you get back on your way. I seem to have made you nervous. I guess I understand that, but I'll tell you that there's no reason for it. I am no threat to you whatsoever. But if your right hand even twitches toward that piece you've got under your shirt, I will have a bullet in your brain before your muzzle clears the leather."

Chapter Sixteen

Shared courage under fire notwithstanding, Jonathan made sure that Dylan was disarmed before he climbed into the Lear for the flight out. The takeoff was harrowing yet not terrifying, and since Jonathan was sitting in the passenger compartment with their new guest, he didn't have to worry about their altitude versus speed. He made a point of not speaking with Dylan during the trip, preferring instead to watch how he comported himself. Was he overly twitchy? Did he avoid eye contact?

As it turned out, he slept. And snored.

Their route took them out over the Pacific, looping clockwise around Nicaragua to land at a private commercial airfield outside of San Salvador. There, they would refuel and file an official flight plan back to the United States.

Dylan awoke on touchdown, stretched, and awaited the next step. Pointing to the duffels on the floor, he said, "How are we going to explain all the firepower?"

"We won't have to," Jonathan said. "I have lots of helpful friends in this part of the world."

Boxers taxied the tiny jet to the fueling area and shut down the engines. Jonathan waited for him to exit the cockpit and lower the door. "Did I miss anything good?" Big Guy asked.

"Not a word," Jonathan said.

"I think I was being tested," Dylan said with a wink. "How'd I do?"

"You might want to get yourself checked out for sleep apnea," Jonathan said. "You snore like you're choking."

"Leave all the cargo where it lies," Boxers said. "The folks here are all trustworthy."

"They're terrified of you," Jonathan corrected.

"That's what I just said." With fear came trustworthiness. A lesson Jonathan had learned again and again over the years.

When the stairway was clear, Jonathan let Dylan go next, and then he brought up the rear. He waited while Boxers chatted up the ground crew, and then when that was done, he pointed over to a little operations shed just beyond the edge of the taxiway. "We'll chat in there," he said.

"You guys seem to know your way around this field pretty well," Dylan observed.

"What can I say?" Jonathan replied. "This part of the world is a hostage-taking kind of place." The heat and humidity were both redlined, and sweat beaded immediately all over Jonathan's body. Every time he came to Central America, he was reminded yet again of why he disliked the place. And it wasn't just the weather. The man-eating flora and fauna didn't help, and neither did the preponderance of violence.

Walking into the shed was like entering an old homestead. Jonathan had planned no fewer than six rescue operations—both for Uncle Sam and for Security Solutions—from this very spot. As always, the lighting was too dim, but the air conditioning worked perfectly. A Formica-topped conference table dominated the center of the room, surrounded by the same six molded red plastic chairs that had been here since the days of Christopher Columbus. Counter space along the left-hand wall supported a filthy sink whose faucets dispensed colon-seizing water that, if Jonathan's memory was correct, was roughly the color of urine. In the back right-hand corner, a refrigerator hummed noisily. If past was precedent, that fridge was stocked with bottled water, sodas, and probably beer and a half-finished bottle of tequila.

Jonathan headed for the fridge and the potable water. He grabbed three and passed them out. "Grab a seat everybody. Boomer, you've got some 'splainin' to do."

"Where should I start?"

Boxers answered, "Did you kill a bunch of Agency pukes?" Why dance around the elephant in the room, right?

"Yes, I did." Dylan launched his answer without hesitation.

"Well, shit," Jonathan said.

Dylan wasn't finished. "And if I could resuscitate them, I'd go back and do it again."

Boxers chuckled as he spun a chair around and sat in it backward. "You asked for a place to start," he said. "That seems like a natural."

"I know you visited Christyne. I presume she told you about Behrang?"

Jonathan nodded. "I heard he was killed."

"No. Killed puts it too cleanly. The Taliban leader— he called himself Satan—knew exactly where he was going to be, and he knew that Behrang was an informant. They went right to him. They pounced on him, yelling to the villagers that he had betrayed them all and would suffer. They stripped him—"

"We don't need to know the details," Boxers said.

"Yeah, you do," Dylan shot back. "All of my friends from the old days are out to judge me, so the least they can do is endure the details." Tears balanced on his eyelids and he swiped them away.

"They stripped him and they hung him by his hands from a sign mounted to the wall of a coffee shop. Jesus, he couldn't have weighed more than seventy pounds. He pleaded with them to stop and when he kicked out with his feet, they tied them together and then weighted the rope with what had to be an eighty-pound rock. It was like stretching him on a rack."

"Oh, Goddamn," Boxers said. Jonathan's stomach churned. He'd seen the aftermath of Taliban cruelty. He didn't know specifically what was coming, but he knew it was going to be awful.

"He couldn't move, Scorpion. All he could do was scream and plead. He cried out for me. I was *there* for Christ's sake. I watched the whole goddamn thing." Dylan closed his eyes as he relived the moment. His breathing increased in rate and volume. "I stood there and watched the whole . . . goddamned . . . thing."

"You had orders," Boxers said.

"Shut up, Big Guy. You're going to hear this. So here's this little boy who's been one of our greatest intelligence assets—the boy I was going to bring home to my family—strung up naked. And then the cutting began. Long strips of flesh peeled away while he screamed for help that never came. Not from his villagers, and not from me. Some of those bastards laughed.

"I don't know how long it went on. A long time. When Behrang finally started to lose consciousness, they cut his throat and it was finally over. After he was dead, they cut off his head and placed it on the ground beneath his feet."

When Dylan looked up, his eyes were scarlet, his cheeks wet. Jonathan felt ill. He avoided eye contact with Boxers.

"All that because he trusted me. I loved that kid. Yeah, I know that crosses the line of lines, but he was family to me."

"He was outed by the Agency, wasn't he?" Boxers guessed.

A deep settling sigh, one that seemed to work only partially. "Yeah. It seems that the NCA"—National Command Authority—"had more important priorities. Some Kabul political bullshit with tribal leaders. To make it work, the local Agency pukes—Tyler, Baker, and Campbell—agreed to give up the assets in the region. Behrang was just one of three who were sacrificed."

"And Tyler, Baker, and Campbell were . . ." Jonathan was certain he knew, but he wanted to hear it from Dylan.

"They were the three I killed."

"What were you *thinking?*"

"That I was ridding the world of murderous parasites."

"Good for you," Boxers said.

"That's not how it works," Jonathan snapped. "They were federal agents acting under orders."

"They were under immoral orders," Dylan said. "They shouldn't have followed them. I couldn't let that go. And now, according to what you told my wife, more of them are out and about trying to find and kill *me*. That's not how that's supposed to work, either."

Jonathan started to speak, but then stopped. He had to get this right.

"If you're coming to take me into custody, then you need to know there'll be a fight to the death."

"We're not here to do that," Boxers said. Jonathan heard a not-so-subtle threat in his statement. If it came to choosing sides, Big Guy would be with Dylan.

Jonathan bristled, but he pushed it down. "Big Guy's right. I have no interest in doing the bidding of the Marshal's Service. Nor do I plan to reveal that we know where you are. We're here because Stanley Rollins thought you might trust us and meet us. That's all."

Dylan extended is arms. "And here we are. What's next?"

"I've got one," Big Guy said. "I get the business about killing the killers. That's done. As far as I'm concerned, you did fine. I want to know about this traitor shit."

Dylan recoiled. "I need more than that. I'm not sure I know what traitor shit you're talking about."

"I think you do," Jonathan said.

Dylan smirked and gave a noncommittal head bobble. "Let's play the game my way for a little while. What traitor shit are you talking about?"

"Not knowing how long the list is, let's start with the business of leaking secrets to foreign embassies. Is that part of your punishment plan for the CIA?"

Dylan held up a finger. "To be clear. I wasn't punishing the Agency. I was killing murderers. With that account settled, I have no quarrel with Langley. And those leaks were bait to bring you to find me."

Jonathan reared back in his chair. "*What?*"

A grin bloomed on Dylan's face. "You heard right. That was bait."

"For us."

"Well, not specifically for you and Boxers, necessarily, but for somebody from the Unit. Even then, it was a pretty short list. I'm glad it was you guys."

"I'm not sure I like being bait," Boxers said. "Where's the hook?"

"What do you know about the nature of the secrets I've leaked?" Dylan asked.

Jonathan sensed that he'd worked out the choreography of this meeting in his head, and he was determined to stick to it. "Not a thing," he said, confessing the truth. "Only that you're leaking them."

"Uh-huh." Dylan laughed. "They're the kinds of 'secrets' that aren't really all that secret. And certainly nothing that deals with national security."

"Why leak anything at all?" Jonathan pressed. "You've been part of the Community your whole life. We don't get to make the call on what's important and what's not."

"Where did these secrets come from in the first place?" Boxers asked. "Are you just launching stuff out there from memory?"

Dylan finished the last of his water and rose from his chair to retrieve another one from the fridge. He opened the door, lifted a plastic bottle, and stripped the cap. "After I killed Campbell, I noticed that he had a computer case hanging from his shoulder. I hung back for a long time, just watching. It never makes sense to enter the scene of a long-range shot, but that case was really calling to me. I hoped that that computer could give me more insight into who might have killed Behrang. After maybe fifteen minutes, I figured, oh, the hell with it, and I did a drive-by and snatched the bag. Did anyone tell you that the bag was missing?"

"No," Jonathan said.

"Figures. On that computer, I found ridiculously large amounts of classified material. Apparently, Campbell had been tapped for something much larger than what he was doing. I found lots of intel about a wide range of stuff. What I released to the embassies of the world—and you've got to give me credit for not releasing any of it to *The Washington Post* or *New York Times*—was piddly shit about the movement of diplomatic resources from one place to another. I released that the ambassador to Buttscratchistan stopped at the same coffee shop every morning at nine-fifteen. It was stuff that everyone already knew."

"Yet here the United States government is so pissed at you," Jonathan said. He wasn't buying.

"Yeah, how about that?" Dylan challenged. "Why might that be?"

"Because they're paranoid," Boxers said. "This administration has been kicked in the balls half a dozen times from people leaking information."

"But I'm not leaking anything harmful to the administration," Dylan said. "In fact, I haven't leaked anything that is close to the administration."

"You're being deliberately cryptic," Jonathan said. His patience for the dramatic reveal was waning. "If you've got a point to make, make it."

Dylan took a long pull on his water, and sat back into his chair, turning it around to match Boxers' backward pose. "Okay," he said. "I believe with all my heart that I have uncovered a plot to overthrow the president and his administration."

Jonathan's laugh escaped his throat before he could stop it. "Bullshit," he said. "I'm sorry. I don't know what you think you've got, but ours is a government particularly insulated from a coup. That whole separation of powers thing."

"Yeah, it's a stupid idea," Dylan said, but his ears turned red. "That's why I risked my freedom—and my life, as it turned out—to bring this to you. It's because I'm paranoid."

Dylan had every right to be paranoid, Jonathan thought. But that didn't necessarily translate to irrational thoughts or actions. "I think you need to put your cards on the table," he said.

"It's called Operation Serpent," Dylan said before he took another pull from his water. "It's actually pretty brilliant. According to the documents on Campbell's computer, the overthrow of the United States government does not require an invasion of Washington by a division of tanks. Rather, it involves a handful of selective assassinations, followed by a seeding of panic in the media. You get neighbors to distrust each other because of differing political beliefs. You get them to concentrate on guns and race and other social issues that don't mean anything. Whatever it takes to distract the papers, bloggers and TV shows. You get groups to hate each other. Conservatives versus progressives. Gay versus straight. Black versus white. Civil war. While everyone's responding to what the media is spewing—always facile and always mostly wrong—a junta waltzes into power, and it's over. Straight out of Hitler's playbook."

"I don't know how to say 'be less cryptic' any clearer," Jonathan said.

"Steel yourself, guys," Dylan said. "The National Command Authority is planning a coup."

"Bullshit," Boxers said.

"See? I knew someone would say that," Dylan declared with a laugh. "My money would have been on Scorpion, though. Do you think for a moment that I would risk all that I am risking for anything that was less than really freaking important?"

Jonathan sighed and closed his eyes. For the umptieth time in his life, he realized that he'd entered space where he had no business being. "And you got all this from a computer file."

"I got a lot of stuff from those files. Campbell had a collection of five or six hard drives in his case. All of them were encrypted, but his computer came complete with the decryption software."

"Was it an Agency computer?" Boxers asked.

"I imagine, but as you might recall, spooks rarely put Company logos on their equipment. Most of the information on the drives was standard intelligence crap, the stuff that every agency churns out—not just *the* Agency. Sensitive and boring. Oh, and it didn't have any Internet connection."

"Disabled?" Jonathan asked.

"Uninstalled."

"I don't understand why you were scouring these in the first place," Jonathan said.

"Would it be disingenuous to try to take the high ground and say I was worried about leaving that kind of intel just out there in the world unprotected?"

Jonathan measured an inch between his thumb and forefinger. "Maybe just a touch."

"Well, anyway, that was part of it. That's why I left my cover to retrieve the bag. Once I had it, though, I started trolling through it to find what I could about the plans to kill Behrang."

"You were obsessed," Boxers said.

"I was committed."

"I think it's clear that you should have been committed," Jonathan said. He tried to make it sound like a joke, but his words came very close to his feelings.

"Yeah, well, that horse has left the barn. Do you want to hear what I found or don't you?"

Jonathan made a sweeping motion with both hands. "The floor is yours."

"There's a group out there on the Internet called the Uprising. Ever heard of it?"

Both other men shook their heads.

"It's a Chicken Little sky-is-falling nutjob militia website like so many others, but this one has the attention of the CIA. And maybe the Bureau as far as I know, but definitely the Agency. They seem to think that this one is real, that it has legs. And they're spending a lot of time trying to track down the guy who calls himself The Commander."

"I'm guessing he's the leader," Boxers said.

Dylan scowled and cocked his head, stroking his chin with the tip of his thumb and the knuckle of his forefinger. "Hmm. I never thought of that. Could the Commander be the leader? I need to give that some thought."

Boxers flipped him off, triggering a chuckle from Jonathan.

"Yes, he's the leader. If you read through the posts and the analysis, you'll see that he likely has a military background. If you read a little deeper, you'll find that a lot of other military personnel have a deep interest in him. A scary-level interest."

"What's the theme of his typical screed?" Jonathan asked.

"What you'd think. Everybody's afraid of the power grab in Washington. The president's casual disregard for the law, the proliferation of signing orders and executive orders, and the fact that no one seems to care because he represents the party in charge, and therefore everything he does has to be supported one hundred percent."

"Sounds like the truth to me," Boxers said.

"That's the problem," Dylan went on. "It sounds like the truth to anyone who's served in uniform. Anyone who's not on Darmond's side of the aisle. The difference with the Uprising is the fact that the Agency believes that these folks are actually planning to do what they say they're going to do."

"I don't get it," Jonathan said. "Why is the CIA even in play? This sounds like a purely domestic issue. Why isn't this with the FBI?"

"Damn good question," Dylan said. "I asked that myself. So I dug a little deeper—really, these guys should be more careful about the kinds of shit they save on hard drives—and I found out that not only was the FBI not involved, neither was the CIA. Not officially, anyway."

"You're being cryptic again," Jonathan said.

"Think about it," Dylan said. He'd become more animated, leaning forward into the table, his elbows rested on the edge. "Here we've got a guy with a computer that is isolated from the Web and he's carrying encrypted files *with* the decryption software installed. It was a stand-alone, rogue machine."

"I don't know what that means," Jonathan said. He wasn't being obtuse. Computers and he had never gotten along well.

"It means that the machine was entirely untraceable. No one could track where it was, the NSA couldn't peek under its skirts to see what it was doing. Yet, all the files it carried had been downloaded from somewhere."

"Which means . . . ?"

"It means that someone was doing an independent research project," Boxers said.

"Bingo to the Big Guy. It think that's exactly what it

means. If the Agency were trying to track down this Commander guy to bring him down, it would be a shared file with a lot of different players. Instead—"

"It's a private quest that involves Agency operatives," Jonathan said, connecting the dots in his head.

"Another bingo. And if bringing the Commander and the Uprising to justice would be a mission for a multi-agency task force, an independent effort to find him would be . . ." He waited for his audience to finish the sentence for themselves.

"There's an effort to find and support the Uprising," Jonathan said. He saw the logic in his head, but he hadn't test-driven it yet, wasn't sure that he should trust his first instinct.

"Right," Dylan said.

Boxers held up both hands, as if to stop an approaching train. "No, no, no. Nothing's that easy," he said. "You can't just say, yada, yada, yada, so therefore the government is planning a coup. There have to be a thousand possible reasons."

"There are a million *possible* reasons," Dylan agreed. "Possibilities are limited only by imagination. *Reality,* on the other hand, happens only one way. Remember what I said to you about the Uprising's strategy? About there being no need for invasion and tanks?"

Jonathan found himself nodding like a kid caught in the rapture of a good ghost story.

"It only takes a few well-placed assassinations," Dylan reminded. He waited for the rest.

"Congressman Blaine," Jonathan said. "Chairman of Ways and Means." It seemed so obvious now.

"And Haynes Moncrief," Boxers said. He looked disappointed at being dragged into the direction the conversation was going.

"What about Haynes?" Dylan asked. "He was my first CO."

"Someone tried to kill him the other night." Jonathan explained.

"What happened?"

"He was on his way to the Metro in DC and a homeless guy confronted him with a shotgun. Haynes blew him away with an entirely illegal pistol, and it looks like he'll soon be under indictment."

"For murder?" Dylan sounded incredulous.

"For the pistol," Jonathan said.

"You're shitting me. He defended himself?"

"Yup. But he did it illegally."

"I think all of that is bullshit," Boxers said. "Haynes Moncrief is under arrest for not having the decency to die and get off the president's back."

"Give it a rest, Big Guy," Jonathan said. By no means an apologist for Darmond's disastrous presidency, Jonathan refused to adhere to the blogosphere's line that the president was somehow a traitor. He thought the president was misguided and an egotist, and ultimately harmful for the nation, but he'd been duly elected twice, and even a man with no enemies in the media-that-mattered had limited power to undermine two hundred fifty years of American progress. He couldn't wrap his head around the notion of Darmond being that Machiavellian. Machiavellian, yes, but just not that much so.

And despite the president's shortcomings, Darmond

was still commander-in-chief, and the apparatus that reported to him had no right to undermine that. Could that be what was actually happening?

"So, let me get this straight," Jonathan said. "You figured all of this out, and you therefore thought that the best way to seek help was to send secrets to foreign enemies."

"It worked, didn't it?"

"Did you consider making a phone call?" Boxers asked.

"Who would I call? There's that small matter of being wanted for murder." He tossed up his hands. "What's the old saying? There's no arguing with success. You're both here."

Jonathan scrubbed his scalp with his fingertips, a tell for frustration. "So, now that you've shared this tidbit, what do you expect us to do with it?"

"I have no idea. I just didn't want to be the only one who knew. From there, I defer to you. You have better connections."

Jonathan looked to Boxers for help and was rewarded with broken eye contact.

"Okay, let's think this through," Jonathan said. "We'll assume that your theory is correct—that people in senior levels of power are in the process of planning a coup. Who do we tell?"

"You know who comes to *my* mind," Boxers said. "Our special asset."

Jonathan knew he was referring to Wolverine. "It's a little early for that one." He deliberately avoided the gender-specific pronoun because Boomer didn't have a need to know. "We need more information." To Dylan, he said, "How confident are you in your conclusions?"

"Confident enough to expose myself like this."

"Isn't there a chance that you're misreading the tea leaves? That there's another entirely plausible and reasonable explanation for what you've seen, but that you need to squint at it a little differently?"

A shrug. "Anything's possible, Dig. I won't say that there's no other conceivable explanation—that's your call." He reached into the ditty bag he'd been guarding so closely and produced two computer drives. "Here it is," he said. "All of it. These are the drives I took off of Campbell. They're yours now. I'm out of it."

"No, you're not," Boxers said. "You can't light a fire this big and just walk away."

Dylan stood. "Watch me."

Boxers took three steps closer and towered over the other man. "No," he said. "*You* watch *me*. Sit back down while sitting is still an option for you."

Dylan seemed shocked. "What's that all about? I'm not the enemy." He sat down, though.

"We don't know who you are yet," Jonathan said. "We know who you *were* and we know who you claim to be, but the rest is up for grabs. We're going to need you to stay close for a while."

Dylan's features darkened. "What do you mean by 'stay close'?"

"That means you need to come back to the States with us."

"The hell I am."

"We're not going to turn you in. You're not even

going to have to go through customs or immigration. But what you're talking about is huge. You've already gone through those files, so you know your way around. That's a lot more than my team and I can say. I have a computer wizard back home that can do amazing things with records such as these, but she's going to need your help to reconstruct what you've already found."

"I cannot afford to go back to the United States. I'll be a sitting duck."

Jonathan's patience was fraying. "This isn't about you, Boomer. In fact, this is about stuff that's way, way bigger than you. Or me or Boxers, for that matter. You're talking about a coup to overthrow the United States government. As opposed to the possibility of you getting caught."

"For shit you already told us you did," Boxers added. "Let's not forget that we found you pretty easily."

"Because my wife pointed you in my direction," Dylan said. "And because I agreed to meet."

"It was still easy," Jonathan said. "No one can stay underground forever. Sooner or later, getting caught is in your future. When that happens, you get dead or you go to jail. There's really no third option. If you come with us, we'll keep you under wraps."

"How?"

Jonathan growled his frustration. "Jesus Christ, Boomer. You want details? I don't have those yet. Baby steps, okay? If you've had your ear to the Community rumor mill, then you know I'm pretty good at helping people disappear. Granted, I've never done that for someone on the top of Interpol's most wanted list, but like I said before, baby steps. You come back, we'll get you to a very secure place out in the country, and you can work with my staff in complete secrecy to figure out what is going on."

"But I already told you what is going on."

Jonathan stood. "We're not going through this again. You're coming back with us. You need to decide whether it's going to be willingly or in zip cuffs."

"Either way works for me," Boxers said.

"Will I be able to see my family?"

"Probably not," Jonathan said. "They're under pretty tight scrutiny. I don't think that's a risk you should be anxious to take."

Dylan hadn't moved from his seat. "You seriously would truss me up and take me against my will?"

"It's one of my best things," Boxers said.

"But neither of us wants it to be that way," Jonathan assured. "Come on, Boomer, tap your inner patriot. This is the right thing to do."

"I just don't know what more I can add," Dylan said. Jonathan could tell it was a last-ditch hedge.

"We'll all find that out together," Boxers said.

"Even if we accept everything you've said as gospel, and you've landed on the *what* of it all, we haven't touched on the *why*. Or, even more important, we don't know the *who*."

"The Commander was very good about covering his tracks," Dylan said. "The who is going to be tough."

"And I know just the gal for the challenge," Jonathan said. He made a circular, beckoning motion with his hand. "Come on," he said. "For the adventure if not for the patriotism."

Dylan laughed as he stood and walked toward the door. "Do people actually respond to corny lines like that?"

"As a wise man told me not ten minutes ago, there's no arguing with success."

Chapter Seventeen

Thanks to some interference run by Stanley Rollins, Boxers received clearance to make US landfall at Hurlburt Field in the Florida panhandle. An extension of Eglin Air Force Base, Hurlburt had been the home to countless Special Forces training operations and launches over the years. Ordinarily, civilian aircraft were not allowed, and that was where Rollins came in. He made a few phone calls, and it was done. Enough spooky shit transpired at Hurlburt that whoever might have had questions knew better than to ask them.

It hadn't been an easy negotiation, though. "I need access to Hurlburt," Jonathan had said on a secure line.

"Does that mean you're coming back with precious cargo?" Rollins asked.

The question sat uneasily on Jonathan's stomach. "I'd prefer not to answer that, Colonel."

"Why?"

"I'd prefer not to answer that, either."

"Listen, Scorpion, if you have him, then I want to debrief him."

"That's not the deal," Jonathan said. "I don't want

you or anyone from the Puzzle Palace anywhere near us. I just want to make landfall at Hurlburt so I don't have to deal with all the Homeland Security crap. I want to touch down, drink some of Uncle Sam's gas, and then take off again. That's it."

"I want to talk with him."

"You're assuming I have him."

"Don't play that game with me, Scorpion."

"Let's not forget who invited whom to whose party, Colonel," Jonathan said. This point was nonnegotiable. He'd given his word to Dylan. Perhaps he hadn't had the authority to do so, but this wouldn't be the first time with that scenario. "I don't want to see troops, I don't want to see government agents when we land. I don't even want to see a Walmart greeter. Are you understanding me?"

"It's not your field, Scorpion. It's Uncle's field. You don't get to call the shots."

Why did life have to be this complicated? "Why did you reach out to me for this mission in the first place, Colonel?"

As sigh on the other end of the phone. "Because you're the best at what you do. Is that it? You just want to be sucked up to?"

"Screw you, Colonel." He said it with enough smile in his voice to maintain reasonable doubt over how much he meant it. "You told me that you trust me. Remember that?"

"I remember a lot of what I say."

"Then remember this better," Jonathan said. "I'm not playing games here. I told you from the very beginning that I'm not doing the Marshal Service's job for them. My mission is to get to the bottom of what's going on and to bring a PC to safety. You have to trust that what I'm asking you to do is all in service to those goals."

Silence.

"Okay, Colonel?"

"Yeah, okay," Rollins said. "I'm going to trust that you know what you're doing."

"I appreciate that," Jonathan said, and then he hung up before Rollins could wiggle off the hook.

Rollins was true to his word. Upon touchdown the only people they saw on the ground at Hurlburt were the ground crew technicians. As soon as Big Guy killed the engines, a tanker truck was there, delivering the much-needed gas that would get them back to a commercial aviation airport outside of Fredericksburg, Virginia. The Federal Aviation Administration would have had a panic attack if they'd known that Boxers had flown as many hours as he had over the past two days.

Jonathan was aware, though, and he recognized the need for sleep. It only made sense, then, that Jonathan be the one to drive the Batmobile out to the Compound. Fisherman's Cove was much closer, but given Dylan's infamy, Jonathan didn't want to risk that many innocents in case his hunters cornered their prey. Their aircraft had been touched by a lot of people today, and it would have been foolish to ignore the possibility that one of them had placed some sort of tracker on the plane. If that were the case, then Fisherman's Cove would be the most likely place for the hunters to come hunting. Precious few people even knew about the Compound.

By the time Jonathan pulled the Batmobile through the gates to the Compound, it was nearly ten o'clock at night. Darkness had fallen, Big Guy and Dylan were both snoring in their respective seats, and the guard team looked more than a little startled to see the boss arriving at such a late hour.

"Mister Horgan," the guard said. "You *are* here."

The emphasis startled him. "Why do you say it that way? Had someone predicted that I'd be here?"

The guard pointed up the hill to a car-shaped silhouette that lurked off the road a bit. "Him. His name is Rollins. Logbook shows that he was here a few days ago. He tried to talk his way in, but of course we wouldn't let him. We told him that we had no knowledge of any plans for you to come this way tonight. I'm sorry if we should have let him in, but—"

Jonathan silenced the kid with a raised hand. "No, son, you did exactly the right thing. How long has he been sitting there?"

The guard checked his watch. "Almost three hours."

Jonathan smiled. "Huh."

"He gave us his cell number and asked us to wake him when you arrived."

"Don't do that," Jonathan said. "Let him sleep. And if when he wakes up and asks, you haven't seen us."

The kid looked confused. "Okay," he said.

"And if he gets out of his car, shoot him," said Boxers from the passenger seat. His eyes were still closed.

Confusion went to terror in the guard's face. "*Seriously?*"

"No," Jonathan said. "Not seriously."

Boxers laughed, a rumbling, contented sound that made the car vibrate.

The guard didn't know what to say.

"Look at me," Jonathan said to him. "And listen to

ne. Do *not* shoot him if he gets out of his car. Understand?"

"Yes, sir. I understand."

Jonathan studied the kid's expression for a while
onger. In his experience, few creatures in the universe
were more dangerous than a young man with a gun that
he had permission to shoot. "Okay," he said. "Keep up
the good work."

"Yes, sir." The kid seemed to be resisting the urge to
snap to attention.

"Good night," Jonathan said. He rolled up the window and waited for the gate to rumble open. "Jesus,
Box," he said. He wanted to sound angry, but laughed
in spite of himself.

"I just saw an opportunity," Boxers said. "Can't
blame a guy for trying."

It turned out that the adjutant who sat perpetually
outside General Karras's office was a local boy named
Tommy Piper. He was twenty-three years old—older
than Ian would have guessed—and was kin to a long
line of local Pipers. The line was destined to stop with
him, however, thanks to an explosion in the mines that
killed his father and two brothers when Tommy was
only eleven. His mother hadn't taken the stress well,
and in trying one night to drown herself with a few
belts of moonshine, she drowned herself for real while
skinny-dipping in the quarry. Social workers had sniffed
around Tommy for a few years, but this was West Virginia, where eleven-year-olds had been working hard
for generations, and the government do-gooders ultimately lost interest in him.

One day at a time grew into a month at a time, and then, in the normal course of things, he evolved into an adult with little ambition but tons of street smarts. When he got word of Karras's Patriots' Army, he jumped at the opportunity to become a member—of anything, probably, but this in particular—and he impressed the right people.

Ian had grown to like Tommy, and the sentiment appeared to be mutual. He greeted Ian with a bright smile. "Good morning, Colonel," he said.

"Hello, Tommy. Is the Old Man available?"

"Yes, sir, he is." He lifted the receiver on his phone and pressed the button. When Karras answered, Tommy said, "Colonel Carrington to see you, sir."

Karras said, "Send him in."

When he hung up and lifted his gaze, Tommy looked offended. "Why are you laughing?"

Ian waved the concern away with broad strokes of his hand. "No, no, it's not about you. It's the phone. You can hear every word from the other side of the wall. What's the point?"

"It's the way the general wants it, sir." His answer came straight, devoid of irony.

"Then so he shall have it," Ian said. He opened the inner door and let himself into Karras's office. If this were a real army with a real general, he'd have entered smartly and snapped to attention. As it was, he just entered.

Karras looked up from the stuff on his desk. "Good morning, Colonel. Why are you giving my adjutant a hard time?"

Ian pulled out one of the metal torture seats and

helped himself. "I suppose it's what I'm good at." He waved his fingers at the flotsam that cluttered Karras's desk. "What the hell do you do with all that paper?"

"Mostly I wish that it wasn't there." He chuckled. "We feed a lot of people here. We burn through lots of ammunition and we buy a lot of structures. All of that has to be contracted and paid for." He laughed at what he saw in Ian's face. "That's the difference between government procurement and insurrection. Cash flow has to be managed."

Ian acknowledged the point by arching his eyebrows. He'd never given that a lot of thought. Uncle Sam employed legions of rear-echelon types to manage that stuff. It ever occurred to him that it would fall on the shoulders of the man who claimed to be in charge.

"Please tell me that's not why you're here," Karras said.

"Actually, no. I've got some strategic issues we need to discuss."

The general's eyes brightened. "Sounds a lot more interesting that what I'm doing now. I'm all ears."

"I think we need to reexamine our strategic model. A couple of weeks ago, you told me that the general wanted to move away from my single-shooter teams. I thought he was right then, and I think he's even more right now. The same problems that existed for the single shooters exist for the three-man teams we've been assembling. Such a small group has to be prepared to perform that many more operations. We just don't have the availability for that kind of training."

Karras sat taller in his seat. It was his tell for getting

defensive. "If you're suggesting an entirely different strategy, then this conversation is over. General Brock was very specific—"

"Just listen for a bit."

Karras recoiled. He looked unsure whether to be offended or amused.

Ian didn't wait to find out. "I think we need to shift the strategy to larger shooter teams." He was talking eight-man teams who would be organized and trained as stand-alone operating units. They'd be cross-trained, but every operator would have a primary job and a secondary job. All would have combat medic training— or, in this case, advanced first aid, because that was the most advanced level of instructor they could field.

"We need to make these teams cohesive, dependent upon each other. If the shit hits the fan—*when* the shit hits the fan—even if they lose sight of the larger mission in all the mud and blood, they'll at least fight for each other. And when it comes time to take the important shot—that history-making twitch of a finger that sends the bullet downrange—they'll have the emotional support of their team to give them that last dose of courage."

"Doesn't a larger team sacrifice some element of security?" Karras asked. "There's that many more people who'll know the mission upfront, and that many more people to be caught and turned."

Ian acknowledged, "That's one way to look at it, but as I see it, those concerns are outweighed by their converse. There's that many more operators to defend each other if the police get too close. That many more people to keep their buddies from yapping. Call it a wash, security-wise, but operationally, I think it's hands-down the best way to go."

Karras leaned back in his chair and tented his fingers over his chest. He looked at Ian the way a chess player tries to read his opponent's mind—pursed lips, squinted eyes. After maybe thirty seconds, he said, "What's the operational impact of this change? Are we talking a small modification of the training regimen, or something bigger? If you're thinking that everything we've been doing so far is a wasted effort and we have to start over again, I'll tell you right now that I can't sell that."

"That's not it at all," Ian assured. "It's more an organizational change than anything else. I want to reorganize the troops into squads, and I want to make them autonomous. They eat together, they train together, but they do not interact with the other teams in these capacities. I want to pit the teams against each other in ways that make them compete for everything."

"Won't that destroy morale?" Karras asked. "Life is lonely enough up here on the mountaintop. Why make them feel even more isolated? Friendships have already been formed. You can't accomplish what you're talking about without pulling those apart. At least some of them."

Ian fought to suppress his satisfaction. It was exactly where he'd hoped Karras would go. "General, with all respect, this is not a social experiment. The Patriots' Army is not about comradery or ideology or shared social experimentation. It is about accomplishing a mission that is dangerous and bloody and will likely leave us with no friends among those who will not understand the need for change. If we fail, we face charges of treason. I can imagine no lonelier position than that. Individual soldiers will have virtually no chance for survival when the hunt for them starts. But well-organized teams will have a better chance."

"I understand that," Karras said, "but why isolate the teams from each other?"

"To build dependence within the team and independence from others."

Karras's eyes narrowed again as he considered what he'd heard. Ian had zero respect for the man as a military mind, but he'd come to admire his management skills. He was smart in a way that Ian imagined would have made him a rich man if he'd applied his skills to his stepfather's business.

"Where does that leave *us*?" Karras asked.

"I don't understand the question."

"As you say, if things go wrong, life is likely to get ugly. I hear your point about these coherent units fighting and dying for each other, but won't that be their primary loyalty? To each other, I mean? What about loyalty to the rest of the army?"

"You can't get that," Ian said, opening the door to another point he'd been wanting to make. "You and I are ideologues. I believe that General Brock is as well, along with your father and any other benefactors of this place. But the soldiers—that group of two hundred young men who are so gung ho to fight—are nothing of the sort. Some are, I suppose, but not on average. I see it in the lack of military discipline among the majority, the lack of respect for rank. For the most part, those boys are angry men, adventurous men, *bored* men who are anxious for a fight. They want to shoot people, and they're willing to shoot anyone we identify to be the enemy."

Karras formed a T in the air with the fingertips of one hand, and the palm of another. "Time out, there, Colonel. I've known these men for longer than you, and I think you're selling them short."

"No." Ian said it with percussive finality. "I don't sell them short, you sell them long. You *want* them to be loyal to something greater than themselves, but I'm telling you that that's simply not the case here. More to the point, that lack of loyalty is not necessarily a bad thing. We are going to dispatch them on missions to kill. There's no way to put some shiny cloak of morality around taking a life. The fact that the killings are necessary in order to put the country back on the right track matters in real time only to people whose fingers are not on the trigger or the knife. In that moment immediately before the life is taken, in the moment *when* it is being taken, all that matters is getting it done and living through the ordeal. Morality issues come into play only after the fact, and then only for those who have difficulty living with what they've done."

"I'm talking loyalty, Colonel. Why are you talking about morality?"

"Because they're the same thing," Ian said in a raised voice that he quickly modulated. How could Karras be so dense? "Pick any war you can think of. Pick one where the other side was clearly the bad guys. Those bad guys didn't think they were being immoral in killing our kids in uniform. They were merely being loyal to the cause that sent them to war. To those bad guys, our boys—the ones who were loyal to God and country and to the National Command Authority—were immoral monsters."

Karras raised his voice, too. "How does—"

"It doesn't matter," Ian said, cutting him off. "As long as our Patriots' Army soldiers do their jobs and accomplish what we ask them to do, it doesn't matter what their loyalties are. You and I and the Uprising and all the rest are irrelevant to them, and it's unreasonable for us to expect it to be any other way. If we reorganize them into the small operating teams I'm talking about, they'll at least be loyal to each other, which will make them dedicated to their missions."

"But where does that leave *us?*" Karras asked. He emphasized his frustration with a slap on the desk. "Literally *us?* You and me and the rest of the command structure?"

Ian reared back in his chair. Was the general really so clueless that he couldn't see something so obvious? "If we prevail, General—if everything goes right with nothing going wrong, if the public hears our battle cry and rise higher and faster than the police and the FBI and every other alphabet group can stop them—then we'll be leaders of the new American order. If, however, any of that does not happen—and I suspect that much of it won't—then we die."

Karras paled. "For God's sake, Colonel, you're a *leader.* That kind of pessimism—"

"Never confuse pessimism with realism, General. I am one hundred percent behind the mission. One *thousand* percent behind doing what is necessary to undo everything that Darmond and his clowns have done. That is the mission and I believe that is achievable. But the rest—the part where the people rise—is a pipe dream. The American people aren't risers anymore. They're lazy, and half of them love the handouts and the Socialist agenda. They value uninterrupted cable television service over liberty. So, we will die for our cause. In the short term, we'll be labeled as monsters, but in the longer term, I have faith that we'll become known as heroes."

"As martyrs," Karras said. It was hard to tell whether the thought pleased or repulsed.

"If you'd prefer," Ian said. "In the longer term, we'll become known as martyrs."

Chapter Eighteen

Jonathan smelled bacon. It was 8:45 the next morning, and he felt hungover, despite the fact that he hadn't had a drop to drink last night. Rough mornings were just one of the list of fines that were due after many years of abusing his body.

But bacon? What the hell?

He rolled out of bed naked and pulled on yesterday's jeans, slipping a shirt over his shoulders and his Colt into his waistband at the small of his back. He couldn't imagine that an attacker would invade the place and then cook breakfast, but almost all of Jonathan's todays were built on the shoulders of yesterday's caution.

He padded barefoot out of his bedroom on the second floor, and down the hall to the open stairway that led in a long spiral down to the living area. None of the boards creaked because he had paid an enormous premium for the quality of construction that prevented creaking. It wasn't a stealth thing, it was a quality thing.

While he didn't know who had gathered in his kitchen, the fact that no alarms had gone off and no shots had been fired clued him in to the fact that the threat was minimal.

He was halfway down the stairs when he heard a familiar laugh. Venice. She'd driven out from Fisherman's Cove, and of course she'd arrived early. Some things were as reliable as the rising sun. There was another voice, though, a male, that he didn't immediately recognize. Whoever it was, he seemed to be getting along well with the presumed hostess.

At the bottom of the stairs, Jonathan button-hooked to the right, and there they were. Venice Alexander and Roleplay Rollins were having a happy conversation across the bar-height kitchen counter. If they heard him approaching, they made no indication.

"Good morning," Jonathan said as he crossed the threshold from hardwood to stone floor.

Venice and Rollins turned in unison, she from her work at the stove, and he from his lazing at the bar. "Good morning," Venice said. Her voice was three clicks too jovial, telling Jonathan that she probably realized that Rollins's presence had crossed a line.

"Hi, Digger," Rollins said. "I know I'm a surprise, but Venice was nice enough to let me in."

"I don't believe you wouldn't let him in last night," Venice scolded. "How juvenile."

Jonathan felt a ball of anger in his belly. "Maybe he's a terrorist and I kept him out for a reason."

Rollins recoiled, but Jonathan ignored him.

"That's still no reason to be rude," Venice said.

"Did it occur to you that I might have reasons for not wanting him to be here?"

"You know I'm sitting in front of you, right?" Rollins said. "Is this the part where you kick me out?"

"No, that's for me to do," Boxers' voice rumbled from behind them.

"He would have me shot," Rollins said. "Yes, I heard."

"As far as I know, it wasn't a secret," Boxers said. He nodded toward Venice. "Smells great."

She waved. Historically, Big Guy and Mother Hen had not gotten along very well, but recently, Boxers seemed to be trying harder. "How many eggs do you want?"

"Let's start with three," Boxers said. "We'll negotiate from there."

Venice sifted her gaze to Jonathan. "Dig?"

He held up two fingers, a victory sign. "I'm not sure I've seen you be this . . . domestic."

"That's because you're never up in time for breakfast," Venice said, turning back to the stove. "I send Roman off every morning with a good meal." That was her son by an otherwise disastrous marriage. He was a middle-schooler now, with all of the angst and attitude that came with it.

"He's with Mama this morning?" Jonathan asked. Venice's mother had been Jonathan's default mother after his own had died when he was a kid, and everyone with half a brain treated the woman with equal parts love, respect, and abject terror.

"And loving every minute of it, I'm sure," Venice said. That brought a chuckle from both Jonathan and Boxers.

"Where's the guest of honor?" Rollins asked. "And don't tell me he's not here."

Dylan Nasbe emerged from the second guest room from off to the side of the kitchen. "I'm not here," he said.

Rollins's expression hardened. This was not the face of a man who was happy to be reacquainted. "I didn't think you'd come back."

Dylan held out his hand for Venice. "We haven't met. I'm Dylan. You must be Venice." He over-pronounced the word as if to show off that he understood.

"Pleased to meet you. I've certainly heard a lot about you. Will two eggs do for you, too?"

"That'd be great. Thank you."

Rollins sighed loudly. "You know, as much as I appreciate this pantomime of domestic bliss, I'd appreciate it if we could get down to—"

"Shut up, Colonel," Jonathan said. "This isn't your meeting. You're the party crasher, and we will proceed along the lines that I dictate. It's really important to wrap your head around that."

Rollins turned red, but he didn't say anything.

Jonathan walked to the coffeepot and poured himself a cup. "Dylan," he said, "I think it would really help if you caught everyone else up to where we already are."

Jonathan ate while Dylan talked, keeping his eyes on Rollins. If, in fact, a coup were in the offing—a wild thought at its base—who better to involve than a leader from the Unit? The colonel possessed many skills, but he'd always been a terrible poker player. Jonathan bet that he'd know if his former commander's expression of surprise was genuine. As it turned out, there was no expression of surprise at all. There was merely an expression of utter disbelief.

It seemed genuine, though.

"You have these drives with you?" Venice asked when he was finished with the first round of the story and the parrying of objections.

"Actually, your boss has them."

Jonathan recognized his cue. He rose from his chair, walked to the wall nearest the stairs, and revealed a safe by sliding a picture out of the way. He spun the dial, turned the lock, and pulled open the rectangular steel door. Inside sat a Glock 23 .40 caliber pistol, five 13-round mags, three fragmentation grenades, and the two hard drives Dylan had given him the day before. He removed the drives then closed the door to the safe.

"Paranoid much?" Rollins asked.

"Prepared much," Jonathan replied.

He handed the drives to Venice, who walked them into the living room. "The connections are in the coffee table, right?" she asked.

"Nothing's changed since last time you were here." That last time was the occasion for a sleepover-picnic for the Alexander family—Mama, Venice, and Roman—along with Jonathan's good friend Father Dom D'Angelo and JoeDog, the black Labrador retriever who had adopted Jonathan as her occasional caretaker. After significant debate, Mama had granted Jonathan permission to introduce her grandson to the pleasures of killing targets in the woods. Back then, the camouflaged computer connections had been employed for video games and movies.

Three minutes later, Venice had a laptop booted up, the images from which were visible to all on the 55-

inch flat screen that dominated the space over the fire-place. When everyone was seated, the group looked like they might have been watching a football game to-gether.

"Okay, Dylan," she said. "Walk me through it. I know what you think. Now show me why you think it."

When you're working in a vacuum of information, random events can shape themselves into patterns that develop into assumptions that lead to obvious conclu-sions that, while self-apparent, are also wrong. Given the nature of the work performed by Security Solu-tions, those incorrect assumptions were the event that Venice dreaded most. Digger Grave depended upon her and her analyses to make judgments that often led to situations resolved by gunfire. The *obvious* was no more than a wild-ass guess if the underpinning facts were not correct.

When starting her analysis with so preposterous a notion that the military structure of the United States was emulating the failed strategies of the Third World, her bull-fritters meter was dialed up to its highest gain. She pushed back against Dylan's attempts to bully her thorough the step-by-step analysis of the information he'd gleaned, telling him no less than five times that she was not interested in the conclusions he had drawn for himself. "You're here to answer my questions," she said at one point, "not to offer your opinion. If I want that, I know exactly where you are sitting, and I will ask for it."

After about twenty minutes of sifting through the various random threads of data, though, she reached out and asked Dylan to reveal the connective tissue he saw between websites and e-mails and blog postings. She realized that while she could probably have done it on her own, the sorting effort would have taken hours, if not days.

Dylan led her through his thought process. It started with a group called The Uprising, which at its surface sounded like any one of a thousand nutjob militia websites that called for the reclamation of lost rights recently seized by the federal government. What set this one apart from the others, it turned out, was the fact that it attracted the attention of the Central Intelligence Agency and the National Security Agency.

"It can't be too right wing," Boxers quipped. "It hasn't attracted the IRS." He laughed, but no one else did. Given the fallout, it was just too soon.

"And here's where it gets complicated," Dylan said. "This should have just been accepted as rantings from those who rant. But this one—this *one*—blog rose to the attention of the CIA. Now if you dig a little deeper . . ." He directed Venice down the communication paths. "Look at all the respondents to what the Commander has written. Read the syntax of the postings. These are educated people, people who know how to construct sentences. If you scroll through these, pay attention to the words and phrases that are used."

Dylan clicked on one from DsgrntldAgt. "Look at this. Disgruntled Agent uses the phrase National Command Authority. Who uses that phrase outside of the Community? And here. And note the handle. 'Agent' is at the very least provocative." He directed Venice to another contributing account. "There. WarFighter writes, 'I lost too many friends to see it all be for nothing.'"

"You're being generous with the spelling," Venice said. The actual post talked about "two menny freinds."

"But there are dozens of instances like that," Dylan said. "This site is attracting the attention of not just people who have a capability to organize and do harm, but also the attention of the government."

"Isn't that what the government is paid to do?" Jonathan asked. "Pay attention to those who make threatening gestures toward the underpinnings of the nation?"

"You can't pick at this," Dylan said. "You can't pull it apart piecemeal. There is clearly a trend. And we're talking about hundreds of posts. Maybe a thousand or more. Dozens of posters."

"Dozens of crazy people among three hundred million tired, jaded, but arguably sane citizens," Jonathan said. "Given the sample size, I don't hear the alarms you're hearing."

"That's because you haven't spent as much time with all of this as I have," Dylan said. "Here, let me have the mouse." He took the tool from Venice's hand—he was lucky to have not lost an eye in the process—and he started plowing through the evidence. Over the course of the next forty minutes, he conducted a guided tour through his paranoid world.

As Jonathan watched, he saw a pattern emerge. So many of the angry posters projected an insider's view to the world of warfare and clandestine operations. There was talk of friends lost to IEDs and of sources who were burned—spook-speak for betrayed and executed. This was not just a select few, but dozens of posters, all with separate handles and avatars. If Jonathan read the syntax and the sentiments correctly, they were looking at agents of the Secret Service and the

CIA and the FBI, whose participation in such a blog would have resulted in immediate termination and potentially even criminal prosecution. By far the most prevalent poster profile, however, resonated to Jonathan's ear as current or former military. They were pissed that a near-victory had been surrendered, and that the sacrifices of so many had been squandered by a president who, in their estimation, had never sacrificed anything for anyone.

The anger registered with Jonathan as very real, as did the vows for revenge. But this was the stuff of crazy talk everywhere. There had to be dozens—hundreds—of websites just like this one in every corner of the Blogosphere. What made this one—this *one*—the subject of so much concern to Dylan?

"It's the organization of it," Dylan explained. He continued to manipulate Venice's mouse. "As I go through these next pages, notice the Commander's subtle but very real call to action." He moved his mouse to a threaded conversation between the Commander and Darmondcide4. "Look at this exchange," Dylan said. "Darmondcide—no points for being subtle on the handle, eh?—spouts hateful stuff and alludes to special violent skills. Now look at the response. The Commander writes, 'you should read Sun Tsu's *Art of War* on March 25 on booksrock.com.'"

Dylan clicked some more. "Now look here. Booksrock dot com shows a lot of book reviews from thousands of titles. But if you look up *The Art of War* and scroll to March 25, look at what you find. This rave review for a forgotten book is signed 'National Truth Teller 3-23-27.'"

"I think I'm getting dizzy," Rollins said.

"Then hang on to your ass," Dylan responded. "Because this ride is about to get really wild. The National Truth Teller is an online e-zine with a few thousand followers."

"Never heard of it," Jonathan said.

"That's because you can read without moving your lips," Dylan said. "It's a site that is one hundred percent antiestablishment, one hundred percent anti-mainstream media, but only about twenty percent wrong in their reporting of facts. They've never smelled a conspiracy they didn't buy, if only for stroking their sales base." He clicked away from Booksrock and over to the National Truth Teller.

"If we go to the March twenty-third issue—the 'three twenty-three' from the Booksrock signature line—and then to page twenty-seven, look what we find." He navigated to the spot, a classified ad, and then magnified the image to make his point. He read the text aloud. "'Freedom isn't free. True patriots know that. Coffee Central, Shepherdstown, WV 4/1. You'll know if you make the cut.'"

After reading the ad, he looked up, as if expecting a round of applause. The others gaped.

"I'm not following you," Venice said. Jonathan thought it was good that hers was the first voice to be heard. His assessment would have been harsher.

"He's recruiting an army," Dylan said, as if it were the most obvious thing in the world.

"Of course he is," Boxers said. "I see it plain as day."

"You're being sarcastic," Dylan said.

"A little bit, yeah."

"It's a pattern that plays out over and over again," Dylan said. "Now, if we go back to the Uprising page and do a search for Sun Tsu, look how many times it shows up." He clicked and revealed a list of at least two dozen mentions. "But the references to the book review for *The Art of War* cover all kinds of whack-job publications, all on different dates, and all referring to different public spaces in and near West Virginia. All of them low-key. Several independent coffee shops, several independent bookstores. He never repeats the locale, either."

"That doesn't mean he's recruiting an army," Rollins said.

"In context, it's a pretty good guess," Jonathan countered. "Not conclusive, but certainly intriguing." He turned to Venice. "Okay, wise mistress of electrons, what can you do to help us out here?"

She pondered for a few seconds. "Can you give me a list of the locations where the meetings were set up?"

"Sure," Dylan said. "I mean, we can compile it just by looking at the various posts. Why?"

"Give me the list and I'll show you."

In addition to being a computer genius, Venice was also something of a showman. She reveled in the drama of her discoveries when they worked, and Jonathan had learned a long time ago that it was senseless to try to rush her through anything.

Ten minutes later, Dylan had his list. "There you go," he said. "Now what?"

Venice motioned for Dylan to surrender his spot at the computer to her. "Now you guys go and play for a while. I'll let you know if I find anything."

* * *

After refilling their cups, Jonathan and the other men took seats in the rockers on the front porch.

"These are really nice digs, Dig," Dylan said as he took in the vistas. The Virginia countryside seemed to roll on forever. Green fields gave way to lines of trees, which gave way to more fields and the occasional stream. Not visible from here were the five- and eight-acre natural ponds on the property.

"I don't get out here as much as I'd like," Jonathan said. "I'm not as much the country boy as I pretend to be. Too much time in the boonies, I suppose. I've come to like traffic noise."

"Yeah, like Fisherman's Cove has real traffic," Boxers scoffed. Big guy was a true city-dweller. His home lay in the center of downtown Washington, DC.

"Boomer, suppose you're right," Rollins said. "What's next? What do you expect to do with this information?"

"I don't like Boomer anymore," Dylan said. "That was my Unit name, and I think we can all agree that I've lost the right." He delivered those words without sadness or remorse, strictly as a statement of fact. "And I don't have a plan from there. I just wanted to pass the word along. Dig's the one who dragged me back to the US."

Rollins shifted his gaze to Jonathan.

"You're looking at me as if I have a plan," Jonathan said. "This is all as new to me as it is to you. I hasten to add, by the way, that of all the people in the know, you're the only one with eagles on your shoulders. I should be asking you for the plan."

Rollins's face folded into a deep scowl. "Yeah, well,

that's kind of problematic, isn't it? The eagles are a long way from stars. This is a tad above my pay grade."

"Then bump it up," Boxers said.

"How? And to whom? And on what basis? I wasn't bullshitting when I told you I was my own in this. Uncle Samuel has no idea that I'm here, and he damn sure doesn't know about my approach to you."

Jonathan cocked his head. He didn't understand. "So, why?"

Rollins shifted uncomfortably in his chair and threw an awkward glance toward Dylan. "He might have done some bad stuff, but he's still family. He's still from the Unit. Like I told you in that first meeting, I couldn't stand the thought of him being hunted down by Agency pukes. That just would have been wrong."

Silence enveloped them. Why was it, Jonathan wondered, that insults and ballbusting came so easily to men like him, but genuine expressions of tenderness made him so uncomfortable?

"I honestly thought that was all bullshit," Boxers said. He slurped some coffee. "Might be that you're not the asshole that I thought you were, Stanley."

There was the Big Guy Jonathan knew so well.

"So, you *can't* pass this up the chain of command," Jonathan said. "If I'm hearing you right, that would for sure torpedo your career."

"Worse than that, it would get me thrown in jail. I'm under standing orders to do pretty much the opposite of what I'm doing right now."

"What about the men under your command?" Dylan asked. "What do they know?"

Rollins shrugged. "They know they're pissed about

you being targeted," he said. "But they don't know that I'm doing anything about it."

Boxers laughed. "I believe we are living the definition of irony right now," he said. "We're all in a tizzy here because it looks like some asshole is trying to negate the National Command Authority, yet every one of us is doing the same thing."

"But we're not advocating overthrow," Rollins said. "We're trying to prevent an injustice—"

Boxers held up a hand. "You don't have to rationalize anything for me, Colonel. I've never had much respect for the chain of command. It's just interesting to see that particular point of view spreading so fast and so far."

Dylan said, "This all brings us back to the colonel's original question. What are we going to do with this information if it all turns out to be what I think it is?"

"We stop them if we can," Jonathan said.

Boxers rumbled out a laugh. "There's that *we* shit that always gets me in trouble. And just how are we going to do that?"

"Details," Jonathan said. "You always get bogged down in the details."

"I think the details are pretty damned important," Rollins said.

Jonathan scowled and cocked his head.

"That was that irony stuff again," Boxers said. "He does that a lot."

"Yes, I do," Jonathan said. "But in this case, irony and reality are pretty close dance partners. If what Boomer—sorry, Dylan—is suggesting is correct, we're going to have to do something. I don't know what that something is, but this isn't something we can just turn away from."

"Are you sure?" Boxers asked.

Jonathan waited for the rest of his point.

"Think about it," Big Guy said. "Think about all the nonsense Darmond and his administration have tried to pull off in the last few years. Think of all the scandals and the shortcuts he's taken with the Constitution, all without repercussions because the electorate is stupid and the media is in his back pocket. Why in the world would we risk our lives—hell, why would we risk a temporary inconvenience—to save his sorry ass?"

Jonathan understood the frustration, and the angry place he was coming from, but surely Boxers didn't need an education in the basics of why they did what they did. "There's right and there's wrong," he said. "And I don't mean the useless stuff that boards of supervisors and congresses pass as the laws of the day. I don't give a crap about those. But there is an absolute right and an absolute wrong. Here in the U S of A, a coup is an absolute wrong."

"And you think the four of us can stop it?" Dylan asked.

"I have no idea," Jonathan said. "And I'm not one for suicide missions. I don't charge into the mouths of volcanos. But I do believe in making a difference, and it's looking—if Venice's research bears out what you think is going on, and I believe it will—like we will be our only resource to stop what's looming on the horizon."

"What about Wolverine?" Boxers asked.

"Who's Wolverine?" Dylan and Rollins asked in unison.

"No one you need to know about," Jonathan snapped. He fired a death glare to Boxers for bringing up her name. "Wolverine doesn't belong in this, either. To include her, we'd have to out Dylan, and I've promised that I wouldn't do that."

Dylan bristled. "Hey, if you're expecting me to feel guilty because you dragged me here—"

Jonathan shook his head. "It's nothing like that. I apologize if that's what I implied. I don't begrudge the promises I've made. They are what they are, and there's no guilt implied."

"I just don't see what four people can do," Rollins said.

"That's a step ahead of where we need to be," Jonathan said. "We don't really even know the scope of the problem yet."

As if on cue, Venice called from inside, "Hey guys! Come on back in. I've got news."

Chapter Nineteen

"Take your seats," Venice said. "I found some really interesting stuff." At the end of the room, the big screen had been divided into three segments, each showing high-angle images typical of security camera footage, but from different locations that looked oddly similar.

"Our friend the Commander seems to like coffee shops," she explained. "These three views are of the security footage from shops that all use ProtecTall Security. You'll see that the time stamps on the videos match the projected dates from the book reviews."

"Really?" Rollins asked. His expression showed something between shock and awe.

"How did you get this?" Dylan asked.

Venice beamed. "A lady never reveals her secrets," she said. Jonathan knew that ProtecTall Security was the most common (and perhaps the cheapest) monitoring company in the world, and that Venice had long ago cracked their system. She could worm her way into other systems as well, but this one company was easie an the others. Or, so she'd told him. The bottom line as that if information resided out in cyberspace some-here, there was a very good chance that Venice could ind it and read it (or watch it) at will.

"I've synched the images to the times of the meets," he continued. "All of them around the same time, oughly between one and three in the afternoon, always a the middle of a workday. I don't know why I feel at's significant, but it feels like it might be."

"An employment test maybe?" Boxers suggested.

"Or even a loyalty test," Jonathan said. "Is this Up-ising cause more important than what you have in our life otherwise?"

"Or it could just be a trap for the lazy and unem-loyed," Rollins said.

"Or any of the above," Venice said. "I was thinking at it was more to fit the schedule of the guy running e meeting, but I could be wrong. The important part something like this is the pattern. First that a pattern xists, and second what the nature of the pattern is." he pointed to the screen. "I've already perused these nce just to get a feel for what I might see, and when I peed it up a little, there's another pattern developing. 'an you see it?"

It was Venice's habit—her very *annoying* habit—to resent information with fifty percent too much drama, ut Jonathan knew better than to try to get in the way f that. She was good enough at what she did to get a ye on pretty much any peccadillo she chose.

He watched the three scenes on the screen. With the peed cranked up, the baristas darted about at comical peed. Common to all three scenarios, the shops started out fairly empty of customers, and then as they filled the crowds seemed to build quickly, and yes, Jonathan saw a new pattern.

"They're all men," he said.

"*Young* men," Venice corrected. "And all of a certain soldierly body type."

She was right. With only a couple of exceptions, the men who gathered in the shops were white and solidly built. More than a few tipped the scales toward the skinhead white supremacist stereotype, and in each of the documented meetings, they seemed to find each other among the crowd. Maybe there was a secret hand gesture or handkerchief code.

"But they're not doing anything," Boxers said. "Most of them aren't even buying a cup of coffee. Deadbeats."

"I think they're waiting," Jonathan said.

"For what?" Rollins asked.

"I don't know," Jonathan said.

"I don't think *they* know," Dylan said. "Look, they're just hanging around, avoiding eye contact. It's like a seventh-grade prom."

Jonathan laughed. That was exactly what it looked like. A bunch of guys all striking disinterested postures while trying to impress someone, though they didn't yet know who that someone was. "Let's not get ahead of ourselves," he said. "I know what this looks like, and I know how it fits into our assumptions, but let's take our time."

The jumping-to-conclusions error was one Jonathan had repeated with startling regularity, along with all of the terrible consequences.

"I think you're going to shift your view here in

ouple of seconds," Venice said. "Keep your eyes on
he center panel."

Jonathan watched. And watched. He was about to
ry foul when Venice pointed to the screen and said,
There. Look at the newcomer. He just came in the
loor. Watch him. He's doing the not-interested body
movements, too, but watch his eyes."

Jonathan leaned in closer to the screen—as if that
would do anything. And he squinted. He hated squint-
ng. He hated anything that even danced around the
dea that he might one day need glasses. As he watched,
he new man—tall, dark hair with a goatee—scanned
he room before he walked to the cashier's station.

"Wait a second," Venice said, and she hammered on
he computer keys that froze the other two screens. "I
vant everyone to watch just this one guy with the
beard," she said.

The action started up again. After the man with the
goatee got his order, he retreated back into the room,
standing off to the side, his whole head moving as he
canned the room.

"Could he be more obvious?" Boxers asked. "But
o one's watching him."

"Not true," Venice said. "Take a look at two o'clock
n the screen."

There, a thick-necked young man wore khakis and a
blue shirt—he could have been an insurance salesman
vith a good workout ethic—did not look away. Instead,
e watched the newcomer intensely.

"He's not the least bit intimidated," Dylan said.

"He looks like he wants a fight," Rollins said.

"I agree," Venice said. "So, keep watching."

Goatee-man did nothing for the better part of two minutes, and during that time, the thick-necked kid was the only one to pay him any attention at all.

"It's about to happen," Venice said.

And then it did. Goatee-man pushed himself away from the wall and sauntered—that's really the only verb for the swaggering gait—to thick-neck and handed him something that looked like a business card. They exchanged a few words, and then goatee-man left.

"This gets really interesting," Venice said. "Count aloud. Well, it's too late now, but twenty seconds pass before the kid who got the card stands up. There. He's doing it now. He stands up and walks out of the shop. The rest of them just sit there. After a while, they'll just sort of filter out and disappear. Shortly after this, there will be some impatient and intolerant e-mail blast from the offended. But the Commander will not respond to any of them."

"So what does it *mean?*" Jonathan asked.

"Give it time," Venice admonished. "Look at the other two screens." She'd reduced the center screen to nothing, leaving the television with two images where there had once been three. She clicked a button, and the other images came to life. While the actions played out of synch, they all showed the same transaction. Goatee-man entered the shop, bought some coffee, and approached individual customers in the shop. Those selected customers each acknowledged the approach in their own clandestine way, and then within two minutes walked out of the frame into whatever lay in the rest of the world.

"He's being selective," Jonathan said. "The call to

the shop is to be seen, and then he makes his selections."

"That's the way I see it," Venice confirmed. "I haven't had a chance to cross-reference to the other footage, but it looks to me like it's entirely possible that at some locations, he never selects anyone."

"What's really interesting," Boxers said, "is that none of the people in the shops seem to know who they're looking for. Or, more to the point, who's looking for them."

"That's a hell of a way to recruit," Rollins said. "It'll take forever."

"Not necessarily," Dylan said. "Remember, the Commander's writings all point to small armies doing big jobs."

"The writings are the part that concern me most," Jonathan said. "The part that doesn't make sense. Why would someone plotting to overthrow the government put the plan out ahead of time for everyone to see? Why draw that kind of attention?"

"I think it's safe to stipulate that our friend is a little off," Boxers said. "As in, a total freaking whack job. Whack jobs do whacky things."

Jonathan acknowledged the point. Sane, well-centered people didn't do crazy stuff in his experience. On the other hand, they tended not to be able to cobble together intricate plans, either. It bothered him in this case that the Commander, whoever the hell he was, was both organized *and* crazy.

"Why don't we keep an eye out for the next ad—or book review—and then respond?" Rollins said. "We'll meet the guy at the coffee shop and be done with it."

"I don't think we have that kind of time," Dylan said. Then, as if in response to the confused looks, he added, "The killings have already started, remember? The plan is underway."

"If only we knew what it was," Jonathan said. He looked to Venice. "What are the chances you can track down the real identity of this Commander dude?"

"Probably pretty slim," she said. "I'll check, but I imagine that given the stakes, he's been pretty conscientious about covering his tracks through cyberspace."

"We've seen it before," Jonathan said.

"But not often," Venice said. "I'll see what I can dig up, but I think you might want to develop alternative plans."

"*Alternative* plans!" Boxers scoffed. "You need to have a plan to start with before you develop alternatives."

"Let's talk about that," Jonathan said.

"Not in here," Venice interrupted. "I can listen to you talk or I can try to find answers for you. I can't do both. Go play outside again."

Rollins looked stunned, as if he didn't know whether or not to be insulted.

"Don't even think about talking back, Stanley," Boxers said as he unfolded himself out of his chair. "Trust me. It's easier just to say okay."

They were reassuming their places on the front porch when Dylan pointed down the hill toward the curving drive that led to the house from the front gate. "You expecting company?" he asked. A ten-year-old

SUV was making its way up the hill ahead of a rooster tail of dust.

Jonathan looked to Boxers. "Jolaine?"

Big Guy nodded. "Yeah, I called her this morning."

"Did you consider checking with me first?"

"Would you have said no?"

Jonathan considered that. "Probably not."

"Then quit your bitchin'."

"Who's Jolaine?" Rollins asked.

"A relatively new associate with our firm," Jonathan said. "She's a helluva shot and she's got a lot of heart."

"You just described a Girl Scout," Dylan said.

Boxers laughed. "Yeah, right. Be sure to tell her that to her face."

Jolaine Cage had joined Security Solutions the hard way, by being on the other end of a mission not too long ago. There may actually have been a time when she'd been a Girl Scout, but those times had ended somewhere in the blur of multiple deployments to The Sandbox as a private security contractor. Back then, her specialty had been personnel protection, but she'd evolved into the covert side of Security Solutions over the months that she'd been associated with Jonathan.

"I thought it was tough to join your band of merry marauders," Dylan said.

Jonathan and Boxers shot him similar looks simultaneously and he blanched. "It's time for you to be careful," Boxers growled. "She has more right to be here than you do. You don't know what she's been through and you don't know what she's capable of. I know both and from what I saw down in Panama, I'd put her against you any day of the week."

Jonathan suppressed a smile. He was as defensive as the next guy when it came to discussing his staff, but it was rare to hear Boxers get on so high a horse. There'd been rumors of romance between Jolaine and Big Guy, but if it existed, they'd been careful to hide it. This was Jonathan's first indication that the rumors might be true. Such relationships were never good in the long run as far as operations were concerned, but given his own past, Jonathan was in no position to say anything.

The red Chevy Blazer pulled to a stop next to the Batmobile, and Jolaine climbed out. Maybe thirty years old, she wore her dark brown hair in a tight ponytail and sported very little makeup. To Jonathan's eye, she didn't need it. Not beautiful by the anorexic standards of Hollywood, he thought she was pretty in the wholesome way that made people like her at first glance. She wore khaki cargo pants from 5.11 Tactical, a blue T-shirt, and an open-front light blue collared shirt that he was reasonably certain concealed the Glock 23 that seemed always to ride on her right hip.

She paused in her stroll up to the house and put her fists on her hips, her head cocked to the side. "You're all staring at me," she said. "Did I do something wrong?"

"Not at all," Boxers said. "We were just startled by the company."

"You told me to come."

Big Guy beckoned her closer. "Okay, *they* were startled by the company."

Jolaine's scowl deepened. "Okaaay . . ."

"Come on up and join us," Jonathan said, waving her forward. "Let me introduce you around."

It took a few minutes to bring her up to speed.

"So you're the big traitor to the country?" Jolaine asked Dylan. Her face showed an interesting mix of humor and affront.

Dylan dropped a beat before answering. "I suppose if someone here has to carry that title, it would be me."

She held his gaze for a few seconds. To Jonathan, she said, "I think he's a good guy."

"We're kind of ahead of you on that," Jonathan said.

"I just thought you'd want to know."

Jolaine was an interesting case. Joining Security Solutions almost literally through the back door on the heels of an operation in which she'd performed brilliantly, she'd shown none of the hesitation typical of a newcomer to a tactical group. In fact, she'd assumed a level of familiarity and equality that Jonathan could have talked himself into taking as offensive. From the beginning, though, she'd shown the hots for Big Guy, and Jonathan wasn't about to get in the way of that.

"So, what's our next step?" Jolaine asked.

"We were just getting to that," Jonathan said. "Venice is trying to pull up an ID on anybody as a place to start. Everything else is predicated on that."

"Let's say it comes down to an identifiable militia movement," Rollins offered. "Is it your plan to invade and overrun?"

"We've done that before," Jonathan said.

"Several times, in fact," Boxers added.

"But it's still five steps too early to be talking about that," Jonathan said. He lowered his tone. They'd reached a pivotal point in these discussions, and he needed to settle a big question. "What are you willing to do?" he asked. "If all of this turns out to be real and the shit hits the fan, are you all willing to be in it till the end? Even if it goes to a shooting war?"

The words hung in the air for a few seconds. "You know better than to ask me," Boxers said, breaking the silence. "I live to shoot." Truer words were never spoken. While Boxers was not homicidal—not *exactly*—he was the most lethal human being Jonathan had ever known.

"I'm in, too," Jolaine said, but neither she nor Big Guy were the ones Jonathan wanted to hear from.

"Sure," Rollins said. "What the hell, in for a dime, right?"

"When was the last time you aimed and fired a weapon at something with a heartbeat?" Boxers asked.

"More recently than I'm allowed to tell you," Rollins said. He'd caught the not-so-veiled accusation buried in the question, and he clearly did not appreciate it.

Jonathan turned to Dylan. "Well, Boomer, you started this. How far are you willing to go?"

Dylan took his time answering. "It seems that I don't have a lot to live for, one way or the other. If I have to settle for a blaze of glory, that's not so bad, right?"

"Don't think that way," Jonathan said, his tone suddenly very serious. "Not even as a joke."

"What?" Dylan said.

"Blaze of glory sounds like a suicide mission. We don't do those."

Rollins scoffed, "A rose by any other name."

"No," Boxers said. "It's not."

"What are we talking about?"

"We're talking about winning," Jonathan said.

"That's the only outcome I will accept, and it is only possible if everyone on the team visualizes victory."

"You're kidding, right?" Rollins said. "When did you go all woo-woo?"

"I'm saying that battles are won or lost in the planning stage," Jonathan said. "If any of you honestly believe that we might fail, I want you off the team. Right now."

"*Might* fail?" Rollins asked. "That's a pretty low bar."

"No, it's not," Jonathan said. "And it depends on the definition of failure, which in this case means that the bad guys win."

Dylan cocked his head. "Doesn't failure mean that the good guys lose?"

"Depends on the definition of loss," Boxers said, stealing Jonathan's line. "If any of us die to make the bad guys lose, then that's a net win." He let the words settle on the group, and leaned way back in his chair. "Come on, this isn't new. The mission has never been about survival, at least not per se. The mission is about the *mission*. The precious cargo, if that's in play, or in this case, the derailing of a really bad plot. We're just the pawns."

Jonathan gaped. He wasn't sure he'd ever heard Boxers say that many words in a row, and he wondered if Big Guy was posturing for Jolaine. In the end, it didn't matter because he agreed with every word.

"Fine," Dylan said. "However you want me to put it, I'm in. I started it, so I'll finish it."

"I'm still lost," Jolaine said. "Who, exactly, are we going to be fighting?"

"Bad guys," Jonathan said. "To be determined."

Jolaine scowled and cocked her head. "Excuse me?"

"Venice's trying to untie some knots," Boxers explained.

"Ah," Jolaine said. "That's why you're on the porch, right? She kicked you out."

Chapter Twenty

"I have something," Venice announced after she summoned the team back inside. "Oh, hi, Jolaine. I didn't know you were here."

Recognizing her place as a rookie, Jolaine waited for the others to choose a seat before taking a hard-backed chair for herself.

Venice sat near the fireplace this time, looking back at her audience as she spoke. "I decided it was best to focus on the Commander," she said. "Since he's the one constant in the equation, I thought—"

"Did you run the goatee guy through the facial recognition software?" Jonathan interrupted.

She glared at the interruption, then realized that he'd pissed her off on purpose. "Not yet," she said. She allowed a small smile. "But I will. In the meantime, we've got the Commander as the constant."

The screen behind her displayed countless lines of code. At least that's what Jonathan assumed it to be. Lots of formless words and numbers.

"I was trying to find a pattern," she went on. "Our boy is pretty computer savvy. I think he's using a lot of different computers for his postings, so I can't nail down a common IP address."

"So you found another way," Boxers prompted. Of all the permanent members of the team, Big Guy had the least patience for the drawn-out reveal.

"Of course I did." She clicked the screen and more gibberish appeared, only this time, Jonathan assumed that he was supposed to understand it. "Internet access isn't free, right? You have to pay for it. People can switch out computers all they want—they can even modify the IP addresses if they're good—but you can only have but so many credit cards and Internet service providers. So, that was my big cross-reference." She pointed to the screen. "Can you see it?"

Jonathan's patience frayed. "Come on, Ven—"

"No," Boxers interrupted. "This is fun. Let's take our time. It's only the future of the Free World in play. What's the hurry?"

Jonathan winced.

The offense taken displayed clearly on Venice's face as her chocolate skin reddened. She swallowed it and turned to address the screen, away from her audience. "I cross-referenced the various IP addresses and the ISPs and the credit card numbers, and I got quite a few hits."

She clicked again, and this time Jonathan understood everything he saw. This time it was four columns, IP address on the left, and then moving right, Internet service provider, credit card number, and the name of the cardholder. While he understood the essentials, he also noted that all of the cardholder names were different. "Don't we assume that these are all fake names?" he said.

"Of course we do," Venice said. "I told you he was computer savvy. He'd be a fool to use his real name."

Jonathan felt deflated. He'd been *so close* to understanding what was going on.

"And yes, I traced the names down, and we have to assume that they are all fake."

"And that's what you have?" Rollins asked. "That doesn't seem like much."

"I think she's holding back on the punch line," Jolaine predicted.

Venice flashed a grin. "Oh, what a tangled web we weave when first we venture to deceive."

"Practice," Boxers said.

"What?"

"Oh what a tangled web we weave when first we *practice* to deceive. You said *venture*. Walter Scott would not be happy."

Dylan gave him a you've-just-grown-a-second-nose look. "You're kidding me, right?"

Venice continued, "One lie leads to another. Sooner or later you make a mistake. Apparently, it was important to the Commander—whatever is real name is—to pay his bills, so on these credit cards—which, by the way, he used only for ISP purchases—he paid exclusively by money orders."

"Which are traceable," Jonathan said.

Venice's grin widened. "Yep. He prefers convenience stores. The vast majority came from a Shop-Mart in Glen Burnie, Maryland. I figure that's either near his office or his home."

"How do we drill deeper?" Jonathan asked.

"By looking harder," Venice said. "Remember, I said that the vast majority came from Glen Burnie. There are two exceptions—the most recent payments. They both came from Bud's Hardware Store in Whitesville, West Virginia." She clicked again, and a map appeared. "I checked, and Whitesville is in the heart of Coal Country, surrounded on all sides by a whole lot of nothing." The satellite image showed exactly that, vertical tree-crowded walls interspersed with deep valleys. Whitesville proper seemed to have maybe one hundred structures, all lining a riverbank.

"So that's his most recent known location," Dylan concluded.

"Exactly," Venice confirmed. "The name on the card he used is Victor Carrington."

"You almost need to say that name with a British accent," JoLaine said in a tortured cockney.

"How does that help if the name is false?" Rollins asked.

"There are only five hundred residents in the town," Venice said. "Towns that small keep an eye out for new faces. A new face named Victor Carrington would probably leave a mark on people's memory."

"Suppose he was just passing through?" Dylan asked. "The fact that he bought from there doesn't mean he's living there."

"I don't know," Jonathan said. He rose from his chair and approached the map on the screen. "This isn't what you'd call a commuter-friendly location. Who would pass through there who was not going there?" He looked to Venice. "Can you search property records, hotel records? See if Victor Carrington has left any other footprints?"

"That will take time," Venice said.

"It'll take the time it takes," Jonathan countered. "I figure you've got at least eight or nine hours."

The comment drew the same confused look from everyone in the room. Jonathan clarified, "I figure it will take at least that long to drive to Whitesville, West Virginia."

Chapter Twenty-one

Ian Martin felt good about the way his troops were adjusting to their individual teams. He'd appointed both Little and Biggs to be team leaders, and they'd pleased him with their leadership skills. He still had no idea who they really were—he knew the true identities of precious few of the men—but he didn't care. Some, he was sure, were exactly who they claimed to be, but he didn't know which ones. He figured that the fewer details he knew, the better off everyone would be.

Let's face it. Even he could become a security risk if he was pushed hard enough.

In the end, he'd settled upon twenty eight-man attack teams. Every member of every team was first and foremost a rifleman. It was the main tool at their disposal, and none of the other tools would matter if they couldn't shoot straight. And truth be told, shooting straight was proving to be a bigger problem than he had anticipated. Apparently, they'd been allowed to play on the shooting range for a long time, and in the process ingrained a lot of bad habits that it was his job to counteract.

In addition to rifles, he was training specialists within each of the teams. The communications man concentrated not just on team coordination, but on confounding the enemy, as appropriate. The explosives specialist was responsible not just for the demolition of the target, but for breach entries when called for. Finally, there was the team medic. The remaining five served as understudies for the primary specialists, but their primary job was to keep the enemy's head down while the specialists plied their trades.

Presently, Ian sat astride a brown and white palomino horse named Wellington in the thick woods surrounding Camp Wainwright. Wellington's hooves stomped the thin grass of the steep deer trail, but Ian held him in place. Ian wore a helmet with a thick face piece, and an orange vest on which he'd painted the words, *Don't shoot the judge.*

Down on the slope below, Teams Delta and Hotel were engaged in an advanced form of Capture the Flag. Their weapons were real—the same weapons they would deploy in combat—and the ammunition was nearly real. Loaded with a significant charge of powder, the bullets were actually tiny marker pellets, thus earning the training ammo the name *simunition*. It hurt like hell when you were hit in an unpadded part of your body—thus reinforcing the need for body armor—but the ammo was nonlethal, though Ian imagined that a shot to the balls would be fairly crippling. Thankfully, that had happened only a couple of times. Once the pain subsided, everything worked as it should.

The structure of the game was little different than the version Ian had played as a child, back when the opposing team was tagged by hands rather than shot

with simulated bullets. This way, however, the strate
gies involved a concern with snipers that he'd neve
faced at summer camp.

The game began with base camps established a hal
mile apart. At each camp, the team flag—red for Delta
yellow for Hotel—had to be displayed in plain sight
At an appointed hour, the game went live. To win,
team had to penetrate the opposing force's defenses
capture the flag, and return it to their own base camp
with at least one team member still "alive." For the pur
poses of the game, a simmunition hit anywhere on th
body was considered fatal, and the "killed" soldier ha
to stop at the point of impact and sit on the ground wit
his weapon at his side. He would remain there until th
game ended, which could take many hours. In th
worst case Ian was aware of, some poor bastard from
Alpha was stuck dead on the ground for eighteen hours
The game did not end until someone had won, or unti
all team members on both sides were "dead."

The Delta-Hotel conflict was into its sixth hour now
and from atop his horse—why walk when you ca
ride?—Ian had taken a particular interest in the Hote
soldier below him on the hill. He sat "dead" on th
ground, his rifle beside him, and he'd been there fc
over an hour. Thing was, as far as Ian knew, this sectio
of the battlefield hadn't yet been challenged. Tomm
Piper, one of the other judges for the day, had sum
moned Ian to the spot, suspecting that they had a de
serter in their midst.

"That's him," Tommy said, pointing. "The coward i
playing dead to avoid the fight."

"Put your arm down, Tommy," Ian said. "And kee
your voice down. We are not a part of this conflict, an

we are impartial. We are also the most visible people on the battlefield. A smart commander will pay attention to our eye lines to gain advantage. Let's not give anyone the satisfaction."

"A coward is no one's advantage," Tommy said.

"Your concern is noted, but I believe it's too early to pass judgment."

"With all respect, Colonel—"

"Shut up, Tommy."

In the near distance to Ian's right, the woods erupted in a fierce exchange of gunfire. That was the direction of Hotel's base camp. Ian's mind played it out as a full-on assault, devouring hundreds of rounds. Then it stopped.

The bud in Ian's ear crackled, "Hotel's flag is in the grasp. All defenders dead. Declare Delta the winner."

Ian keyed his mike. "Negative," he said. He spoke on a designated judges channel. "This is Liberation Six. The game continues until Delta returns the flag to their base. How many Delta remain?"

"They're down to two," said the other judge, whom Ian could not see. "They attacked Hotel base with four, lost two. Four KIAs lost previously."

Ian smiled. "Do I understand that Delta base is undefended?"

"Affirmative."

Ian nudged Tommy's shoulder with his stirruped toe. "Watch this," he said. "I think it's going to get interesting."

Ian heard movement and talking from below and to the right. The sounds and actions of soldiers who no longer gave a shit.

Directly below, the dead Hotel soldier they'd been

watching coughed. To Ian's ear, it was louder than it needed to be, but it had the effect of silencing the noisy approach. By the time Ian caught sight of them, the two Delta members had remembered themselves, and they were moving as professionals should—their weapons to their shoulders. Biggs was the leader, and he wore Hotel's yellow flag as a bandanna around his neck.

"There!" the other Delta guy said, pointing toward Ian's man.

Biggs pivoted his aim and then relaxed. "He's already dead." He lowered his M4 and let it rest against its sling.

The partner shouted, "Hey, you! Are you dead?"

The sitting soldier flipped him off.

"Oh, yeah?" the partner said. He prepared to shoot.

Biggs pushed his muzzle down. "Shooting the dead will get us disqualified." He emphasized the point by pointing in Ian's direction.

"Told you they keep an eye on the judges," Ian said to Tommy under his breath.

The partner got the point and lowered his rifle. "Hope you're not sitting on an anthill," he said. "I'd hate to see your losing candy ass all covered with bites."

Hotel guy said nothing.

"Okay, watch this, Tommy," Ian whispered.

Biggs and his minion fell back to chatting mode as they walked past the casualty. When their backs were turned to their enemy, and less than twenty feet separated them, the Hotel soldier slowly and silently placed his hand on the grip of his rifle. With the grace of a dancer, he pivoted his from his butt to his knee as he brought the M4 to his shoulder.

Biggs and his pall were literally knocked to the ground as they were nailed with half the contents of a thirty-round magazine. The soldier pulled the half-empty mag from the rifle and slipped in a full one, placing the half-spent mag into the front pocket of his trousers. He strolled to Biggs just as his prey was struggling to find his feet again. "So, are you going to take that flag off of your neck, or do I have to remove your head to get it?"

"What the hell!" Biggs yelled. He looked ready to kill.

"I wasn't dead," the Delta soldier said. "You asked me, and I never answered. I've just been waiting there."

Biggs shot a look up the hill to Ian.

"He's right!" Ian called. "Mr. Biggs, I believe you've been schooled."

"Add Whitesville to the long list of places where I don't intend to retire," Boxers said as he guided the Batmobile down Coal River Road.

"What do you bet the cost of living is low?" Jolaine said from the backseat. She sat next to Dylan and in front of Colonel Rollins.

"And what do you bet the suicide rate is off the charts?" Boxers replied.

Jonathan smiled. But even he, who found Fisherman's Cove to be the best place on earth for its bucolic slow pace, would go crazy living in a town this small, this slow. "There's Bud's Hardware just up there on the left," he said, pointing.

Boxers parked along the curb on the opposite side of the street.

"What's the play?" Rollins asked.

"Big Guy and I will go in and ask Bud a few questions," Jonathan said. "Why don't you guys go over to Mary's Diner there and get something to eat? We'll join you after our chat."

"Works for me," Dylan said, and he opened his door.

"Yeah, me, too," Boxers said. "It's not like I'm hungry or anything."

"Are you whining?" Jonathan asked as he pulled open his own door.

"No, I'm bitching. There's a difference. I don't whine when I'm hungry, I bitch when I'm hungry."

"This is the part where small animals get nervous," Jolaine said. "He starts seeing them as merely undercooked meals."

When they were all gathered on the outside of the car, Jolaine said, "I think I should go with you."

"I don't want to overwhelm the guy. Scare him off."

"So you bring Gigantor?" Rollins quipped. He backed off—literally—when Big Guy's body language switched from bitching to menacing.

"Over the years I've found that people listen to him," Jonathan said with a wink to Boxers. "He's got that . . . *sincere* way about him."

Big Guy added, "Jolie's got a point, Boss. There's a good chance that a guy named Bud might be more inclined to listen to a pretty young lady than a couple of weathered old grunts."

Jolie? Where the hell did that come from? "Watch the 'old' shit," Jonathan said. "I might feel like it in the mornings, but I'm not old yet." Still, he got Boxers' point. "Yeah, okay, Jolaine, you come with us." He looked to

Dylan and Rollins. "I'll take a club sandwich and a Diet Coke. Won't take long."

"How about you, Big Guy?" Rollins said. "Which page of the menu should I order for you?"

"I think it's time for you to run away, Stanley," Boxers replied, and he started walking away.

Jolaine looked to Jonathan. "What is it with those two?"

"That's a very, very long story," Jonathan said. "Just let it lie."

"But why—"

"Just let it lie."

Boxers arrived at the door to Bud's first, but walked past it and waited at the end of the block.

"I don't get it," Jolaine said as she and Jonathan joined him. "Aren't we going in?"

"I didn't want to gather in front to have this chat," Boxers said. "Dickhead had a point back there. You two should go in and chat him up while I stay at the door and intimidate the townsfolk."

Jolaine's shoulders sagged. "Oh, Box . . ."

"What?" he said. "That sounded like pouting, didn't it? No, I actually like intimidating townsfolk."

Jonathan pulled on her elbow. "Really," he said, "it's one of his best things." Sadly, that was a statement of fact. "I'll go in first and just look around, then you come in and ask the questions. Okay?"

"Sure."

As was his habit before walking into just about any place, Jonathan pressed his right elbow against his side to make sure that his .45 was nestled in the holster where it belonged. He normally preferred a more substantial cover garment than the T-shirt he was wearing, but to savvy observers, the presence of a jacket in thi heat would raise unwelcome suspicions.

The sleigh bells slapped as he entered the dark, nar row space. At first the cluttered rectangular spac looked empty, but then he saw movement in the back where an older guy wearing a denim shirt and a pair o suspender-supported jeans emerged from what had t be a little office. "Can I help you?" the man called.

From this distance, Jonathan couldn't actually se the firearm on the man's hip, but he could tell from th pull of the waistband that it was there. That wasn't concern, necessarily, but it was a data point. "I'm in th market for a socket set," Jonathan said. He had to be i the market for something, right?

The manager pointed to his own right, Jonathan left, to a point along the back wall. "Right back here Got a pretty good selection, if I say so."

Rather than walking directly toward the man, Jon athan turned and walked to the leftmost wall, the turned right to walk to the back of the store. He wante to take in as much as he could. He noted the back doc straight ahead. The lit EXIT sign above it seemed t contradict the heavy steel bar that blocked it shut. I nothing else, that was an indication that Bud—if tha was the guy's name—was concerned about break-in That could mean the presence of security cameras, an that, in turn, could mean their big break.

"Where'd you go?" the man asked.

"I'm coming." Jonathan kept his tone light. "This i like stepping back into my childhood."

The man with the gun appeared at the end of Jon

athan's aisle, a big smile on his face. "I get that a lot. Where you from?"

"Are you Bud?" Jonathan asked, sidestepping the question.

"Last time I checked."

The sleigh bells announced the arrival of another customer. Jolaine, Jonathan presumed.

Bud held up a finger to interrupt himself, and then pointed to the shelf directly in front. "The socket sets are right there. Take your time. Got another customer." He disappeared. "Well, hello, young lady. What can I do for you?"

It never failed, Jonathan thought. Something about the presence of a young woman made men transform.

"Hi," Jolaine said from beyond the shelving. "I'm hoping you can help me."

"I'll do what I can."

Jonathan examined the back door more closely. That iron bar was held into the steel door by welded brackets, and it spanned across both sides of the steel door frame, which in turn was mortared into the brick. "Well, that's pretty close to impenetrable," he mumbled.

"My uncle moved out here a few months ago, and I was wondering if you could help me find him."

Jonathan cringed. He should have coached her on what to say. Her cover story had a verifiable element, and that was a mistake. The lesson he had to learn more often than any other, it seemed, was that it was always a mistake to overestimate people's capabilities—even the most competent ones.

"Sounds more like a job for the police than a hardware store owner."

"Well, we think he's been here."

Oh, shit.

"We? Who's we?" Jonathan could hear the man's guards falling into place.

Jolaine recovered as best she could. "My family and me."

"Are they here with you?"

"No, sir, I took on this mission myself."

"What's this uncle's name?"

"Victor Carrington."

"Never heard of him. What makes you think I might have?"

Jonathan recognized the sound of shutting down. This wasn't going to work.

"He sent my mother—his sister—a money order from here."

"From here. You're sure about that?"

Maybe this wasn't going as badly as Jonathan had feared. He became aware that he needed to do something other than listen. How long could it take to pick out a socket set? He pulled one off the shelf and strolled along the back wall. He wanted to peek into Bud's office.

"Positive," Jolaine said.

"And when might that have been?"

As Jonathan had expected—hoped, actually—a tape deck and security monitor sat on Bud's desk. That meant there was a camera, and that meant he had some work to do tonight.

"About a month ago."

"What does your Uncle Victor look like?"

Shit! And that was why you didn't use verifiable references. Jonathan dropped the socket set. The metal case clanged against the tile floor. "Dammit!" he shouted.

"You okay back there?" Bud called.

"I'm fine," Jonathan called back. "Just got some butter fingers is all."

"You need help?"

Jonathan snatched the box up and walked toward the counter. "Sorry about the noise. I found what I wanted." And indeed he had. The security camera was mounted high on the wall behind the cash register, aimed to record anyone who bought anything. He also noted the guns in the case and he realized why the security precautions were in place—including the cannon on Bud's hip.

Jonathan nodded toward Jolaine. "Hi, Miss."

"Hello." She looked a little confused, but made no indication that they knew each other.

Bud turned back to her as well. "You were going to tell me what your uncle looks like."

Okay, so the distraction didn't take. It was worth a try.

"He's sort of medium," Jolaine said. "Medium height, medium build. I guess he's in his fifties." As bluffs go, it was a pretty good one. When in doubt, describe everyone in the world.

Bud turned his attention back to his paying customer, but said to Jolaine, "Nope, don't know nobody who fits that description."

Jonathan suppressed a smile. "Do people still buy money orders?" he asked. "Sorry for eavesdropping, but I haven't seen a money order in years."

"We don't sell a lot," Bud said. He looked up, as if sensing that he might have said something wrong. "But we sell enough to keep selling them. And I'm sorry, I never caught your name."

"Horgan," Jonathan said, extending his hand. "Rick Horgan." And if he somehow dropped his wallet—not likely—it was filled with carefully forged documents that would confirm that.

"Any relation to Zeb Horgan up near Wheeling?"

"No, not that I know of. It's not exactly a rare name. How much do I owe you?"

As Bud figured the retail price and tax on a calculator and transferred it to an old-fashioned NCR receipt book, Jonathan motioned with his eyes for Jolaine to leave.

"Can I give you a phone number in case you remember anything about my uncle?"

"I won't remember anything," Bud said.

Jolaine left. Jonathan said nothing.

"You movin' in around these parts?" Bud asked as punched the numbers into an antique cash register that was older than anyone in the room.

"Just passing through. Seeing the sights."

"And you just happened to want a socket set?"

Bud wasn't buying any of this, and Jonathan wasn't going to chase a lost cause. He paid in cash and left.

As he stepped out onto the sidewalk and turned toward Boxers and Jolaine, he mouthed, "Get out."

Jolaine didn't get it, but Boxers did, and he pulled her around the corner. They'd just disappeared when Bud stepped out the door, too. The Colt on Jonathan's hip begged to leave its holster, but Jonathan ignored his inner paranoia. Instead, he turned and faced Bud, some twenty yards away. "Everything okay?" he asked. "Did I leave something in the store?"

Bud covered. "No," he said. "I just wanted to test the weather."

"While I've got you," Jonathan said, "let me ask you. Is the food over at Mary's good?"

"As good as you're gonna get in this town," Bud said. "Try the chicken-fried steak."

Chapter Twenty-two

His belly full—his club sandwich was waiting for him, so he didn't get a chance to try the chicken fried steak—Jonathan sat on a picnic bench at a roadside break station, surrounded by his team. Behind them, the Coal River flowed freely and heavily, testament to the first year of adequate rain and snowfall in quite some time. The Batmobile stood beside them. This was a place designed for families to kick back and stretch their legs after long hours on the road. Given the number of spiderwebs covering the area between the benches and the tabletops, and the lack of trash in the bins, Jonathan deduced that it hadn't earned its price as a tourist concession.

Jonathan was in the middle of a strategy session for tonight's operation. "If we get the security tapes—or disks or whatever—then we get a face. With a face, we have a shot at getting a name."

"Sorry I couldn't get anything on the goatee man," Venice said through the computer on the table. "And for striking out on any more information on Victor Carrington."

"That just means it's an alias," Jonathan said. "One he doesn't use very often."

"How are we getting in?" Rollins asked.

"You're not getting in anywhere, Colonel," Jonathan said. "I don't want to have to construct a cover story for a Unit commander getting arrested. I want you and Dylan in the alley behind the store, keeping an eye out, just in case."

"In case of what?" Dylan asked.

"In case of *anything.*"

"Where will I be?" Jolaine asked.

"Across the street in Mary's, watching the front."

"Won't it be closed?"

Jonathan gave her a look, let her figure it out for herself.

"Oh," she said. "We're breaking in there, too, aren't we?"

"Yes, we are."

She blushed, and Boxers put a tender hand on her shoulder. Sooner or later, Jonathan supposed he'd get used to using *tender* and *Big Guy* in the same thought string, but it was proving to be harder than he'd anticipated.

"We need a place that's under cover so you can keep an eye on the street. Hanging out where people can see you will just raise a lot of questions. The good news is that I didn't see any sign of alarm systems when we were there for lunch."

"How do you plan to do all this breaking in, Boss?" Boxers asked. "You said the back door is impenetrable."

"We could always use thermite," Dylan said.

"Why not a load of C4?" Jonathan asked sarcastically.

Boxers clapped his hands together. "Now you're talkin'."

"In a perfect world we'll be in and out and no one will know the difference," Jonathan explained.

"So, what's the plan?" Boxers asked.

"Old school. We pick the lock," Jonathan said.

Boxers' shoulders fell. "But that's so boring."

Coal River Road was as solid a definition of the phrase dead after dark as Jonathan had ever encountered. Granted, they'd waited until after midnight to move in, but even so, the buildings along the road seemed unusually dark. Only a couple of lights glowed from windows, and they were all from the second floors above the commercial buildings. Jonathan figured they must be apartments.

They'd parked the Batmobile in a pullout about half a mile away, then walked one at a time through the woods along the river to work their way to the edge of town. Jonathan made them travel light with their various burglar tools carried in day packs that looked on the outside just like any hiker's day pack. Expecting no violence, Jonathan limited his team to their sidearms of choice and a couple of spare mags of ammo—nothing that couldn't be explained away if they encountered a cop along the road.

In many ways, this was the kind of op that troubled Jonathan the most. Over the decades, his training had focused on speed and overwhelming force. Collecting intel via breaking and entering was a level of tradecraft that was better left to Agency guys.

Consistent with their loose cover story of being hikers on a trip, they wore woodland camouflage of the type normally worn by hunters. All black would have made them far less visible, but it also would have blown their cover. Life is balance, right?

The designated gathering spot was the Dumpster behind Mary's Diner. Jonathan brought up the rear, and by the time he arrived, the others had already made their way inside. A wad of anger bloomed in his gut. Independent action was commendable to a point, but he didn't like them breaking in without him being there. What if something had gone wrong? They hadn't established comms yet, and—

"Get rid of the pinchy face, Boss," Boxers said as Jonathan entered the kitchen through the open back door. "The door was unlocked."

"Why?"

"How should I know?"

"Doesn't that raise a concern with you?"

"I don't remember you being this twitchy before, Dig," Rollins said.

"It's Scorpion," Jonathan corrected. Once an op went hot—once *any* op went hot—the use of real names was forbidden. Choosing from a list of three options Jonathan had offered, Jolaine had chosen She Devil. Rollins rejected Roleplay and settled for Madman. He certainly liked it better than Big Guy's suggestion of Asshole as a moniker. "Everybody comm up."

Jonathan saw to it that no corners were cut when it came to communications equipment. The ability to see and hear your enemy, in combination with the ability to see and hear your team, made all the difference between the success and failure.

Tonight, Jonathan, Boxers, and Jolaine wore custom-molded wireless transceivers that tucked snugly into their ear canals. When their satellite radios were set to VOX—voice-activated transmission—vibrations of the bones in their head brought the transmitter to life, and every word they said would be live, both between themselves and to the rest of the team, including Venice, who monitored everything from Fisherman's Cove. When set on PTT—push to talk—a transmit button would have to be depressed in order to transmit a message.

As transient newcomers, Boomer and Madman would work Secret Service style, with a generic monitor in their ear and a microphone cord strung down their sleeve. VOX was still an option for them, but it was an awkward one. Jonathan monitored everyone's progress. When they seemed set, he reached behind to depress the transmit button on his radio. "Mother Hen, Scorpion. Do a radio test for us, please."

Five seconds later, Venice's voice came clear as crystal through his earpiece. "Black Team, Mother Hen. Radio check. Respond when I call you. Madman."

Rollins raised the wrist mike to his lips. "Madman's okay."

"Boomer."

"Boomer's okay."

"White team. She Devil."

Jolaine had positioned a transmit button in the center of her chest, beneath her camo shirt. She pressed it. "She Devil's okay."

"Words cannot express how much Mother Hen hates that handle," Venice said. "Entry team. Big Guy."

"Here."

"And Scorpion."

"Scorpion's okay and we are set. Everyone keep the channel clear except for essential traffic. Mother Hen, do you have any eyes at all?"

"Nothing I like," Venice said. "I've been able to tap into the ATM fisheye from the Commerce Bank, but it's no one's version of a clear picture."

"Monitor what you've got and let me know if you see anything out of the ordinary."

"Oh, you want me to *tell* you if I see something? I thought you wanted me just to keep that a secret."

Rollins laughed. "I'm liking her more and more," he said off the air.

"Yeah, give it a couple of years."

"Big Guy, do you have traffic?" Venice asked. "Give what a couple of years?"

"Shit!" he spat. He damn near turned himself inside out switching off VOX. Then he pressed his transmit button. "Disregard, Mother Hen."

"We'd all be wise to consider that a lesson learned," Jonathan said through a chuckle. "Nobody on VOX unless I order it."

"Oo-uh," Dylan said.

"And we don't oo-uh here," Jonathan said. "We're all civilians now."

"Not all of us," Rollins said.

"The night is young, Stanley," Boxers said. Then, to get ahead of Jonathan, "I mean Madman. This might not turn out to be your best career move."

"Focus, gentlemen," Jonathan said. He loved the banter as much as the next guy, but he had his limits. "Boomer and Madman. Questions?"

They both shook their heads.

"I prefer verbal," Jonathan said.

"No questions." That came in unison.

"Okay, then. Git. Let us know when the alarms are disabled." The plan was simple and direct—and again, untraceable if they went about it correctly. Madman would keep an eye out while Boomer disconnected the phone line—it was merely a matter of dislodging a plug that could easily be reset—and then disconnecting the exterior to the local alarm by unscrewing the connectors. Whoever had put this system in place had not planned for a sophisticated burglar.

Jonathan checked his watch as they left through the back door of Mary's. It shouldn't take more than five minutes, he figured. In fact, it took just under four. His earbud popped. "Exterior's clear."

Now it was Jonathan's turn. If big steaming holes had been an acceptable side effect of entering the hardware store, then popping the door would have been Boxers' job. As it was, Jonathan had decided on the more subtle approach of lock picks, and as with all things more subtle than not, that fell more naturally into his wheelhouse.

"You wait here with She Devil," he said to Big Guy, "until I get the lock undone."

"Shouldn't I be watching your back?" Boxers asked. He didn't like it when Jonathan worked without backup.

"It'll only take a few minutes," Jonathan said. "It's

going to be obvious enough if someone drives by and sees me working the door. With both of us, it'd be too much." He wasn't going to argue the point, so he walked back outside as he was talking.

Over the years of doing this kind of work, he'd learned that one of the hardest things to do was to look intentionally nonchalant. When you genuinely had nothing to be concerned about, it was easy to stay unnoticed, in large measure because you didn't care if you *were* noticed. It's when people try to be invisible that they stand out like a bright light on a dark night. Jonathan believed that people generated a different kind of energy when they felt nervous, and that it was that energy that triggered discomfort in others.

Think about it. You can pass a thousand people in a shopping mall without noticing any of them, yet there'll be that *one guy* that gives you the creeps. It's not anything he's said or anything he's done, it's just a *feeling*. Countless studies had shown that those discomfiting feelings—those feelings of "stranger danger"—were real and needed to be paid attention to.

In Jonathan's line of work, the challenge lay in not giving out the vibes for others to intercept. He thought of that kind of thing as the woo-woo element of his job, and he believed that it was impossible to teach it to others. The woo-woo elements led inevitably to platitudes that resonated as hollow and empty to those who didn't believe in them. If you projected confidence, people felt confident in you, and their belief resulted in results worthy of the confidence. It was a big cycle. To project victory guaranteed victory. To consider failure to be an option guaranteed failure as the only outcome.

Or something like that.

As Jonathan stepped out from behind Mary's Diner, dressed in camouflage with a pistol concealed on his hip and a leather pouch of lock picks in his hand, he pretended that he belonged, and believed that no one who saw him would think otherwise.

Assuming that Bud hadn't invested more in his cylinder lock than he had in his burglar alarm, Jonathan anticipated no problem getting through the door.

Coal River Road was empty from horizon to horizon as Jonathan stepped from the street up to the sidewalk. He opened the flap on the pouch, and his fingers worked by feel to find the two tools that he would need—the tension bar and the rake. By the time he reached the door, his hands were ready to go. It was darker than he'd like, but this was an operation that shouldn't take a lot of visual examination. And night vision was out of the question because of the bizarre space-man look that it presented to observers.

Simple locks like standard cylinder locks found on glass doors that were typical of retail establishments posed little challenge to anyone with even a vague knowledge of what they were doing. These were pin-tumbler locks. The keyway slit at the front of the lock formed the center of a rotating cylinder which, when rotated, caused the bolt to either insert or retract itself from the receiving slot in the door jamb. Two lines of pins—one on the top and one on the bottom—jutted into the keyway like tiny stalactites and stalagmites and their presence physically blocked the cylinder from turning. The ridges on the key pushed these pins out of the way, removing the blockage and allowing the lock to turn.

The process of picking a lock required the burglar to

push the pin tumblers out of the way manually. To do this, Jonathan would insert a tension bar into the lock to put rotational torque on the cylinder, and then use a pick to physically push the pin tumblers out of the way. As they cleared their individual slots, the cylinder would turn a tiny fraction, just enough to keep the pins from reinserting themselves.

Some burglars worked well with a tension bar that was essentially an L-shaped piece of metal that they'd stick into the keyway to add torque to the cylinder. Jonathan preferred a Y-shaped tension bar that never entered the keyway, but rather grasped the slit on the top and the bottom. He held it in place with his left thumb and applied upward pressure with the first knuckle of his forefinger. With the tension applied, he inserted the rake—a general purpose thin metal pick with a squiggly head—into the keyway and literally raked it along the heads of the pins, first along the top and then along the bottom. With each pass, the cylinder turned a little, and after maybe seven seconds, the pressure released, and the cylinder turned all the way.

Jonathan returned the picks to his pocket and keyed his mike. "We're in," he said.

Two seconds later, Boxers' hulking form emerged from the shadow of Mary's Diner, and he walked a straight line across the street to join Jonathan on the sidewalk in front of the door. Jonathan smiled as his big friend approached. He was one of those people who attracted attention no matter what. Big Guy was still five feet away and moving when Jonathan pulled the door open and stepped inside. Boxers was with him ten seconds later.

Jonathan spun the cylinder again to lock them in.

"NVGs," he said. In unison, the two burglars dropped to a knee, shrugged out of their day packs, and removed a four-tube night vision goggles array. They slipped them over their heads and as Jonathan flipped the switch, the darkness became green-tinted daytime.

"Money order records and security camera recordings," Jonathan said, reminding them both of the limits of their mission. "Other than those missing things, no sign that we were ever here."

"You know I was listening last time you said that, right?" Boxers said.

Jonathan ignored him. More out of habit than necessity, he drew his .45, and led with it as he advanced into the empty shop. Yes, it was overkill, but he could never remember a single time in his many-year career when he'd said, "Dammit, I wish I hadn't drawn my weapon." The converse, however . . .

The entire room became brighter as Boxers turned on an infrared flashlight and scanned the room with the beam, which would appear as invisible to anyone who was not equipped with night vision. The effect was to add less-green light to an otherwise green environment.

They moved deeper into the store. The plan was for Boxers to search the area around the cash register and the gun display while Jonathan tossed the office in the back. Jonathan assumed that Bud had no reason to hide the materials they were looking for, so the whole mission couldn't take more than—

"Freeze," Boxers said in a tone that Jonathan had heard too many times over the years.

Once heard, it meant exactly what it stated. Freeze. As in, stop whatever you were doing in exactly the posture you were holding, and lock every muscle. That's what Jonathan did. "What?"

"Look down at your feet," Big Guy said. "Three feet ahead and at shin level."

Boxers had illuminated the area with the beam of his IR flashlight, and Jonathan actually saw the shadow of the trip wire before he found the trip wire itself. He was still a step and a half away, but trip wires were always concerning. "What does it go to?" he asked.

"Interesting question," Boxers said. "I'll get back to you on that."

Frozen as he was, with the majority of his weight on his left foot, Jonathan felt particularly unbalanced as he watched Boxers' light sweep the room.

"I'm almost positive you can redistribute your weight," Big Guy said.

"Almost positive."

"Sixty percent, easy." Boxers rumbled out a laugh. "But let me hide behind this shelf before you do it."

"I hate you," Jonathan said. He understood Boxers-speak, though. All of that tranlated to *you're safe where you stand, but go no farther.*

A trip wire meant a booby trap, and the presence of a booby trap fundamentally changed the nature of the game. Bud was prepared to kill to protect that which he valued, and people who were willing to set one trap were more often than not willing to set several. The evening just got longer.

"Found it," Boxers said. "It's a good old-fashioned shotgun trap. When was the last time you saw one of those?" To put tension on the trip wire was to pull the trigger on a shotgun. Nothing good came from that.

Jonathan watched as the tension drooped out of the trip wire. He knew that Boxers had moved the gun and eliminated the threat. "Pretty aggressive move," Jonathan said. "In my part of the world, that would get you sent away for life."

"I believe you could say that the same would be true for the intruder," Boxers replied. Jonathan could see his smile even in the night vision. "He must have some pretty cool shit to hide. We're clear."

Clear but on notice.

They got to the sales counter first. "This is mine," Boxers said.

"I've got the office."

"Entry team, what is your sitrep?" Per the plan, Venice had called in for a situation report.

"We're inside and on schedule," Jonathan said. She didn't have to know about the booby trap.

Even with night vision, the view inside the back office was dim. It wasn't that he couldn't see as much as it was he couldn't make out the fine detail. Reading, for example, was difficult. Jonathan withdrew his own IR penlight from its pocket on his sleeve, and he pressed the button to bring it to life. That made all the difference in the world.

Bud's office looked exactly like what you would think something called "Bud's office" would look like. Maybe ten by ten, the place looked like it had been hit by a cyclone. Papers lay upon papers, which had been stacked upon food wrappers placed upon papers. The desk itself was of hearty wooden construction—the kind of desk that hadn't been made in seventy years. Bud had cleared out a one-foot-by-one-foot rectangle of space on the desk, directly in front of the old wooden desk chair. Jonathan figured that was the space he allowed himself for actually doing work.

The floor around the desk was likewise stacked with stuff. Much of it appeared to be incoming inventory. Jonathan cared about none of it. His mission here was to stay focused on the recorder deck. Somewhere in its files lay the picture of the man he needed to identify and take down. It took a couple of seconds to orient himself to the machine. It was a tiny thing, barely bigger than the disk that it recorded, and he had trouble finding the eject button. Finally, he found it and pressed it and was rewarded with a familiar electronic whir as the disk drawer opened up in the old cup-holder style and offered him the CD. Fortunately, Bud was an organized man and he had labeled the front of the disk with the start date. Three weeks ago.

Jonathan thought about that. If Bud labeled them that meant that he kept them. That meant there were others. How on earth, amid all of this clutter was he ever going to find—

The little file box sat next to the recorder. Made of what appeared in the night vision to be gray plastic, it looked like a repurposed recipe card file. Could it be that simple? Yes it could. As he lifted up the lid, he saw more disks. They were filed vertically, all in white sleeves with clear plastic windows. And each one was labeled with a start and end date. There had to be two years of files here. Jonathan took the last three months' worth, slipped them into his pack, then put the file box where it belonged.

Now it was time to find the receipts for the money orders.

"Hey, Boss, I found the money order files," Boxers said in his ear.

Jonathan keyed his mike. "Roger, and I have what we need in here." All that remained was for Big Guy to find the files from the appropriate date, shoot a picture of it, and then they could be on their way.

Jonathan worked his way out of the office toward the front of the store.

"Scorpion, She Devil," said Jolaine's voice over the air. "We have a big problem. Call it huge."

Chapter Twenty-three

"**I**'m at gunpoint," Jolaine explained. "It's Mary. As in Mary's Diner. And she's not happy. Sorry to rat you out, but I told her about both you and Big Guy. She wants you back here right now."

"Well doesn't that blow dead bears?" Boxers said.

A bit of imagery that Jonathan didn't need. He didn't know how Jolaine had gotten herself caught, but he understood the subtext of her message. She hadn't mentioned anything about Dylan and Rollins.

Jonathan pressed his transmit button. "Black team stand by. I'm opening the back door." Just like that, being untraceable didn't mean as much anymore. He moved to the reinforced metal door and pulled on the steel bracing bar. Clearly it had been in place for a long time. It didn't want to move.

"Outta the way, Boss," Big Guy said. He nudged Jonathan aside and pulled on the bar. It resisted his efforts, too, but only for a couple of seconds. As it cleared its mounts, Boxers lifted it up and out of the way, setting it to the side of the doorjamb. By the time he had it stabilized, Jonathan had pushed the door open.

Madman and Boomer stood side by side, just beyond the swing of the door. "You heard?" Jonathan asked.

"Yeah, what happened?" Boomer asked.

"Doesn't matter," Jonathan said. "Jolaine didn't mention you two, so we have time. Go back to the Batmobile, grab a couple of long guns, and radio me when you're in position to take a shot."

"You're going to shoot Mary?" Rollins asked.

"I hope not," Jonathan said, though he didn't understand why the thought was more horrifying than shooting anyone else. "But if comes to a team member o. Mary, Mary's having a bad day. Questions or problem with that?" He focused his glare on the colonel. Role play Rollins had a history of putting his own men second.

Jesus, old grudges die hard.

"I'm on it," Dylan said. He turned on his heel and was gone. It took Rollins a few seconds to get with the program and follow him, but he did.

"Okay, Big Guy, we're on."

Jonathan led the way back through the hardware store, toward the front door. Before they'd taken more than a few steps, Boxers reset the blocking bar. "I'd hate to see someone rip Bud off," he said.

"Scorpion, She Devil. I need you to expedite."

"On our way," Jonathan said over the air. The he added, "Mother Hen, channel three." While Jolaine wore a custom earpiece for her radio, sometimes transmissions could be heard by others as a distant buzzing He didn't want to raise suspicions. "Big Guy stay on channel one." If something went wrong with Jolaine Boxers would know about it.

"Mother Hen on channel three," Venice said.

"Mother Hen are you caught up with the recent traffic?"

"Affirmative. And I am monitoring local emergency frequencies to advise if someone calls nine-one-one."

Amazing. He had gone to channel three to tell Venice to monitor the local emergency frequencies and advise if someone had called nine-one-one. "Okay, good work," he said into the radio. "Return to channel one."

"So what's our play?" Boxers asked as they walked out of Bud's front door.

"Plan Whiskey Indigo," Jonathan said.

Boxers laughed. "Wing it," he said, translating the acronym. "This is why I've always admired your skills as a tactician."

The reality was that there was no plan to plan. Clearly, Mary had gotten the drop on Jolaine. Beyond that, they knew nothing, and therefore, the possibilities were endless. Most of them unpleasant. On the plus side, if Mary's intent had been to kill Jolaine, she would have done it by now. He drew his Colt.

"Keep your weapon low, but do not disarm," Jonathan said. "I'm not sure what the game is here, but Mary needs to know that the one guarantee in life if she pulls that trigger is that she will die."

"Works for me. How do you want to enter?"

"Good question." Jonathan keyed his mike. "She Devil, Scorpion. We're approaching the diner. How do you want us to enter?"

A few seconds passed. "Through the back door," Jolaine said. "Be sure you're unarmed and your hands are up."

"Tell your hostess that we're coming in armed, but that we have no desire to shoot," Jonathan said. He had no idea if Jolaine would deliver that message—it was a tough thing to do while staring down the bore of a gun—and he didn't care. The subtext was meant for her anyway.

"And I'll be the one to kill her," Boxers said over the air.

Jonathan recognized the attitude as Boyfriend Boxers, but he still found the new sensibility to be unsettling. "Go get 'em, tiger," he said off the air.

They crossed the street, and button-hooked around the edge of the diner. "We enter with purpose," Jonathan said. "No fear."

"I'll try to manage my terror."

No one had yet to turn on the lights in the diner, though the glow of the emergency exit sign was surprisingly bright. Even more light spilled in through the long front window. Jonathan led, as he usually did—if things went south, Boxers could shoot over his head, but the opposite was a nonstarter. Keeping his Colt at a low-ready, he visually swept the kitchen for threats. Finding none, he never broke stride as he crossed into the dining room.

Their waitress from this afternoon—a harried forty-something who could have been pretty if she didn't look so exhausted—sat in a booth ahead and to the right, facing the kitchen door. Opposite, with her back turned, he recognized Jolaine. Between them lay a 12-gauge coach gun whose barrels had been trimmed all the way back to the foregrip, its business end pointed at Jolaine's chest. The pistol grip appeared from this angle to be homemade, and the waitress's hand was wrapped around it, her fingers on the triggers. Both hammers were pulled back, and the weapon was ready to go.

"Hi," she said. "I'm Mary. This is my place, and I want to know why you think you belong here. She Devil here doesn't want to tell me. So why don't you boys put your guns down so I don't have to repaint the place and we can have a nice chat."

"Why don't we shoot you instead?" Boxers growled.

"Because I think you care about this young lady," Mary said. In the dim light, Jonathan could see the serious set of her face. "If I'd wanted to shoot, this one would be dead already, and I could've reloaded to take out both of you. I'd rather just have a peaceful chat."

Jonathan had long prided himself in his ability to judge people, and he liked this lady. He liked folks who spoke their mind plainly. He also imagined that someone who could appear so calm under circumstances like this possessed a toughness that he'd rather not get crosswise with.

"Holster up, Big Guy," he said. Holding out one hand to Mary in a *be cool* gesture, he slowly slid his Colt back into the holster on his hip.

"The hell are you doin'?" Boxers asked.

"Mary wants to talk, we're going to talk. Sometimes, you have to acknowledge when the other guy—excuse me, the other gal—has the upper hand." Then he shifted the tone of his voice. "Besides, as she already noted, with three targets and only two barrels, if she goes rogue, she's guaranteed to be one-third of the casualties. More likely one-half."

Boxers hesitated. He didn't like this, but in the end, he followed his orders and slipped his M9 back into its holster.

Jonathan pointed to the shotgun. "Now it's your turn," he said.

Mary shook her head. "Not yet it's not."

"At least take your fingers off the triggers," Jonathan said. "Right now, a sneeze can end in disaster."

She considered that. "Okay." Her first two fingers formed into a wide V outside of the trigger guard. "That make you happy?"

"Happier," he said. He flashed the grin that historically had worked wonderful things for him. "So, what do you want to talk about?"

"Have a seat there at the counter," Mary said, nodding to the padded round stools. "Take a load off, but keep facing me."

Jonathan complied, lifting a butt cheek high enough to hook the edge of the stool. Boxers sort of squatted to end up at the same level. Something about the awkwardness of his movement made Jonathan chuckle.

"You're quite the tall fellow, aren't you?" Mary asked.

"You okay, She Devil?" Boxers asked.

Jolaine nodded.

"Say something," Boxers said.

"I'm fine. I just feel stupid. She came right up behind me. Could've cut my throat if she'd wanted to."

"Well, Mary, thank you for not cutting my colleague's throat," Jonathan said. He wanted to keep things as light as they could for as long as they could. "Now, about that conversation."

"You can start with why you're in my diner in the middle of the night."

Jonathan winced. "You know, if I were in your position, that's exactly the question I would want to know the answer to. But try another one, because that's one I can't answer."

"Can't or won't?"

"A little bit of both," Jonathan said.

His earbud popped. "Scorpion, Boomer. We're in position, eyes on target."

Jolaine and Boxers looked to him simultaneously.

Mary caught the motion, and clearly sensed something significant. "What is it?"

Jonathan scratched the back of his head. "Okay, Mary, here's the thing. I really need you to raise both of your hands and move them away from your gun."

She gave him a look. "Why in the world would—"

"There's a very talented shooter out there, probably across the street, who has you in the crosshairs of his sniper scope. He just told me over the radio that he's ready to kill you."

Mary's features sagged, and she pivoted her head to look out through the window into the night. "I don't see anyone."

"Look at me, Mary," Jonathan coached.

She turned.

"I'm going to spin a little on this stool to show you that when I reach around my back, I will not be reaching for a firearm, but rather for a two-way radio." As he spoke, he did exactly what he described. "Okay, now I'm going to press a button."

He twisted back to face Mary and said, "Boomer, Scorpion. Don't shoot yet, but light up our hostess with a visible laser."

"Rog." Two seconds later a luminous red dot appeared on Mary's chest. It moved in tiny circles as Boomer struggled to hold stationary.

Mary froze in place as she saw it. It's a terrible feeling to know that someone could make you die in a millisecond.

"Like I said, Mary," Jonathan coached, "I need you to slowly raise your hands straight over your head, like you want to touch the ceiling."

She did just that, and when Mary's arms were stretched as far as they could go, Jolaine reached out and spun the shotgun back around toward her captor. For an instant, Jonathan feared that she was going to shoot her in retaliation. He was relieved when Jolaine pulled the stubby weapon close to her and stood. She hurried back to Boxers and stood next to him. Neither showed a public display of affection, thank God. Not that Jonathan had anything against romance, he just didn't want that kind of emotion to gum things up.

"Okay, Boomer," Jonathan said into the radio. "Continue to monitor, but don't take any shots unless I tell you."

"Roger, Scorpion. Madman wants to know what you want him to do."

"Madman, stay with Boomer," Jonathan replied. "Keep an eye on the rest of the town while you stay on target."

"How many of you are there?" Mary asked. Her demeanor had become significantly less aggressive.

"Can't answer that one, either," Jonathan said. "Frustrating, isn't it? Let me ask you one. Why didn't you call the police when you found a burglar in your restaurant?"

"I had my trusty shotgun," she said, but the smile told him that even she knew that it was an unsellable lie.

Jonathan waited for the rest.

Mary folded her hands and placed them demurely

on the table. "I didn't call the police because I suspected that none of us wanted that. I suspect that I know something about why you're here."

Jonathan folded his arms. "Is that so?"

"You're not police yourselves, are you?"

"No, we're not," Jonathan said.

"Not FBI, not CIA, not some other secret government cover?"

Jonathan hesitated. He hated telling lies because they created too many tentacles, any one of which could uncover the lie and once that was done, trust was gone, too. "For your purposes—for the way I think you're thinking of *other secret government cover*—I'll say no. Best not push that one too hard, though."

Behind him, Boxers sighed loudly. If it were up to Big Guy, no questions would ever be answered, and no details of any op would ever be shared. As for the trust thing, Jonathan had never known Big Guy to give much of shit about that.

"Fair enough," Mary said. "I figured out the cop part because you broke in, and cops aren't allowed to do that. And as soon as I saw you in town today, I knew that you weren't just casual strangers in town. Your necks are too thick." She winced and glanced over at Jolaine. "Sorry, She Devil. I meant that in a good way. So that leaves the who and the why. I'm going to go out on a limb and guess—I'm going to *hope*—that your presence here has something to do with that nonsense that's going on at the top of the mountain."

Something flipped in Jonathan's stomach. "What nonsense are you talking about?"

Mary's features hardened. "If you're going to insult me or my intelligence, then to hell with you. I'll just sit quietly, and sooner or later you're going to leave. I don't believe for a moment that you'll shoot me in cold blood. So it's up to you. You do what you need to do with what I know or without it."

Boxers coughed out a laugh. "Jesus, you're a tough lady." Coming from Big Guy, that was nearly an expression of love.

Jonathan keyed his mike. "Boomer, Scorpion. You can take eyes off our friend Mary. You and Madman come on in and join us."

They acknowledged, but Jonathan stayed focused on Mary. "Okay," he said. "You win. We believe that the activities at the top of the mountain are an effort to overthrow the United States government."

"God*damn,* Scorpion," Boxers said.

Jonathan figured he wasn't telling her anything she didn't already know.

"I *knew* it was something like that. So if you're not with the government, who are you?"

"No matter how many times you ask that question, I'm not going to answer it."

"Then tell me whose team you're on."

Jonathan started to answer, then stopped himself. "What are my choices?"

"Them or us?"

He hesitated again. Defining terms was important. "Who's us?"

"Patriotic Americans."

He knew that she was going get annoyed soon, but Mary clearly didn't understand that she kept answering in double entendres. "You need to understand, Mary, that I've done a lot of fighting in my lifetime, and almost all of it was against bad guys who thought they were good guys. The Nazis were patriots, right? Just for the wrong side. If you've been keeping up with the news, you'll know that over the past few years, there are a lot of folks who believe that all the patriots have left Washington."

"Are you one of those?" Mary asked. She seemed suddenly nervous.

"I'm asking *you,*" Jonathan said.

Mary shifted in her seat, then jumped as Dylan and Rollins entered the room. "Well, maybe this *is* where you shoot me, but no, I am not one of those people. I personally have no time for that asshole Darmond or any of his asshole policies or asshole crooked cronies, but they are the assholes we elected. Twice, God help us. If people rise up against them, what's to stop the people from rising up in the future against a government I like?"

"We're on the same side, Mary," Jonathan said. "Anarchy is anarchy, and it's never to anyone's benefit. Our job is to verify that they're doing what we think they're doing and to interfere with their plans."

"How will you do that?"

Jonathan shot a thumb over toward Boxers. "If I told you that, Big Guy would take your shotgun and beat me to death with it."

"Damn straight I would."

Mary laughed.

"I went first," Jonathan said. "Now it's your turn. By the way, meet Boomer and Madman. They're on my team, too."

Both of the newcomers looked confused. And they'd have to remain that way, at least for a while.

"Do you know who Mr. Wainwright is?" Mary asked.

"No," Jonathan said.

"Well, he's about the most important person in town He owns almost all of it. He got his money from coal and then he's spun it out in a thousand different directions. We're talking more money than any of us could possibly imagine. Starting about two, maybe three years ago, Mr. Wainwright started building fences. Big, scary fences. Thick steel construction, barbed wire on top Must be miles of it. The contractors who installed i used to eat here, and I heard them talking. Said they'd done work on a fence for the NRO—whatever that is— and that this fence is comparable to that."

Jonathan recognized the NRO as the National Reconnaissance Office, an agency that made the CIA look like an open source research library.

"What's he doing that he needs so much security?" Jonathan asked.

"My question, exactly," Mary said. "I even asked i to one of those contractor fellas. He looked like I'd said a dirty word in church. Looked around to see if anyone else might have heard, and then he told me to be careful what I said. Never saw them in here again. And let's be honest, there ain't a lot of options in Whitesville."

"What do you *think* might be going on?" Jolaine asked, earning her a subtle poke in the ribs from Boxers, and a gentle shake of his head. There's a rhythm to questioning people, a protocol. One of the fundamentals was never to split the attention of the person being questioned.

Seeing that Boxers had taken care of the rebuke Jonathan let it go. It so happened that Jolaine had asked the question he was going to ask next.

"I can't imagine," Mary said. "Well, I *can* imagine

ut what I imagine makes me even more nervous. Any-
ody with that much money and that much fear of
eing caught is doing something that he shouldn't."

"What about the police?" Jonathan asked. "Have you
poken to them about it?"

Mary offered a bitter laugh. "Sweetie, in this county—
ell, in this *state*—Mr. Wainwright could rape little
hildren in the middle of the street and not get arrested
or it. The Council would pass a retroactive law mak-
ng it legal to do that, limited to the date he did it. Are
ou catching my meaning?"

"All I'm hearing is that the politics in West Virginia
re the same as the politics in Washington," Dylan
aid. "Laws are for sale."

"Amen to that, Good Lookin'," Mary said.

Jonathan felt an inexplicable flash of jealousy at the
ood-lookin' thing.

"Then I guess he finished the fences," Mary contin-
ed, "because the contractor people all went away."
he gathered herself with a sigh. "And then the other
eople started coming." She stopped. Did she think
hat she'd just made sense?

"What other people?" Jonathan prompted.

"People like you," she replied. "Wide shoulders, thick
ecks. Young people. Not all of them had the thick
ecks, but there were a lot more trim bellies than fat
nes, and they all looked so serious."

"Who are they?" Jonathan asked.

"I don't know. Not by name. But they'd pass through
own, always in trucks driven by the same people, and
hey headed up the mountain. As far as I know, I've
ever seen any of them again."

"They're building a compound," Boxers said.

"And what good can possibly come from a com
pound?" Mary asked. It was hard to be sure in the dim
light, but Jonathan thought he saw tears balanced on
her lids.

"You're upset," Jonathan said.

She seemed embarrassed. Quickly swiped the tears
away. "It's just sad," she said. "I've lived here my whole
life, and everything is changing. Everyone is so *angry*
all the time. And now this. Something violent is com
ing, I just know it. You hear them shooting up there all
the time."

"And still no police?" Jolaine asked. Clearly, she
was a slow learner.

"What's illegal about shooting?" Mary asked. "I can
lay a lot that's bad at the feet of a bought-and-paid-for
police department, but that's not one of them. It's just
so sad."

Jonathan sensed that he was missing something. He
could understand it all being scary and disturbing and
about a thousand other adjectives, but *sad* eluded him.
"Is someone close to you involved in what's going
on?" he asked. It was the most obvious source of sad
ness that he could think of.

Mary placed folded hands on the table again and
talked to them. "There's a boy in town. His name is
Tommy Piper. Sad, sad case. I don't know that anyone
knows who his daddy is, but his mama was a real piece
of work. She just up and left one day. But Tommy was
that poor kid who never seemed to have enough to eat
and never had a bath until five or six days after he
needed one. He was maybe thirteen when his mama
left—maybe twelve—and the word around town was a
hundred percent agreement that he was better off with

ut her. The poor boy had nothing, and the fear around
own was that Social Services was going to come
round and take him into the system. Well, we all know
hat boys that age have no place in the system. They're
oo old to be cute and too young to be anything but vic-
ms."

"You took him in, didn't you?" Boxers asked. If ever
here was a teddy bear for kids in trouble—a huge,
ethal grizzly with a big heart—it was Big Guy.

Mary nodded. "I did. I had a spare bedroom, and a
usiness where he could learn a skill, so why not? I
on't say it was easy, but it was easier than it could
ave been. That boy has a solid heart, but oh, brother,
vas his head a mess. I guess that's what happens when
ou grow up wild. Stupid stuff, like stealing things
rom the diner and hiding them in his room upstairs."

Ah, Jonathan thought. *She lives upstairs. That's how
he sneaked up on Jolaine.* He felt like an idiot for not
esearching that more closely.

"Sounds like you did the right thing for the right
easons," Jonathan said, hoping to move her closer to
er point.

"Thank you," she replied. "Yes, I think so, too. But
ou know? Towns like this have long memories. He
vas never really accepted as anything other than the
nongrel kid with the neglectful mother that we're all
mbarrassed was ever tolerated by the community.
ommy never found his group. He was never accepted
y the other children in school and his grades showed
. He didn't finish his sophomore year in high school.
o now he was sixteen, no education, no skills, work-
ng in a small-town diner. I worried about him, but I
vas never his official foster mother, you know? I had

no legal authority over him. He worked here and sle
here and was just sort of rudderless."

"You're speaking of him in the past tense," Jonatha
said. "Is he . . . ?" He didn't want to finish the end o
such an obvious sentence.

"Oh, he's still alive," Mary said. "He's just one o
them. Up on the hill. I don't know how they met u
with each other, but he got recruited early on, and
think he was just so happy to be a part of someth
that he jumped at the chance. One day he came do\
stairs with a backpack stuffed with stuff, and he sai
'Mary, thanks for everything, but I'm moving on.
Then he gave me a big hug.

"Now, you have to know that hugs are not a part o
Tommy's style. It worried me. I asked him what he wa
going to be doing and he said that he couldn't tell me
But it was big, he said. Really, really big. He was i\
so *excited*."

"You must have been happy for him to be happ_
Jolaine said.

"I should have been, shouldn't I? And I guess a pa
of me was. You want somebody you care about to b
happy, of course. But I knew there was somethin
wrong about all of that, and Tommy went up there eve
before the shooting started."

"Have you seen him since?" Jonathan asked.

"A few times. I guess he knows he's got a free m\
and pie waiting for him whenever he wants it."

"How is he?"

"I have to admit that he looks terrific," Mary sai
with a shrug and a tentative smile. "He's filled
quite a bit—in a good way—and he seems more co

ent than he used to be. But he wears a uniform all the time now, at least every time I see him."

"What kind of uniform?"

"Looks like army to me, but I don't really know the difference. A lot like what you people are wearing."

For Jonathan, all of this confirmed what he'd been suspecting all along. It seemed clear that they'd stumbled upon the location they were looking for. Now, the question was what to do about it?

"What does he tell you they're doing up there?" Jonathan asked. "How does he explain all the shooting?"

Another deep sigh from Mary. "I'll tell you the God's honest truth about that," she said. "After that response I got from the contractor guys, and after the nervousness I see from everyone around town about that place, I don't ask him anything. I don't want to run him off."

"Is he a violent kid?" It was the first time Rollins had opened his mouth.

Mary recoiled in her seat. The question seemed to have taken her off guard. Perhaps it was too on the nose. But she took it seriously. "Which one are you?" he asked. Are you Boomer or Madman?

"Madman, ma'am."

"I wish I could answer this differently, but this is part of what's been bothering me from the beginning. Tommy's not a violent boy, but he's an impressionable boy. I think he'd do just about anything to impress somebody he respected. Tommy doesn't have a lot of time for authority."

"So, let's get back to why you didn't call the police,"

Jonathan said. "You're hoping that we can interfere
with all that's going on up there, don't you?"

"I'd have thought that was obvious by now," Mary
said with a touch of annoyance.

"Okay," Jonathan said. "I think we have a plan. But
you're going to have to make a phone call to Tommy."

Chapter Twenty-four

Never a sound sleeper, Ian Martin had learned over the years to ignore the routine sounds of nighttime. In a hotel, for example, because of the context, he could filter out the movement of people in the hallway—the very sound that would launch him out of bed prepared to fight if he were at home. Here in Camp Wainwright, the common sounds included not just the fauna of the night, but also the rumble of low conversations and the crunch of gravel as soldiers moved from one place to another.

To hear the sound of a car door, however, was a thousand percent out of the ordinary, and it ripped him from sleep to full alert. He rolled out of his rack to go to the window and pulled the blinds aside. Sure enough, someone was opening the door to one of the camp SUVs. It was too dark to make out the identity, but the silhouette clearly showed the outline of a uniform.

Ian spun on his heel and snatched his M4 from its resting place next to his headboard and headed for his bedroom door. He cleared the living room in six long strides, pulled open the door, and stepped out into the coolness of the night just as the soldier was climbing into the driver's seat.

"Hey!" Ian yelled. "Stop!"

The engine cranked.

Ian took off at run, clad only in boxer shorts, and pressed his rifle to his shoulder. He shouted louder, "Stop, goddammit!"

The vehicle remained still. Ian approached cautiously. This was entirely new territory. He had no template to work from. He approached from behind the driver's door, squinting through the darkness to see who it was, and to assess the level of threat he posed.

Tension drained from his shoulders as he saw the profile of Tommy Piper sitting behind the wheel. The boy's eyes looked wet, and he looked shaken.

Ian slung his rifle and used his left hand to pull open the door. Tommy was a mess. He wore yesterday's clothes, his hair was on sideways, and he'd clearly been crying. "Jesus, Tommy. What's wrong?"

"I have to go into town," he said.

"It's two in the morning."

"I know. I have to go."

"Tommy, look at me."

The boy pivoted his head. His eyes weren't right, reflecting a head that wasn't right.

"Talk to me, son. What's going on?"

"It's Mary. She's sick. She needs me."

Ian felt more tension drain. Homesickness was the bane of many soldiers' existence, most often among the very young and the newly married. It was worst among new fathers. He was surprised to see it in Tommy.

Rumor had it that the kid didn't have personal ties to anyone outside the camp, other than the lady who ran Mary's Diner. Apparently, she was some kind of foster mother to him. The lack of close ties was one of the factors that made him such an excellent adjutant. He could be trusted not to gab with people he shouldn't be gabbing with.

"It doesn't work like that, Tommy. A soldier can't just leave camp. We have work to do. You know that we're in a high-security lockdown."

"Please, Colonel," Tommy said. The edge seemed to have worn off of his panic, but he was still distraught. "She lives just at the base of the mountain. She's the only person who's ever given a shit about me, and she's never asked me for a thing. If she called, then something is wrong."

Ian had been in camp now for six weeks, and this was the first burst of emotion he'd seen from Tommy. It hurt his heart. "The orders are no exceptions, son. That includes you. Hell, it includes *me*." That last part wasn't true, but he hoped it sounded convincing.

"Please, Colonel. *Please*. The office doesn't open until seven-thirty. That gives me five hours. I promise I'll be back before then. I *have* to go, sir. One way or the other, I *have* to go."

Ian heard the veiled threat of desertion, but he shrugged it off. The fact of the matter was that due to their daily proximity, Tommy got away with transgressions that others would not. And that was a slippery slope. Once an officer started making exceptions based on personal preferences, the fabric of discipline unraveled.

"*Please,* Colonel. I need you to do this for me. I swear to God I'll be back early in the morning. You know you can trust me."

Ian looked at the kid's eyes. Justified or not, Tommy needed this. Sometimes, good leadership required making exceptions. "Look," he said, "I feel ridiculous standing out here in my skivvies. Follow me for a minute."

"But Colonel, I need to go."

"I hear you, Tommy, but listen to me. I need you to follow me to my quarters." This time, he didn't wait for an answer, but rather turned and headed back toward his open front door. He was relieved when he heard Tommy climb out and close the truck's door. He noted, however, that the kid left it running.

Ian entered the living room, turned on the light, and walked straight to the little desk he used for personal matters. He snatched a ballpoint and scribbled out a message. *Tommy Piper, General Karras's adjutant, has permission to leave Camp Wainwright for a short period. He will return in the morning. Refer any questions to the undersigned.* Then he signed the note with a flourish.

Tommy had come no farther than the doorjamb, but he stood in a posture that was neither relaxed nor at attention.

"Here," Ian said, offering him the note. "This will get you out and back in without a headache."

Tommy looked genuinely relieved. Emotional, even. For an awkward couple of seconds, Ian feared he might start crying again.

"Thank you, Colonel," the boy said. "I'll never forget this."

"Forget what?" Ian said with a wink. "I'll see you at work bright and early tomorrow morning."

Tommy stood there for a moment more, then snapped to attention and tossed off a picture-perfect salute. "See you tomorrow, sir." He closed the door behind him as he left.

It took twenty-five minutes for the doubts to materialize in Ian's head. He'd gone back to bed and might have already been asleep when it hit him. Camp life was defined by routine, the utter lack of the extraordinary. So why was Tommy Piper, who'd never, so far as Ian knew, been contacted by this foster mother—or anyone else for that matter—suddenly contacted tonight?

Sure, he'd said it was a medical emergency, but how can one verify such a thing? The emergency could have happened on any day or any night, but why this day and this night? Why must it come at a time when the camp was asleep and therefore most vulnerable?

Ian tried to slow himself down. Sometimes things just happened. Emergencies by their very nature did not follow a schedule. Certainly, Tommy Piper was loyal to the cause. He was above suspicion, and as such, Ian felt anger at himself for even considering the thoughts that were troubling him now.

But he felt what he felt. And that niggling voice in the back of his head had saved his life more than once.

Rolling to his side, Ian turned on the lamp next to his bed and picked up the phone. He dialed a three-digit extension. On the third ring, the man on the other end said, "Duty office."

"It's Carrington," Ian said. "I want you to triple up on the guard detail tonight."

"Is there a problem, sir?"

"Not officially, no. Call it an uncomfortable feeling."

"Want me to sound the general alarm?"

Ian considered that. His misgivings were *that* strong. Absent an identifiable threat, though, it made no sense to pull everyone out of the rack and into full gear. How would he know when it was time to release them back to their quarters?

"No," Ian said. "Just triple the guard."

"Sir, are you aware that a soldier left the camp under your signature?"

"I am," Ian said. "Mr. Piper is a big part of my concerns."

"We need to take this to the FBI," Rollins said at a whisper. They were up in Mary's apartment, away from the others as Jonathan watched through the window for signs of this Tommy kid. "We've found what we needed to find. Now we need to turn it over to the professionals."

"You're welcome to leave anytime you want, Colonel," Jonathan said.

"Oh, so we're dick-knocking now?"

"Keep your voice down." Jonathan pivoted his head to look Rollins in the eye. "This is about finishing what we started."

"But the feds have a thousand times more resources than we do," Rollins insisted. "Christ, they could use air power if they needed to."

"But they won't," Jonathan said. He peeked through the curtain again.

"You can't know that."

"But I do." He turned back to Rollins. "Let me hear your pitch to the FBI."

Rollins looked confused.

"You know," Jonathan continued, "tell me what you would tell them."

"I'd tell them that there are a bunch of terrorists training on the top of the mountain."

"Who are they?"

"What?"

"I'm the FBI," Jonathan said. "You're you. Let's do some role-play—pardon the pun."

Rollins's face reddened.

"I have a point," Jonathan said. "Play along. Who are these terrorists?"

"I don't know them by name."

"How do you know them, then?"

Rollins waved him off. "I'm not—"

"You started this, Colonel. Stick with it. How do you know there are terrorists at the top of the mountain?"

"We have evidence."

"And how did you get that evidence?"

Rollins started to answer, but then the lightbulb came on over his head. "We don't have any evidence that they could use."

Jonathan pointed at his nose. "Bingo. Add to that the fact that the source of our inadmissible information is the federal government's secret Public Enemy Number One, and that whole law-and-order response gets tough." He turned back to the window.

Rollins was silent for the better part of a minute—Jonathan's favorite part of that particular minute—and then he said, "You really love this stuff, don't you?"

Jonathan thought about ignoring the question, but it triggered something in his gut. He looked back again. "Yes and no," he said. The man asked an honest question, so if Jonathan was going to answer, he owed him an honest answer. "I don't love the ops. I'm past the adrenaline-junkie shit of my youth. Every time I do this, it takes longer and longer for the soreness to go away. But I do love the clarity. There are good guys and bad guys. Getting past all the relativistic crap I laid down on Mary—all of which was true—I don't get involved in that. I am Batman, breaking all the rules for all the right reasons. I like being Batman."

"What does that make Big Guy?" Rollins's eyes sparkled as he asked the question.

"Just scary," Jonathan said. "At the end of the day, he's just very scary."

Outside, beyond the window, Jonathan heard a vehicle arrive. He spun back to the window in time to see a white, nondescript SUV pull into a parking space out front. A tall, skinny guy in a uniform spun out of the driver's door and made a beeline for the diner's front door.

"Okay, team," Jonathan said. "We're hot."

Tommy Piper was at least ten years younger than Jonathan had pictured him in his mind. He was merely a boy, maybe twenty years old if he lied a bit. Certainly not old enough to buy a drink. The kid entered through the front door of the restaurant—clearly he had a key—and he tore up the stairs, bursting into the apartment that was Mary's home, and that used to be his.

"Mary?" he called. "Mary, where are— Who the hell are you?" His expression turned from fear to anger when he saw Jonathan and his team standing in a loose circle around the living room.

"Sweetie, I'm fine," Mary said, standing from her spot on the sofa. "I'm sorry to scare you, but it was the only way we could think of to get you to come down off the mountain for a visit."

Tommy's eyes never moved from Jonathan, who had taken a position closest to the door. "Who the hell are you?"

"That's a little complicated, Tommy, but for now, how about you call me Scorpion?"

"That's not a real name."

"No, it's not, but it will do."

Mary moved to the boy with her arms spread, ready for a hug. "I'm sorry I scared you."

He held out his hand and stiff-armed her in the chest. "Right," he said. "I get that. Who the hell are these people?"

"Will you take a seat?" Jonathan asked.

"No."

Boxers slipped behind Tommy to physically block the door. It was okay if the kid didn't want to sit, but he wasn't going to bolt out, either.

Jonathan shifted his weight to one side and crossed his arms. "Let me start with who we're not. We're not cops and we're not FBI and we're not any government agency who can send you to jail."

The words resonated with relief on Tommy's face, giving Jonathan two data points simultaneously. The kid was aware that he was breaking laws, and he wasn't willing to pay too high a price for breaking them.

"But to be perfectly honest, we are very close to people who are all of that. You know that you've been committing the worst kind of treason up there on the mountain, right?"

As color drained from his face, Tommy's eyes burned right through Mary. "You brought these people into our house?"

"She didn't bring anyone anywhere," Jonathan said. "We showed up on her front step and she got stuck with us."

"But I'm also worried about you, Tommy," Mary said.

Jonathan winced. Mary's part in this drama was finished. She brought the kid to the house. Now he wanted her to shut up. He didn't want this to get personal.

"Who are you to worry about me?" Tommy snapped.

"Easy, kid," Boxers threatened. "The lady cares about you. Show some respect."

Tommy whirled to give Big Guy some lip, but clearly did the math and decided not to. Boxers saw it and smiled. "Smart," he said.

"Here's the thing," Jonathan said. "If we've done our research right—and we usually do—you and your pals up on the mountain are planning to commit murder. I confess I don't know the details, but whether it's one person or a thousand, someone famous or just another guy, murder is murder, and that means a quick trip to a padded table and a sharp needle. Know what I'm saying?"

Tommy's eyes darted all around the room. If he was planning a reply, it wasn't finding traction in his mind.

Jonathan continued, "Within a couple of days or a couple of weeks, it's all going to come down around your ears. I'm certainly not going to keep your secret, and when I tell the people I intend to tell, you'll learn a thousand lessons about what it means to piss off Uncle Sam."

Without thinking, it seemed, Tommy helped himself to a hard-backed chair to Boxers' left. His color was looking progressively less right. "Are you arresting me?" he asked. His voice was barely audible.

"You haven't been listening," Jonathan said. He kept his tone soft, reasonable. "I'm not a cop. I have no power to arrest you."

"So, what do you want?"

"Information," Jonathan said. "Treason Camp is ending tonight."

Tommy scowled as he considered the words, and then he laughed. "What are you, five people? We've got two hundred up there."

"We're very good at what we do," Jonathan said.

"Nobody's that good. Are you bulletproof, too?"

It was a throwaway question, and Jonathan didn't honor it with an answer.

"I'm not a snitch," Tommy said. "I'm not a sellout. Why should I tell you anything?"

Jonathan had been waiting for that question, and he took his time. He grabbed the matching chair from the other side of the door and pulled it over. He spun it around so the back faced Tommy, and he straddled it. "I'm betting on the fact that you're a survivor," he said.

"After the fan has scattered all the shit that is going to hit it, people will go to jail. People will die, and those who don't will see their lives ruined." He pointed at Tommy's nose. "You've got a lot of life ahead of you. It'd be a shame for you to spend the next sixty, seventy years staring at the same concrete wall, only seeing the sunlight through bars or chain-link."

"You said you can't arrest me," Tommy said.

"That's right. But those who can are going to depend on me to point to the ones who should live in a cage. Help me out, and I won't point to you. Help me out, and you're free and clear."

Tommy shot a look to Mary. "Please, Tommy. Listen to him."

"How do I know I can trust you?"

"I'd be interested in hearing all of your other options," Boxers said.

Tommy whirled to look at him. Look up at him.

"I can't," Tommy said. "They're my friends. My family."

"They're murderers," Jonathan said. "Did you know that your man in charge, Victor Carrington, has already murdered one man and tried to murder a second? Did he mention that to you?"

Tommy just stared. Jonathan sensed that he was searching for an angle to work.

"Please, Tommy," Mary said. "You need to do the right thing."

"That's what they're doing," he said. He slapped his thigh for emphasis. "They're doing the right thing. They're taking the country back from the bastards who hijacked it."

"The bastards who hijacked the country were elected

by the people who are being hijacked," Jonathan said. As Tommy became more agitated, Jonathan softened his voice. "Think it through. Imagine you win. Imagine the wildest win possible. Say you rally a million people to your side. Then what? What's the next step? You kill a few politicians you don't like, along with a couple of senators and congressmen and maybe a few judges. What happens next?"

Tommy's eyes darted around the room. He seemed to want to be anywhere but here. "Things . . . change."

"No, they don't," Rollins said.

"Shut up, Madman," Jonathan snapped. He didn't need any help. "We've got a million-plus soldiers in uniform, Tommy. Thousands of federal law-enforcement officers and hundreds of thousands of police officers of various stripes. I suppose you'll pull a few of those to your side, but not all of them. Not a quarter of them. What are you going to do with the state legislatures and the town councils and the courts? You cannot win."

"Then why do you care so much?" Tommy asked as if it were a killer question, an argument ender.

"To plug the bleeding before it starts," Jonathan said. "As bad an idea as your operation is, it can be effective enough to hurt a lot of people. It's enough to send the economy into the toilet and create panic in the streets. If that's the picture of victory, then you can have a victory, but you have to know that it can't last. The American people will demand order, and sooner than later, they will all turn against you. You. Cannot. Win."

Tommy shook his head. "I won't turn on my friends."

"Then save your friends' lives," Jonathan said. "You say there are two hundred of them up there. I only want one of them. As far as I'm concerned, the rest of them are free to go."

"You don't mean that," Tommy said.

Jonathan crossed his heart. "Hand to God. If I can get my hands on just one, then everything else falls apart and goes my way."

Tommy looked like he might cry. He looked to Mary, and then he looked to the ceiling. Jonathan gave him all the time he needed to sort through his options. "Take me, then," he said.

Jonathan smiled. He almost wanted to give the kid a hug. *Greater love has no one than this, that one would lay down his life for his friends.* How many times had he discovered himself in that same space? "I admire the sentiment, Tommy," he said. "And I mean that from the bottom of my heart. But you're not the one I'm looking for."

Tommy cocked his head.

"Victor Carrington," Jonathan said. "Him alone. I don't need the others."

Tommy's face sagged. No matter what followed— no matter what recovery Tommy attempted—Jonathan now knew that Victor Carrington was someone important. He'd mentioned the man twice, and had gotten the same reaction two times.

"I don't know who that is," Tommy tried.

"Don't," Jonathan said. "Don't insult our intelligence. That's just wrong."

Tommy stared.

"You need to wrap your head around the fact that you really have no options," Jonathan continued. "I know that sucks—even though it saves your life—but that's the way it is. You can help us, or you can spend the rest of your life in prison. I need you to choose quickly."

Tommy continued to stare. It seemed to be too big for him to comprehend.

"Listen to the man, Tommy," Mary said. "They're giving you a way out."

"I don't want a way out. I don't *need* a way out. What we're doing is for the good of everyone."

"You're going to lose," Jonathan said. He didn't know how he could be any clearer. "If we don't win a total victory tonight, then the FBI and the army and God knows who else will be here within the next few hours to finish it for us. If it gets to that, you and your surviving friends—however few there are—will all go to jail."

"And you'll be dead," Tommy said.

"No, we won't," Boxers said. "Look at me, then look at you. Which one of us do you think has survived more battles?"

Jonathan didn't appreciate the interruption, but he did appreciate the thought.

"Why do you want him?" Tommy asked. "You know, assuming I know what you're talking about."

"We're going to bring him to justice," Jonathan said. "I put it that way to be one hundred percent honest with you. Whoever he is in reality, he's fomenting traitorous activity, and he has to pay for that."

"He's doing the will of the people," Tommy said.

"He's doing the will of a few people," Jonathan corrected. "I hate to keep harping on the same point but he's doing the will of a precious few, all of whom are destined to end up dead or in prison. Mary tells us that you're a smart kid. Tell me that this hasn't occurred to you."

"There's only one reason for secrecy," Jolaine said. Apparently, she had a hard time dealing with any period of time that existed without the sound of her voice. "And that reason is to hide something."

"And who are you?" Tommy asked. Exactly the reason why she should have kept her mouth shut. Until that moment, Jonathan and Boxers were the only people in the room as far as he was concerned. Now, he was aware of a crowd, and Lord only knew what might come of that.

"They call me She Devil," Jolaine said.

"Why?"

"She Devil, you shut up, too," Jonathan snapped. "That's her name for the same reason that my name is Scorpion. The very rough translation is that it's none of your business." He paused to regroup, to change his approach.

Jonathan stood from his chair and swung it around to sit normally. When his butt was back in the seat, he leaned forward and rested his elbows on his knees. The posture of a concerned father. "Maybe we got off on the wrong foot," he said. "We brought you down off the mountain on false pretenses, and then we startled you when you came through the door. Nobody likes that."

"No kidding."

"But Tommy, I really want you to do some serious thinking here. Consider what your options really are. Let's start with what's *not* going to happen. We are not releasing you to go back up to the top of the mountain. That's not in play. So your options are to help us and stay out of prison, or go to prison. In that context, I don't understand why you're not one hundred percent on our side."

"Because they're my friends," Tommy said. His voice caught on *friends,* and Jonathan remembered what Mary had told them about his youth.

Jonathan let those words hang in the air for probably a full minute. Entire wars were won by young men who fought to protect their friends. God knew that loftier nationalistic ideals were nowhere on the horizon among junior soldiers once the shooting started.

"Look at me, Tommy," Jonathan said softly. It took awhile, but he waited for it. "I can't tell you how thankful I am that I have never been in the position I'm putting you in. Loyalty is important. It really is. But for every man who finds himself in a tough spot, the time comes when he must ask himself what it is that he's loyal to. Think about the mess in Washington. Whether you want to look at President Darmond or at either party in the House or the Senate, the reason why we're in the crappy times we're in is because those assholes are loyal to something other than the people they've sworn to represent."

Something sparked behind the kid's eyes. Jonathan sensed that he had begun dancing close to the rhetoric the kid had been hearing up in the camp.

"I don't pretend to know what it is," Jonathan continued. "Whether it's their party or the hatred of the other side, or just plain greed, they have locked up our system of governance for reasons that have everything to do with themselves, yet nothing to do with us. Can we agree on that much?"

Tommy seemed startled to be presented with an actual question that demanded an actual answer. He thought for a few seconds. "Sure. I can agree with that."

"Good. I'm glad. Then you can understand how people can become loyal to things and people and causes that ultimately have less to do with the greater good than they do with self-aggrandizement."

Tommy stared some more. Jonathan thought he saw tears. That was almost always the precursor to a breakthrough. He went for it.

"Tommy, your friends are plotting bad things, and they're trying to take you with them. That makes them not your friends. They've been using you."

Tommy shifted his eyes toward Mary, who was instantly on her feet. He stood, too, and as they embraced, the disappointment and embarrassment poured from the kid. At the sound of the soft sobbing, Jonathan looked toward Boxers, who had his arm—his hand, actually—draped around Jolaine's shoulder. No one wanted to witness anyone else's pain.

"Listen to them," Mary whispered in his ear. "Please listen to them. I don't want you to come to harm."

A minute passed, maybe more. Finally, the kid found control. He kissed Mary on the cheek and pushed her away. "What do you want me to do?"

Chapter Twenty-five

"**H**ow accurate is this photo?" Jonathan asked. All of them—Jonathan's team, plus Mary and Tommy—stood in a cluster around the screen of Jonathan's laptop computer. Venice had uploaded a satellite photo of the top of the mountain.

Tommy studied the image carefully. It showed a sheared-off mountaintop with all manner of buildings, mostly of prefab construction. "I can't tell you building by building without really studying it," he said, "but it looks pretty close."

"Take your time," Boxers said.

Tommy did exactly that, probably five minutes in silence to process all of the details.

"Let me help," Jonathan said finally. He pointed to the cluster of trailers in the lower, southeastern corner of the site. "These look like barracks to me. Is that right?"

"Yes. That one there is mine." Tommy pointed to one of the trailers in the image.

"How are the barracks arranged? How many people in each trailer?"

"Ten," Tommy said. "Five to a wall. The latrine is at the end."

Jonathan noted the military term for toilet. "Showers, too?" he asked. The question had no purpose other than determining the relative size of what he was looking at.

"No," Tommy said. "The showers are here." He pointed to a separate trailer. It made sense, when you thought about it. Running zoom pipes out of commodes was an order of magnitude less complicated than providing high-volume running water. To focus the showers in a single facility made a lot of sense.

"Are you telling me that two hundred men all shared the showers in one little trailer?" Rollins asked.

"We're on shifts," Tommy said. "Assigned times."

Much of what Jonathan saw in the rest of the image was fairly self-explanatory. Shooting ranges look like shooting ranges, no matter where they are, and the big tent is always the mess tent, both observations confirmed by Tommy.

"What are those buildings on the top of the hill?" Jolaine asked, pointing to the middle-top of the screen.

Dylan scrolled in closer, highlighting a series of twelve buildings, six to a side, flanking an access road and each served by what appeared to be gravel walkways.

"That's officer's country," Tommy said. "Quarters and offices. That's the motor pool right there." He indicated a parking lot just to the north of the northernmost building.

"Which one is Carrington's?" Jonathan asked.

Tommy said nothing for several seconds, then he said

taller in his seat and declared, "You'll never get through to him. You'll never get through the security."

"I find that hard to believe," Jonathan said. His heart raced at the thought of the kid volunteering in a fit of pique the information he expected to be most difficult to wring out of him.

"Multiple fence lines, each of them patrolled. One gate in each fence, and they're guarded by some serious soldiers. They'd as soon kill you as look at you."

As Tommy spoke, Dylan scrolled back up to about two hundred feet. The image moved, and then he dialed back in again. "These are the gates here, right?" he asked.

Tommy stopped himself. He blushed and his ears turned bright red. He said nothing, but clearly he understood what he had done.

"Let's go back to the buildings on the hill," Jonathan said.

"I'm not talking to you anymore," Tommy said.

"I bet you're wrong," Boxers said.

"Not now," Jonathan said. The kid didn't need to feel any more threatened than he already—

The sound of vehicles racing up and stopping abruptly outside drew Jonathan's attention. Rollins, who'd never left the window, said, "We've got company, people."

Jonathan darted to the window and as he saw the rest of his team coming to join him, he pointed to Jolaine. "She Devil, you keep an eye on Tommy."

Outside, two SUVs that looked remarkably like the one Tommy had driven pulled to a stop in the middle of the street and disgorged four people each for a total of eight. They all carried some form of AR-15 variant, and they headed as a group toward the door of the diner downstairs.

"Shit," Jonathan spat. "We're in trouble. Mary, is there a back door from here?" He drew his Colt. Suddenly, eight rounds plus a spare magazine didn't feel like nearly enough.

"Only downstairs," she said.

The very downstairs where the armed posse was swarming.

"Fire escape?" Jonathan asked. Surely even a burg like this had fire codes.

Mary pointed to a room in the back. "The window," she said.

The whole building shook as the invaders slammed the door open and entered the diner.

"She Devil, you take Tommy and head to the fire escape. Boomer, you and Madman are next. Big Guy and I will hold them off and join you."

"I'm up here!" Tommy yelled. "They've got guns! They're going out the fire escape!"

Rollins was closest, and he punched the kid in the head. The force of the blow should have knocked him out, but instead, it seemed to energize him. Tommy leapt from his chair and charged Rollins, knocking him off-balance. In a move that Jonathan found impressive, the kid grabbed Rollins's gun hand with both of his own and twisted the pistol free.

"Don't!" Jonathan yelled.

Tommy had the M9 in his hand, but he fumbled with the trigger.

"Tommy!" Mary yelled.

Outside, the pace of motion on the steps peaked. The entire second floor seemed to vibrate.

Tommy's grip settled on the pistol and he swung it toward Rollins.

Jonathan shot the boy through the temple from a range of five feet. Through the pink mist of bone and brain, he saw a lamp shatter from the bullet that passed all the way through.

Mary screamed, lunged at Jonathan.

Jonathan swatted her away and pushed her to the floor. He kept her there with his knee planted between her shoulder blades as the apartment door flew open from a massive kick that actually cracked the length of the door panel.

Jonathan saw a rifle poised to fire and he shot the face behind it. And the face behind that one. To his right and rear, Boxers didn't have an angle on the door itself so he fired through the wall adjacent to the opening. More people fell.

With his weapon up and ready, Jonathan rushed the door, emptying his remaining five rounds blindly through the opening. As the slide locked, he thumbed the mag release and dropped the empty from the grip. By the time it hit the carpet, he'd seated the spare mag and slammed the first of seven fresh bullets into battery.

As he passed through the doorway into the hall, he didn't even try to step around the first two bodies, but rather walked on them, on their torsos, for the best balance in an inherently unbalanced stance. He encountered two more bodies in the hallway itself, one clearly dead of a head wound, and the other writhing from a gut wound and a neck wound that pumped blood at an unsustainable rate. Apparently the vest he wore was not ballistic after all. Jonathan lifted the man's rifle away and pulled two of his spare mags out of their pouches.

He racked the bolt to make sure a round was cham
bered, and he double-checked the safety to make sure
was off. He noted that this was a civilian model of th
AR-15, with no full-auto mode. He slung the rifle ove
his shoulder and stuffed the mags into his back pock
ets.

"Call an ambulance," the wounded man moaned.

"Where are the others?" Jonathan asked.

"Oh, man, I'm hurt. Please, get me an ambulance."

"You're not hurt, you're dying," Jonathan said
"Where are your friends?"

The light in the man's eyes dimmed and then wer
out. Jonathan felt a tug. Killing people was never easy
always took a piece of you away, but watching them di
carved a bigger chunk.

"Did I get him or did you?" Boxers asked. Some
times, Big Guy just pushed too hard.

Gunshots cracked in the night outside, at first just
single shot, and then a sustained exchange. Jonatha
heard pistols and rifles, and knew right away that they'
found the dead men's friends.

"Scorpion! Scorpion! We're under fire. Black sid
off the red corner."

"Arm up," Jonathan said, but Boxers had alread
slung two of the rifles. Rollins, meanwhile, stood in th
doorway watching. He seemed stunned. "Madman!
Jonathan barked.

"Leave him," Boxers said.

Yep. Jonathan switched his radio to VOX. "Scorpio
and Big Guy are on the way," he said.

Dylan's voice said, "Expedite. She Devil's out c
ammo, and I nearly am. If you button-hook to the re
side, you should be able to flank them."

At the base of the interior stairs now, Jonathan charged forward toward the diner's front door. "Are you and She Devil under cover?"

"Affirm. Behind a Dumpster in the back."

"Stay there and stay down. We're coming into position." It troubled him that the shooting had subsided. Typically, that meant the enemy was making a move. "If you see a shadow up close, shoot it. It will not be a good guy."

Jonathan led with the rifle pressed into his shoulder, walking at a low crouch, fully aware that Boxers was two steps behind in the same posture. As he stepped through the door into the night, he swept left and right and found no threats.

"Come out from hiding!" someone yelled. "We see you behind that container. Your friends are dead upstairs. You cannot get away."

"I don't feel dead," Boxers whispered on the air. "Do you feel dead? You don't look dead."

Jonathan ignored him. Boxer got positively jolly during gun battles, and this one clearly was not over yet. In the distance, he heard an approaching siren.

As they turned the corner to the left, his heart rate increased. The four bad guys had fanned out in a jagged line that ran perpendicular to his position, and they seemed to move with fair precision as they approached the Dumpster. Even in the dark, Jonathan could see the bullet punctures in the steel.

"You take the two on the right," Jonathan whispered into his live mike. There would be no warning, no challenge.

Before Big Guy could acknowledge, gunfire erupted from the second floor of the diner—from Mary's apart-

ment. Enormous muzzle flashes strobed from the win
dow. Eight, maybe ten rounds in rapid succession.

Jonathan dropped to his knee and swiveled to con
front the threat.

"That was me," Madman said over the air. "Chec
them, but I think I got them all."

Jonathan broke his aim on the window and pivote
back to the soldiers in the alley. None moved, all glis
tened. He and Boxers approached the sprawled bodie
cautiously but deliberately.

"Just when I think I understand Stanley, he goes an
surprises me all over again," Boxers grumbled.

It took less than twenty seconds to determine tha
they were all dead. "We're clear," Jonathan said on th
air. "Four sleeping inside, four in the alley." The soun
of the siren grew louder.

Dylan and Jolaine stepped out from behind th
Dumpster. "That siren is the police," Jolaine said. "W
need to get out of here."

Jonathan turned and craned his neck toward the soun
of the approaching emergency vehicle. He could se
blue lights painting the facades of buildings at the en
of the street. "Nope," he said. "No time. Drop all fire
arms that don't belong to you and gather on me."

"Hope you know what you're doin', Boss," Boxer
said softly.

"Remember," Jonathan said. He was still on VOX
"We don't kill cops."

"You remember that I do not go to jail," Boxer
replied.

Rollins cleared the front door of the diner at abou
the same moment that Dylan and Jolaine sidled up
Jonathan switched his radio back to PTT.

"What's the plan?" Rollins asked.

"We're gonna talk," Jonathan said.

"Come again?" Jolaine said.

"Y'all welcome to the team," Boxers said. "One thing about my friend Scorpion is he always keeps you guessing."

"What are we waiting for?" Dylan asked.

"For the cop to decide what he wants to do." The vehicle had stopped short of the diner, and now had turned its lights off.

"I think he's a-skeered," Boxers mocked. "He's not going to come to us."

"Okay, then," Jonathan said. "We'll go to him." He looked to the sloppily parked vehicles. "You three take that one," he said, pointing to one of the SUVs from the raiding party. "Drive down to the Batmobile, grab it, and then drive both vehicles back here."

"Why?" Rollins asked.

"You know, Madman, I hate the *why* thing at times like this," Jonathan snapped. "Just do it."

"What are you two going to do?"

"The talking," Jonathan said.

Boxers chuckled. "Yeah, because that's what I'm so good at."

"When you drive past the cop, he might try to stop you, but don't stop," Jonathan instructed. "Don't threaten him, and don't ram him, but don't stop, either. Drive up on the sidewalk if you have to."

"Oo-uh," Rollins said. Apparently, some habits were hard to break.

"Boomer, you drive the Batmobile," Boxers said. "I don't want Madman's cooties on the spot where I have to plant my ass."

"Jesus," Jonathan muttered.

Big Guy rumbled a laugh.

"Showtime," Jonathan said. "Let's go."

As the other three swarmed out toward the SUV, Jonathan stepped out of the alley into the street and waved to the cop car. The headlights came on, as did a floodlight, which nailed them in the eyes, effectively blinding them.

"Halt," said a voice over the siren speaker. "Come no closer."

"Let's split," Jonathan said. "You walk down the left sidewalk and I'll go down the right."

"Split the target, split the fun," Big Guy said. "You're Whiskey Indigo-ing again, aren't you?"

"I'll tell you later," Jonathan said, and they split their course. He was betting on two facts, both of which were pretty sure things. One, that the cop was alone on his patrol, and two, that he was scared fairly shitless. That would make him at once skittish and open to negotiation.

"I'm telling you to stop!" the cop said. With only one floodlight, he had difficulty figuring out who to illuminate. The beam switched from one side to the other.

"We mean you no harm, officer!" Jonathan shouted.

"Stop them!" came a shrill voice from behind. It was Mary. Jonathan could only imagine how much counseling she was going to need. "They're murderers!"

"I'm not telling you again to stop!" the cop announced.

Jonathan stopped behind a parked Chrysler to up his odds a little for the next part. Behind him, he heard the SUV that contained his team approaching up the street.

As he calculated it, they had room to pass by the patrol car, but it would be tight. Jonathan beckoned for the truck to drive up on his edge of the sidewalk, and he pressed up tight against the parked Chrysler to let them pass.

"I'm going to shoot!" the police officer said.

"No, you're not," Jonathan shouted. Then he lowered his voice. "Can you hear me if I speak at this volume?"

"Yes," the cop said into the public address speaker.

"And I can hear you just fine without that," Jonathan said.

"Stop them!" Mary yelled. "They killed Tommy Piper."

"I swear to God I will shoot you!" the cop shouted.

"And I swear to God that the survivor will kill you!" Boxers shouted. "Turn off the friggin' speaker!"

"We mean no harm, Officer," Jonathan said. He kept his tone modulated to be the essence of reason. "And as much as *I wish my friend would keep his mouth shut!*"—he shouted that part for Boxers to hear—"he raises a good point. Because we mean no harm, and because you cannot shoot two targets at opposite poles at the same time, you should avoid shooting either one."

"Who are you?" the cop asked. He shouted that time through his open window. Down the length of the street, lights were coming on. Less than three minutes had passed since the end of the gunfight, but it felt like much longer.

"I'm a man with a mission," Jonathan said.

"He's a murderer!"

"Excuse me, officer," Jonathan said. Then he turned to face back toward the diner and shouted, "Mary, please shut up!"

Back to the officer. "I won't deny that there's been some unpleasantness here tonight, sir," he said. "Truth be told, the coroner and undertakers are likely to be working overtime for a while, but I swear to you, sir, that I was not the aggressor. The late Tommy Piper who Mary refers to was in fact about to shoot my friend when I shot him. He chose to work for the bad guys. We, on the other hand, work on the side of the angels."

"Are you confessing to a crime?"

"No. I'm confessing to a bad night. The rest is up to a jury."

The cop, who was faceless in the midst of all the bright lights, took his time for the next part. "I need to arrest you," he said.

"Yeah, well, that's not going to happen," Jonathan said. "Not tonight. I've got a lot of important things to do, and going to jail isn't on the list."

"So you're resisting arrest," the cop said.

"No. I'm refusing arrest. Is that a crime?"

A pause. "I don't understand."

"I don't blame you," Jonathan said. "It's a confusing situation. And it's a situation that—and I mean no offense here—you have no control over." Beyond the police car, at the far end of the street, Jonathan saw approaching headlights. One big vehicle and one bigger vehicle. That had to be the cavalry.

"You can't just shoot up my town and get away with it," the cop said.

"I didn't do that," Jonathan said. "People tried to

shoot up my friends and me, and we shot back. That's a different proposition."

Another pause. Longer this time. "I can't just let you go."

Tommy's SUV and the Batmobile pulled in behind the cop car. "I understand where you're coming from," Jonathan said, "but sometimes principle finds itself at odds with reality. In this case, the reality is that you can't possibly stop us."

On the far side of the cop car, Boxers was already moving toward the driver's side of the Batmobile. "Are we cool, Officer?" Jonathan asked.

"No," the cop said. "Of course we're not cool."

Jonathan considered that. Admired it, even. Who cannot admire honesty in the face of overwhelming firepower? "I'll tell you what," Jonathan said. "Remember I told you that we were on a mission?"

He actually waited for a response. Finally, the cop said, "Yes, I remember."

"Good. Well, our mission is at the compound that you know about, but I'm guessing you ignore, up there on the top of the mountain. If you want to come and arrest me, that's where I'll be. When you get your reinforcements, come on up and we'll talk." He shielded his eyes from the blinding light and saw a twelve-year-old behind the wheel. Okay, maybe twenty-five, but he looked twelve. "Do we have a deal?"

"Who are you?" the cop asked again. "Are you FBI or something?"

"Go with *something*," Jonathan said.

"What are you going to do?"

Boxers was already in the driver's seat of the Batmobile, and he tapped the horn. Jonathan regarded the kid with the badge who sat behind the wheel of the police cruiser. He considered how much life he had in front of him, and how terrified he must be, not just of this confrontation, but of the activities that swirled around him every day that required him to pretend to be ignorant.

"We're going to end it," Jonathan said at last. "I can't promise that all the danger will be gone by tomorrow morning, but a lot of it will. In two weeks, there'll be nothing left."

"Then you have to be FBI," the cop said. His tone was significantly lighter than before.

"I'll stick to my guns," Jonathan said. "We're *something*. And we're on the side of the angels."

"But you killed people tonight."

Jonathan inhaled deeply and noisily through his nose and let it out as a silent whistle. "You and your buds are going to do an investigation," he said, "and that investigation will show what it shows. One of those things will be that Mary of Mary's Diner lost someone close to her. She lost him because I shot him through the head, but I shot him through the head because he, Tommy, the friend, was going to kill *my* friend, code named Madman, because Madman was an idiot and let Tommy get his gun. All of this happened because we lured Tommy off the mountain to give us information on what's going on up there, and the shitheads in charge launched a hit team to keep us from doing that."

The cop said nothing.

"Are you still there?" Jonathan asked.

"You don't have enough people," the cop said.

"You're not the first person to tell me that," Jonathan replied. He stepped out from behind the car and started walking toward the Batmobile. His path took him directly past the driver's window of the cop car. As he passed, he stopped and offered his hand. "My name is Scorpion," he said.

"That's not your real name."

"Obviously."

"Officer Parks," the cop said. He shook Jonathan's hand.

"I really am sorry for the mess," Jonathan said. "That's a lot of bodies and a lot of blood, and I'll tell you up front that no matter what fingerprints or physical evidence you or the crime scene guys find, you'll never find us."

"Because you're *somebody*," Parks said.

Jonathan smiled. "But of course, in this case, being *somebody* is tantamount to being nobody."

Chapter Twenty-six

The two-vehicle caravan traveled blacked out, navigating via night vision goggles. At this hour—just shy of four in the morning—there was no oncoming traffic to be concerned with. Boxers led behind the wheel of the Batmobile with Jonathan riding shotgun and Jolaine in the backseat. Rollins and Dylan followed in the other vehicle and stayed close to their rear bumper.

Jonathan had entered the coordinates of the camp's key components into his handheld GPS. The first milestone they needed to reach was the outer gate, which was still eight miles away. He keyed his mike. "First chance we get, we're going to pull off on a side road and plan." The truth of the matter was that the team hadn't spoken as a group since they'd left Officer Parks wondering what had just happened, and there were issues that needed to be discussed.

Boxers found a dirt road off to the left—might have been a driveway—and pulled in far enough to leave room for the other vehicle behind them. Jonathan had long ago disabled the interior light, but when the follow vehicle opened a door, the splash of illumination washed out his NVGs for a second and ruined his night vision.

Without waiting to be told, Rollins hit the dome light with the muzzle of his pistol, bathing them in manageable darkness again. They gathered around the hood of the Batmobile. "Now is it time to tell us what that shit was all about in town?" Rollins asked.

"How about you start with what happened in the apartment, Stanley," Boxers said.

"The kid knocked me off balance and got my gun," Rollins said. "Shit happens."

"The kid weighed a hundred thirty pounds soaking wet," Big Guy said. "How does someone that size knock a professional soldier off balance?"

"Look here, Lurch, I'm not going to stand here—"

"Shut up, Madman," Jonathan snapped. "Excuses don't count, and you know it. They never have. You jeopardized the mission and got that boy killed. Own it."

"You're the one who shot him."

"So he wouldn't shoot you," Jolaine said.

"And what was going on with you in the hallway afterward?" Boxers pressed. "You looked like you had a stroke. Maybe pissed yourself."

Rollins peeled his NVGs off his head and donned an aggressive posture. "What are you implying, Lurch?"

"I'm implying that you locked up," Boxers said. "And if you want to continue to breathe through any natural orifice, you'll remember my name."

Rollins turned to Jonathan. "Are you going to let this go on? Is this the way the famous, vaunted Scorpion preserves unit cohesion?"

"Those are officer words, Madman," Jonathan said. "Desk words. Out here, cohesion is organic. It's earned or it's not. You froze in there, and you owe us an explanation." He removed his own NVGs so he could look his former commander in the eye. Jonathan had no doubt that this was new territory for Stanley Rollins. Somehow, he'd been one of the few to earn his way up through the ranks of the Unit by kissing asses along the way. Out here, though, there was no rank to pull.

"Let's not forget that I was the one to eliminate those final bad guys," Rollins said.

"From a sniper's nest," Boxers reminded.

"You took them out," Jonathan said. Then, to Boxers, "He took them out, no doubt. That's good. Well done. Thanks for that. But you also froze in the apartment. You can talk around it all night or you can explain what happened."

It had long been a tradition in the Unit for operators to confess their errors, to own up to them, and to institute a plan that would keep them from happening again. It was never a comfortable moment—and some operators never regained trust after a mistake—but it was essential. There was no slot for an operator who put his own ego above the safety of the team.

Rollins took his time. Jonathan would have waited all night. "He startled me, okay?" he said. His tone was combative, but it was an important first step. "I let my guard down, and then he was on me. I didn't expect it, and then I was looking down the barrel of my own pistol. I guess I peeked at the face of God and realized that I wasn't ready to meet him."

"So, you were startled," Dylan said. Jonathan read his comment as a peace offering.

"Exactly."

But they weren't done. "What about in the doorway?" Jonathan asked. "After the initial burst of gunfire, Big Guy and I charged the hallway, but you were still standing there."

"What is this, Scorpion? A chance to settle scores? A chance to make me look bad?"

Jonathan answered from the heart. "God's honest truth, Madman. You've already made yourself look bad. I'm giving you a chance to redeem yourself. Ain't none of us hasn't already been where you were, but to function with the team, you have to own up to it." He waited. "That was your cue."

It was hard. Jonathan could see it weighing on the colonel as a near-literal, physical weight on his shoulders. Maybe a first in Stanley's ass-sucking, miserable life.

Rollins scanned the faces of his colleagues. Jonathan thought he was looking for some kind of reprieve, and was relieved that he apparently found none.

"I'd never seen someone killed who looked so much like us," he said, finally. Both the content of the statement and the honesty it represented shocked Jonathan. And he was hard to shock. "I've killed skinnies and I've killed Hadjis, and I've killed my share of . . . Central Americans. But blond, blue-eyed, and so young. Never been there before." When he spoke that last sentence, he drilled Jonathan with his glare.

"You're welcome," Jonathan said.

"I confess it took me a while to recover," Rollins said. "Are we square now?"

"There's likely to be a lot more of that," Jonathan

said. "I don't expect to find a lot of Somalis at an abandoned coal mine in West Virginia."

"I'm not a racist," Rollins said. "I understand the mission. Yes, I had a moment of hesitation, but let's get back to the fact that I was the one who eliminated the threat of the other shooters in the alley."

"Duly noted," Jonathan said. Beyond the frustration, he read the colonel's explanation as sincere. People who shoot other people for a living often find refuge in the clichés about differences. It's a difficult transition to do the job that needed doing in full knowledge that in the eyes of the law, you were committing murder.

"The police are going to come after us," Dylan said. "Why aren't you worried about that?"

Again, Jonathan gave it him straight. "Because that's a concern for later. I don't think they're going to be a big problem for us, given the target we're going for, but if they are, we'll deal with it. I think it's significant that even though I told them where we were going, I don't hear a parade of emergency vehicles coming this way."

"You think they're on our side, don't you?" Jolaine asked.

"I'm kind of betting on it," Jonathan said.

"Why would they be on our side?" Dylan asked.

"Because they're frightened of what they know is going on in their backyard, and they're equally frightened by their powerlessness to stop it."

"Did you discover a crystal ball I'm not aware of?" Rollins asked.

"The boss has good instincts," Boxers said. "Otherwise, he'd have gotten me killed a dozen times by now."

"So, we assume we don't have to fight to the front and the rear," Dylan said. "What's the plan?"

"Stand by one," Jonathan said. He moved back to the shotgun seat of the Batmobile, opened the door, and removed a nylon bag from which he removed his laptop. As he did, he keyed the mike on his radio. "Mother Hen, Scorpion. Are you still awake?"

Fifteen seconds passed. "I'm right here."

"Has anything come from your talks with my special friend in Florida?"

Lee Burns, a former Unit operator, had invested millions and made hundreds of millions from a geosynchronous satellite imaging system he called Skys-Eye. Marketed for use by petroleum companies who wanted to scour the globe for better oil fields, Lee also made a decent living from others who were willing to pay for a high-tech peek into specific places. Because he had known Lee personally, Jonathan told himself that the man only provided real-time satellite imagery for the good guys, but when he thought about it really hard, he worried that the math didn't work.

"If you had booted up first, you wouldn't have to ask," Venice said. "Turns out he had birds watching the oil fields in Pennsylvania anyway. You're just a sideward glance."

He typed in the appropriate information and an image appeared on his screen. It looked much like the static satellite shot that Venice had provided earlier, but this one showed images of people on the ground.

"These images are perfect," Jonathan said. He oriented the laptop so the rest of the team could see it. He clicked a few keys and the image switched from visual to infrared. "SkysEye is persnickety," he said to the team. "The images are clean, but they only refresh every four or five minutes. That means we're largely looking into the past. Still, it's instructive. Look here." He pointed to a cluster of white human-shaped forms against a black background.

"That's the outer gate," he said. "Looks like they've got eight sentries on it."

"Those are the ones we can see," Rollins said.

Jonathan scrolled out. "Those are the ones we have to worry about," he corrected. "There might be others, but those are the ones we have to worry about initially. When it comes time to strike, we'll wait for the most current image and work off of that."

"That's a doable number," Jolaine said. "It's all about marksmanship. Five of us, eight of them."

"So, we're just going to shoot them outright," Rollins said. His tone carried an edge of disbelief.

"We could always ask them to surrender," Boxers said.

"They're the enemy," Jonathan said. "All of our intel, such as it is, indicates that the guards at the gates are shooters. If we take that to heart—and I think we have to—then we have no other choice."

"The trick is getting them all simultaneously," Dylan said. "That's hard to do when you have fewer shooters than people to be shot."

Jonathan sensed that Boxers was about to say something snarky, and was grateful when he chose not to. "We can work that out," Jonathan said. "Just make sure your weapons are suppressed, and that your first, say, three rounds are subsonic. If we get close enough— which we will—then we should be able to shoot our- selves into a free pass through the front gate."

Jonathan and his team understood that *silencers,* as the lay public thought of them, did not exist in reality. The *phut-phut* sound that people had come to believe in from the movies simply did not exist. Even if the baffles of the suppressor at the end of the barrel had been capable of diffusing the sharp crack of the propel- lant that launched the bullet downrange, the bullet it- self traveled faster than the speed of sound, which created its own explosion—a sonic boom—as it traveled through the air. By using subsonic rounds—bullets that were designed to fly slower than the speed of sound—they had the greatest chance of penetrating the compound without creating a big stir.

"If we can get past that spot," Jonathan continued, "we have options available to us."

"So, being assigned to that gate is a death sentence for the sentries," Rollins said.

"Exactly," Jonathan replied. "That's the price of be- ing a bad guy." He didn't understand why the colonel was having such a hard time understanding these basic tenets, and he really didn't care. "Is this going to be a problem?"

"I don't think so," Rollins said.

"I need something stronger than that," Jonathan said. "Mine will be among the asses on the line, and if there's any doubt—"

"I'll do my job," Rollins said.

"There's the inspiration I was looking for," Boxers said.

"Okay, stop," Jonathan said. "Madman erred, he atoned, and now we're ready to go."

"I don't think we are," Dylan said. "I don't have a clue what the plan is."

"I'm not sure I know what the mission is," Jolaine said.

Jonathan settled himself for the explanation with a deep breath. "The mission is to nab Victor Carrington—or whatever his real name is—and bring him in for questioning. The questioning, in the meantime, should reveal the details of whatever the larger plan is. That means getting all the way in to the heart of the compound, making the grab, and then getting out again."

"Let's not forget the part about living to see another day," Boxers said.

"First and foremost on my mind," Jonathan replied. "The trick is to level the playing field. That means operating in darkness."

"Don't we know that they have night vision?" Dylan asked.

"Yes," Jonathan said, "but we also know that they have electrical power, and that they illuminate the camp at night."

"That means they're not using their night vision," Rollins said.

"Exactly. So once we're in, we need to get to their power plant—"

"That's it right there," Big Guy said, pointing to the

computer screen. "You can tell by the heat signature. Nothing looks like a power plant but a power plant."

"How do we know it's the only one?" Rollins asked.

"If you see another, point it out," Jonathan said. "Otherwise, we roll the dice on a better-than-average bet."

"How do you want to handle it?" Dylan asked.

The power plant was just inside the second fence line, sitting more or less by itself beyond the enlisted quarters.

"We need the darkness," Jonathan said. "Without that, we're five targets among two hundred shooters."

"That's bad, right?" Boxers said.

"That's *very* bad. Big Guy, you, Madman, and I will take the generator. When the place goes dark, Boomer and She Devil will take out the guards at the second gate. Then, while we rush to Officer's Country to make the snatch, Boomer, you and She Devil will create a diversion by tossing a thermite grenade at the base of a trailer."

"They're going to go like kindling," Dylan said.

"Yep," Jonathan agreed. "Here's hoping that the soldiers inside are confused and move quickly."

Dylan asked, "After the compound is dark, where do you want us?"

"In support," Jonathan said. "That's the best I can do right now. We're going to have to play the rest of it by ear. There's bound to be some resistance."

"I think that is the understatement of the night," Boxers said. "Some resistance."

"It's all about speed, people," Jonathan said. "Shock and awe. If it moves and has a gun, shoot it. You're each fully loaded with five-five-six, right? Four hundred rounds?"

The team looked at each other. "More or less," Jolaine said.

"That's a lot of firepower," Jonathan said. "Y'all have moved through this space before. It's about keeping people's heads down."

"And not catching a stray bullet," Rollins said.

"Well, that, too," Jonathan agreed.

"Once we have Carrington," Dylan said. "Then what? How do we get down off the mountain?"

"We drive like crazy," Jonathan said.

"Really?" Rollins gaped. "That's your plan?"

"Unless you have some air assets we haven't thought of."

"This is feeling a little like a suicide mission," Jolaine said.

Boxers snapped his finger. "Stop. We don't do suicide missions. We wreak havoc and bring people to justice, but we do not do suicide missions."

"Listen to Big Guy's words," Jonathan said. "We're about to cross the full-commitment point, the point of no return. If you have doubts, this is the last opportunity to express them."

As he scanned their faces, they all looked away. Except for Boxers, who'd heard the speech a thousand times and responded with a huge smile and two thumbs up.

"So, are you done?" Big Guy asked. "Is it time to go mess people up?"

Jonathan didn't like the feel of the group. Just as

lovers shouldn't go to bed with angry words between them, warriors should not face down an enemy in the midst of anything but complete trust.

"Okay, listen up, everyone," he said. "There are those among us who will never be friends, but that fact should not take away from our willingness to die for each other. We have to be a *team*. If there are any among you who cannot reach that place—and I'm looking at you, Big Guy and you, Madman—I need you to tell me right now. Because once we get back in those vehicles, there's no turning back."

"I'm good," Big Guy said.

"Me, too," Madman agreed.

"What about you two?" Jonathan asked, addressing She Devil and Boomer.

"What about us?" Boomer said. "We've been nothing but easy."

"Okay," Jonathan said. "Before we move, I want everybody in black. I mean ink stain black. Balaclavas included. Full body armor, including chest and back plates. Kevlar lids. Full soldier, understand?"

In the flatbed of the Batmobile, each of the operators had his or her own duffel, complete with the appropriate equipment. Boomer and Madman had to make do with loaners, but Jonathan had enough in the storeroom to make the selection easy. When they were fully kitted up, all of them wore a slung long gun—Boxers and Dylan with 7.62 millimeter HK 417s, and the others with M27s, modified HK 416s chambered in 5.56 millimeter. In addition, Jonathan and Boxers each carried holstered MP7s along with their regular sidearms. For good measure, Dylan wore a pistol-grip Mossberg 12-gauge slung under his arm.

In their rucks, each team member carried a couple of GPCs—general purpose charges made of C4 with a tail of detonating cord—a spool of detonating cord, a few grenades, and an assortment of triggers and detonators, plus one claymore mine apiece. Throw in ten spare mags of thirty rounds each for the long guns, and assorted spare ammo for the pistols, plus essential first aid gear, and it was a knee-sagging load.

"You sure you can carry all that?" Boxers asked Jolaine.

It was the wrong thing to ask, and her glare showed it.

"I meant no harm," Big Guy said. Jonathan felt a pang of sympathy. Boxers was good at a whole lot of things, but none of those things involved sensitivity.

"I want everybody on PTT," Jonathan said—push-to-talk. "After the first guards are down, we're essentially splitting into two teams, and I want you to be vivid and complete in your descriptions of what's going on. Are we clear on that?"

Nods all around.

"Okay, do a radio check." Jonathan pressed the switch on his radio and said, "Scorpion, radio check."

"Mother Hen reads you loud and clear."

And so it went, person to person, voice to voice.

"NVGs on," Jonathan said, and the team pulled the $30,000 four-tube arrays over their eyes. "Boomer, you and She Devil are Alpha. Big Guy, Madman, and I are Bravo. Alpha holds back until Bravo announces that we're in position. After that, we're game on. Everybody good?"

Affirmatives all around.

"Okay, hands in," Jonathan said. He placed his right hand out, palm down, and waited for the others to stack their hands on top of his. "To success," he said.

They bounced their hands, and then they were ready to go.

Ian looked at his alarm clock, and adjusted to the fact that he was not going to get any sleep tonight. He should have heard back from *somebody* tonight. It was nearly four in the morning for heaven's sake. If he hadn't heard from Tommy Piper, then he certainly should have heard from Biggs or Little. Yet he'd heard nothing.

In his bones, he knew that something was wrong. That's why he had sent Little and Biggs—Dumb and Dumber—into town with a team to bring Tommy back. Ian had let his emotions get in the way of sound thinking, and now he was caught in that netherworld between knowledge and intuition. He knew that he had no reason to sound the alarm, but that little voice in his head—that devil on his shoulder—kept whispering that it was time to go to full alert.

Yet that was a step forward from which there was no step back. He worked with amateur fighters who were becoming more talented with each passing day, but they did not possess the discipline of real soldiers. If he brought them to full alert, then there had better be a fight to be fought, otherwise there would be no response to the next alarm.

He considered waking Karras to inform him of his concerns but he decided against it, largely for the same reasons. Karras was more a panicker than a tactician. He would respond at two hundred percent to whatever input Ian fed to him, and while under most circumstances, that would be considered a good thing, in this one, it just put a huge burden on Ian to be correct.

Resigning himself to a very long night, Ian turned on the lights, showered, shaved, dressed, and got a head start on the day.

Chapter Twenty-seven

Boxers parked the Batmobile in the road, in the dark, two hundred yards from the main gate of the compound. As he climbed out, Rollins took his place behind the wheel. Twenty-five yards ahead, Boomer and She Devil had pulled to a silent stop, waiting for word that the rest of the team was in position. It worked to their benefit that tonight brought a new moon, meaning no moonlight at all. That meant that the bad guys could see virtually nothing, beyond the wash of the light mounted on a pole overhead. On the downside, that lack of visibility always brought a kind of hyper-awareness that translated to disturbingly fast trigger fingers.

Jonathan took the right side of the road while Big Guy took the left. They moved swiftly yet silently despite the one-hundred-plus pounds of gear they carried. As with any invasion, the first moments made all the difference in the world. The plan in this case was to use overwhelming force in the least offensive way.

Jonathan found a spot among the trees that gave him

a panoramic view of the first checkpoint. As they had expected, a total of eight guards had amassed around the lift-up gate. Each of them was impressively armed with AR-15 variants and sidearms but only the sentries closest to the gate seemed to have an inkling of a mission. Five of them happened to be on Jonathan's side of the road.

"I'm in position," Jonathan said. "I have five targets and they're all in the open." Of course, as soon as the first of those targets fell dead, the in-the-open part would likely reset to something closer to run-for-their-lives. Or, in the worst case scenario, it would reduce to fight-for-their lives. Jonathan possessed enough ego and enough confidence that either choice would end the same for the bad guy.

"I've only got three," Boxers whispered. "Want to change sides?"

As he often did at times like these, Jonathan ignored him. "Okay, Alpha, you're on. You have the lead, but we have eyes on. If bad guys start falling, adjust accordingly."

Jonathan wedged his left side into a solid spot in a tree trunk, and wedged his M27 into the soft spot of his shoulder. Through his scope, he had a perfect, full-bodied image of the rightmost sentry, as he would for any of the others if he scanned. Once he confirmed that the guards were not wearing night vision themselves, he thumbed the button for the infrared laser that would paint the target he wanted to shoot. Because the beam was IR, it was invisible to anyone who was not wearing night vision. Of all the force multipliers he and his team utilized—read, *cheats*—the ability to turn night into day was hands down the greatest. And because the night was so well lit for him—and had been for so many years of operations—it was sometimes startling for Jonathan to realize just how blind his adversaries were when they died.

He saw the headlights of Alpha's vehicle approaching from the left-rear, but he looked away, concentrating on that rightmost sentry—the one he would shoot first. Jolaine and Boomer stopped at the gate. Through his radio, Jonathan heard Dylan say, "We're coming back from town."

"They didn't like it," Boxers said over the net. Jonathan could see nothing from Dylan's side, the driver's side. He increased the pressure on the trigger. The sentry still seemed clueless. And he seemed very young, though well armed.

"We're hot, we're hot!" Boxers said. In that instant, through the periphery of his NVGs, Jonathan caught two muzzle flashes from what would have been Jolaine's weapon in the shotgun seat. Jonathan painted his target's left eye and felt the trigger break, launching a bullet downrange. Simultaneous with the vague *bang* that escaped his weapon's suppressor, he noted the splash of gore as the target fell, but he'd already moved on. He shifted his aim a couple of clicks to the left, where he found another sentry reacting in panic, raising his rifle to his shoulder. Jonathan killed him before the sentry was halfway to being set.

And then there were no targets.

"Clear on the right," Jolaine said.

"Clear on the left," Dylan agreed.

"Nice job," Jonathan sad. "Now to phase two." He

considered combining the teams back into a single vehicle, but decided against it. This way, if they needed to split up for operational issues, they could. Also, the lighter SUV—the one without the armor plating and bulletproof windows—was more agile. He also decided against stashing the bodies. With the gate wide open, if anyone happened to drive up at this hour—and he thought that to be unlikely—the fact that the guards were gone would raise a loud enough alarm. Plus, speed mattered, and he didn't want to take the time.

Before getting back in the car, he did, however, take the time to drop an infrared strobe at the gate, just in case the ride out was more intense than the ride in.

The camp designer had chosen to place the electrical generator building inside the first fence, but outside the interior ring, probably to allow for more secure servicing. If a repair truck was necessary, it could do what it needed to do without actually entering the main part of the compound. Getting to it, however, was going to be a tricky proposition.

While the outer ring fence was only dimly lit, the closer they got to the inner fence, which was quite some distance away, maybe half a mile or more, the night started looking more like day. Because of the steep terrain, there was no line-of-sight visibility to worry about yet, but that would come soon.

Jonathan looked to his GPS. He could see the generator building, but he cursed himself silently for not being more thorough in his markings. "Stop a second," he said, and Boxers brought the vehicle to a halt. "Mother Hen, Scorpion," he said into his radio.

"Go ahead."

"Do you have eyes on us?"

"Not a current one, no. The image won't refresh for another two minutes."

"Do me a favor, will you, and upload the specific coordinates of the generator building access road to my GPS."

There was silence for a few seconds and then she came back with, "Did someone drop the ball on research?" There was a time, not too long ago, when Venice stayed away from light banter and focused exclusively on the mission. Jonathan missed those days. "Okay," Venice said. "The numbers are on the way. Need any others?"

This was the problem of planning an op on the fly. You forgot important stuff that you didn't realize you needed until you needed it. "Affirm," Jonathan said. "Give me every intersection on the map."

"Okay," she said. For whatever reason, Venice never used military jargon, preferring *okay* to *roger.* Jonathan never asked because he didn't much care, and she was so damn good at what she did that it didn't matter. "You have the buildings, right?"

"That's affirmative," Jonathan said.

"Okay, numbers will be up as I get them." In the worst case, Jonathan knew that that would be five minutes, max.

"Break, break," Jonathan said over the air. "This is Scorpion. Final check before we go hot. Boomer."

"Check."

"She Devil."

"Ready."

Jonathan turned to his drive du jour. "Madman."

"Check."

And, finally, "Big Guy."

"O Captain! my Captain!"

Jonathan laughed in spite of himself. "You know that poem doesn't end well for the captain, right?"

"Color me ambitious," Boxers said. "And quit thinking so hard."

The ambient light troubled Jonathan. Given that they were surrounded by two hundred armed men, they remained at a distinct disadvantage as long as they were visible. The silence of the night bothered him, too. The camp produced its share of mechanical noises, but for the residents here, they had a sense for what was normal and what was not. If they'd had any decent training at all, they would have learned that anything out of the ordinary is cause for alarm. Because of its weight and girth, the engine that propelled the Batmobile produced a grumble that Jonathan wagered was unique to the sounds of the camp.

"That's our access road right there," Jonathan said, pointing to the barely discernable driveway that cut through the barely present grass. Ahead, on the far side of a short hill, a bright glow filled the sky, washing out his night vision. He flipped the switch on the four-tube array to transition to infrared. Because of the brightness of the background, the light-amplification technology of the standard NVG setting could miss objects or people hiding in the shadows. Because infrared (IR) worked off of the heat emitted by the objects he observed, even the best camouflage couldn't conceal a healthy human being. There was a price to be paid however—as there was always a price to be paid for any technology—and in this case, the price was detail

While night vision looked like green daylight, IR imagery looked like a moving X-ray.

"Alpha, Scorpion," Jonathan said into his radio. "Hold tight here at the intersection and give us cover. Big Guy and I are going to make things dark again."

"You know that's going to create a panic, right?" Rollins said off the air.

"I'm kind of counting on it. I'm betting it gets pretty damn dark out here," Jonathan said. "If they shoot each other, we don't have to worry about them shooting us."

"I really don't feel comfortable out in the open like this," Boxers said. "Can't we move the vehicles under the trees over there?" He pointed to a copse of hardwoods a hundred yards away.

"No," Jonathan said. "I hate the noise. With the sentries dead, and out of sight of the second gate, I think noise is our greatest enemy."

Boxers laughed. "Well, give it a couple of minutes. We'll have more enemy than we know what to do with."

"Madman, you stay put. Keep the engine running, but don't give it any gas. Deploy outside to give us some measure of cover. I don't know what it's going to look like in there, exactly, but we'll set the timers with enough to get us back before things go boom." He let the words set for a moment. "You good?"

"I don't like being out in the open."

Jonathan slugged him playfully in the shoulder. "You don't like not being in the middle of the shit," he said. In the parlance of the Unit, he'd just bestowed a compliment—that Rollins wanted to be in the middle of the battle instead of on the outskirts—and it seemed to resonate as such.

Rollins nodded once and opened his door. "Don't take too long," he said. "And remember to keep Big Guy between you and the explosion."

Even Boxers laughed at that as he climbed out the passenger side with Jonathan. "I hate that son of a bitch, but he's not all bad."

Jonathan and Boxers moved in unison, Jonathan facing front, and Boxers keeping up step-for-step moving backward. Between the two of them, by sweeping continuously one hundred eighty degrees, they could keep an eye on every compass point. The fact that a very experienced, very capable team was covering their six o'clock, the most likely route of discovery and attack, made him feel more comfortable, but they still needed to move fast.

Jonathan moved his NVGs up and out of the way as they crested the hill, and he stooped to a crouch. Boxers followed without looking. They'd done this enough as a twosome that they'd learned to think each other's thoughts and anticipate and read each other's moves. Keeping his right hand on the grip of his M27, he used his left to fish though a pocket on his vest to find the ten-power monocular that allowed him to assess the scene in close-up detail. At first glance, what he saw disturbed him.

He pressed the transmit button that now resided atop the chest plate in his vest. "All teams, Scorpion," he whispered. "I count two, three, four, *five* bad guys on the exterior of the power plant."

Behind him, he felt Boxers whirl around to get a look for himself.

"Do you need backup?" Rollins asked.

"Not yet," Jonathan replied. "Stand by."

"Want me to take four of them and you can chase one of them down and beat him to death with your pistol?" Boxers whispered.

"I really do hate you, you know."

"O Captain! my Captain!" Boxers said.

"And sometimes I hate you more than others." Jonathan didn't like what he saw. Why, on a regular night just like any other night, would there be so many people guarding the power plant? Surely, that was not sustainable in the long term. "I think they're on alert," he said.

"For good cause, as it turns out," Boxers replied. "You want the three on the right or the two on the left?"

Jonathan scanned some more with his monocular. If they were in fact on alert, they weren't very disciplined about it. Rather than deploying in an arc around the building, they stood in a single cluster, engaged in conversation. Whatever alert might have been issued had not been taken seriously.

"Kinda get the sense that this isn't the first time they've been rousted?" Boxers whispered.

"Exactly what I was thinking," Jonathan said.

"So, I take the right?" Big Guy asked.

Jonathan hated this part. For every soldier—real, wannabe, or poser—there existed no more thankless job than that of sentry. You spent endless hours staring out into nothing, only to be the first poor bastard dropped by the enemy during an incursion. The best a sentry could hope for was to see the bad guys approaching and sound the alarm. If he lived that long, he'd done his job. There was no more random way to leave this mortal coil than what lay ahead for these poor souls.

"Affirmative," Jonathan whispered back. He flipped the selector switch with his thumb. The cluster of targets stood maybe eighty yards away, too far away for the IR lasers to be useful. With his NVGs tilted out of the way, he would depend on the simple optics of his telescopic sight. He'd set it for ten-power, which allowed him to fill the sight picture with the images of the young men he would kill. Because he was at eighty yards instead of the fifty yards for which he'd zeroed in the scope, he settled the reticle slightly above the target's head, anticipating impact just forward of the bad guy's ear. His first target was about three inches taller than his second, so it would take some skill to get both shot right. He took five, maybe ten seconds to rehearse the necessary pivot.

When he was set, he said, "I'm going full-auto in five, four, three, two . . ." When he got to the silent *zero,* his trigger broke, and bullets flew. His first target took two rounds essentially through the same hole behind his eye, and the second died in a millisecond as the first impact sheared off the top of his head.

"Clear," Boxers said. Jonathan thought he'd heard Big Guy's shots, but was it really three rounds? They recorded as one.

"Clear," Jonathan said. *Pleasant journey to the other side, boys.*

Thinking as one, they held their positions, unmoving, as they swept the area for additional targets. After thirty seconds, when none had shown themselves, Jonathan whispered, "Let's go."

They advanced quickly yet carefully down the hill, their weapons at the ready. Jonathan ignored his sight and the tunnel vision they brought in favor of

anoramic view. Because it was nighttime and the area
was well lit, it was disturbingly easy for a badguy to
tay in the shadows if he knew what he has doing. It was
he rare amateur who had that level of training, but
onathan and Boxers had both lived as long as they had
by assuming the best-trained enemy with the worst pos-
ible motivations. In these conditions, the most telling
iveaway would be movement. The human eye had dif-
iculty discerning forms in the dark, but it compensated
y being hypersensitive to movement. Jonathan figured
t had something to do with his great-great grandfather
o the nth power who managed to survive by adapting
o the fact that every living being he encountered was a
otential predator.

The power plant building was bigger in reality than
t looked in the satellite imagery. The footprint was the
ame—call it twenty feet by fifty feet—but it was
nuch taller, every bit of fifteen feet of ceiling. Inside,
he generator churned just as it was supposed to, but as
hey got closer, Jonathan worried about the noise
rowning out the sound of approaching bad guys.

"Moving," Jonathan said. A walkway of sorts—a
vorn path, really—led from the access road to the left,
r green, side of the building. Jonathan knew that the
Jnit had abandoned the old color-coded side designa-
ions in favor of compass points, but old habits died
ard. Besides, in Security Solutions, Jonathan got to
vrite the SOPs.

With the exterior wall of the building now able to
ive them cover on one side, they shifted in what looked
ike a choreographed motion to press their shoulders to
he wall—Jonathan's right and Boxers' left, because
3ig Guy was walking backward.

"I feel like I'm on a damn stage," Boxers said. Th lights were that bright.

"Yeah, well, we're gonna fix that." The closer Jona than got to the building, the more impressed he wa with the stoutness of its construction. This wasn't som pole barn thrown up at the last minute. This was a soli building with corrugated steel walls, erected on poured-concrete base. He wondered if it had been buil for this purpose, or if Carrington and his crew had hi jacked it for their own means. Not that it mattered.

His heart sank as he arrived at the door. The stee panel had been set in a steel frame and the lock was high-security job that had an old analog keypad entry He'd been hoping for a padlock and hasp, or at the ver least a pin tumbler lock like the one they'd found i Bud's.

"We're gonna need to use a GPC to get in here," h said.

"That's a lot of noise," Boxers said.

"I'm open to suggestions."

They both stewed on the problem for a few seconds and then Boxers finally said, "I'm on it."

Jonathan pressed his transmit button. "Alpha, Scor pion. We're going to have to do an explosive breac here. That's going to wake some people up about fiv minutes before we want them awake. Get eyes on th sentries at the inner gate. Let me know if we can tak them out before we shoot the GPC."

Dylan looked to Jolaine. "Is he serious?"

"Scorpion is always serious once we're hot."

In his ear, he heard Rollins ask, "Where do you want Madman?"

"Right where you are," Jonathan said. "When it's time to go, it will be time to go right friggin' now. Alpha, acknowledge my last, please."

Dylan said, "I copy that you want us to advance in the light. Is that correct?"

"Affirmative," Jonathan said. "Try not to be seen."

"Well, no shit," Dylan said off the air. "Roger," he said to Jonathan. "This is crazy," he told Jolaine.

"We don't know that yet," she said. She opened up her laptop, bringing up the detailed satellite image of the compound. Dylan watched over her shoulder as she clicked in the details and did the calculations. "That bunch of trees over there," she said, pointing thirty yards distant, "looks to be part of a constant chain of cover. If we hang to that, we should be able to get pretty close to the sentry station. That will also put us pretty close to the first objective."

Dylan saw what she was describing, but didn't like it. "We can't bring the truck up there."

"Obviously. We'll have to hoof it."

Dylan's gut reaction was instant and emphatic. "What about the rest of the gear?"

"We bring it with us."

"I don't like this," Dylan said. "If we kill the sentries in the light, then the entire plan gets knocked sideways."

"We have to adapt," Jolaine said.

"No," Dylan countered. "We need a workable plan."

"There's always a plan," she said, shrugging into the straps. "Scorpion *always* has a plan. He adapts quickly."

"But *we* don't have a plan," Dylan objected.

Jolaine gave him a hard look. "No, we don't, but w
have the next best thing. Orders. Everybody is count
ing on us to do what we've been told to do."

"This is crazy." The key to survival in the SpecOp
world was to plan the shit out of everything. Ever
contingency had a countercontingency. Superior plan
ning, superior firepower, and overwhelming force
Those were the secrets to living long enough to retire

Jolaine started walking. "Are you coming with me
or am I going alone?"

He had to hustle to keep from getting left behind a
he donned his ruck. He was still getting it settled on hi
shoulders as he started across the field. Jolaine had t
wait for him after she'd reached the tree line. Like him
she had rocked her NVGs out of the way, and it wasn
till he got very close that he saw the anger in her eyes

"Listen to me, Boomer," she said. "I don't know
about your past—other than the bad stuff—and I don
much care. I know that you served in the Unit wit
Scorpion and Big Guy right before everything wer
bad, and I know that Madman had a big role in wha
did go bad."

Dylan recoiled from the words. How much had Dig
ger shared with his new civilian friends?

"All of that is past now," she went on, "and becaus
you're on my team, I choose to trust you and your judg
ment." She thrust a finger at his face. "But don't eve
second-guess the command structure of this team i
my presence again."

Dylan scoffed and held up his hands in surrende
"Hey, I didn't say I wasn't—"

She didn't let him finish. "I don't care what you were or weren't. I saw hesitation, and hesitation scares the crap out of me. These are the best operators I've ever worked with. If they say green is red and that shit smells like roses, then my first assumption is that they are correct. If you have a problem with any of that, then we need to part company right now."

This was officially new territory for Dylan. He'd never gone into combat with a civilian before—or a woman for that matter—and the only times that he'd ever played fast and loose with well-established, heavily tested and toned rules, it had always been on his own terms. It was also a new experience to encounter Jolaine's intense level of personal loyalty to the boss. He wondered where that came from.

It took less than ten minutes to walk the distance along the tree line. As they approached the road, the trees thinned to the point of barely being visible. In the distance, maybe fifty yards away, and uphill, he could see where the road met the fence and presumed that to be the location of the gate. This area was very brightly lit from lights atop twelve-foot poles. Dylan thought he saw four people milling about, so he brought his rifle up to verify through his scope. He dialed in ten-power magnification and confirmed what he'd thought.

"Mother Hen, She Devil," Jolaine whispered over the air. "Can you confirm four sentries at the inner gate?"

A moment passed. "Mother Hen counts six. Plus two in the woods south of the tree line, unless that's you."

"That is us," Jolaine confirmed.

"When you pull out, do you see any others?" Dylan asked. His question drew another glare from Jolaine, as if she considered herself the only one qualified to talk on the radio.

Venice took awhile with her answer for this one. "Negative, Boomer. Those at the gate are the only humans I see out in the open. There's a small herd of deer, though, directly to your east."

"Can you take two from here?" Dylan asked. As soon as the words were out, he knew he'd made a mistake. He'd accidentally emphasized the word *you*, making it sound as if he'd questioned her marksmanship as a function of his own.

"Anything you can do, asshole," she said.

He considered apologizing, but realized that it wouldn't matter. Therefore it could wait. Standing to his full height, Dylan pressed his weapon against the trunk of a stout hardwood and settled the stock into the soft part of his shoulder. He achieved his desired cheek weld against the pad on the 417's stock, and without looking, he verified that the selector switch was clicked to full-auto. Taking out two men with automatic weapon fire was tricky, but it wasn't as hard as most people thought, provided you knew what you were doing. The first target would be dead well before the sound of the gunshot arrived, and by the time the second target realized there was a problem, he'd be dead, too. "On your count, She Devil," he whispered.

"You're taking right, I'm taking left, correct?"

"If that's the way you like it," he replied. Actually, because he was standing to Jolaine's right, it was the only solution that made sense, but for some reason it felt good to be a little shitty.

"Targets acquired?" she asked.

"On your count," he repeated.

"In three, two, one . . ."

A millisecond before Dylan's trigger broke, his first target stooped down, out of the sight picture. It was a clear miss, and rather than chasing Target One with the ten-power scope, he shifted to Target Two. He sent five rounds downrange in less than a second, and the target died instantly.

While the suppressors on their weapons muffled the report of the rifle, and all but eliminated muzzle flash, they'd burned through their subsonic loads, and the whip cracks of passing bullets told the survivors that they were under fire.

Someone up there started shooting back.

Dylan had never heard rifle fire sound so loud.

Chapter Twenty-eight

"**W**ho's shooting?" Boxers said, his head whipping around to the source.

"Shit," Jonathan spat. "They started the war without us. Open the goddamn door."

Boxers dropped to one knee and readdressed the slab of C4 explosive he'd packed against the latch assembly on the door.

Jonathan grabbed Big Guy's discarded ruck and took five giant steps back to leave Boxers a clear path for retreat. Big Guy pulled the pin on the seven-second fuse, plugged his ears with gloved fingers and moved back to Jonathan's position on the corner nearest the driveway.

GPCs were dependably loud, but this boom seemed louder because of the silence of the night and the shock wave's reverberation through the corrugated steel wall

The sound was still rolling through the hills when they pushed themselves off the wall and streamed back to the shattered door. The charge had blown a nearly perfect round hole in the steel where the lock assembly used to be, and had knocked the frame askew. Boxers got to the door first, stuck his beefy hand through the still-glowing hole, and pulled. It took two enormous yanks, but it opened, squealing metal-on-metal as the surfaces separated.

Stepping inside, Jonathan turned on the light. Why not, at this point? An industrial generator hummed in the center of the building, its exhaust pumped through ductwork out into the night. The total footprint of the machinery, including the service catwalk and appurtenances, covered an area of about twenty feet square. Someone had invested serious bucks into this thing.

"We just need it to be effective, Big Guy," Jonathan said. "We don't need it to be pretty. Just kill the power." He knew that left to his own devices, Boxers—who rightly considered himself a master of the explosive arts—could engage in overkill.

"You might want to step back outside," Big Guy said. He lifted a thermite grenade from its pouch on his vest, and walked toward the main buss bar panel. He pulled the pin, placed the grenade on the top of the box, let the safety spoon fly, then quick-stepped out of the way. Little more than a can filled with a mixture of fine aluminum powder and iron oxide, thermite grenades had notoriously unreliable fuses once the safeties were disengaged, and once ignited, they burned white-hot through just about any surface—including the copper conductors that lay behind the panel door.

Jonathan stood just outside the door, scanning the night for threats. "Hey, Madman," he said into his radio. "We'll be ready to go in about thirty seconds." Behind him, he heard the hiss of the thermite igniting, and he felt a blast of heat. Two seconds later, Boxers approached from his blind side and lifted him up and moved him over a couple of feet.

"I don't want you to get hurt," Big Guy said. Then he pulled an M67 frag grenade from his pouch and pulled the pin. "Frag out," he said, and he tossed the bomb inside the room. As the grenade left his hand, the thermite did its job and the camp went black. Four seconds later, the ground shook from the grenade. Responding to the disapproving look he got from Jonathan, Big Guy said, "I feel better when I can hear the boom."

Ian's head snapped up at the sound of the rifle shot. Had there been a negligent discharge? He'd worried about the firearms discipline in this place ever since he'd arrived. But he thought for sure that with the extra training—

A second gunshot. Then a rapid burst of them. Then an explosion.

"Dammit!" His hand snatched his radio from its charger and he keyed the mike. "Gate One, Gate One, this is Carrington. Report."

Nothing.

"Gate One, respond."

Nothing.

The lights went out. He was bathed in blackness. The lights were out everywhere throughout the camp. "Good Christ, we're under attack," he said to himself. He keyed his mike again. "Communications, this is Carrington. Sound the general alarm."

"Communications" was the radio designation for the central command post that occupied a reinforced concrete bunker in the middle of the compound. When it was completed, it would have its own electrical supply and would serve as a kind of castle keep for moments just like these. *When it was completed.* As in, three or four weeks from now.

"We don't have electricity, Colonel," said a young voice from the radio. "We got no general alarm to sound."

God*dammit.*

His heart racing, Ian tried to piece together the next steps. It had been a long, long time since he'd been in a real shooting war, and back then, he'd been the aggressor. He tried to make the pieces fall into place.

When he realized that shooting had stopped, he also realized that his sentries were either dead or had run away. He'd tried to put the best of the best on perimeter security, but it was never possible to know what people were going to do once the shooting started.

Whatever the facts turned out to be, the perimeter had been breached—whether by one or by a hundred, he didn't know. But it was time to get the soldiers organized. He grabbed his vest and his M4 from its spot next to his bed and headed for the door.

If the sentry had stayed on the ground, he probably would have survived. Instead of accepting his gift of life for what it was, however, and no doubt panicked by the sudden deaths of those surrounding him, he chose to return fire to the night, first a single shot, and then a long burst, his shots all going wild. But flying bullets were flying bullets, and given enough time and a large enough number, sooner or later the odds got bad for anyone downrange.

Dylan was distantly aware of the sound of the GPC being shot as he settled the reticle of his gun sight on the sentry's muzzle flashes. Before he could pull the trigger, though, Jolaine let loose with a long burst that silenced the other shooter.

"Let's go," she said, and she was moving again.

There was an odd X-factor in play, Dylan thought. It was as if she didn't recognize him as part of the team so much as a burden to be born, a rookie to be babysat. When this was all over, he was going to have some words with her about that. For now, he followed.

After seven or eight steps, the tree line ended, leaving them exposed to the lights that—

Finally, darkness fell. Real darkness, too, the kind you only get out in the middle of nowhere, exposing a clear sky that looked cloudy with stars. Dylan pulled his NVGs into place and vision returned. Up ahead, beyond that second gate, commotion grew. People were waking up—literally and figuratively—to the notion that something was wrong. Gunfire, explosions, and then darkness all triggered fear, and fear triggered confusion.

That last part—the confusion—was what he and Jolaine had been assigned to maximize.

With the advantage of darkness now, they advanced toward the gate at a run, instinctively keeping low. Dylan kept his rifle up and ready, scanning continuously for any targets that might present themselves. Digger's orders could not have been clearer. Anyone with a gun would die. Anyone who ran away with a gun in their hands would die, too, because retreating and surrender are entirely different things. Those who merely retreated often formed up again to reengage. By not killing them the first time, you exposed yourself and your team to the risk of death on the flip side.

Ahead of him, Jolaine vaulted two of the dead sentries without slowing, then dropped to a knee about eighty feet farther in. He mirrored the posture next to her. "Is there a problem?" he asked.

"Just want to make sure I have my bearings," She Devil replied. "Those are the barracks over there, do you concur?" Pointing with her whole hand, as if it were a karate chop, she indicated what looked like a residential arrangement of trailers downrange and to the right.

"I concur."

"All right, then," she said. "Let's do our job."

Ian stepped out into the darkness of the front stoop and was dismayed to see so little activity. Shots had been fired, for God's sake. There'd been explosions. Where was the . . . panic? "Wake up, everyone!" he yelled. He fired a long burst of 5.56 millimeter rifle bullets into the ground just beyond the stoop. "We're under attack, goddammit!"

He strode down the steps of his quarters and across the gap that led him to the next quarters. These officers were of lesser rank, and occupied four to a building. He pounded on the door with the butt of his rifle, then threw the door open. "Where are you?" he yelled. He stared into the darkness, where he saw movement but no faces. "I want every man in this room dressed, armed, and out of here in less than one minute. Less than ten seconds. Find your teams, organize them, and be prepared to fight."

"Who are we fighting?" Little asked.

"Whoever's fighting us back. Weapons and ammo, men. Right by God now!"

Dylan and Jolaine advanced in lockstep on the cluster of house trailers that served as barracks for the residents of this place. Dylan had a hard time thinking of them as soldiers. Alpha's mission was to roll a thermite grenade to the base of one of the trailers. Nothing was more disorienting to anyone—soldier or civilian—than waking up the knowledge that your world was on fire. Given the fact that trailers such as these were constructed mostly of plywood and glue, that world would ignite with startling speed.

The plan was both simple and brutal, and in his heart, Dylan was happy that the barracks residents had had a chance to wake up. Since the first moment when they'd discussed the plan, he'd been plagued by images of people burning to death in their beds. Friend or foe, that's a shitty way to go.

By the time they got to the end of the street, there were visual and audible signs of movement within the darkened residences. Time was running out for the attackers to have maximum benefit of their diversion.

"How many thermites do you have?" Jolaine asked him.

"Four."

"Me, too. You take left, I'll take right. I figure every other building will do it. Ready?"

"Whoa, whoa," Dylan said. "Our orders are to light one structure. We want a diversion, not a wholesale execution."

Even through the distortion of night vision, Dylan saw the serious set of Jolaine's face. "We're here to win," she said. "The more fires we set, the bigger the diversion, the better our chances of survival."

Dylan didn't know what to say. This was crazy.

"Give that look to someone else," Jolaine said. "Self-righteousness works better coming from someone who didn't kill American agents from a couple hundred yards away."

"Hey—"

"Suit yourself," she said. "I have a job to do, and apparently I'm doing it alone."

She took off at a jog down the center of the street, her rifle slapping against her body. As she passed the first trailer on her right, she lobbed a grenade. It rolled under the steps to the main door and ignited with ferocious intensity.

Dylan stood still, anchored in place for five, maybe ten seconds—long enough for her to lob her second grenade to the base of a trailer on the left-hand side of the road—unsure what to do. This was horrible. This was murderous.

The sound of panic growing in the first trailer snapped him out of his fog. Even if Jolaine was a psycho, she was still a member of his team. He owed her security. With his rifle up and at the ready, he took off after her. By the time he caught up, the first trailer was well involved in fire, and people had begun spilling out into the street. Four other trailers were also on fire.

And the screaming had started. There are no screams

like those of a man on fire. He had heard it many times in his past, and every time was a new exercise in nausea. Warfare would be many times more gratifying if it weren't for the killing it required.

With the new source of light—the fires—he lifted his NVGs away and turned to see Jolaine's face. He wasn't surprised to see her smiling.

"Scorpion, Alpha," she said into her radio. "Diversions are active. We're going to take out targets as they present. Advise when the primary is achieved, and we'll join up."

"Scorpion copies."

Dylan was horrified. "Now we're going to snipe people as they flee a burning building?" he asked.

"Only if they're armed," Jolaine replied.

"Jesus, that's murder."

She hit him hard with a glare. Her NVGs up and out of the way, the intensity of her eyes was well north of frightening. "I figured this was the part you'd be best at."

"Did I just copy that Boomer and She Devil are going to kill people as they run out of their burning quarters?" Rollins asked over the engine noise as he barreled toward the gate at the second ring.

"That's what I heard," Boxers responded. The fact that he didn't editorialize indicated to Jonathan that Big Guy was as horrified by the thought as he was.

But he kept his mouth shut. He couldn't think of a single instance in his career where a discussion of the morality of an ongoing mission inured to the benefit of the ongoing mission. As they passed through the gate, he ignored the bounce as Rollins rolled the Batmobile over a sentry's corpse. "Do you know where officers' country is?"

"Committed to memory," Rollins said. "Oh, my God," he added, pointing toward the roiling plume of flames.

"Holy Christ," Jonathan said. "How many fires did they start?" It was a rhetorical question, the answer to which was, *too many.*

Big Guy looked uncomfortable sitting in the seat that wasn't driving. In the backseat, as he was with Jonathan, he looked like he might explode. For all of the misery that was being inflicted, though, not a single shot had been fired since that initial volley—except for a one-off a few seconds ago that seemed to come from the top of the hill they were approaching.

"This is feeling too easy," Jonathan said. He was a little surprised to actually hear the words. He'd been intending to just think them.

"I hate it when you say stuff like that," Boxers said.

Ian saw the fires burning down the hill, and he knew right away that it was the barracks complex. From the color of the flames and the size of the inferno, he knew that it was not a natural fire, and he sensed that it was in fact a diversionary measure. Whoever his attackers were, they knew what they were doing. These were military tactics, but was it even possible that the military would be involved? He could wrap his head around the notion that the FBI had gotten wind of what they were doing, and if that were the case, they might mount a raid that was military in scope, but they would never risk the lives of innocents by setting fires. By running the rats out of the ship.

Yet laws existed to prevent the military from using military tactics on American soil. Truth be told, he'd counted on it, just as countless terrorist groups had counted on American laws to take them a step closer to victory.

But if this was a military operation, where were the helicopters? Where were the drones? The drones in particular were a signature of the Darmond administration, which showed no compunction about vaporizing American citizens without benefit of due process.

"Colonel Carrington," a voice called from behind, from the darkness. "Where are your defenders?" It was General Karras. In the dim, deflected light of the fires, he looked like he might have showered before stepping outside his quarters.

"They're down the hill where you insisted they be," Ian said.

He heard the pops of individual gunshots in the distance.

"And I'm guessing they're being killed, either en masse or one at a time."

"Then do something!" Karras yelled. His eyes showed something north of fear yet south of terror.

Ian spun around, turning his back on Karras, and headed for the next building in officers' country. "What a great idea," he mocked under his breath. "Do something. Why didn't I think of that?" He stepped to the next building and pounded on the outside wall with the butt of his rifle. "Wake up! Get out here! We're under attack!"

Behind him the door to the barracks building he'd just left opened, and four men streamed out. All were armed, but none were fully clothed. He saw underwear and boots, shirts, pants and barefoot, boots and pants and shirtless. Every permutation, it seemed, but for now, the weapons were the important part.

"You four!" Ian shouted, pointing to them. "Fan out and form a defensive perimeter."

They started to move, then one stopped and turned. "How do we do that?"

This was the nightmare. They'd planned their security around keeping people in, rather than keeping them out. The tactics to which the men had been trained were all about small unit offense. He'd offered up nothing for defensive fighting. It had always seemed too unlikely that the camp would have to be defended. Who'd attack it, after all?

Ian walked to the young man who'd asked the question, put his left hand on his bare shoulder and pointed with his right with a wide, horizontal sweeping motion. "Out there," he said, shouting to be heard by the others. "Form an arc around this complex of buildings. Keep ample space between you. Don't fire until I say to fire."

"Who are we shooting at?"

Damn good question. "Don't fire until I give the command," he said again.

At first, it seemed that the residents of the enlisted barracks had chosen to burn to death. For the longest time—although it was probably no more than a few seconds—no one moved. Dylan and Jolaine both had time to take positions at the far end of the street. Dylan used a stout tree for cover on the left side and Jolaine had hunkered in behind a serious tree stump on the right.

Then the yelling started and doors started flying open. Men spilled out of the burning trailers first, most dressed only in undershorts, several in less than that. A few T-shirts, all barefoot. Dylan watched, transfixed, through his scope as the scale of the disaster they'd created continued to escalate.

At the far end—the barracks he thought of as Trailer One—one of the evacuees was clear of danger before he turned and ran back inside. As far as Dylan could tell, he never came out again. He pretended that he couldn't hear the screams of those who were being burned alive. On Jolaine's side of the street, from what would have been Trailer Three, one man dragged another man out of the inferno, only to collapse on the ground. Neither of them moved after that. Dylan felt sick. He'd faced down what had seemed like certain death countless times over his career with the Unit, and he'd always found the physical strength and the strength of character to pull himself through. If faced with the certainty of burning to death, however, he believed he'd eat his own bullet before he'd allow the flames to consume him.

Suddenly, the streets were filled with soldiers. Those who streamed from the trailers that had been spared the horrors of the thermite raced to help those who fled from the infernos.

Across the street, Jolaine's rifle burped. She fired a second time, and then a third. "Am I working alone here?" she bitched in his ear.

Dylan snapped his head back in to the game. *Anyone with a gun dies.*

And per their training, no doubt, many—maybe most of those fleeing from the unburned structures—had spilled out into the street carrying rifles, either in their hands, or slung over their shoulders.

Dylan checked to make sure that his selector switch was settled on single-fire and he settled his reticle on a soldier's head. The trigger broke, his rifle barked and the man fell. At this range, there was no consideration of additional elevation or Kentucky windage. At this range, you pressed the trigger and the target dropped.

The terrified soldiers didn't seem to understand that they were under fire. Dylan settled his reticle on another soldier, took a settling breath, and didn't shoot. "I can't do this," he said, apparently into an open mike. This was murder. And no matter what Jolaine chose to think, this was *different* from the agents he'd killed. They had betrayed him. They had betrayed Behrang, too. Those killings had been *justified*. Those men had been trained killers.

These poor bastards . . . They weren't even soldiers. They were amateurs with guns and delusions.

Who'd already killed a congressman, and had attempted to kill a senator. He tried one more time to shoot. It wasn't in him.

But Jolaine kept shooting. And men kept falling. It took the longest time, but when the reality finally sank in, the terror among the men blossomed to full-blown panic.

* * *

"Hey, Scorpion," Rollins called over his shoulder. "Have you considered that we're going to be silhouetted against those fires as we approach?"

"Have you considered that you've got the steering wheel and the gas?" Boxers replied.

Jonathan ignored them both and keyed his mike. "Mother Hen, Scorpion. Time's getting kind of short here. If you have a picture of Carrington available, now would be the time to share it."

"Workin' it."

The sporadic gunfire from the barracks down the hill was less intense than Jonathan expected. He interpreted it as either a lot of fatalities or a lot of panic. Either one suited him as well as the other.

Apparently reacting to his own observation, Rollins swung a hard right at the base of the hill that would have taken them to officers' country. The Hummer bounced hard as the wheels left the paved surface and ran into the grass, tossing Jonathan into Boxers' side. It was like colliding with a stone wall. Rollins drove with both speed and purpose across the grass, and then perilously close to the woods on the right side as he advanced to whatever landmark he had in mind.

"Think he knows where we're going?" Boxers asked.

"I hope so," Jonathan said. "At this pace, we're going to be there very soon."

"Put your weapons down and no one will get hurt!" Dylan yelled to the swirling mass of panic that was the street in front of the barracks.

"They can't hear you," Jolaine said over the air.

Then, as if to emphasize the point, one of the idiots down there opened fire in their general direction. It wasn't close, but it was the thought that mattered.

"Full-auto," Jolaine said.

"No! What about the wounded and unarmed?"

"The wounded and unarmed are either dying or arming themselves. The smart ones are running." She opened up with a long burst. People fell.

This just wasn't right. It was like fishing with dynamite. With the ammunition they were shooting, after a bullet hit its target it was likely to penetrate all the way through and hit another. Maybe more. At a cycling rate of six hundred rounds per minute, it was devastating. Not a problem when the guy on the other end of the sight was armed, but this was different.

Well, it used to be different. While many ran, too many stayed, and they were, indeed, arming themselves.

Dylan moved the selector to full-auto, picked a cluster of armed survivors, and opened up.

Chapter Twenty-nine

The renewed sound of gunfire encouraged Ian. He hoped it meant that his troops were fighting back. The gunfire was sporadic, though. Hesitant and unsustained. Less encouraging. More officers had joined him from the other barracks, and they'd expanded the defensive circle.

And somewhere out there, beyond the single arc of shooters that defined his defensive perimeter, he heard the sound of a vehicle on the move. "Do you hear that?" he asked to whomever stood nearby. He'd hoped it would be General Karras, but he wasn't sure where the good general had disappeared to.

"Stand fast, gentlemen," he said to the twenty or so soldiers who had dispersed themselves in a wide protective arc. "I believe they're sending an assault vehicle our way."

"They've killed everybody down below, haven't they, Colonel?" someone asked from the line.

"It was a surprise attack," Ian said. "We can repel it."

A few seconds passed.

"*You* can repel it," one young man said. He stood. "This isn't what I signed on for. They're killing everybody down there."

"What's your name?" Ian challenged.

"You don't know? Why should I tell you?"

Ian brought his M4 to his shoulder. "Because I don't want to kill strangers for desertion," he said.

"My name is the same as it was two months ago when you didn't give a shit what it was," the kid said. "I'm out." He made a show of throwing his weapon to the ground and started walking toward the woods.

"Don't make me shoot you!" Ian shouted.

"Don't do anything you don't want to do," the soldier said.

Just like that, Ian found himself in a place he'd never been before. He'd read stories of General George Washington executing conscripts who'd deserted or who disobeyed orders, and while he'd understood the decision on principle, he'd never considered the practical elements. Was there any psychological formula that showed fear of execution to be a positive motivator?

"Stop!" Ian yelled.

"I'm leaving," the soldier said. He continued to walk.

"I will shoot you in five seconds," Ian said, raising his rifle to his shoulder.

"Do what you gotta do."

Ian's bullet literally separated the kid's head from his shoulders, in a massive pink spray of bone and brains.

Ian turned to face the others, but took care to make

sure that the muzzle was pointed in a safe direction. "Any questions?" he asked.

As if in unison, the others turned to face the direction of the approaching threat. Individually and as a group, he knew that they were ready to throw him to the first wolf that presented itself.

This was going to be a difficult night.

"Scorpion, Mother Hen," Jonathan's radio crackled. "Check your handheld. I think I found Victor Carrington."

Jonathan fumbled for his phone/lifeline, and entered the appropriate codes to bring it to life. "You think or you know?"

"Given the time constraints, I think the two are about equal, don't you?" Venice said.

His phone lit up with the image of a tall, slender man at what clearly was the checkout stand at Bud's Hardware. "Okay," Jonathan said. "I have the picture. Do you have an identification on who it is?"

"That'll take a couple extra minutes," Venice said. Her tone showed him that she was not happy with his lack of appreciation for what she'd already accomplished.

"This is who we're looking for," Jonathan said, passing the phone to Boxers.

"He looks like everybody," Big Guy said. He handed the phone and its image up to Rollins.

Madman glanced at the phone, then turned his eyes back to what he was doing. "Light discipline's a lo

harder when you're looking at lighted pictures," he
said.

Point taken.

Ian was horrified by what he'd done. He'd murdered
that young man. That wasn't discipline. That was murder.

The reality crystalized for him with horrifying clarity. The Patriots' Army wasn't an army at all. It never
would be an army. It lacked the discipline and any pure-
ness of purpose. They were a team of attackers. The
mission was a noble one, a necessary one, but it was so
based on anger and revenge that there was no room to
stand for anything else. While armies trained equally
for offense and defense, the Patriots' Army had trained
only for offense. That had left them vulnerable to attack.

But how much could Ian reasonably be held to anticipate? He'd focused his training on the missions they
were facing, not on the defense of the camp. That had
been a distant goal, but it had never elevated to primary
importance. And now it was the weakness that would
kill them all. There was no reasonable scenario in which
law enforcement authorities could attack him. There
was no constitutional construct that would allow the
military to intervene. And if the military was even
close to intervention, General Brock would have inter-
vened. At the very least, he would have issued a warning to his own army.

So, who were these people who were tearing everything apart? How many of them were there? Why had no alarm been sounded?

And where were they? Literally, *where?* Engine noise did not occur naturally, so where was its source?

More of the officers poured from their barracks and gathered around him. Eight, maybe ten more men, bringing his effective force to nearly thirty.

"The colonel shot Dennis," someone said from the darkness. Ian interpreted it as an attempt to foment mutiny.

"As I will shoot anyone else who tries to run. This is not the time for cowardice. This is a time for action and valor." Those words were meant to inspire, but they sounded flat even to him. It's the rare soldier who would rally around a man who would kill his colleague. "You are officers in this army, gentlemen. You are the leaders."

"Jesus Christ, they're killing everyone down there," a newcomer said. "Why aren't we down there helping?"

"Because that's exactly what they want us to do," Ian said. "Those fires are a diversion."

"Those fires are an attack, Colonel."

"Our forces are in disarray," Ian said. "We cannot shoot from here because we cannot see the enemy. If we go to their fight, they win. We stay here and defend until such time as we can plan a counterattack."

"How many are there?" another voice asked.

"To hell with how many," said yet another unknown. "*Who* are they?"

"We don't know any of the above," Ian said.

"But we know they have vehicles. We heard them."

In fact, where was the engine noise now? At first, it had been at their twelve o'clock, directly in front, but now it sounded dispersed, seeming to come from several directions at once. And it was getting closer. Louder.

So, why couldn't he see it? Why wasn't the vehicle silhouetted against the fires that raged below?

"They're circling around," Ian declared. "They're flanking us."

"My team is down there, burning to death, *Colonel*," one of the officers said. This one had the courage to step up and confront Ian face-to-face.

"Then let's get to the business of killing the bastards who killed them. Fan out. And form a defensive circle."

The officer didn't acknowledge, but he obeyed.

"General Karras!" Ian called.

"I think I saw him running the other way," a voice said. "Sir."

This was sickening. Dylan wished that he could unsee all of it. The dead were merely dead, but the burned would suffer for a lifetime. He had little sympathy for those he shot because they were armed. And they'd learned. Apparently word traveled fast among the living because almost as one, they dropped their weapons and put their hands in the air.

He and Jolaine issued no orders. This was the victims' moment, and they would live or they would die based on the decisions they made.

The smart ones ran. They scattered, heading to the woods or down the road toward the gates where they would no doubt find the remains of their security force.

The courageous ones stayed to help their wounded colleagues.

Into his radio, he said, "She Devil, if you shoot any of them, I swear to God that I will shoot you."

"What the hell kind of radio traffic is that?" Boxers asked, off the air.

"Let it go, Big Guy," Jonathan said. He had an image in his head of what Jolaine and Dylan were dealing with, and he preferred not to go there. It sounded to him as if Jolaine was having twenty percent more fun at her job than she should. That made her a liability, and he'd have to deal with that—

"We've got a runner," Rollins announced, pointing through the windshield. Up ahead, a guy was running directly at them across a field. In night vision, he was clearly visible, but if he knew that the Batmobile was there, he made no indication. He was fully dressed and appeared to be in full panic mode.

Rollins said, "He's got stars on his collar."

"Get him," Jonathan said. "We need the intel."

They didn't even need to chase him down. He literally ran right at them. When he was still thirty feet away, Jonathan opened his door and stepped out. Boxers mirrored him on the other side.

The runner heard the noise and skidded to a stop. He clearly considered pivoting and running.

With his MP7 up and at the ready, Jonathan said, "Don't move or I'll kill you." His voice was barely louder than the engine. Sometimes, speaking softly carried more threat than barking an order.

The man froze.

"Okay," Jonathan said. "Make no loud noises. In fact, make no noise at all. You cannot see me, but I can see you as if you were standing in daylight. Give me two thumbs up if you understand."

His eyes huge, clearly terrified, the man held both hands high and wide and jutted both thumbs straight up. He said nothing.

"Very good," Jonathan said. "Now, I want you to lie facedown on the ground and remain silent. Do that, and we won't hurt you."

The man complied precisely.

"Okay, Big Guy," Jonathan said. "Your turn."

While Jonathan kept the beam of his IR laser sight squarely on the top of the prisoner's head, Boxers moved out into the night with a set of plastic zip cuffs and bound the man's hands behind him. He assumed that Big Guy said something to him, but Jonathan couldn't hear the words. Instead, he watched the shiver reverberate through the prisoner's body. When Boxers lifted on the man's bound arms, he stood readily and walked back to the vehicle.

"Turn around and sit down," Jonathan instructed, "and hold your feet out to my friend. We need to zip those, too."

"Who are you?" the prisoner asked. He turned sideways in the seat and offered his feet to Boxers.

"Think of us as the people who haven't killed you yet," Jonathan said. "Who are you?"

"I'm nobody," he said. "I'm just a soldier."

"You're wearing stars," Boxers said.

"We're looking for Victor Carrington," Jonathan said. "Is he here?"

"I don't know who that is."

Boxers drew his pistol and pressed the muzzle against the man's knee. "I know you can't see images in the dark" he said, "but try to envision the future. I threaten to shoot your knee. You get all brave and shit and say again that you don't know who Carrington is. Then, I blast a bullet through your knee just as I promised, and you're, like, all in agony and shit, and then we ask you again, and you tell us what we want to know because it really, really hurts to get shot in the knee. only now you walk funny forever."

The man looked terrified. And he should have, because Boxers was not bluffing. It's not how Jonathan would have handled it, but it was what it was.

"Okay," Jonathan said. "With that done, let me ask again. Is Victor Carrington up there?"

The prisoner nodded. "Yes."

"Is he in charge?"

A slight hesitation. Then, "Yes."

Boxers saw it, too. He pressed the muzzle a little harder into his knee. "If ever there's been a time in your life where being forthcoming mattered more than anything, this is it. What's the rest?"

The prisoner hesitated.

"Okay, fine, then," Boxers said. He worked the decocker on his M9. That metallic click was a great motivator.

"No! Don't!"

"Keep your voice down," Jonathan reminded him.

"My name is Karras," the prisoner said. "I'm in charge of some things, but Carrington is in charge of the tactical details."

"So, you were running someplace to get a better vantage point to lead from?" Boxers asked.

"Big Guy, stop," Jonathan said. Taunting the man would not bring greater cooperation. "How well armed are they up there?"

"How many of you are there?" Karras asked.

"Concentrate," Jonathan said. "I ask, you answer. How well are they armed?"

"Rifles," Karras said. "Maybe a few handguns."

"How many people?" Jonathan asked.

"In total, nearly two hundred."

"What about up here in officers' country? How many here?" He deliberately used the term that Tommy Piper had used. He'd take any edge he could get.

"Twenty."

"That's too round a number," Rollins said.

"I got this, Madman," Jonathan snapped. But again, it was the comment he was going to make, and it raised the question he wanted answered.

"Twenty-seven."

"How good are they?" Boxers asked.

Karras hesitated. "I don't know how to answer that."

"Do they have night vision?" Jonathan asked.

"I don't think so."

"That's not an answer."

"They have access to night vision," Karras said. "But not in their barracks. It's kept locked up. I don't think any of them have had a chance to find it and use it tonight."

"How far are we from them?"

"Not a hundred yards. I don't know precisely They're close."

"And how are they deployed?"

"In a defensive circle."

"What the hell is a defensive circle?" Boxers asked. Disdain polluted his tone.

"They don't know where you are," Karras said. "They've deployed in a circle, behind whatever cover they could find."

Jonathan's mind conjured an image from old Westerns, with circled wagons and Winchester repeaters pointing out at every compass point, aimed everywhere. He had no idea if such a strategy ever occurred in real life, but it made no sense to him. In reality, people didn't attack in circles, they attacked at weak points. The "defensive circle" created nothing but weak points.

Boxers leaned in very close to the prisoner. Close enough that even if the man couldn't see him, he could sense his presence. "Think about every word you just told us, and understand that if any of it is false, I won't hesitate to kill you. In fact, that will be my very first bullet, and it will be to a part of your body that will keep you dying for a long, long time. Do you understand what I'm telling you?"

Karras nodded emphatically.

"Say it out loud," Jonathan said. Once vocalized, words lingered longer in the head.

"I understand," Karras said. "Everything I've told you is true. To the best of my knowledge."

Jonathan caught the hedge, but decided to give the guy a break on that. Backing away from an absolute might just be a sign that Karras was working hard to tell the whole truth. He decided to believe him.

"All right," Jonathan said. "Hog-tie him, gag him, and put him on the floor in the back row of seats." If nothing else went right tonight, at least they had a high-value asset to take home with them.

Boxers needed no help to do a task he had done so many times in the past. In three minutes, it was done. It helped that Karras was such a cooperative prisoner. That happened a lot when people contemplated how near they were to dying.

While Big Guy took care of Karras, Rollins said to Jonathan, "What's the plan?"

"We'll leave the Batmobile here," he said. "We'll leave it running so the bad guys will have something to listen to, and then we'll edge up and see what we've got."

Boxers reappeared. "He's all tucked away, nice and comfy." That no doubt meant the Karras was facedown on the floor, wedged between seats.

"Listen," Jonathan said. "I do not want a bloodbath here, am I clear? These poor bastards might call themselves an army, but we all know they're nothing like an army. They're zealots with guns."

"Who are going to try to shoot us," Boxers said.

"And I'm not suggesting that we die on their behalf," Jonathan said.

"Otherwise, it would be disconcerting," Big Guy said.

"So put that into the shape of a strategy," Rollins said.

"We go in slow and easy," Jonathan said. "With

luck, they won't see us or hear us, then we see what we've got."

"We're gonna have a lot of yay-hoos with guns," Boxers said.

"And if they shoot those guns, we shoot back."

"That's a mighty big change to the playbook, Boss," Boxers said. "For the record, I do not approve."

Jonathan understood Big Guy's point, and he even agreed at one level. All reasonable assault protocols dictated that people with guns in their hands be killed before they had a chance to use them. There was no yelling for people to put their hands up, and there was no shame in shooting the enemy in the back. Elite Special Forces team members lived to retirement by bringing overwhelming force to their enemies with terrifying speed.

But monitoring the radio traffic of the slaughter that was ongoing down the hill had gotten to him. He didn't want another slaughter up here. He didn't need that burden on his conscience.

"Think about what you're saying, Scorpion," Rollins said. "We survive against outrageous odds because we have the advantage of technology, training, and commitment. But that advantage only lasts as long as we are willing to leverage it."

Of course, they were correct. This was no time to change the rules of combat that he'd lived by for his entire professional life. It wasn't fair to his team. "Okay, you win. But show restraint. If people try to surrender, we let them."

"When have we not?" Boxers asked.

"You're right," Jonathan said. "But unless we wander

up against something imminent, we coordinate shots. Is *that* understood?"

"Got it," Boxers said.

"Coordinated shots, got it," Rollins agreed.

"Now let's go kill us some soldiers," Big Guy said. There was a smile in his voice. "Oh, lighten up, Boss. I was kidding." A beat. "Mostly."

Chapter Thirty

Jonathan's Bravo Team advanced in a disciplined line, each of them separated by thirty feet. Scorpion held the center position, with Big Guy on his right. Jonathan kept his M27 pressed into his shoulder and advanced in a high crouch. The others moved just like him. Through his NVGs, infrared laser sights cut the dark in bouncing, sweeping lines. The night revealed nothing but wide open spaces and no movement but their own.

"I hear voices," Rollins whispered over the air.

Jonathan pivoted his head to the left and caught Rollins pointing forward and to his left with a bladed hand. "Copy," Jonathan whispered back. *Good God, they're talking. Do they* want *to die?*

A few seconds later, Jonathan heard it, too. He couldn't make out words, but the sounds were unmistakably voices. People didn't realize how efficiently sound traveled on a quiet night. They also didn't realize that the whisper they thought was nearly silent was really quite loud. Back in the day, he'd trained in the art of whispering. Christ, he'd trained on just about everything at one point or another, except maybe buttwiping, but he couldn't rule that out entirely.

As one, Jonathan and his team sank a bit lower to the ground and slowed their approach. At night, in tense situations, movement was easily detected.

Jonathan's Spidey-sense tingled. Something was out of place, but he couldn't put his finger on it. He'd learned to trust that sense, so he tapped his transmit button twice. The double-rasp of breaking squelch on the radio would be interpreted by his team for what it was—a silent order to stop and assess.

One of the greatest dangers Jonathan and Bravo faced right now was overconfidence. Their enemy was without doubt incompetent, but they were well armed, and bullets fired by idiots were no less deadly than those fired by professional assassins. The only difference lay in the ability to aim. The annals of warfare bulged fat with stories of disaster wrought at the hands of amateurs. Jonathan's greatest hero of military strategy and tactics—Jonathan "Stonewall" Jackson (the man after whom he was named)—was shot and killed not by a Yankee sharpshooter, or in a hail of bullets while leading his troops, but rather by one of his own sentries on the night of what was then his greatest victory. It didn't take a talented marksman to kill with a weapon capable of spraying six hundred rounds a minute.

The technical term for Spidey-sense was *situational awareness,* the greatest, most important factor that separated victims from victors. If you toiled in the field of violence long enough, you developed a sense for what belonged and what did not. You learned to trust yourself. You learned that when something didn't *feel* right, that's because it was *not* right.

He swept the area with his sight, left to right, high to low. He switched his scope from light-enhancement mode to heat-seeking mode, and the world viewed through his right eye switched from green-on-green to black-and-white. That's when he saw what he was looking for.

Almost directly ahead of him, a face peeked out from behind a tree. In the green hue of light enhancement, the image appeared as a bulge against the column of the tree trunk. Now, the bulge had eyes. And it was pointing a rifle in his general direction, close enough to pose a hazard. Knowing now what to look for, he switched back to light-enhancement mode. He drew a circle around his target with his IR laser sight. Through his peripheral vision, he saw Big Guy and Madman doing the same thing. Each one of them had identified a target.

Jonathan keyed his mike and whispered, "At will." He heard the suppressed *cracks* of their rifles almost instantaneously, before he could focus on his own target. It was a kid, not yet twenty years old. The age of ninety percent of all soldiers. The kid was turning to examine the noise of his neighbors' fracturing heads when Jonathan launched a 5.56 millimeter bullet through his ear. The brain spray was somehow more unsettling in the artificial light that it was in daylight.

The enemy stirred. They heard the sounds, and they sensed the danger, but they clearly didn't know what to do. One of them, on the far side of the circle, facing exactly the wrong direction, started shooting randomly into the night, endangering Alpha. Rollins took the shooter out with an efficient double-tap from what had to be seventy-five yards. For anyone else, it would have been an unimpressive shot, but Jonathan had perhaps unjustifiably discounted his former commander's skills.

Jonathan pressed his transmit button. "Hold fire unless fired upon. Find cover." They'd made their initial point. Now they needed to see if the enemy could be reasoned with. He scanned the area for cover, and took refuge behind a substantial hardwood. He told himself that it was oak, because oak was a particularly hard hardwood. It had remarkable bullet-stopping properties, and he suspected that the next step was going to bring more than a few bullets in his direction.

"Acknowledge that you've gone to cover," Jonathan whispered over the radio.

"Set," Rollins whispered back.

"Good to go," Boxers agreed.

It was time. Jonathan all but straddled the tree trunk. He pressed his body against the rough bark, and exposed only his weapon and his right eye. He kept his right elbow—the elbow of his shooting hand—tucked in close to his ribs so as not to unnecessarily expose an impact point.

"Patriots' Army, listen up!" he yelled.

Someone on the near end shot at the sound of his voice, sending a bullet into his tree. A good shot. Boxers and Rollins dropped him simultaneously.

"We can see you and you cannot see us!" Jonathan yelled. "We have you surrounded. Your troops in the barracks down the hill are dead and dying and in total disarray. You cannot win. All we want is Victor Carrington. Give him up, and we will allow you to lay down your arms and walk away. Anyone who tries to shoot back will die. Decide." In the distance, on the far side of the circle—which had grossly lost any geometric resemblance to a circle, with some elements moving closer to the center and others moving away, almost all of them moving farther away from the sound of the threat—a soldier raised his weapon to his shoulder. "You in the back!" Jonathan shouted.

He was too late. Boxers had already taken him out.

"You are outgunned and outclassed!" Jonathan shouted. "You don't have to die tonight. We already have Karras. We caught him as he was abandoning you. Running away. Now, we only need Carrington and we'll be out of here."

In the distance, he saw confusion. The chatter grew in intensity and volume. They were about to give their guy up, Jonathan thought.

Ian's heart skipped when he heard the mention of his alias, and it damn near stopped when they invoked Karras's name. The coward. *Now we only need Carrington and we'll be out of here.* He kneeled on the ground, initially facing the wrong direction, but now facing the sound of the man's voice. But he kept his weapon down, the muzzle toward the ground. No sense drawing unnecessary fire.

"On my command," he whispered, "I want this row to turn and engage. If we can—"

"Don't be foolish," the voice called from the dark.

"Too many people have died tonight. You don't have to be among them."

"Don't listen to them," Ian said. He pivoted his body so that it was completely concealed behind the pickup truck he'd been using for cover.

"We don't even know who you are," the voice said. "Our intel says that none of you used your real names to join this outfit, so if you walk away, no one will be the wiser. You've got dead to bury and wounded to care for. Give us Carrington and our business here is over. Unless you make it more complicated than it needs to be."

"He's over there behind that pickup truck!" someone shouted. Ian didn't have to look to know that he was being pointed at.

"Simpson!" someone spat in rebuke.

"He shot Dennis!" was the reply. "I'm not dying for a guy who'll shoot his own troops."

Panic seized Ian. He didn't know what to do. Certainly, getting caught was nowhere on the agenda. Whatever his next step was going to be, he had to decide now.

The officer who'd ratted out his commander made a show of placing his weapon on the ground and standing with his hands stretched high in the air.

"If he leaves, let him go peacefully," Jonathan said in his radio. "That will encourage the others."

"As long as his hands are empty."

"Keep those hands high in the air until you are past the gate," Jonathan instructed. "You'll pass more of us.

If you pick up a dropped weapon, or attempt to seek shelter elsewhere in the compound, you'll be shot without warning. Hold two thumbs up if you understand that."

The soldier popped two thumbs and started walking. He'd taken three steps toward the rear when one of his cadre whipped around and shot him. Boxers and Rollins fired simultaneously to drop the shooter.

"Goddammit, it does not have to be this way!" Jonathan shouted. "Put your weapons down! Give yourselves a chance to live, for God's sake."

But panic had taken hold. Two or three of the soldiers opened up on full-auto in the direction of Jonathan's voice. Jonathan had seen them raising their weapons and had plenty of time to duck behind his tree before bullets slammed into it. He heard cracks through the air of rounds that went wide of the tree, but still close enough to make themselves known.

"Left shooter down," Boxers' voice said in his ear.

"Center shooter, right shooter down," Rollins said.

In the blast of rifle fire, Jonathan didn't hear the softer pops of his team's suppressed weapons, but the silence of the others confirmed their words.

Jonathan pivoted from behind his cover and scanned the scene before him. It was utter bedlam. Against the wild, dancing light of the burning barracks down the hill, a swarm of largely undressed men ran and fell and tripped over themselves trying to get away. It would have been comical had it not been for the corpses among them, each lying so still among the swirling action.

Sudden movement on Jonathan's left startled him. It was Rollins, and he had taken off at a dead run. "Carrington's bolting," Rollins said. "I saw him take off from behind the truck they were pointing at."

Jonathan bolted after him. As he sprinted, his gear flapping against his body, he pressed his transmit button. "Big Guy, get the vehicle before we get too far separated. Break, break. Alpha, Scorpion."

"Go, Scorpion," Jolaine said.

"There are waves of bad guys heading your way. They are in total disarray. Try to find a way to let them go. Try to disarm them. Only engage if engaged."

Jolaine said something in response, but Jonathan had turned back to the business of running. An exercise fiend, he was no stranger to a vigorous ten-mile jog, but he hadn't sprinted in full kit in a while. It bugged him that Rollins seemed to be better at it. That pushed him to run harder.

The man they were chasing seemed intent on not getting caught. He had a rifle in his hands, but he'd made no effort to shoot. Technically, by their unofficial rules of engagement, that made him eligible to be shot, but he was the purpose for their raid tonight. If at all possible, they wanted to take this guy alive.

Son of a bitch wasn't making it easy.

Ian's lungs screamed and his head boomed with the effort of his flight through the woods. He felt angry and betrayed by his men, but mostly he felt fearful of what the future would hold for him if he got caught. Under the Uniform Code of Military Justice, the fact of his conspiracy was justification for the death penalty. But to be caught at this stage of the operation wouldn't trigger that. The judges wouldn't want that.

They would want to see him toiling at hard labor for the rest of his life.

Life in a military prison was a fate worse than death, especially for the crimes he had committed. As unlikely as it sounded, many of the inmates in military prisons were still patriots at heart. They had violated the rules, or in most cases had committed felonies, but they'd committed their crimes while in service to the United States. Ian imagined that the treatment of a traitor at their hands would mimic the horrifying stories he'd heard of the treatment of child molesters who'd served time.

Some lines just could not be crossed. And Ian had crossed one.

His future did not exist. Not anymore. Unless General Brock figured out a way to help.

But Brock would never do that, would he? Of course not. Brock's fingerprints were nowhere to be seen on this operation. He'd never shown his face in the camp, he'd never met Ian on government soil. There had been no written record. He needed only to deny his involvement, and Ian's claims would be ignored. After all, who was more believable to a jury of military personnel, a lieutenant colonel who'd been trying to overthrow the political structure of the United States, or the chief of staff of the United States Army?

He pumped his legs harder. The weight of his M4 was slowing him, but that weapon was his last opportunity to impact his own future. Tree branches tore at his face and his arms as he crashed through the woods, so he turned a hard right and headed out into the open. There, he'd be able to move faster, but the people chasing to catch him—he hadn't seen them, but he'd heard the footsteps—would have a clearer shot. It was a chance he had to take.

Ian had already decided that the invaders were not here to kill him. They'd said as much back in the compound—back when there was something that could reasonably be called a compound—but that could have been a lie to get him to step out into the open.

But now that they had a shot, they weren't taking it. That meant that they wanted him alive.

But he'd never be able to outrun them. Not two of them, who were no doubt much younger than he, and clearly understood the business of warfare. If they caught him, they would send him to prison, where he would die, either of torture at the hands of other prisoners, or of old age. Neither suited him.

His rifle was his only chance. He stopped without slowing, sliding to a halt while pivoting 180 degrees and bringing his rifle to bear. At this range, he couldn't miss.

"He's going to do something desperate," Jonathan said into his radio. It was the only reason he could think of for Carrington to peel off out of cover to run in the open. They followed, but it didn't feel right. "Give him some space."

Ahead and to his left, Rollins responded to the order by slowing his stride just enough to open some distance between himself and Carrington, and allowing Jonathan to catch up.

Carrington skidded to a stop and raised his rifle.

"I got him!" Rollins yelled, likewise stopping and raising his weapon.

"No!" Jonathan yelled. They needed him alive. That was the whole damn purpose of the exercise. He blew past Rollins, spoiling his aim, and drove himself headlong toward Carrington. Even in the darkness, he saw the look of shock in the man's eyes as Jonathan closed the distance without slowing.

Jonathan was three feet away and closing when Carrington popped off a shot. The sound of the report was deafening, instantly stuffing Jonathan's head with a pound of invisible cotton that seemed to fill even his sinuses with sound pressure.

Jonathan targeted Carrington's off-hand for collision with his shoulder, and his nose for collision with the crown of his Kevlar helmet. Both impacts reverberated through Jonathan's body. Jonathan felt a snap on the bridge of his nose as the night vision array absorbed its share of the impact, and knew that he'd broken it. This would be the fifth time for his nose, but he hoped that he hadn't ruined the ridiculously expensive electronic gear.

Jonathan's momentum carried him through and over his target, ending in a shoulder-roll that left his equipment tangled and his flesh torn in the spots where hard metal won over soft tissue.

By the time Jonathan found his feet, Rollins was already standing over their prisoner, covering him with his M4. "He's not moving," he said. "Nice hit, there, Scorpion. Are you okay?"

Jonathan adjusted the night vision array on his head and blew a plug of bloody snot from his nose. "Been better," he said. "Tell me I didn't kill him."

"He's breathing. And, frankly, it wasn't *that* good a hit. But at least he looks worse than you."

"Yeah, well, that's what matters." He keyed his mike. "Alpha, Scorpion. How's it going down there?"

"It's like Zombieland." Dylan replied. "Lots of dazed and confused. Lots and lots of injuries. Burns. And people are flooding out of here."

"Are they armed?" Jonathan asked.

"Not that I've seen. But I can't tell you with certainty that no armed men got out of the compound."

Jonathan considered that. The fear was that the defeated army would regroup and form up for some kind of counterattack. But that would take effective leadership of a level Jonathan hadn't seen here. What would be, would be, and they would need to remain vigilant. But for now, he felt that things were stable.

The Batmobile rumbled up out of the night and disgorged Big Guy, who, predictably enough, looked pissed. "You know I hate it when you do the cool shit without—" He interrupted himself with a laugh and he pointed to Jonathan. "Look at you," he said. "You got a boo-boo." Then he looked down at Carrington's unconsciousness. "Nice." Then, to Rollins, "Was it epic?"

"It was a pretty good hit."

"Can you just package him, please, and let us get out of here?" Jonathan said. Then, over the radio, he said, "Mother Hen, Scorpion. Have you been monitoring radio traffic?"

She always monitored the radio traffic. "Is it time to start ambulances on the way for the injured?"

She'd read his mind. Again. "Affirmative," he said.

"Have them send five ambulances to start, and then they can work out their own tactics from there."

"I copy."

"Scorpion, Boomer."

Jonathan's team stopped at the leaden tone in Dylan's voice.

"Scorpion."

"I think you need to come to the gate. A police officer wants to talk to you."

Chapter Thirty-one

The young cop looked even younger out of the car than he did when viewed through the window. Maybe five-ten, with a physique that Mama Alexander liked to call a swimmer's build, the kid stood tall in his gray-and-green uniform, his legs set wide and his hands resting on his Sam Browne belt, the web of one thumb spanning his pistol, and the other spanning his nightstick.

Jonathan approached on foot while Boxers followed in the Batmobile, and Rollins watched from a little ways up the hill. Dylan and Jolaine flanked the cop from a respectable distance, and all weapons rested in neutral positions.

"Officer Parks," Jonathan said as he closed to within a few feet. He extended his hand. "Pardon my glove."

Parks ignored the gesture of friendship. "You're hurt."

"Not that bad."

"From the town, it sounded like there was a war going on up here."

"Felt a little like that, too," Jonathan said. "If you're here to help us, though, you're a few minutes too late. We're just cleaning up and are on our way out of here. We've called for ambulances to take care of the injured."

Parks cocked his head. "What about the dead?"

"They won't need ambulances," Jonathan said. "They'll pretty much just stay dead."

The cop's face folded into an offended mask. "You think this is funny?"

"I think it's settled business," Jonathan replied. "No, I don't think it's funny. I think it was a lot of hard work, and a lot of gullible young men died needlessly because they listened to nonsense in the past and refused to listen to reason tonight. Nothing's funny about any of that. And nothing is funny about the countless murders that we prevented by being here."

"Well, you did say you were on the side of the angels," Parks said. "I remember from Sunday School that Satan was once God's favorite angel."

And there went Jonathan's patience. "I'm not sure why you're here exactly, Officer Parks, but I am no more inclined to be arrested now than I was a couple of hours ago."

The kid shifted his stance to one leg and he folded his arms. "Me and my team were working the murders down at Mary's, and one of the dead guys showed up as being wanted by the United States Army for desertion. Another one has been in and out of jail since forever. Judging from the physical evidence, I think it's pretty clear that we're dealing with a case of self-defense down there."

"That's good to hear," Jonathan said. He wasn't at

all sure where this was going. Parks seemed too calm, too focused. And too alone.

"So I took what you told me down there," Parks continued. "You said your name was Scorpion, and that you were on the side of the angels. Those are two things you don't hear very often, and the way you said them, I figured it wasn't your first time. So I did some research into some police databases, and I got a couple of hits. It seems that there's another guy out there who uses those same combinations. Violence seems to follow him, too."

The back of Jonathan's neck lit up with a feeling of danger. What did this guy know?

"There's no real pattern to it," Parks went on. "And no real focus. This Scorpion guy has touched lives all over the world, it seems. No one knows his real name, and the guy rarely leaves fingerprints. On the few occasions when he has, the fingerprints prove to be untraceable. They belong to someone who appears not to exist. Isn't that crazy?"

"Huh," Jonathan said. "That's really wild."

"I thought so, too," Parks said. "But here's where it gets really interesting. Wherever this other Scorpion goes, it seems that only bad guys end up dead. There've even been unsubstantiated rumors where Scorpion rescued hostages that the police never knew had been taken."

"Sounds like this guy is quite a hero," Jonathan said.

"Well, yes and no," Parks hedged. He took a step closer. "What Scorpion does is technically murder. It's called vigilantism, and it's illegal in all fifty states. It's that whole due process thing that's guaranteed by the Constitution."

Jonathan's eyes narrowed as he regarded this kid with ever-growing respect. "So, what's your point?"

Parks shrugged. "I don't really have a point, I guess. I just thought that you should know that there's a guy with your name who's wreaking havoc and is a wanted man. For example, if I suspected that you and he were the same person, I'd have to arrest you. But of course I don't suspect you. That's why I felt comfortable coming up here alone." His eyes burned into Jonathan's.

Jonathan didn't blink. He waited for the rest. This kid was tough.

Parks broke it off and turned toward the fires and the injured and dead. "I have no idea what happened up here, but it looks like a terrorist camp of some sort to me. As you said, ambulances are on the way, and word is going to leak out. I'm going to need a way to explain this." He turned back to Jonathan. "Any ideas?"

"Officer Parks," Jonathan said, "you seem to have thought most of this through already. I sense that if I just stand quietly, you'll tell me an idea on your own."

Parks smirked. "I can't say you're wrong. Back in town, Mary mentioned something about you coming up here to grab someone to question him. A fellow named Carrington, I believe."

Jonathan waited.

"Did you succeed?"

Jonathan waited.

"I'm betting you did," Parks said. "I want him."

"Why?"

"For the credit," Parks said. "And for the scapegoat. You can't have this kind of destruction, this much loss of life, without a rationale to explain it. A town like ours can look away from a lot of stuff, but we're talking mothers' sons here. Someone has to answer for that."

Jonathan pressed his mike button. "Big Guy, bring out our guests, please. Boomer, help him."

"I'm doing this, but I'm not liking it," Boxers said.

"Ah, so there's more than one," Parks said. "So much the better."

"Don't count those chickens just yet," Jonathan said.

"Excuse me?"

"I think you heard," Jonathan said. "And in a few seconds, I think you'll understand."

Thirty seconds later, Dylan and Boxers arrived with their hog-tied cargo and laid the men on the ground. Jonathan pointed his rifle at them and thumbed the tactical light on the muzzle, bathing them in a beam that was brighter than bright.

Karras squinted and looked away. Carrington was still trying to figure out if he was alive.

"I'm going to try and pull a Solomon on you," Jonathan said, "and split the baby. The one on the right is Carrington. That's not his real name. In fact, we don't know his real name, but I want to find that out. He's mine. I'm keeping him. The other one's name is Karras, and as far as I can tell, he's supposed to be the boss, but he's a big-ass coward when the going gets tough."

Parks scowled and moved in closer. He withdrew a MagLite from his belt and hit Karras with the beam. It must have been like staring into the sun.

"His name's not Karras," Parks said.

The hog-tied man writhed and tried to force his eyes open. "Watch yourself, Parks," he said.

"Why, Mr. Wainwright," Parks said. "So you're actually the one behind this?"

"Wainwright?" Jonathan said. "The guy who owns everything in town? This whiny asshole is him?"

"His son," Parks said. "Now this should be interesting."

"You know you can't win," Karras—or whoever—said. "I've got more friends in this town than you will ever know. You'll never win against me."

"I believe I can," Parks said. To Jonathan, he added, "This is quite the gift. Fact is, he doesn't get the difference between friends and people who are afraid of him. This thing is federal, anyway, if only because of the weapons involved." He chuckled and rubbed the back of his head. "Mr. W, you are *so* under arrest. I'll figure out the charges later."

Karras let out a stream of curses, but Jonathan paid no attention. In the distance, the night swelled with the sound of approaching ambulances.

"Okay, you can keep your guy," Parks said. "This will be way more fun."

Boxers was already hefting Carrington and returning him to the Batmobile.

"It's probably time for you to get going," Parks said. "Once the ambulances get here, it's gonna be tough." He reached into his back pocket and withdrew a three-by-five index card. He handed it to Jonathan.

"What's this?"

"Once I realized that both Scorpions are on the side of the angels, I took the liberty of jotting down these directions for you. They'll get you off the mountain and onto the main roads without having to pass back through town. Be careful, though, it's easy to get lost."

"You know I'll verify these, right?" Jonathan said as he took the card.

"Doesn't surprise me a bit. In fact, it's kind of a relief. I don't want you around here any longer than necessary."

Jonathan extended his hand again. "Thanks, Officer Parks."

The cop shook his head. "Put that away. And don't think for a minute that we are friends. Get out of here."

Jonathan was liking this guy more and more. He pressed his transmit button. "Okay, teams, let's mount up."

Chapter Thirty-two

Three weeks later

Autumn in Virginia was a time of unparalleled splendor. Not all fall displays were created equal from year to year, though. Some years the trees were more vibrant than others—Jonathan understood it had something to with rainfall amounts, but he'd never researched it—and this was one of the winners. Just barely north of dawn—an unusual time for Jonathan—the hues of yellow and orange and red bled into the splendid blue of the newly bright sky. When you gave it the chance, life could be truly breathtaking.

He sat alone on the porch of the lodge. He wore jeans and a sweatshirt, no shoes or socks, sipping coffee from a logo-less mug. In retrospect, the footwear decision was probably a mistake—it was just a touch too cold—but he was enjoying the peace too much to break it.

Out in the field, directly in front, a small family of deer grazed about, as if to complete the picture of bucolic perfection. They wandered in the comfort of knowing that deer season wasn't quite yet upon them. When the front door opened and Dom D'Angelo stepped out to join Jonathan, they didn't even look up.

"Now there's a picture," Dom said.

"Yes, it is. Good morning. Did you sleep well?"

The priest—who looked distinctly unpriestly in a disheveled puffy gray sweat suit—helped himself to a rocker. "I enjoy peace and quiet as much as the next guy," he said. "But this might take it to a new extreme. And you might consider a night-light in the guest room. I nearly peed in a closet at around four."

"If you didn't drink so much beer, you wouldn't have to pee so much."

"If I didn't drink the beer, you wouldn't invite me out," Dom countered. "Are you considering ruining Bambi's day?" He pointed to the rifle that rested against the railing.

Jonathan pulled it toward him and picked it up. "This is my gift from Haynes Moncrief," he said. "It arrived yesterday at the guard shack, and they brought it up this morning. It's a beauty."

"Looks like a rifle to me," Dom said.

"Cretin. This is a Nosler M48. Eighteen hundred bucks." He opened the bolt, and the deer took off at a run. "Did you see that?"

"Evolution in action, I suppose," Dom said. "And is this Haynes Moncrief the same one of late in the news?"

"Indeed," Jonathan said. He felt oddly sorry about scaring the deer. "It's hard to prosecute so powerful a man when it became clear that not only was he defending himself from attack, but that the attack was part of a plan to overthrow the country."

"I hate to see anybody be above the law," Dom said. "Present company excluded, of course."

"I hate stupid laws," Jonathan countered. And yes, he'd caught the irony in Dom's words, but he chose to ignore it.

There was a moment of silence as Dom sipped from his own mug. "You make terrible coffee. I might as well put a pinch of grounds between my cheek and gum." An awkward silence. "How's your friend Dylan?"

"I can't talk about Dylan," Jonathan said. That was because the entire Nasbe family was being assigned a new life. If you think it's hard to hide someone from the mob, try hiding them from the CIA. Just because Dylan did something heroic and helpful did not clean the slate of the bad stuff. Jonathan wished him well, but he didn't think it could end well for him in the long run. Frankly, Jonathan lost a lot of respect for the man when he decided to suck his family into his disappearance instead of just going away solo.

But it was not for him to judge.

"Okay, Digger," Dom said. "I've been here for fifteen hours. We've drunk through the night and now it's morning, and we still have not had a meaningful exchange. Let's have it. Why am I here?"

Jonathan said nothing.

"Dig, you suck at this. You don't invite me for private getaways unless there's something private that you need to get away from. So let's have it. Consider my confessor hat and my shrink hat to both be on my head."

For as long as Jonathan had been in the business he'd been in, Dom had been his single relief valve. It helped that as both a psychologist and a priest, he was compelled by both manmade and holy laws to keep secrets secret, but mostly, he depended on Dom as a friend. Perhaps his only true friend.

"What the hell am I doing, Dom?" Jonathan asked.

"I need way more than that."

"This op into West Virginia. We killed a lot of people. We maimed even more."

"Forgive me, but you say that as if it's a first time. Meaning no disrespect, you've been killing and maiming people for a long time. What's different?"

While those words were exceptionally harsh, Jonathan knew that Dom meant no harm. One of the reasons their friendship had lasted so long was because they communicated bluntly with each other.

"Jolaine Cage took pleasure in burning people alive."

"Did you take any pleasure out of burning people alive?" Dom asked.

Jonathan felt his ears go hot. "Of course not. I was horrified."

"So how did you channel your horror?"

Jonathan knew that Dom knew, but there had to be a reason for him asking. "She's done," he said. "She's off the teams."

"Done and done," Dom said. "How's Box with that?"

Jonathan shot him a look. "Less than happy. But I think he gets it."

Dom kept watching the tree line. He seemed to understand that Jonathan handled moments like this best without eye contact. "Not to repeat myself, but done and done. You've chosen a path for yourself, Dig, that doesn't allow for a lot of introspection. It's a little late to change, don't you think?"

It was a valid point. Scorpion had committed more murders than Jonathan cared to count over the years, but he got through the day by convincing himself that every killing was justified. People chose the courses they chose, and at the moment when they chose to cross the line that threatened other people's lives, they'd abandoned the most important clause of the social contract. The fact that Jolaine had wandered so far off the reservation didn't rest directly on his shoulders, and the fact that he'd fired her removed any of the burden that remained.

"How did your chat with Wolverine go the other day?" Dom asked.

Jonathan chuckled. "If only the public knew," he said. "It turns out that our Victor Carrington is in fact a US Army officer named Ian Martin. He's a complete whack job, but he's claiming that General Manfred Brock, also of the US Army, is involved with the plot to overthrow Washington."

"I know that name," Don said. "General Brock."

Jonathan turned his head and waited till he had Dom's gaze. "He's the chief of staff of the United States Army."

"A coup?"

"Yep. Of course, there's no proof beyond the rantings of a crazy guy. Wolfie doesn't think anything will ever come of it."

"So the guy just walks?"

"Welcome to Washington," Jonathan said. "Wolfie hadn't even shared the details with the president. Apparently, the Honorable Mr. Darmond does not like to hear bad news unless it is accompanied by hard evidence."

"Unbelievable," Dom said. "I can't count the number of things I've learned from you over the years that I wish I could unlearn."

"Hey, priest-boy," Jonathan said. "You chose to be the sin-catcher."

Dom laughed. "Sin-catcher. I like that." Then he drilled Jonathan with his eyes. "Quit dancing, Dig. I happen to know that you groove on the political intrigue, so don't tell me that's why I'm here. Dig deep, my friend. What's really going on in that addled head of yours?"

Jonathan closed his eyes. In the past, every mission had left him feeling exuberant, confident that he'd made the world a better place, if only for a few people. "Okay, here it is," he said. "I think I made a mistake in breaking up Carrington's operation—Ian Martin's operation. I believe in my heart of hearts that the world would be a safer place if that abortion of an army had been better trained and more successful."

Dom's scowl deepened. "You're not suggesting that you wish you'd been killed."

"Of course not," Jonathan scoffed. "I'm suggesting that the Darmond administration is the most dangerous group that's ever sat in Washington. And we've had some pretty scary groups."

"So, we should just kill the lot of them?

Jonathan waved that off, too. "No. Dammit, I don't know what I mean."

"We get to have another revolution in just three years," Dom reminded. "Election Day."

Jonathan now wished he hadn't said anything. He did not need a lesson in civics.

Dom continued, "And that oath you pledged back in

the day was to support the Constitution, not the president. And certainly not some tin pot who considers himself smarter than the electorate."

Jonathan didn't need a lecture on his enlistment oath, either.

"So, let's talk about what this is really about," Dom said.

"I did."

"Sure you did." Dom crossed his legs and sipped at his coffee. They said nothing as they stared out at the beauty.

Jonathan had spent a lifetime keeping the emotional doors of his mind closed. Locked. Hermetically sealed. He didn't like where his head was taking him because it made no sense to go there. What was done was indelible. The only option was to suck it up and move on. Young people died by the thousands in every war the world has ever fought. Over the years, Jonathan had lost track of the number of young men he had killed. He'd never tried to keep a count. They were the enemy, the force that had to be vanquished in order for larger goals to be met. He offered no apology because there was nothing to apologize for.

So why, today, was he worried that his voice would not work if he tried to talk? Why had he felt this way since hours after they'd returned from West Virginia?

"Did I ever tell you about my observations about stupidity?" Dom asked. He didn't turn his head away from the view. Jonathan didn't answer.

"It goes like this," Dom said. "*Stupid* is a word we throw around with abandon. Stupid is as stupid does, right? You watch Internet videos, and you wonder what went wrong with the gene pool. People make stupid mis-

akes, and when they get hurt—or worse than hurt—we
ay, 'yeah, well, duh.' I know you've seen a lot of stupid in your line of work, and the price can be ridicu-
ously high.

"But there's a special breed of stupid that has always
tugged at me. Call it gullibility. People get talked into
doing stupidly wrong things for all the right reasons.
There's usually a powerful demagogue in the mix somewhere. The gullible hear what they want to hear, and
then they dedicate themselves to that cause. Heavens,
some might say that such is the case with every person
I serve at Mass. People who think that way would be
wrong, of course."

Jonathan let him talk. Dom wasn't given to empty
pontification. He had a point to make and he'd make it
soon.

"I think it hurts to hurt the gullible. I think it must
feel like punishing gullibility with the death penalty."

And there it was. Jonathan felt as if he'd executed
the gullible. He clamped his jaws tight and stared even
more intently at the tree line. What was done was done.

"Tell you what," Dom said, rising to his feet. "You
stay put. I'm going to go get my stole, and you and I
are going to talk."

ACKNOWLEDGMENTS

I've been writing novels now for twenty years. In a very real way, each book represents in my mind a chronicle of my family's journey. Looking back, life's ebbs and flows are inexorably tied in my head to what I was writing when the big events transpired. The death and the births, the frustrations and elations. Life is after all, an emotional sine curve—the thrill ride of a lifetime. Through it all, the one constant—my rock and my best friend—has been the ever-loving, ever-beautiful Joy. She continues to be my everything.

As does Chris. There is no more profound testament to the passage of time than the series of photos shot over the years of my writing, where the early ones show him barely coming up to my shoulders, and the recent ones show me barely coming up to his. No prouder father walks the earth than I.

As I write this, I am one the cusp of a huge new change. After ten and a half years of holding down a Big Boy Job by day and writing my novels in the off hours, I will be leaving the Institute of Scrap Recycling Industries, effective January 1, 2015, making the New Year a new year indeed. A decade is a long time, and during those years I've made some friendships among the staff and our members that I truly hope will endure. Against advice of counsel (see the first paragraph of this section), who fears that I will offend through omission, I choose to throw caution to the wind and name some of the people whose company I have particularly enjoyed, and whose counsel I would particularly miss if we fell out of contact. In no particular order: Ed Szrom, John Geiger, Anne Marie Horvath, Kent Kiser, Joe Pickard, Tom Crane, Chuck Carr, David Taylor, David Wagger, Doug Kramer, Cap Grossman, Veronica Costanza, Jerry Sjogren, Lee Twitchell, Bill Rouse, Anatoly Mendelsohn, George Adams, Rick Hare, Kendig Kneen, Randy Goodman, Debbie Hayes, and Tamara Deiro. And yes, I'm sure there are a few whose names I have neglected to include here, but please know that I meant no offense by doing so.

Jonathan Grave knows a lot about weaponry, explosives, and tactics. He'd know a lot less if I wasn't allowed to pick the brains of some very smart people. At the top of the list are Chris Grall and Lee Lofland, the former for things military and the latter for things police-related. I can't thank you guys enough for your willingness to keep me from screwing things up. Then there are the folks who I believe would prefer to remain anonymous. Thanks to you folks, too.

My appreciation for all that the Kensington team has done to make my books better than they could ever have been otherwise, and then to support them in the marketplace, deepens and grows with every day. Steve Zacharias sits in the big chair, and Michaela Hamilton makes sure that my plots make sense, that the characters come alive, and that I stay below my quota of adverbs (I wrote smilingly). Special thanks to Vid Engstrand, Alexandra Nicolajsen, Karen Auerbach and the rest of the outstanding Kensington marketing team.

And Anne Hawkins. Goodness gracious, nothing would be possible without my wonderful friend and agent, Anne Hawkins.

Turn the page to read an exciting teaser excerpt from
the next Jonathan Grave thriller by John Gilstrap . . .

FRIENDLY FIRE

Coming from Pinnacle in 2016!

Ethan Falk recognized the monster's voice before he saw his face. The voice pierced the white noise of chatting patrons at the Caf-Fiend Coffee House and froze Ethan in place, any thought of the relative cleanliness of the milk steamer forgotten. Perhaps the voice by itself wouldn't have done it. It was the voice in combination with the words. "Be quick about it, if you don't mind."

Be quick about it.

With the lightning speed of imagination Ethan was once again eleven years old, his ankles shackled by a chain that barely allowed for a full step, that prevented him from climbing stairs without crawling. The pain was all there. The humiliation and the fear were *all there.*

Without the voice, he doubted that he would have recognized the face. It had been eleven years, after all. The monster's hair had turned gray at the temples and hugged his head more closely. The features had sagged some and his jaw had softened, but the hook in the nose was the same, as was the slightly cross-toothed overbite. There was a way he carried himself, too—a square set to his shoulders that a decade had done nothing to diminish—even as he stood waiting for his order.

Ethan felt his face flush as something horrible stirred deep in his gut, a putrid, malignant stew of bile and hate and shame. "Look at me," he whispered. He needed the confirmation.

The old woman directly in front of Ethan snapped, "Are you even listening to me, young man?"

Her voice startled him. No, he wasn't listening to her. She stood there, a silver thermos extended in the air, dangling from two fingers. "You're out of half-and-half," she said. Her clipped tone told him that she'd said it before. The heat in her eyes told him that she'd said it maybe five or six times.

Reality had morphed into the past with such violence that her request registered as a non sequitur. "Huh?"

"My God, are you deaf? I said—"

The monster turned. Raven, Ethan's nominal girlfriend and fellow barista, handed the monster his drip coffee, and as he turned, Ethan caught a glimpse of him full-face. Ethan's heart skipped. It might have stopped.

The lady with the thermos continued to yammer about something.

Please need cream or sugar, Ethan pleaded silently. That would put him face to face with the man who'd ruined so much. The man who'd beaten him, torn him.

But apparently the monster preferred his coffee black. He headed straight to the door, not casting a look toward anyone. Whatever his thoughts, they had nothing to do with the sins of his past.

Perhaps they had only to do with the sins of his future.

". . . speak to your supervisor. I have never—"

"No," Ethan said aloud. The monster could not be allowed to leave. He could not be allowed to torture others.

He could not be allowed to dominate Ethan's life anymore with recalled horrors.

Another customer said something to him, but the words—if they were words at all—could not penetrate the wall of rage.

Ethan needed to stop him. Stop the monster. Kill the monster.

He dropped the stuff he'd been holding—a tiny pitcher for the steamed milk and the spoon through which to sift it—and was deaf to the sound of them hitting the floor. People looked at him, though. Raven at first looked confused, and then she looked frightened.

"My God, Ethan, what's wrong?"

Ethan said nothing. There wasn't time. The monster was on the loose, out in the world, preying on other people. On other children.

Raven tried to step in front of him to stop him—*how could she know?*—but he shouldered past her. He moved fast, not quite a run, but close to it. Fast enough to catch every pair of eyes in the shop.

As he passed the pastry case, he snagged the knife they used to cut bagels. It had always been the wrong style for slicing bread, with a straight edge instead of a serrated one, but they'd learned as a crew that if you kept a straight-edged knife sharp enough, it will cut anything.

The whole rhythm of the shop changed as he emerged from behind the counter with the knife. The old lady with the thermos put it down on the counter and collapsed into a fetal ball on the floor, covering her head and yelling, "I'm sorry, I'm sorry! I'm so sorry!"

In a distant part of his brain, Ethan felt bad that he'd inflicted fear on the poor lady—all she'd wanted was a little customer service—but in the readily accessible portion of his brain, he didn't give a shit. Closer still was the thought that maybe next time she wouldn't be such a bitch.

The crowd parted as Ethan approached the exit with his knife. He didn't slow as he reached the glass door, choosing instead to power through it as if it weren't there. The blast of autumn air felt refreshing after the stuffiness of the coffee shop. Invigorating. Head-clearing.

Where is he?

The shop lay in a suburban strip mall in the suburbs of Washington, DC. There weren't many people milling about, but this was lunch time, so there were more than a few. The monster could have gone only so far. He had to be here somewhere. He had to still be within view.

Ethan saw a guy from a Subway sandwich shop chatting on the corner with a hot girl from the quick-quack medical place next store. She wore checkerboard scrubs that strained in all the right places. Ahead and to the left, a lady in a red jacket carried a take-out order from the ribs joint. ("You bring your appetite, we'll supply the bib.") Beyond that lady, taillights flashed on the back end of a pickup truck, followed by the backup lights.

"Shit, he's getting away."

He stopped himself from chasing, though, because he knew that the monster wouldn't be in the pickup. It was too far away. Not enough time had passed to get that far.

Ethan pivoted on his own axis to look the other way. He stepped around the corner of the coffee shop to look past the drive-through traffic. To scan the parking lot.

There he was.

The monster walked easily, as if he had not a care in the world, on his way to the rest of his day.

Ethan moved without thinking, taking off at a run. He'd changed a lot, too, in the past eleven years. His shoulders had broadened, and he'd grown to six-two. The monster no longer had a chance of holding him down with a hand on his chest and a knee in his belly.

The monster had no chance of winning this fight.

Ethan ran at a full sprint, closing the distance in just a few seconds. When he was only ten or fifteen feet away, the monster seemed to awaken to the danger and he turned.

Good, Ethan thought. *Get a good look at me, you son of a—*

The monster led with a punch that came from nowhere and caught Ethan with withering force just in front of his ear. Light flashed behind his eyes.

But Ethan still had the momentum, and the collision took both of them to the ground between parked cars. The monster's head sheared a side view mirror from its mount, and then pounded hard against the pavement.

John Gilstrap

They landed in a tangle, with Ethan on top, in the command position. As his vision swam from the punch and the fall, he knew that survival meant fast action. The monster bucked beneath him, trying to throw him off. The guy didn't seem scared at all. He seemed angry. If he got free—

Be quick about it.

Despite all the squirming and writhing on the ground Ethan's right hand was still free, and it still grasped the knife. He raised it high and hesitated.

In that instant, the monster seemed to understand what was going to happen.

"All units in the vicinity of the Antebellum Shopping Center, respond to the report of an assault in progress. Code three."

Officer Pam Hastings pulled her microphone from its clamp on the dash and brought it to her lips, keying the mike. "One-four-three responding." With the white mike still in her grasp, she used the first three fingers of her right hand on the rocker switches to light up the roof bar and the front and rear emergency lights. She cranked the siren switch all the way to the right—to the Wail setting.

Known throughout the Braddock County Police Department as a lead-foot (with the Internal Affairs reports in her record to show it), she didn't even think about the future paperwork as she mashed the accelerator to the floor and let herself be thrown into her seat back as the 305-horsepower Ford Police Interceptor accelerated from cruising to holy-shit-fast in zero-point-few seconds. In that same amount of time, at least four other units likewise marked responding. Nothing drew a crowd of cops quite like violence in progress.

Pam didn't know where the other units were coming from, but she was only a quarter mile away, and that meant that she would be first on the scene.

"Units responding be advised that we've received multiple calls on this. Callers report a man in the parking lot next to the Caf-Fiend Coffee House with a knife in his hand. One victim appears to be down."

To be sure, that raised the stakes. If the callers were right—and when multiple callers had the same story, the situation was almost always as reported—Pam was cruising into the middle of a murder in progress. That was the best case. There was no ceiling on what the worst case might be. She used her right thumb to release the snap on her thumb-break holster. If she was going to need her weapon, she was going to need it quickly. Milliseconds counted.

Peripheral vision became a blur as Pam pushed the speedometer to its limit down Little Creek Turnpike, switching the siren to Yelp as she approached intersections. Someone was being killed, and people needed to get out of her way. The penalty for being a little too slow might be the ultimate one, but she'd learned over her thirteen years on the job that if you move with enough conviction—whether on foot or in a vehicle— people will move to let you pass.

As Fair Haven Shopping Center whizzed past her on the left—a blur of colorful signage and logos—she lifted her foot off the gas to prepare for the hard left onto Pickett Lane, named after the famed Civil War general. She tapped the brakes but didn't jam them, taking the turn twenty miles an hour faster than the intersection was designed for, but a solid fifteen miles an hour slower than her tires could handle. Her seat belt kept her from being launched into the passenger seat by the centrifugal force.

The ass end of her cruiser tried to kick out from her, but Pam wrestled it back in line with gentle pressure on the wheel. The casual observer wouldn't have seen even the slightest fishtail.

Straightaway.

The engine growled as she pressed the accelerator to the floor. Up ahead, as far as she could see, the traffic parted. She saw cars in the median, a truck up on the curb on the right. Somehow, they knew. Somehow, they always knew. This was the part of the job that she loved more than any other.

The Antebellum Shopping Center was now in view, ahead and on the right, and she slowed. It was one thing to get to the scene quickly; it was something else to rush into an ambush. Because weapons were involved, county protocols required that she wait for backup. But because someone was in the process of being murdered, she decided to disobey the rules. The fact that the murderer had a knife and she had both a .40-caliber handgun and a 12-gauge shotgun within easy reach made the decision a little easier. Still, violence in progress required a careful approach.

Pam cut her siren and slowed to twenty miles an hour as she turned in to the shopping center. She pulled the mike from its clamp again and keyed the mike. "One-four-three on the scene."

"Four-four-seven. Hold what you've got. I'm ninety seconds out." That would be Josh Levine, a cool kid with a big heart and a bit of a crush.

Pam opted not to respond. A good guy was being stabbed to death. Ninety seconds was quite literally a lifetime. Waiting was out of the question. But she wasn't going to go on the record violating protocol. Sometimes it truly was easier to beg forgiveness than ask permission.

A crowd had gathered in the parking lot outside the Caf-Fiend Coffee House, naturally forming the kind of semicircle that inadvertently directed Pam's eye directly to where the threat stood. The gawkers closest to her beckoned her forward, while the ones who were farther away continued to stare and point at the hazard.

"The situation is critical," Pam said into the radio. Translation: *I'm triggering the protocol's exception clause.* "Other units expedite." Translation: *Run over anybody in your way if you want a piece of the fun.*

She threw the transmission into Park, kept the engine running, and stepped out of the cruiser.

"He's up there!" a lady yelled. "Shoot him!"

Pam ignored her. In fact, she ignored everything but the facts as she saw them play out before her. With her Glock 23 at low-ready, she approached carefully yet steadily, sweeping her eyes left and right, ever vigilant for an unseen threat, perhaps an accomplice. She tried to focus on her tactical breathing—four seconds in, four seconds held, then four seconds to exhale. It made all the sense in the world when she learned about it in the classroom, but it was pretty damned hard to do in real life.

The intensity of the combined energy from all the people watching her seemed to create its own form of heat. Crime scene gawkers were a funny lot. Roughly a third of them thought you were a god, a second third thought you were Satan incarnate, and the rest didn't give a shit. They were the ones with the cell phone cameras. She saw three devices on her periphery, one of which hovered in the air at the end of one of those extender rods that had become ubiquitous among the selfie crowd. Of the thirty or so people who had gathered, she noted that none of them had pressed forward to help the victim or to confront the attacker. That was her job. The crowd's job was to film it and to offer criticism after the fact.

She'd nearly made it to the front of the crowd when she caught her first glimpse of the gore. Two cars were painted with it, as was a nice-looking, terrified young man in the apron of a Caf-Fiend barista. The kid looked confused. He looked at the knife in his hands as if it belonged to someone else.

Pam raised her Glock to high-ready and rested the front sight at the center of the attacker's chest. "Police officer!" she yelled. Her voice cracked just a little. She hoped it wasn't obvious to anyone else that she was in way over her head. You train for the scenario where you single-handedly confront a murderer, but you never really expect it to happen on your watch. "Put the knife down or I will shoot you!"

The attacker held out his free hand as if to ward her off. "No!" he said. "I'm not the killer. He's the killer. He's a kidnapper, a rapist, and a killer!"

"Put the knife down!"

"You don't understand. I'm the victim here. He's . . ." The kid's face seemed to clear for an instant, and he looked at his hand. At the blood. "Oh, my God." Then he looked at the bloody man who lay motionless at his feet. "Oh God, oh God, oh God."

Pam moved her finger inside the trigger guard. The experts all agreed that inside of twenty-one feet, a man with a knife could kill a cop before the cop could pull a firearm from its holster. Correcting for the fact that she was scared shitless, but that her gun was already trained on the badguy, a finger on the trigger pretty much canceled out that research. Still, if he took a step toward her, she was going to blast his heart out through his spine.

"Listen to me!" Pam yelled. Her voice was firm and strong this time. "Put the knife down and lie down on the ground."

"I'm the victim!"

"You're the victim with a knife," she replied. "You're putting me in danger, and you're putting all these other people in danger, too. Put the knife down, do what I tell you, and then I'll listen to your side of the story."

In the distance, the sound of sirens crescendoed. One of them would be Josh Levine. If he thought she was in mortal danger, he would shoot before talking.

The assailant didn't move.

"What's your name?" Pam shouted.

The kid seemed confused. Perhaps it was the ordinariness of the question.

"Your name," Pam prompted. "What is it?"

"Um, Ethan. Ethan Falk."

Pam lowered her weapon a few degrees. "Nice to meet you, Ethan Falk. I am Officer Hastings, and I am here to arrest you. Whether you're innocent or guilty, victim or perpetrator is not my concern. All I know is that right now, there's a man on the ground at your feet, and you're standing over him with a bloody knife. What would you assume if you were in my position?"

"It looks bad, doesn't it?"

The comment struck Pam as funny and she smiled. "I think we all can agree that this does look bad. So how about you put the knife—"

"But I didn't do—"

"Listen to me, Ethan! Do you hear those other sirens? Those are other cops, and when they arrive, they're going to see you still standing there with a knife. They're going to see the blood, and there's going to be that many more guns pointing at you. You don't want that. Please just drop the knife and—"

He dropped it. The knife landed on the victim's back, but not point-first. Baby steps.

"Thank you, Ethan," Pam said. "Now, keeping your hands where I can see them, I need you to step forward into the road—"

Just then, a Toyota driven by a soccer mom in a pink top sped down the parking lot aisle that separated cop from felon.

"Jesus," Pam cursed. "Really?" Refocus. She stepped out into the roadway and over to her right, keeping more or less the same distance between herself and her suspect.

"Four-four-seven is on the scene." Josh Levine had arrived.

Pam moved her left hand from her weapon to the microphone on her epaulette. "Come in easy, Four-four-seven. I have the situation under control, but it's fragile. I don't need a lot of noise and mayhem." To her suspect: "Ethan, I need you to take two big steps forward into the street and lie flat on your face, your hands out to the side."

He still seemed to be caught somewhere between reality and someplace else.

"Come on, Ethan, I know you can do it."

"Don't shoot me."

"I won't shoot you if you don't threaten anyone. Come on, two big steps forward, and then just sprawl on the ground. We'll get past this one step and then everything else will be easy."

Josh Levine burst out of the crowd on Pam's left, Mossberg shotgun pressed to his shoulder. "You heard her!" he shouted. "Get on the ground! Now!" He pressed in three steps too close, ruining the safe zone that Pam had been trying to create. "I said now!"

"Josh, shut up!" Pam shouted. The words were out before she had a chance to stop them. But once out, they needed to be followed up. "I've got this. Step back." In the back of her brain, she was distantly aware that she was making some great video for the cell phone crowd.

"Look at me, Ethan," she said. "Not at him, at me. He won't hurt you. But do you see how nervous you're making everyone?" She dared a couple of steps forward, if only to earn the frightened glances that were going toward Levine. More sirens approached, and more units marked on the scene. The entire Braddock County Police Department was descending on them.

Ethan took two exaggerated steps forward, taking care not to step on the body, and ostentatiously avoiding the stream of blood, to stand in the middle of the street. If the Toyota had come by at that moment, he'd have been launched over the hood. He walked with his hands out to the side, cruciform, his finger splayed.

"You're doing great, Ethan," Pam said. "Now, I just need you to—"

Levine rushed him. With the shotgun one-armed into his shoulder, he closed the distance in two or three quick strides. Grabbing the back of the kid's shirt at the collar, he kicked his right foot from underneath him while at the same instant driving him forward and down. Ethan barely had enough time to get his hands out in front to prevent his face from being smashed into the pavement.

With the kid down, Levine kneeled on the small of his back and pressed the muzzle of the shotgun against the base of the kid's skull. "I've got him!" he announced. He looked to Pam. "You cuff him."

Pam's shoulders sagged. She holstered her Glock and approached the two men on the ground. "You didn't have to do that," she said when she was within easy earshot. "I had this under control."

"Yeah, but I have him under arrest," Josh said. "That's better. Are you going to cuff him or chat?"

Anger boiled in Pam's gut, but she swallowed it down. Cuffing Ethan was a cakewalk. He did everything he was asked to do, and by the time that fifteen-second process was completed, at least ten more cops had arrived.

"I've got this," she said to Levine.

He cocked his head. "Why are you so pissed?"

"Because you didn't have to hurt him," she said.

"You know he killed a guy, right?"

Pam didn't answer. She helped Ethan to his feet and Mirandized him. She did her best to ignore the citizens who crowded her as she escorted her prisoner to her cruiser, and she didn't acknowledge any of the other officers. It was the damn cameras. She just wanted to be out of their range.

"Watch your head," she said as Ethan lowered his butt into the backseat.

"Officer Hastings?" They were Ethan's first words since he'd been pressed into the pavement.

Pam made eye contact.

"That man kidnapped me when I was eleven years old. You look it up. It was terrible. He was a monster. I'm sorry for what I did, but he was . . . a *monster*."

Just from his tone, Pam believed him. "Okay," she said. "Make sure you tell your lawyer. And the prosecutor if you decide to talk to him. The FBI will have a record of your rescue, and that will surely help."

"But I wasn't rescued by the FBI," Ethan said.

"Then how did you get away? Did you escape?"

Ethan shook his head. "No, I was rescued, but not by the FBI. I was rescued by a guy named Scorpion."

"Who?"

"That's all I know. His name was Scorpion."

"That's not a name."

"Of course it's not a name. But that's what he called himself. He saved my life."